OF BLOOMING EMBERS

FATE OF THE EMBERED
BOOK TWO

ROWYN ADELAIDE

Cover Design: Rowyn Adelaide

Edited by: Katie Awdas, Spice Me Up Editing

Map Art: Melissa Nash

*For anyone who has been told that they weren't enough **and** that they were too much. They can't have it both ways. Besides, you are perfectly, wildly enough just as you are.*

Among shattered hopes
    and phantom breeze.
    Fated promises,
    Sealed in moonbeams.

— ROWYN ADELAIDE

ALSO BY ROWYN ADELAIDE

FATE OF THE EMBERED SERIES

Of Withering Dreams

Of Blooming Embers

Of Hollowed Stars

EXCLUSIVE UPDATES
FOR READERS

JOIN ROWYN'S AUTHOR NEWSLETTER

Be the first to learn about Rowyn Adelaide's new releases and receive exclusive content!

WWW.AUTHORROWYNADELAIDE.COM

PLAYLIST

Books are life. But so is music—at least to me! In no particular order, the following songs inspired me while I wrote this story. Below, come find me and my book playlists on Spotify!

- "Crimson and Clover (cover)" - Joan Jett & the Blackhearts
- "Hot Blooded" - New Constellations
- "The Killing Moon" - Echo & the Bunnymen
- "You're Dead" - Norma Tanega
- "Cherry Bomb" - The Runaways
- "Daisy" - Ashnikko
- "Sweet Dreams (cover)" - Ravens Rock
- "Let's Dance" - David Bowie
- "Light My Love" - Greta Van Fleet
- "FEEL" - BURY and Beneld
- "Paint It, Black (cover)" - Bishop Briggs
- "Beggin'" - Måneskin
- "Take My Breath Away (cover)" - EZI
- "Angry Too" - Lola Blanc

- "Decode" - Paramore
- "Lights" - Ellie Goulding
- "Make Me Feel" - Janelle Monáe
- "Running Up That Hill (cover)" - Meg Myers
- "Burn Alive" - The Last Dinner Party
- "Numb" - Linkin Park
- "Somewhere I Belong" - Linkin Park
- "Going Under" - Evanescence
- "That's How I'm Feeling" - Jack White
- "How Villains Are Made" - Madalen Duke
- "You Put a Spell On Me (cover)" - Austin Giorgio
- "The World We Made" - Ruelle
- "Bad Dreams" - Teddy Swims
- "Bullet With Butterfly Wings (cover)" - Violet Orlandi
- "Fire For You" - Cannons
- "Emergence" - Sleep Token
- "Misery Business" - Paramore
- "Brutal" - Olivia Rodrigo
- "Come As You Are" - Nirvana
- "Hollaback Girl" - Gwen Stefani

Of Blooming Embers Spotify Playlist

AUTHOR'S NOTE

This is the second book in the *Fate of the Embered* series. Before diving into *Of Blooming Embers,* you should read the first book, *Of Withering Dreams,* as it is a continuation of the story. I am thrilled to finally get this story out into the world. I've always loved romance novels, especially ones with atmospheric world-building, magic, action, quests, and mystical beings. While some elements and names may be similar or very loosely related to Greek mythology, this is not a retelling or close representation of those tales or culture. This is a dark fantasy romance that was inspired by nature, magic systems, the world of dreams and imagination, Fates and Oneiroi (Dream Gods), mythology, etc.

At the back (*because spoilers*) of the book, there is a **glossary** and **pronunciation guide**. If you utilize the glossary and pronunciation guide, **PLEASE** be mindful that they are together and may contain **spoilers** if you look them up before reading.

Please enjoy the second installment of my dark romantasy series, and keep an eye out for the rest. Read on for an important **content warning**.

CONTENT WARNING

Of Blooming Embers is a dark fantasy romance (a.k.a. dark romantasy) with morally gray characters, explicit content, themes or hints of trauma and abuse, hints or talk of potential sexual assault (NOT described explicitly on the page), scenes with blood and gore, torture, violence, characters struggling with mental health and/or well-being, anxiety, grief, and other complex emotions. There are open-door sex scenes, talk of parental and loved ones' deaths, death, loss and grieving, cussing, characters with dark pasts and dark deeds, and supernatural elements.

Dark fantasy romance is a subgenre of fantasy romance that explores darker themes and worlds that may be considered disturbing, unsettling, traumatic, or frightening to some. However, it is not considered the same as dark romance, which often explores the darker side of love and relationships, power/control dynamics, fear, obsession, violence, abuse, etc.

I want to be clear that *Of Blooming Embers* is NOT considered a dark romance.

I think the difference is important to note for those who enjoy dark romance specifically. I don't want to lead you astray if you were expecting certain tropes and themes that are often included in dark romances and the relationships therein.

Your mental well-being is important, so please review any trigger warnings before reading. If you are sensitive to scenes with the noted content, then this isn't the book for you. I want you to stay safe and love what you read. If you decide to read this story, then buckle up and enjoy this enchantingly wild ride!

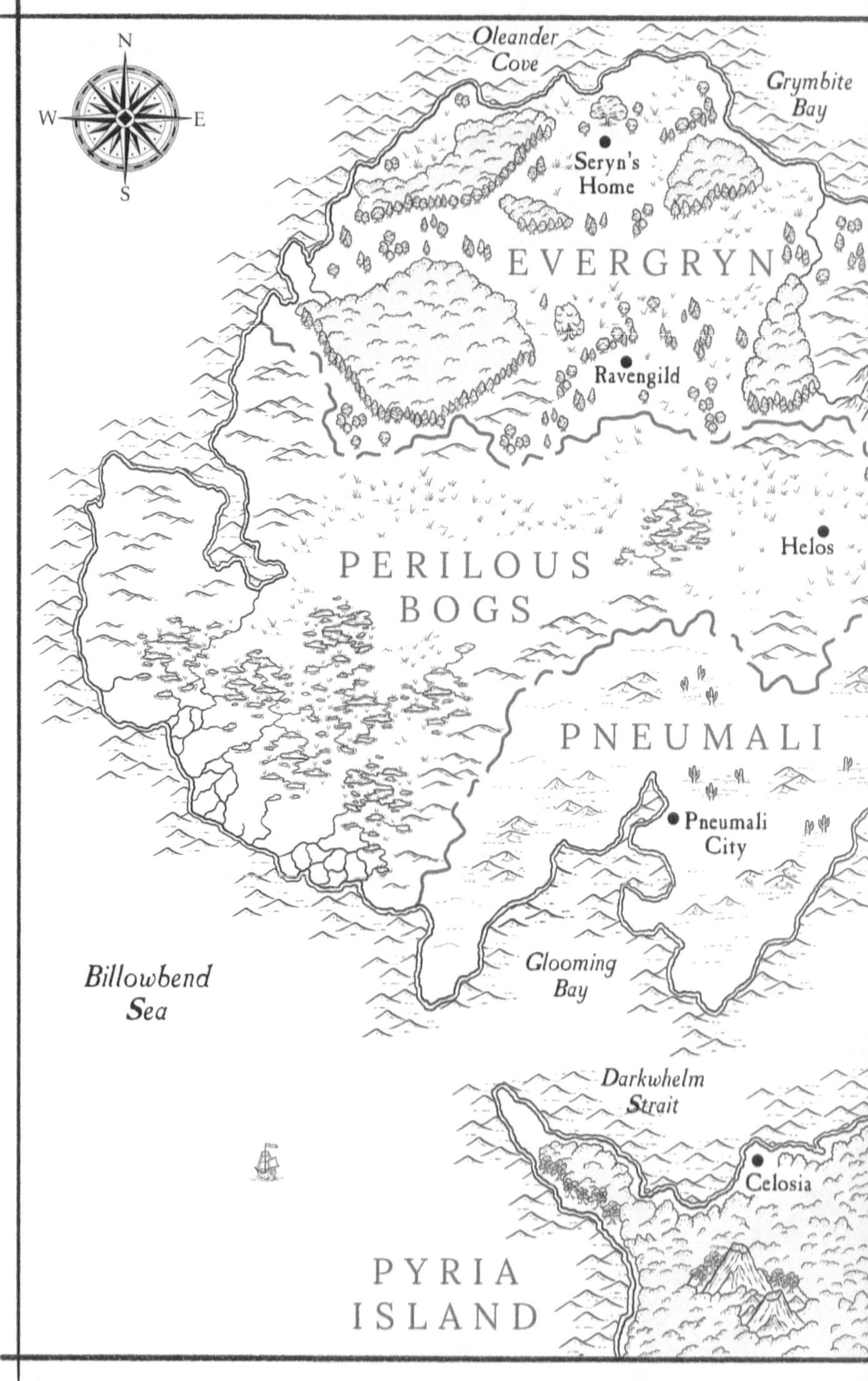

N
W E
S
Oleander Cove
Grymbite Bay
Seryn's Home
EVERGRYN
Ravengild
Helos
PERILOUS BOGS
PNEUMALI
Pneumali City
Billowbend Sea
Glooming Bay
Darkwhelm Strait
Celosia
PYRIA ISLAND

Ourea Peaks
Oneiroi Abyss
Lotus Loch
Inksalt Loch
Ceto
HAADRA
Aerides Loch
Gulf of Eidolon
MIDST FALL

PROLOGUE

"What do you mean, this was a mistake?" Seryn's bottom lip wobbled before she tucked it under her front teeth, pressing the bright enamel into the plump skin. I swallowed a groan before it escaped.

Her hands dropped from my chest. The chilled autumn air scurried over the space they had occupied, the warmth from her touch obliterated. My hands itched to reach out and gather her to me. Never let her go. I dug my short nails into them, the bite of pain a welcome reminder of what an absolute failure I was.

I looked above at the thick grymwood canopy. Mottled beams of light stabbed through the brambly crown. Perhaps one of the massive, decaying trees would collapse on me, its grizzled trunk smashing my brains to pieces. Eyelids scrunching tightly, a deep exhale left me. My nostrils flared in disgust.

I scraped my fingers through my trimmed, dark waves, the strands tugging at my scalp irritably as I dragged my gaze over her distressed face.

My cock stirred at the memory of her soft mouth on mine, pink and wet. Appalled at myself, I squinted, molars clenching.

Pull yourself together.

Her eyes glistened like the color of frost floating atop the vivid blue waters of the Oneiroi Abyss. I would gladly drown in their depths, and at this very moment, I would deserve it.

Fucking idiot.

Lurching, my heart punched the back of my ribs. Straining toward her as if ready to tear itself from me and latch onto her. If I could do just that, I would. There was no other choice but to break her, though.

Break *myself.*

We'd had a few perfect months. From this spring until now, I'd spun in her orbit while reality sank its teeth into me, gnawing at my logic until I could no longer ignore its bite.

If I weren't a bleeding moron with no self-control, we wouldn't be in this mess. I wouldn't have to split us in two.

Wouldn't have to lie.

Lie until she believed I didn't want her.

Until she loathed me.

When we were younger, Kaden, Seryn, and I would often journey north to Oleander Cove right before summer's end. The frigid pool beckoned us, its azure waves lapping at the pebbled shore.

Every single time, Seryn would kick off her leather slippers and squeal as she ran, laughing and hiking up her dress. Dead grym needles hid among the stones, most definitely piercing the pads of her feet, but she never cared as she tore into the surf.

The sun would skim over her auburn curls as she twirled, setting its gleaming strands aflame. A satisfied, gleeful smile would bend across her mouth as she splashed Kaden, who was no doubt at her heels.

My brother was never far from her side.

An aching twinge coursed through my teeth as the enamel

ground together. I turned my attention away from her unbearably beautiful face. Hatred oozed over me like thick, warm blood coating my skin.

If she cared for me like I did her, what I had to do next would surely sever any budding feelings.

Kaden will be pleased. My chin dropped, a growled huff falling from my lips.

"Gavrel?" Her soft plea snapped my attention back.

If I told her everything—about the danger she was in—she would no doubt scoff at my concern, thinking we could face whatever lay ahead together.

But Melina would destroy her if we were found out, and I couldn't allow the Elder to harm her in the same way she'd harmed the others. It was unacceptable.

The leather of my boots creaked as I widened my stance. My emerald eyes bored into hers, plummeting into their depths. I had to get this over with. Otherwise, her tears would drown me. Flood over the wall of numbness I'd built around the hammering muscle within my chest.

"This ..." My hand waved between us, steady when my insides were anything but. "... it can't go on. I apologize if you thought this was more than it is, and for my part in leading you astray." My jaw was so tight, every word was going to rip it off at the hinges as I cut through the thread connecting us.

Torn in two, my heart heaved. Could she feel the pain slicing through my very soul?

She stepped back, her chest rising and falling rapidly, nails digging into the fabric across her chest. Disoriented, her eyes widened, and she blinked a few times as if waking from a dream. Her lashes swept closed, trapping the line of salty tears beneath.

A sweet-smelling breeze fluttered through her curls. Burning acid frothed inside my guts. The sun stroked her strands as the scent of astra poppies slapped across the angular ridges of my face.

Against my will, my boots shifted forward, hand gravitating toward her.

Seryn opened her eyes and breathed deeply through her nose. Resignation settled into the straight line of her mouth. My hand dropped, following her clipped words as they fell heavy at my feet. "Well, I suppose there's nothing left to say."

Without another glance, she spun, marching toward her cottage through the grymwoods, their branches arching over— claw-like twigs reaching for her greedily. The flames of her hair flickered at her back and shoulders, consuming her.

Consuming us *both*.

But it didn't fucking matter.

I had already cremated my own heart.

Cold, black ash was all that remained.

1

SEASONS OF OUR LIVES

SERYN ~ NOWADAYS

My bones ached, the muscles of my leather-clad thighs screaming as they gripped the thick saddle between them. Atop a pair of burnished mares, Gavrel and I moved through the dense forest of Evergryn. For the last few days, we'd journeyed past endless grymwood trees. The farther we got, the grayer the hues that sank into the grain of the imposing trunks.

They surrounded us from every angle, their desiccated branches raking at the surrounding spaces, poking their nearest comrades, trying to get their attention as we passed.

My horse followed Gavrel's, dark hooves crunching over dead grymwood needles, dried grass, and rocks as it cantered rhythmically.

Gavrel's massive hands gently pulled on his animal's reins, and I did the same, a rumbling huff puffing from my steed's flaring nostrils as we slowed.

My lips pressed into a firm line as I studied Gavrel's back. His sheathed broadsword bumped against the corded muscles.

We had spoken little during our trip. Each second dragged across the day. We had secured supplies and food at various villages along the way, ate in silence, slept on separate bedrolls under the bristled canopy and blackened skies, awakened, and did it all over again.

Sometimes, the corner of Gavrel's mouth would curl ever so slightly, but then his brow would fall as he sipped in a quick bit of air, remnants of stifled words catching in his thick throat. Perhaps he knew I didn't have it in me for idle conversation or to deconstruct our past.

Perhaps he didn't either.

Good.

I breathed in the damp, foggy musk. It smelled of timber and rot. We surveyed our surroundings, ears tuned to the faintest echo of any movement not our own.

So far, the plan to head east, toward Haadra, was the right one. There had been no sign of the two Akridais, the Elders' elite Druik enforcers, stalking us. No doubt Elder Melina Harrow's fury was mounting with every passing day in which our chained bodies weren't dropped at her feet. I pushed the delicate frame of my chin forward, the bitter taste of disgust rippling over my tongue before I swallowed it back.

With a deep inhale, I ran my hand over the coarse mane of my mount. Luckily, Gavrel had brought a cache of coins from his earnings as a commander, so we were able to barter for the horses in a small village early on our journey.

Thank the Ancients.

I lifted my eyes to the aether, my brow crinkling. *Do the Ancients deserve accolades any longer?*

Where were they as Midst Fall crumbled around us? As the Elder Laws oppressed mortals and Druiks alike, the heel of the oligarchy's mandates digging into our spines, our voices muffled and choking in the dirt. Where were they as the Dormancy stole seasons of our lives—our minds ravaged by malignant dreams?

My nostrils flared with a frustrated exhale, and Gavrel turned to me as my mare fell in step beside his. His expression remained stoic and unflinching. Impassive. He was always brooding; his plump mouth set in an unwavering slash across his face.

Heat zipped down my spine, and I shifted the rucksack on my back, its weight distracting my attention away from Gavrel's heartbreakingly beautiful. Fucking. Face.

A line of wariness and exhaustion dented the space between my brows as I dug my molars into each other. The fingers of my left hand squeezed around the reins, the cool, carved tourmaline of my ring humming against my forefinger.

My gaze roamed upward, searching for pockets of sunlight pushing through the crown. I ground the base of my thumb into my belt satchel. Two glass vials squeaked against each other between the leather.

I had too many resurfaced recollections to sift through since taking the embered Mirage Orchid elixir several days past. Murky memories of Gavrel and me embracing two springs ago weaved with those of Kaden's arms around me during the last Dormancy.

My best friend's head between my thighs under the Elysium Tree in Surrelia.

His teeth nipping at my neck.

Me straddling Gavrel under a clear, starry night in the woods behind my cottage. Igniting as I rubbed against him while he sucked and bit at my breasts.

Me whispering, *finally*.

A rush of heat sped over my skin and pooled within my very core. Biting the inside of my cheek, I clenched my thighs.

Shame twisted in my gut. The image of Kaden, traces of

anguish marring his usual smirk, stomped through the lust of my first intimacy with his brother.

These were the moments when I wished Derya hadn't made the potion. That I'd remained oblivious to all the erased experiences in which the Dormancy and Melina had swept into the crevices of my mind. Others, I clutched tightly within my chest, the knowledge of them burning through every cell and pushing me onward.

My father, Gideon, one of the Elders' Somneia spies, dooming Gavrel and Kaden's mother, Hestia, to death by culling.

Melina's abuse and torment of countless Midst Fall citizens, including two of her fellow Elders.

She possessed a warped and wanton lust for dominance at any cost. She had specifically erased my memories of my ember's origins, and that was ... something. It pointed to her insecurities. Her fears.

Within every shadowy corner of my mind, ashes of drifting recollections settled. Along the edges, a few things were clear, and the reflections of reclaimed fragments cast light over them.

Elder Harrow was wary of my gifts, just like she'd been of my mother's. Perhaps she suspected that Mama and I were Scions, primed to undergo Ascension and take her spot.

Damn Melina to the Nether Void. I didn't want her place as an Elder, and I suspected Mama hadn't either. Nonetheless, we paid Melina's price.

I squeezed my eyes tightly, trapping the thought of my mother—and the hope that she was still alive—behind the lids.

"We're close," Gavrel announced, and my attention snapped to him. Melina was obsessed with Gavrel. Covetous and jealous enough to erase my memories of our fleeting relationship.

A heavy sigh fell from me, and I tucked an errant curl behind my ear, mollified that the rest of it remained in a messy plait.

I studied the strong, angular line of his profile as he reached into the pocket of his black trousers, removing a wrinkled scroll. Gavrel had sent missives to Rhaegar and Xeni by harbinger starlings from the village where we had acquired our mounts.

I grimaced, thinking of the small gray spotted birds. They were temperamental beasties, but they took their job of delivering messages across the realm seriously. You just might get pecked for their efforts, though.

Turns ago, while stationed in Pneumali City, Gavrel had sent his brother a scroll by harbinger. Kaden had warily untied the message from the bird's leg, and the scrappy thing stabbed him in the thumb with its tiny yellow beak before puffing its feathers and flying off. Kaden acted as if he had been impaled. My mouth curled at the memory.

With a breathy, amused exhale, I straightened in my seat and refocused on Gavrel.

We'd find Kaden. There was no other outcome I'd accept. I only hoped Gavrel's dream—what he believed to be a premonition—was correct, and that we'd find Kaden safe in the Perilous Bogs.

Gavrel rolled the fawn-colored paper, nodding as he tucked it away. I followed his line of sight toward a tall boulder nestled between a pair of thick trees.

Only Xeni had replied, her message relaying that she would meet us at this location via a hidden portal from Haadra, her home region.

A couple of days ago, Gavrel had revealed that his Draumr team and the Akridais knew the locations of several secret portals throughout the realm, which could only be accessed and activated by those with ember. Throughout the turns, these portals had helped them traverse the expanse of Midst Fall and swiftly complete various missions.

The star-shaped scar on my neck tingled with anticipation as we dismounted and secured the horses. Although it had been part of me my entire life, its constant buzz served as a reminder of both my failings and my potential as a Druik. If a shade hadn't attacked me in the Stygian Murk last autumn, leaving the hidden talisman undisturbed, would my path have been different? Or would my gifts have eventually overpowered the rune's spell?

Realizing such thoughts were futile, I breathed out steadily through pursed lips, allowing my ember to flow in rippling waves under my skin.

Dimly glowing auras flared to life as we made our way to the boulder. Grayish greens flickered about the grymwoods as they clung to the last vestiges of their existence. Shades of brown and amber twinkled over various living surfaces, and a streak of smoky black trailed after a plump raven as it flew over our heads and into the distance ahead.

The intricate, ten-point star on Gavrel's right hand pulsed into existence, a white glimmer lurking under the delicate, intersecting lines.

During our journey, I often forgot about his rune tattoo because it remained invisible in the mortal realm in the same way that my ember was tucked away.

It blazed for a moment as a misty vortex spun in the center of the rock.

My heart fluttered as amber orbs twirled within the haze like beckoning fireflies. A petite, yet solid, frame stepped through the opening. Xeni's features emerged, the fog clinging to the rich, tawny brown skin of her face and hands as she exited the portal.

Meticulously, her golden-brown eyes swept over her surroundings before landing on us. She adjusted the baldric across her torso as the glow from her hand tattoo flickered out.

"Commander." She nodded, standing tall in her dark Draumr uniform. One eyebrow rose slightly as she studied Gavrel's black tunic and breeches with clear, assessing eyes. Curiosity shone in her deep, burnished pools. Warriors rarely wore anything but their uniforms.

Gavrel offered her a kind smile. "Any news about the state Helos is in?"

Helos, the capital of the region, was situated in the swampy easternmost part of the Perilous Bogs. If you could call the grouping of ramshackle huts a city.

According to Gavrel, about a hundred dwellings huddled together, their bases resting on a system of wooden supports and walkways. The city was in a constant state of survival against the harsh, mucky landscape and leftover floodwaters gifted from Haadra and Ourea Peaks, the impenetrable line of melting, snow-capped mountains to the north.

"There's major overflow from the lochs. Navigating south isn't advisable," Xeni reported matter-of-factly.

"We'll chance it." My confident tone belied the rapid pulse under my scar. Air stuck in my throat. Even without the deluge, the Bogs were dangerous to traverse, but we needed to get to Kaden.

She pursed her lips, digging a small scroll from her pocket and handing it to Gavrel. "I also received this missive. Addressed to you." One of her delicate eyebrows lifted. "Arrived early this morning."

"That's ... odd," he muttered, unrolling it. His eyes quickly studied the curling letters. A frown pulled at the corners of his lips as he ran a hand through his wavy hair and then looked at me with a heavy sigh. He looked to the east. "We'll continue to Ceto then."

I rubbed my fingers across my forehead. "We don't have the time."

"This"—he gave me the yellowed paper—"might help us find him. Besides, the closest portal that leads to Helos is somewhere near the Ourea Peaks along the Haadran border."

My mouth pressed together, but then slackened as I read the note.

You'll find your next path.
With the seer, you'll meet.
On the morrow at The Oracle's Seat.

I crumpled the parchment. "We're following some cryptic note from Ancients knows who?"

"It's the best lead we have," he said and moved toward the twirling opening, his rune igniting. "Let's move."

I shook my head, knowing he was right. If it was a trap, then so be it. Choosing to venture into the Perilous Bogs could cost us days. Weeks even. But finding the portal to Helos would be a boon indeed.

Xeni hesitated, her stance shifting away from the boulder. My fingers clutched Gavrel's sword belt at his shoulder. Boots faltering, he faced me.

My head bobbed toward Xeni. Her chin lifted. "I'd hoped to be stationed in Evergryn, sir. Unless you require my assistance?"

A sly smile slipped across my lips, and I pulled her into a firm hug. Her body stiffened, but then relaxed ever so slightly before I released her. "Letti took the Mirage Orchid tonic. I'm sure she'd be ecstatic to see you, and I'd be in your debt if you watched over her."

Her eyes widened, the corners of her mouth gently tipping upward. A beautiful rush of mauve swept across the gentle slopes of her cheekbones. She looked away as she smoothed her hands over the starched fabric of her overcoat.

"You can stay in my cottage next door," Gavrel offered, not wasting any further time as he gave her directions and directives to monitor my father and not allude to me or my sister regaining our memories.

The warriors clasped each other's wrists in farewell before Xeni swung atop one horse, guiding the other beside her. She bobbed her head once and then turned toward her destination.

Toward Letti.

My heart thumped heavily as the image of my sister hovered behind my eyes.

Gavrel's soft, gravelly words pulled me back. "Ready, Little Star?"

The muscle behind my ribs fluttered within its cage at the nickname slipping from his lips.

My shoulders pushed back, the seam of my mouth tightly clamping together. With more confidence than I felt, I strode past him into the coiling haze.

Better to tumble through a damned portal than to fall to pieces at his feet.

2

ROOTS

SERYN

*O*ur bodies flung through the blurred, twirling aether before being deposited unceremoniously inside a dimly lit grotto. A briny scent saturated the cool air. As I breathed deeply, my feet fumbled for balance on the shifting gravel.

Fingers wrapped around my biceps, steadying me. I gulped and pulled away from Gavrel's touch, ignoring how his warmth sank into my flesh and moved toward the sun-drenched opening of the hollow. He followed behind like a silent, prowling shadow.

"Inksalt Loch," he stated, stepping into the light and surveying the expansive pool before us. Beyond, he studied the sprawling mountains lining the horizon, their massive summits reflecting in the glassy, brackish water. Decidedly, he turned and moved toward the marshy path behind me.

I inhaled, questions about to tumble from my lips as I trailed him, but Gavrel spoke before I had the chance. "We need to gather some supplies before navigating the mountains. We can reach Ceto before nightfall, find a place to rest, and head out in the early morning."

"But we should try to find the seer tonight—"

"If we're rash, Kaden is lost to us. Besides, the message said, 'on the morrow,'" he interjected.

I huffed, shifting the nearly empty rucksack on my back and ignoring the quiver in my legs. My energy was depleted, and we were dangerously low on rations, but I didn't care. We needed to find my best friend. Gavrel's *brother*.

The corners of his eyes softened. "If we don't care for ourselves, we won't have the strength needed to reach him. We need to be intentional." His long stride slowed, matching mine.

My upper body deflated as I sighed, knowing his words rang true. It would be quicker to head into the city than to hunt game when it was scarce in these parts.

My jaw tightened. "All right. Ceto first, then we leave with the sunrise." He nodded, looking before us without another word.

As we navigated the marshland, the reeds swayed in the breeze, and mud sucked at my boots. Air caressed my cheek, and I breathed in, not minding the damp aroma of dried grass and earth. Quiet moments often brought a flood of hazy memories from a life half-remembered, and now was no exception.

Logically, I understood those emotions and experiences were mine, yet the jarring difference between my past and present was profoundly unsettling. It was as if I were looking at a series of blurred paintings from a distance or watching a disjointed theatrical play on an endless loop.

I sighed, and Gavrel's words flit through my mind once more, plucking at the edges of a resurfaced recollection from when I was seven turns old—one of Mama during the Dormancy before she vanished.

With an unfocused gaze, I urged it to fully form, knowing the memory was a vital one.

"What pretty hair you have. Like flames." The male's voice slithered over my back, his hot breath grazing my cheek.

In front of me, Letti squinted at the intruder. With a thunk, the ball she'd been holding dropped onto the grass and bumped into the toe of my slipper. Her bottom lip trembled.

I gritted my teeth, unease fluttering in my belly, while I turned to the voice, tucking Letti into my side.

I recognized him. The Akridai, who was never far from Elder Harrow. He leaned into our space, his greasy black hair curtaining either side of his blunt face. His rancid whisper rasped over us as his spindly fingers reached out. "If I touch, will it burn me?"

Hastily, I stepped back, tugging Letti with me as our backs hit the wooden fence that ran along the training field's brink. He leered, his thin lips shiny and pulling across crooked enamel. His oily, phosphorescent aura simmered above his form, and a sickly glow pulsed under the geometric locust tattoo marring his neck.

Below, the river roared, its waves crashing against the obsidian cliffs on either side. My pulse frantically pounded throughout my small body as if I were one giant heartbeat. My sister whimpered, and I hunched over her, turning my head away from him.

"Don't." The clipped demand gave the Akridai pause. I peeked at him as he straightened, tilting his head at the sound of a woman's voice.

He chuckled humorlessly. "Don't?"

I seized the opportunity while he was distracted, shoving Letti past him. The male's brows scrunched together as my sister made her escape. His attention snapped back to me, splinters sticking in my fingers as I clung to the fence and tried to creep away.

Clucking his tongue, he snatched my wrist and swung us around. My back slammed into his front, and the jagged nails of his other hand dug into my shoulder.

Squeezing my eyes shut, I whimpered at the stinging in my scalp as my curls pulled, trapped under his grip. My nose scrunched at the pungent scent wafting from him.

"Balor." My eyes snapped open, realizing that Mama was the one talking. I'd never heard her sound like that. Chilling. Lethal. "Let. My. Daughter. Go."

Behind Mama, Father backed away, Letti cradled protectively in his arms. There was a small crowd gawking at the unfolding scene. Mama stepped forward, her jaw tight, her golden-hazel eyes boring into the male's. I shuddered, fearful that she would get hurt. We weren't supposed to defy Akridais.

Balor's bony body practically vibrated against me. "Let her go?" he sneered.

All at once, a yellow radiance illuminated behind me, and slippery tendrils of ember slithered around my waist. I gulped, my petrified eyes meeting my mother's.

Before I knew what was happening, the ground left my feet, and my body flung over the fence to a chorus of gasps and stunned cries. My mother darted forward, her outstretched hands reaching for me. A glimmering halo of midnight blazed around her.

Time seemed to move in slow motion as I soared through the air.

My last thought would be one of panicked confusion.

Mama is a Druik?

As the furious river came into view, all my thoughts scattered, carried away by the blood-curdling screech that tore from me.

My body jerked to a stop before I plummeted. A glittering, dusky mist coiled around Balor's embered ropes, cinching them around my waist tightly. My vision swam in my eyes. Hazy tears plunged into the churning water.

"What have you done?" The Akridai bellowed as my mother reeled my body into the safety of her arms. I curled into her glowing form, and her ember flung Balor's away. He glared at us, a severe scowl carving into the dull, pallid skin of his face. The corners of Mama's full lips tipped up.

"Ah, Balor. Run along. I think you've done enough today," a

melodic voice commanded from behind us. His gaze snapped toward the woman, and he hunched forward, his aura slinking back into itself.

"Yes, Mistress." Balor, a scurrying insect, fled toward Morpheus' palace.

My mother squeezed me closer, and I whimpered as my face pressed against her chest. Her pulse quickened, harmonizing with the beating under my star-shaped scar. "Shhh, it's all right, Little Star. I've got you," Mama murmured as her halo dimmed.

The woman clapped her hands over the buzz of hushed words from the crowd. "What do they call you, pet? Who am I to thank for such entertainment? And during the last days of the Winnowing Trials at that."

A rush of air blew from Mama's flared nostrils, and she gently set me on my feet. "Go to your father." Numbly, my feet followed her directive. I glanced at the striking woman. Elder Melina Harrow. One of her perfectly arched, pale eyebrows rose as she scrutinized me.

"Elder Harrow." Mama's voice was steady. The Elder's attention slid back to my mother. "My name is Maya Vawn."

Melina's laughter chimed through the air. "Maya." She paused, her tongue pushing at the inside of her cheek. Tasting the name. "Come, pet. It seems we've a lot to discuss." She sauntered toward the palace, her flowing black dress fluttering behind her. In the cool breeze, her hair lifted from her nape, and a flash of gold reflected in the setting sun.

I blinked, and it was gone.

Hurrying over, Mama crouched, her chilled hands cupping my cheeks. "You were very brave. Thank you for protecting your sister. I know you'll always be there for her."

"Yes, Mama," I sniffled, tears lining my bottom lashes.

She swiped her thumbs under my eyes. Icy dread gurgled behind my ribs as if my heart had fallen into the river and was drowning.

Urgently, Mama continued, "But hear me now. You must also be good to yourself. A flower can't bloom and nourish other living creatures if it doesn't seize the sunlight itself. If it doesn't cling to its roots."

With wide eyes, I blinked while her words knocked around my mind. She stood, kissing the top of my head and then Letti's, and murmured sentiments of love, smiling at us. But it didn't quite reach her eyes; the crinkles at the sides were missing.

Rubbing her lips together, she looked at Father. "Take care of them."

He lifted his chin, his expression softening as he met her gaze. "Of course, my love."

My eyelids scrunched together as the memory faded away. I coughed, trapping a sob in my chest. Gavrel glanced my way, and I subtly shook my head from side to side. He looked ahead, brows squeezing together.

I breathed in deeply through my nose, resting my palms on either side of my neck as I worked on soothing myself. My middle finger stroked my humming scar.

No wonder I was terrified of heights. Images of the Winnowing muddled with this unearthed memory. I shivered at the thought of being suspended over the cliff's edge, whether by ember or by rope. A huff of air whooshed from my nose, and my shoulders sagged.

That was the last time I saw my mother. The moment I had learned of her gift, and it had saved me.

Doomed her.

My loathing for Melina and the Dormancy burrowed deeper into my marrow, hardening my bones until my frame straightened and lifted my head.

All these turns, my last moments with Mama had been stolen. But they were mine once more, and I'd be bloody damned if anyone would take them again.

Marching forward, my hands fell as I pushed my shoulders back. First, food and supplies. Then rest.

One step at a time.

Back to the beginning.

To my roots.

3

THE SLIPPERY CHANNEL

SERYN

*W*e arrived in Ceto, the Haadran capital, by nightfall, just as Gavrel had predicted. My stomach growled as we stepped from the muddy marsh onto a wide, white lynstone bridge. Our boots, caked in thick mud and broken bits of marsh reeds, slurped against the smooth stone as we neared the city entrance.

Gavrel led us along the winding boardwalks supported by thick, crisscrossing wood piles. Canals gurgled between the paths and under footbridges, brackish water lapping at the algae-ridden tidemarks along the walls. Moonlight kissed the pallid, timeworn buildings.

I sighed, nearly bumping into Gavrel's back as he abruptly paused outside a spirited establishment, light, raucous laughter spilling out from its open wooden door.

I looked up at a swaying sign, one eyebrow raising as I read the curling letters. *The Slippery Channel.* I snorted at its name, smirking when Gavrel glanced at me. He grunted and, without a word, stepped through the door. But not before I caught the hint of his dimple winking below the grim line of his mouth and stubble.

The robust comfort of the place barged into my senses. A small fire danced in a hearth at the opposite end, next to a bar lined with people drinking pints. Lively chatter filled the room, bouncing off the walls and well-loved wooden tables.

Scanning the patrons, I couldn't tell if anyone was a Druik. There were no signs of auras flickering in the sea of alabaster attire.

"What have we here? But it can't be—Commander Larkin gracing our presence!" a comely, middle-aged woman called out from behind the bar. She tossed her rag on the counter and marched toward us, her ivory kirtle stretching around generous curves. Some patrons whooped or raised their brews in our direction.

Gavrel bowed as she stopped directly in front of us, her wide mouth beaming. Her smile was infectious, teasing a similar expression from me. I held out my hand, and the woman bounced forward, cocooning my hand in both of hers. "And you've brought a friend. How divine! Welcome to my place. The name is Cordelya Brimwell."

"Nice to meet you. I'm Seryn."

As she spoke, the sun-kissed skin around her bright eyes crinkled. She let go of my hands and touched Gavrel's arm. "What can I do ya for, Commander? Looking for a bed and a pint?" She winked at me, and a small laugh caught in my throat at her audacity.

The corners of Gavrel's lips lifted politely. "Two rooms and some of your stew, if you have any left."

She clapped her palms together. "You're in luck. We have nibbles, we do. This way." In a flurry, she led us to a table in the corner and smacked her hand on it before flitting away.

We settled in the creaking chairs, the patrons of the tavern gulping down their ale, laughing, and sharing stories, not paying us any further attention.

Cordelya swooped back to us, clinking bowls on the table. My stomach rumbled at the savory aroma of spiced fish and vegetables swimming in a hearty broth. "Now, about the *rooms*. We only have the one left. Will that do?" One of her pale eyebrows quirked at Gavrel.

"That's fine. We'll take it," Gavrel replied, frowning and handing her coins. "A pleasure as always, Cordelya."

She laughed, clunking a chunky metal key on the table between us. "You tell that Rhaegar to come visit me. Cross is what I am that he's stayed away so long." She winked at us before making her way to the bar, smiling and touching patrons' shoulders as she went.

Gavrel huffed a wry laugh and lifted his stew-filled spoon to his mouth, pausing for a moment before sliding the savory meal between his full lips. He chewed slowly, and his thick throat bobbed.

"You're humming. Good, yes?"

Warmth ran over my cheeks, and I nodded, swallowing. "Ceto's food rations seem sufficient."

"The region does better than most as long as the fish-harvesters can bring in a plentiful bounty. But the fish have been dwindling steadily over the turns."

My belly grumbled at the interruption, and I continued eating slowly, grateful for the hot meal. A festering ire bubbled within me at the thought of people starving elsewhere.

Of citizens disappearing during the Dormancy, possibly trapped in the Stygian Murk. While the Elders—Melina, Lucan, and Ryboas—were safe in Surrelia, we barely survived. They imposed their laws on the mortal realm for their own benefit.

I could sense Gavrel studying me in silence, but I refused to meet his gaze. The broth slid down my throat, warming me. Heat bloomed in my cheeks under his unwavering perusal.

After several moments, I set my utensil in my half-empty bowl, brushing the pad of my thumb over my lips, the taste of the spices still clinging to them. Both satiated and agitated, I sighed and finally met his eyes. "What?"

He ran the tip of his tongue over his bottom lip, then grazed it with his top teeth. After setting his bowl aside, he picked up the key. "Your face is practically shouting. Anything you want to share?" One eyebrow lifted.

"Pass," I mumbled.

"No remarks about needing to share a room?"

Unhurriedly, I pushed to my feet. "Why bother?" I moved past him toward the steps leading to the second level, tossing my words over my shoulder. "I'm sure you won't mind sleeping on the floor."

A soft chuckle rumbled in his chest. "Not at all."

I rolled my eyes and stomped up the stairs, shoulders stiff with irritation. As we came to our room, Gavrel stepped in front of me, the key clanging against the lock. The sound clinked within my ears, and I ground my molars together.

Thoughts banged around my head, and frustration bubbled in my gut. My skin felt tight around my muscles, itching to lash out and find relief from my resurrected memories—from the stifling need to scream into the void until my throat was raw.

From the heartache festering in my chest each time I looked at Gavrel.

Each time I thought of Kaden being missing, and of our time together in Surrelia.

Rubbing the space over my heart, my forehead creased as I studied the modest room with its narrow bed and extra blankets neatly folded at the end.

I removed my muddy boots and put them next to Gavrel's by the door. The music and chatter from below wafted up through the floorboards.

After removing my belt and dagger, I rummaged through the

attached satchel, tucking the etched protection talisman within my palm.

I was fairly certain Mama had the rune stone implanted in my nape at an early age. I couldn't remember a time when I didn't have the star-shaped scar on the back of my neck.

If her ember was as mighty as my memories alluded, she must have feared the Elders would harm me, assuming I had an equally powerful gift. And she wasn't wrong. My skin vibrated, and I clamped my eyes shut, disgust lining my tongue.

My mother must have been terrified that Melina would think I was the next Scion. The rest of my face crumpled, and my heart stuttered. The rune had likely been the only way Mama had known to protect me—or at least, that was what she'd believed.

With a sigh, I opened my eyes and set my belongings on the lone dresser in the corner. I moved to the window overlooking the canal. A few people strolled along the boardwalks without a care in the world. With the talisman tightly gripped in my hand, the tiny prickle of the rune's energy comforted me.

When I sat on the bed, it squeaked under my weight, but it was clean and comfy. After tucking the stone into my pocket, I curled on my side and closed my eyes as Gavrel used the extra blankets to make a makeshift bed on the floor at the foot of the bed.

His clothes rustled as he blew out the candle, his large frame shifting as he lay down. He was a protective blockade between me and the door.

Through the muffled sounds of the tavern below, I could hear Gavrel breathing. His deep and even rhythm lulled me to sleep, sinking into the chaotic shadows of my mind.

I woke with a start, sweaty strands of hair clinging to my neck. A broken, garbled cry fell from my lips. My ember pounded under the skin of my nape.

Gavrel was beside me in an instant, his weight dipping onto the mattress. "You're safe. Breathe." His hand found mine and rested on top of it, anchoring me to reality.

My fingers curled into the sheets as I breathed in and out, pushing away the smoky images of Kaden screaming, his muscles tense and writhing within a murky abyss.

As my eyes adjusted to the dimness, slices of moonlight trickled in from the window, painting the ceiling in a delicate glow. Gavrel's warmth seeped into my skin as my pulse steadied.

I pulled my hand away from his and then turned away from him and lay back down. When he rose, my heart skipped a beat. A raspy plea flew from me. "Stay."

He stilled; the silence blanketed with our breaths and the babbling waterway outside.

But then the bed dipped once more as he settled behind me and fit the broad expanse of his back against mine. I melted into the comforting, solid feel of him. My ember calmed, now a faint flutter.

After a few minutes, his gentle but firm words broke the silence. "Tell me."

He held his breath. I wrapped my arms across my chest. "Kaden. Somewhere dark. He … he was screaming in p-pain." I stumbled over the last word, choking on it.

No other mortal had dreamed in a long while. The dreams had decayed, withering away into nothing like Midst Fall. But that didn't stop nightmares from seeping into the shadowed corners of our slumber.

As of late, Gavrel and I had been *blessed* with premonitions that riddled our sleep under each full moon. Although tonight, both the moon and my patience were waning.

Why were the Fates toying with me? With Gavrel? Why force these cryptic messages upon us?

My eyes squeezed tightly as Kaden's anguished face flashed behind my lids. We needed to find him. *But what if we failed?* I whimpered, brushing the wetness from my cheek.

Gavrel turned, his muscled frame nearly pushing me off the narrow bed as it creaked in protest. One massive arm slipped under the crook of my neck. His other arm wrapped around my middle, tucking me safely into his chest.

And I let him hold me, snuggling into the warmth of his embrace. Ignoring memories of his arms around me like this from the past. Allowing myself to be soothed by his nearness as my whirling anxieties crumbled once more into a blessedly dreamless sleep.

4

—————

THE LEGS OF A DYING SPIDER

GAVREL

As I held Seryn in my arms, the steady rise and fall of her breathing quieted the rapid thrum of my blood. I navigated the twists and turns of my contemplations, memories of her flooding my mind. Recollections of all the moments we had shared, both together and apart, echoed through the corridors of my thoughts. There were so many things I needed to tell her, yet so many things I never could.

I tipped my face closer to the back of her head, messy curls tickling my nose, letting her sweet scent fill my senses. My Ancients, what I wouldn't give to hold her like this for the rest of our days.

If only I could allow that to happen.

A vicious sourness filled my throat at the thought of Seryn trapped within Melina's clutches. There were too many instances where she'd been in danger. Too many times, Melina had threatened her even before Seryn knew she was caught in the Elder's web.

The first time Melina had erased Seryn's memories was the winter before last. Even then, I was powerless against her. Unbidden, the memory crept into my mind like a festering wound.

In Morpheus' palace, I wandered through the maze of hallways, exhausted from hours of sparring with Rhaegar and my brother.

My thoughts drifted as I beheld the opulence of the place. I yearned for the simplicity and comfort of Evergryn—the days when danger didn't seep into every seam.

For a moment, I squeezed my eyes shut as an image of Seryn's smile flitted into my mind, morphing into the shattered expression I'd put there. A heavy sigh dropped at my feet as I blinked, a daze settling over me.

A little over a turn had passed since I'd shredded our relationship. Understandably, Seryn had made damn sure to spend as little time as possible in my presence since then—and it was for the best.

Of course it was.

I pressed my thumb to the corner of my mouth, as if that could wipe away any lingering doubt.

It's what I'd intended, after all. For her safety. So Melina wouldn't look her way again. If keeping the Elders' eyes off Seryn meant keeping my distance, then so be it.

Melina seemed pleased that Seryn no longer sought me out during the Dormancies, as she'd done more and more the last several turns. I pressed the heel of my palm into the scar on my chest, gritting my teeth.

Soon, I approached a set of massive doors, and my eyes widened at the realization of where my legs had carried me.

Of course, I was at the fucking library. Was I trying to sabotage my best efforts? Seryn loved the library and was likely still working there.

In spite of myself, my curiosity and desire to be near her got the better of me. With knit brows, I stepped inside as if I couldn't help myself. Because, if I were being honest, I clearly couldn't when it came to her.

Bloody void.

"No need to lurk, boy. Get what you need or get out." I winced at the sound of Iben Burlam's ill-tempered tone.

"Indeed. Thank you," I replied, bowing my head in his direction, and moving toward the stacks near the curling staircases in the back.

Because you know that's where she likely is.

Damn me to the Murk.

As I admonished myself, the sunbeams glinted, and a glimmer of flame-colored hues caught my attention. Seryn wandered out from behind a row of shelves, her hand tracing over the words in an open tome before sitting at her favorite table.

I froze, seriously considering diving into an aisle, but before I could take the leap, she lifted her head and sucked in a quick intake of air.

Eyes narrowing, her jaw turned to stone, and she dipped her head toward her book again, shifting her body away from me. Against my better judgment, I shuffled over to her, resting my hand on the back of the chair opposite her.

Patiently, I waited until she looked up with a quirked brow. "Yes?" Just a hint of curiosity laced with her annoyance.

My pulse throbbed under my jawline. "May I?"

"Do as you please," she murmured.

I wish I could.

Situating myself across from her, I feigned interest in another novel on the table, but studied her from under my lashes. She was reading her favorite book again ... the one she always found every Dormancy without fail—a written history about the Ancients.

The corners of my mouth tipped, and I set my volume aside. "Learning anything interesting?"

She sighed, her gaze remaining on the book. "As much as I can."

I leaned forward. "Such as?"

What are you doing, you imbecile?

She turned another page. "Gavrel, is there anything I can help you with, or are you bothering me for a reason?"

Because I can't fucking stay away from you.

"Ah, no reason. I ... I wanted to see how you were doing."

"Fine, thank you," she murmured.

"Er, well. I'm glad to hear it."

She snapped the book closed, color gliding over her cheeks. "Well, I'm glad you're glad to hear it. If you'll excuse me." She stood and marched away from me, down an aisle.

And, of course, I followed because I was a fool. Because seeing her was the only thing that brought me any peace. She stretched onto her tiptoes as she tried to put the book in its place, and I reached over her, helping the volume slide into its spot.

A little gasp slipped from her as my fingers met the back of hers. She pulled her hand away from mine and spun around, her spine pushing *into the shelves.*

My heart tripped over itself; her nearness almost brought me to my knees. Instead, I stepped back, fisting my hands at my sides as my gaze swept over her delicate features.

Even when she was glowering at me, I wanted her. My molars were going to crack if I clenched them any tighter.

Don't do it.

I shifted closer, and she lifted her chin. She was magnificent. My fingers twitched, and before I realized what I was doing, they slipped a curling strand behind her ear.

Her breath caught in her throat, and my fingertips froze at the edge of her jaw. My skin hummed at the contact, and her eyes crushed closed as if my touch caused her pain.

"Seryn, I—"

"What a touching moment. Do let me play." Ice skittered up my nape, and I snatched my hand away from Seryn as if I'd been burned. Eyes snapping toward the intruder, Seryn's shoulders wilted.

Melina sauntered toward us, and I positioned myself in front of Seryn. "Mistress, I was looking for you."

"Melina," she snapped.

She preferred that I call her by her name, forcing me to make our connection personal. Bitterness coated my tongue. "Melina," I conceded. Anything to make her leave.

"Were you?" Her incisors glinted as she raised one eyebrow. "How fortunate I found you then. Who do we have here, Gavie Gav?"

Disgust rippled up my vertebrae at the moniker.

She knew who Seryn was.

But she wanted me to say it. Wanted to watch her prey while they squirmed.

The leaden words tumbled to the floor. "Seryn Vawn, my brother's friend. Our neighbor."

"Oh, how interesting." Melina waved her hand for me to move aside, tilting her head to peek at Seryn. Like embedded stones, my feet wouldn't budge. One hand rested on the pommel of the dagger attached to my side, itching to unsheathe it. Slowly, Melina slid her tongue over her top lip, looking at me from under her dark lashes. "Move, Commander."

My fingers tensed, and I squared my jaw, shifting. Melina's narrowed eyes slid down Seryn's body, and Seryn smoothed her hand down her dress as if wanting to rid herself of the intrusion.

"Good day, Mistress," Seryn murmured. "Gavrel was helping me put a book away."

"Ah, she speaks. How chivalrous our Gavie is, is he not?" Melina purred, sidling closer.

Dread roiled within my stomach, and my breath hitched.

Seryn frowned, eyes darting between me and the Elder. Could she sense the impending threat? She stacked her spine, tucking her hair behind her ear. "He's not my Gavrel, but I appreciated the help."

"How clever you are, pet." Melina grinned, inching closer now. She tapped one finger against her crimson lips. "Now, who do you remind me of?"

It was as if the air was sucked from the library. Everyone else had left; there was no one to witness what Melina would do next.

"Melina, I'd like to meet you in your study," I said, noticing two Akridais situating themselves at either end of the aisle. Seryn's chest rose and fell in shallow breaths.

Elder Harrow's halo spilled around her, and my chest cracked open. "Commander, we'll reconvene later. I do so enjoy our playtime, but I'm quite busy at the moment. Shall we have some fun, pet? It's been a while since I took a trip down memory row." Melina snapped her fingers, and her enforcers slunk closer.

Her ebony smoke slunk around Seryn, caressing her. Seryn swallowed, terror widening her eyes.

"I do so love reminiscing. Let's see if there's anything amusing in that head of yours, shall we, pet? Or will you be like Maya and Gavie? I must admit I've been curious about you and your sister over the turns, but you haven't piqued my interest until quite recently. What with how Gavie pays you attention. Helps you with your books. Your mother was quite the challenge, but you ... you seem rather ... fragile."

Seryn's strangled response flew from her mouth as her hands fisted around the dark energy. "My mother—"

Melina nodded, and a gust of oiled air knocked my body backward. "Run!" I roared, fighting hopelessly against my invisible fetters, knowing the demand was futile.

And it was. Melina's power slithered into Seryn's mouth and ears while she screamed and clutched at the sides of her head.

Horrified, I watched as Melina's eyes fluttered, her body arching as she clawed her way through Seryn's brain. She licked her lips, savoring whatever it was she saw. Whatever she was stealing from the woman I'd break for again and again.

Seryn's head whipped from side to side, a look of anguish contorting her features. Her body trembled, and tears stained her dress.

"Ah, you have been a naughty ... naughty boy, Commander," Melina bit out, and her fingers jerked in front of her like the legs of a dying spider. "But don't fret. A departed memory means it never existed at all. Doesn't it?"

Damp air filled my lungs as the present resurfaced. Fury and anguish filled the empty spaces within me, shoving my shame and regret aside.

Melina would bloody well pay.

She would *never* harm Seryn again.

We would show her the meaning of agony, of being nothing more than a memory to be erased. She would learn that the departed don't always stay buried.

Conviction rumbled low and deep in my chest.

Seryn shifted, her back pressing harder into my chest. I tightened my arms around her, kissing her crown and surrendering to the contented slumber that finally claimed me.

5

REVERIES

GAVREL

*E*arth and nectar. I trapped my bottom lip behind one incisor, wishing I could taste the sweetness invading the air. My hips moved of their own volition, pushing into the soft heat wrapped around them.

With palms cupping a plump ass, my fingers pressed into warm curves. My cock jerked, seeking more friction.

I nuzzled into the crook of her neck, breathing her in as if she were oxygen.

A low growl vibrated in my throat when I tugged her lithe body closer, her heat tighter against my throbbing cock.

One of her arms wrapped around my middle, her nails digging into my back. The other twined around my nape while her fingers burrowed in my thick strands. Tugging on them. Pulling me into her as if we could melt together.

Rhythmically, her warm center ground against me.

A shudder ran up my spine, pushing a moan along the edges until it burst from my throat.

34

"Asteria." The gravelly murmur fled from me.

A plea.

A prayer.

I wasn't sure, but I needed to be inside her. Now.

I missed her embrace. Craved it.

My eyes snapped open as a sharp squeak broke through my lusty haze.

I was dreaming.

A tangle of messy auburn curls met me. Their soft strands tickled my jaw, catching in the stubble lining the squared angles as I pulled away.

I was most definitely *not* dreaming.

Slowly, I lifted my head, and my bottom lip slid from my bite. Her honeyed scent clung to my nostrils. I wanted to swim in it. Bite her skin as if she were made of the peaches she so loved, and then soothe the mark with my tongue.

Seryn's cheeks matched the color of her hair in the early morning light. Her irises burned brightly, the color of a glacial sky. She gulped. "I'm … I'm sorry."

I wasn't.

Within me, I felt her need coursing in waves.

She blinked when she realized how entwined we were. As if the warm limbs coiling around my bulky frame weren't her own.

I didn't move. Perhaps because I wished to avoid frightening or embarrassing her. But mostly because I didn't want to. I licked my bottom lip, and she followed my tongue's path, her nails gently pressing into my scalp and back.

Delicately, her nostrils flared before her eyelids fluttered, a moth ready to flee toward the light.

As she hastily untangled herself, I breathed in, trapping a muffled groan. Standing, I adjusted my arousal as she busied herself with her boots and belongings. With a ticking jaw, I tugged my own on, pulling the laces snug. "Ready?" I asked and secured my baldric across my chest.

Avoiding my eyes, she nodded and turned to leave. The edges of dawn's radiance spilled over her leather-clad, round backside as she scurried out of the room. At the view, my petulant cock twitched within the confines of my breeches, clearly not wanting to listen to reason.

Fucking void.

This was going to be a long journey.

Correction, it had *already* been a long journey. Every moment alone with her was torture.

Being near her.

Her sweet scent caressing me.

Sleeping next to her among the grymwoods.

The impenetrable silence and unspoken words between us.

Often, the rarity of quiet moments in my days left me longing for them. However, her reticence was troubling. She was working through her newly resurfaced memories—the pieces slicing through her one after the other as they unearthed themselves.

Aching worry scurried over my skin, and my muscles tensed, my cock somberly settling in my breeches.

Throughout the last several days, she'd been ill-tempered and despondent. I couldn't blame her. I wanted to take her pain away, but she didn't want any help from me.

At least, not yet.

Probably never.

I sighed, shifting my pack and weapon on my back as I followed her out of the room. The weight of our footfalls plunked over the inn's rickety steps as we descended.

Over the turns, the constant effort of evading the consequences of my choices had been exhausting.

Every day, the jagged pieces of regret wedged between my

ribs, clawing at the bony cage and trying to dig in. Trying to pierce my heart and drown me in my own blood. My jaw tightened, fists strangling the leather of my baldric.

Oddly, a morbid sense of relief lined the soiled edges of my remorse and shame. Now that Seryn remembered everything—now that she was coming into her powers—a sense of something urgent and terrifying nipped at my heels.

I wanted her to tear my heart in two. Needed her to punish me for everything I'd done over the turns. Help me forget the fear and regrets I carried deep within my mind while everyone else's conscience was wiped clean every spring at the end of the Dormancy.

My thoughts soured as Melina's malevolent grin sliced into my thoughts, her cold, delicate fingers stroking over me whenever she pleased.

Uninvited.

She was in Surrelia, along with her lapdogs, Lucan and Ryboas. It was time for me to cut my leash. No longer would I bend to her whims.

To her cruelties.

To *my* cruelties.

I swallowed, my windpipe dry. Brittle.

With Seryn and Kaden coming into their ember, a spark of—dare I say—hope was kindling within me. They weren't as fragile as they once were and would only grow more capable over the coming turns.

They had to.

I rolled my shoulders, shifting my rucksack as we left the sleepy tavern.

Seryn peeked at me as I stood next to her on the boardwalk. The dawn painted the lynstone of the buildings in shades of peach and neon pink. She was radiant; the mortified flush on her face still lingered.

Growing up, I'd always been protective of her, as if she were my younger sister. She was all gangly limbs and mischief. However, over time, things changed. As a teenager, she'd sought me out more often, and I noticed her bashful glances frequently. It wasn't until she'd turned eighteen that I truly began to see her as the beautiful, stubborn woman she had become. She ignited something deeper within me. As if I blinked and could no longer view her as I once had.

She was *more*.

I wondered if she remembered the first time we ever kissed two springs ago. The first time she'd come undone in my arms.

We moved through the twisting boardwalks of the city. I shook my head, trying to dislodge the bittersweet recollections as they flit through my mind, but to no avail.

During a beautiful spring day two turns ago, Seryn asked me to walk with her to and from the village. Later that afternoon, we walked home through the grymwoods. I didn't wish to be away from her, so I foolishly asked her to sit with me awhile and watch the stars paint the twilight.

She talked about adoring the night sky—about Asteria, the Ancient of Stars, weaving her burning ember through the aether.

"I'm sure the stars would worship at your feet ... Asteria," I said.

Fuck.

She'd smoothed her thumb over the crease between my eyebrows, teasing that it would permanently etch into it as fear and longing spun through my mind.

"If you'll keep touching me, I'll make sure of it," I murmured absently.

Fucking Fuck.

One thing led to another, and we collided, the gravity of our orbits too powerful to resist. In a fit of passion, we'd kissed, grasping at each other, and as she rocked against my clothed erection, I witnessed our undoing as she came.

After, she cupped my jaw tenderly and simply whispered, "Finally."

"Finally," I rasped in hopeless agreement, the word laced with shame and fear, knowing I would destroy her.

A sharp twinge in my chest brought me back to the present. I scrubbed my hand over the aching scar over my heart. I glanced at Seryn as we walked, and my fingers twitched with the need to touch her now.

But I couldn't.

I'd lost that privilege.

Long ago, I had stomped on what we had. Tearing the roots up with my bare hands. My nails dug into my palms.

Back then, we'd never fully consummated our relationship. *Unlike Seryn and my brother.* A burning knot pulled tight within my chest at the thought. The muscle in my jaw pulsed, and I squeezed my teeth together until they ached. She was free to do whatever she desired. It's all I'd ever wanted for her, but it didn't stop me from wanting to tear my fucking heart out because it wasn't me.

Last night, when she'd asked me to stay—when she allowed my arms to wrap around her—I could have passed on. Given my physical form to the dirt and gone to Surrelia, sated and content.

"Which way?" Seryn inquired as we arrived at a crossroads, her eyes still avoiding mine.

I inclined my head slightly to the right, moving in that direction.

She sighed, following me as we made our way through the winding boardwalks. Closer to the edge of town, we hastily bartered for some dried foods, supplies, and a set of smaller knives with the merchants.

Seryn slipped the sheathed blades carefully under some straps on her tall, black boots. I swallowed as she stood, my fingers twitching as soft light caressed her curves. She surveyed

Ceto's gentle beauty, her eyes pensively following a fisherman's rickety boat as it drifted under the bridge we were crossing.

Jaw ticking, she froze. My hand went to the dagger at my waist as I followed her line of sight. There, in the window of a shop, was a tall banner. Melina and the Elders' likenesses were drawn in admirable detail. Their hair fluttered as if they stood in a gentle breeze, their gazes gallantly staring off into the distance. In big, bold lettering, the slogan "Through Dormancy, we blossom!" was scrawled.

Seryn moved toward the propaganda, and I stepped into her path. She sneered; her collarbone painted in angry pink splotches.

I cleared my throat. "We should—" My words fell short as a flash of velvety pewter caught my eye near the merchant stands on the other side of the canal. Scooping Seryn around the waist, I pulled her into a narrow alley between the shops and pressed my body into hers against the chilled wall. A garbled sound of distress shot from her lips.

"What the void, Gav?" she hissed, her fingers digging into my sides. "You really need to stop dragging me around like a doll."

A half-smile ghosted across my lips as I cautiously peeked around the edge of the building. Two males stalked toward us— a stocky Akridai and a lanky, young Draumr—following the pointed fingers of the weapons merchant.

Damn him.

The enforcer's metallic cape flapped in the morning breeze. "Melina sent reinforcements," I whispered.

Seryn gulped, her fingers clinging to the sides of my tunic. She shivered, breathed in deeply, and then nudged me away and lined up her spine in a column against the wall. Her chin lifted as she finally met my eyes, hers frosting over as we moved deeper into the alleyway. "Let's go."

We reached the other end and veered down another path along a different canal. Our boots slapped against the planks as we ran. Seryn stopped abruptly, and I nearly collided with her before she spun around, her head angled toward the way we'd come.

She fisted my baldric at the sound of footfalls rushing down the alley, tugging me through an open door to our right.

My brows rose as I glimpsed the creaking sign hanging above the door.

The Oracle's Seat.

I wouldn't bother questioning our good fortune.

If Tyche, the Ancient of Luck, had led us to where she wanted us. I'd take it.

As we stumbled into the shop, the musty smell of ancient papers, earthy incense, and melted wax met us. My heart pounded against the inside of my ribs as I surveyed the dimly lit room.

Various mystical artifacts, thick books, crystals, and dripping candlesticks were scattered along the abundant wooden shelves and counters. There, to our left, was a small stairwell leading to the next floor.

Without warning, Seryn darted toward a different doorway in the back, swatting away a pair of velvety azure curtains sweeping over each side. In frustration, I rolled my eyes and then looked back. Advancing shadows approached the board-walk in front of the door, and I bolted through the egress behind her.

"You've arrived. Come, sit." The feminine, melodious words fluttered around us. Seryn paused, gripping the hilt of the dagger at her hip. My heels dug into the plush rugs strewn haphazardly around the cramped space, squinting toward the voice.

Flickering candlelight danced over the walls, painting the stunning female in a soft, sputtering glow. The waves of her hair were so pale that it looked like fine threads of gold with various metallic beads glinting among sporadically braided strands. Her white, flowing dress pooled on the colorful rugs beneath her feet.

"I've been waiting for you," she crooned, fixing her gaze upon Seryn. One corner of her mouth tipped as she turned her attention to the worn oracle cards in her hands. She swept her palm over the room's round table and left behind an arc of cards.

Moving to Seryn's side, I studied the woman for any signs of ill intention. She didn't appear to mean us any harm, but you never could be sure. I squared my stance, blocking the way we'd entered, and heard no signs of others following us.

Seryn hesitated, but then cautiously took a step toward the table. Her head tilted as she moved closer, studying both the female and the divination spread across the velvet-covered tabletop.

The seer's hand hovered over the arc, gilded eyes flashing with every card she plucked and laid on the table in a diamond. Images of various Ancients and lore painted the deck's colorful faces.

Spellbound now, Seryn drifted nearer still, her attention flitting over the cards as she sat across from the stranger. I moved beside her, the knuckles of my left hand turning white as I clamped my fingers around the top of the chair.

"Ahh, just as I suspected." The female tapped the card in the west, sighed gently, and then touched the one in the south position. Beneath her fingertip, the image of a running stag with two arrows protruding from its back lingered. "You've journeyed a great distance through the mist and decay. Forced your way into the sunlight so the shadows would lift. Even so, they nip at your heels."

Remaining silent, Seryn pressed her lips together as the seer's eyes bore into hers. Seryn's chair creaked as she shifted. One eyebrow rose on the female's face, her mouth gently curving.

Without looking, her first two fingers touched the card to the east. The image of three ethereal females mocked me. Their glowing forms huddled together, a whirlwind of golden string twirling around them. "What you seek will be found, but the path will prove arduous. Shadowed truths unveiled."

She glanced at me, the metal of her irises glinting before she looked back at Seryn. In my ears, the pounding of my heart thundered.

Her fingertips tiptoed over the table and then pressed into the card at the pinnacle, pushing it toward us and leaning forward as if sharing an intimate secret. "Poseidon's spear." She lifted her hand, propping her delicate chin upon her knuckles, revealing the image on the last card. "On more than a single occasion, you'll find the beginning in the aqueous depths. Allow your gifts to guide you."

"What do you—" Seryn started as I barked, "What location?"

Seryn glanced at me, and I nodded once. She continued, looking back at the seer, "The portal is somewhere in water?"

The female smiled serenely and leaned back; her chair silent despite the weight of her riddles. Breathlessly, she mused, "Oracle cards rarely lie. It's odd more mortals don't embrace them."

Rolling her eyes, Seryn pushed herself to her feet. "Looks like all our problems are solved, Gav. All we need to do is find the portal among water"—she ground her molars together, throwing her hands up and letting them slap onto her thighs before her voice climbed a few octaves—"somewhere in this entire Ancients-forsaken, bloody drowning, salty fucking water region!"

"Sometimes, you must let the journey unfurl. If you were given a direct path, providence might fray. Might ripple through the strings of other fates tethered to yours." Rising gracefully, the seer offered us a placating smile as she took a step back into the corner where the candlelight couldn't reach. "You must go now. I hear hydor lilies are in season."

Seryn and I looked at each other, matching expressions of confusion and annoyance etched into our features. When we looked back, the female had vanished. She was a reverie swept away by the shadows.

6

HYDOR LILIES

Cautiously, Gavrel scanned the front of the shop. With no sign of Melina's minions, we rushed over to the door.

A short stub of a man wearing dingy robes in a patchwork of blue velvet wobbled down the stairs. His pudgy cheeks puffed as he sputtered, "What were you doing in the back of my—"

My brows shot up, and then a mask of contrition spilled over my face as I interrupted him with a mumbled apology and hurried outside after Gavrel.

Gavrel marched across a footbridge and down another alley, checking each corner before progressing. His gaze continually swept over me as if I were the twilight about to slip away into the morning sun.

Finally, as we left another backstreet, we reached the edge of the city. Relief washed over me at the sight of the lynstone bridge and marshy land whence we had arrived.

We darted toward the exit, but before we could set foot on it,

45

a young man in Draumr uniform appeared from between two shops. With a yelp, I crashed into him, knocking us both onto our backsides.

The rasp of Gavrel's sword being drawn had me scrambling away from the guard while reaching for my dagger. The Draumr slowly got to his feet, his palms held out in front of him. "Commander Larkin?" he asked, his eyes wide and curious.

Gavrel squinted at him, taking an ominous step forward, blade blinking in the sunlight.

"Wait. Wait, please," the guard entreated as he righted his overcoat and lifted his chin. Standing, I leaned in just a fraction and rested my hand on Gavrel's left biceps. The man continued, "It won't be long until my companion finds us. Please, listen."

Gavrel's blade dropped a fraction. "Speak."

"Your second-in-command sends a missive." A quick breath of air filled my lungs, my eyebrows lifting. The guard looked down the alley he'd shot out of and then back at us. Gavrel lowered his weapon further, and the young man leaned in, speaking furtively. "Rhaegar sent word through our *network*. Said that mortals were better messengers than"—he curled the first two fingers of each hand in the air near his cheeks— "blasted harbinger starlings."

He glanced behind nervously. "He'll find you in the Bogs post haste, but asked that you leave word with Neoma Skiya of your final destination once you arrive in Helos."

Gavrel sheathed his sword and patted the young warrior on the shoulder before walking toward the bridge once more.

The guard nodded to me and turned to leave the way he'd arrived. "May the wings of the Raven carry you."

"Uh, thank you," I muttered as I moved past him, falling into step with Gavrel. "Do you think it's a trap?"

"No, that message was surely sent by Hale. The man loathes birds."

I chuckled, the feel of it odd in my throat. "He seems to have issues with most small, winged creatures." Rhaegar didn't enjoy pixies either.

His dimple flashed before he shifted his rucksack and pushed ahead.

Hastily, we moved through the marshland, mud sucking at our boots and wispy, tan reeds stroking against our bodies. Briny wind tossed loose strands about my cheeks.

Bending, I plucked a thin, broken stalk from under my foot. I ran the grain through the pressed pads of my thumb and middle finger. "How long do you think it'll take for Xeni to reach Letti?" I murmured.

"She'll make haste. I'd say a few days."

My chin dipped. "I wish I'd gotten to know her better. I'll remedy that once we return home."

"You'll get the chance." He slowed, the corners of his mouth tipping. "Xeni is a woman of few words, but she'll do what she must in order to protect Letti."

"I've no doubt." I tossed the reed to the ground. "What are we going to do about my father?"

Gavrel's jaw ticked. "I don't know yet. When we find Kaden, I fear that he'll take the decision from us regardless."

A grimace settled over my features. He was right. Kaden would likely lose the precarious command he had over his temper.

And it bothered me that the thought didn't pain me as much as it should. Did I care about Father? Yes, but he'd been so distant and uncaring my whole life that the weight of his demise didn't sit heavy upon my shoulders.

With a deep exhale, my eyes roamed over the wide expanse before us. Far in the distance, the Ourea Peaks poked at the sky.

"Are those huts?" I asked, focusing on a spattering of slanted, grass-roofed structures along the horizon to our left.

"Likely abandoned long ago. Haadra used to be filled with marsh dwellers, but the Withering made it nearly impossible to survive out here. Citizens either fled to the city or starved." His voice rumbled, ire lacing his words.

I breathed in, a sodden gloom coating me. The only sounds that accompanied us for the next several hours were those of the salted air pushing through the reeds and the squish of our boots as they trekked through endless puddles.

Either the critters in this region were long lost to the Withering, or they were hiding, silently watching as we crept through the sopping wetlands.

We reached Inksalt Loch as the sun prodded its pinnacle in the sky. I scanned the water, following its gentle ripples to the right. Close by, a single coral bloom bobbed in the current.

I crouched. A smile curved my mouth, mimicking the gentle bend of the petal as I ran a finger over it.

"Hydor lilies are in season," Gavrel mumbled as he strode to the right, following a thin tributary connecting with the loch.

With one eyebrow lifted, I stood, brushing my hands over my thighs.

"She said, 'hydor lilies are in season' … the *lotus*." His dimple peeked out from the side of his grin, and the shock of it had my head jerking back. He so rarely allowed his face to express joy in that way.

"Why, Gavrel, I had no idea you were so interested in flowers," I teased.

"The seer was directing us to *Lotus* Loch."

Bugger me.

Hydor lilies were also called *lotus*. My heart tripped and then caught up with itself as we hastened our strides along the meandering river.

My thoughts drifted along with the current. I wondered how Letti was doing, how she'd react when Xeni found her, and if Father suspected she remembered everything. If he cared even a little that I was gone, but my chin fell, already knowing the answer. Did he at least regret what he'd done to Hestia?

My heart pounded erratically as the image of Kaden screaming in the darkness replayed, and then skipped several beats entirely as I wrapped my arms across my middle.

I scrunched my eyes closed, remembering Gavrel's biceps cocooning my body this morning. The warmth of his front pressed snugly against my back. Heat climbed from the base of my spine to my neck, and my ember purred within me.

Heart fumbling, my focus wandered along the crisp mountain ridges as I tried to distract my thoughts from scurrying back into this morning's wake-up call.

A low hum of frustration vibrated in my throat. I blinked and glanced at him. He was studying me from his peripheral, as he often had during our little *adventure*.

One side of his mouth tipped up before settling back in place again. I pulled my eyes forward as a burning rush of heat swept over my face and scalp. Did he know what I was thinking? Ancients, I hoped not.

Absently, I played with the end of my messy plait, tugging on the end before tossing it back over my shoulder. My fingertips brushed over my neck.

A tingling caress stroked down my spine as I recalled my half-asleep body rubbing against his this morning. I'd relished the feel of his solid limbs tangled around mine. His hands squeezing my backside. His hardness pressing against my core.

Pulling my thoughts back, Gavrel coughed lightly, hands tightening on his baldric. He sucked his bottom lip into his mouth, and I wished it was me doing that.

Bloody void, you wanton wench.

Kaden was likely suffering, trying to survive, and I was lusting after his brother. My forehead wrinkled at the thought of my best friend's anguish, his body contorting in pain. My contemplations continued to spiral and bleed into one another.

Confusion.

Longing.

Rage.

Concern.

Nostalgia.

Frustration.

Overwhelming emotions skittered over my bones, poking and prodding me. Trying to find their place within the cracks of my very being. I wiped my damp palms along the sleeves of my dark tunic as I hugged myself.

Breathe in.

Breathe out.

A subtle brush of Gavrel's biceps against mine brought me back to the present. He wasn't looking at me as we forged ahead, but the corners of his eyes were soft. Comforting.

He was holding back, allowing me to shuffle my memories back in place. Allowing me to acclimate to the onslaught of feelings thrashing around my skull. Giving me the space to soothe myself while letting me know he was here.

Kaden was the sun. Shining. Conspicuous. I'd always counted on his constant comfort and warm presence. My head leaned to one side, neck stretching with the motion. I peeked at Gavrel, considering him. He'd always been around as well, discreetly watching over those he cared for like an unwavering shadow. He wanted Kaden to shine and was content with lingering in the background.

I breathed in and then out to the count of four again, allowing the crisp, clean air to soothe me as we trekked through the reeds and mud. As my pulse calmed, a final, shaky puff of air pushed from between my lips.

Gavrel and I would have to address our past. It bubbled beneath my skin, yearning to unleash itself. The compulsion to do just that was almost as intense as my ember wanting to drain others dry. A prickle stroked in an upward curve along my nape as if it was smiling against my skin.

Within the hour, a mesmerizing array of hydor lilies scattered over the clouded surface of Lotus Loch.

My scar tingled as we walked along the edge. Tentatively, I allowed my ember to trickle out, its energy sighing with relief as it wavered around me, unveiling the spectacular halos dancing around the water, mountains, and flora.

A sparkling haze twinkled above each flower, but as my eyes traversed the pool, their auras sparked and popped the closer they got to a section not far from the shore.

Pointing, I gulped. "There."

Without question, Gavrel stepped into the water. The blooms swayed around him, and his tattoo glowed as he held his hand out to me.

I breathed in and exhaled as I placed my palm in his. Lapping at my skin, the wet chill seeped into my clothes and bones as we trudged deeper. The briny liquid was so murky, it devoured any part of me that was immersed, my top half bobbing with the flowers.

The silty bottom sucked at my boots as we pushed forward, and as we grew closer to the crackling lotus, a humming energy crescendoed—a watery drone that vibrated among us.

Briefly, Gavrel turned his attention to me, one eyebrow raised, head tilting.

The water was waist-high, but with our next step, my aura and Gavrel's rune exploded with brilliance. We plunged into the icy depths, the muck no longer meeting our feet. The cloudy liquid pressed into me from all sides, its grip yanking me down.

I gasped before my head submerged, and salty liquid filled my throat. Trying to propel myself upward, my hand ripped from Gavrel's as I flailed.

The memory of me almost drowning as a child intruded my thoughts. My heart thrashed about, lungs screaming. Buzzing filled my skull, and despite sinking into the gloomy depths, a scorching light pulsed over the insides of my scrunched eyelids.

Not caring if it hurt, I opened my eyes, seeking a way to save myself. A stinging burn swept across my pupils before a massive shadow swooped past my left. Without warning, something tangled around my calves, wrenching.

Trying to escape as the squirming shackles tug me sideways, I jerked to my right but didn't get very far. I pulled my dagger from its sheath, and within a few seconds, the blade severed my restraints with a squishy snap.

Milky claret swirled around me as I sheathed my weapon, panic vibrating within every fiber of my body. My ember rammed against my flesh, urging me to tear at the water to my right.

An obscured blaze of light whirled into the opaque depths. Frantically, I pushed ahead and heeded my gift's counsel.

Just as my fingers stretched toward the vortex, the current pulling me in, the glint of massive, needle-like teeth snapped precariously near my left. A muffled scream tore from me, and a burst of bubbles fled my mouth, the maelstrom greedily gobbling them up.

The dim outline of the creature's bulbous form lunged at me again, as its bulging, phosphorescent eyes locked onto me. I could just make out numerous eel-like tentacles writhing and stretching from the beast's rotund mass, reaching for me.

I shut my eyes tight, not wanting to see the creature any clearer as it dragged me into its jaws. My heart slowed, and my lungs jerked, no longer able to withstand the lack of oxygen.

All at once, my whirling thoughts stilled, and absolute acceptance washed over me.

Pain was fleeting.

Perhaps the Fates were offering me a way to find Kaden and Mama.

After all, death was just another part of the journey.

7

DOOMBARKS

SERYN

Before the beast could claim me as its meal, something shackled around my wrist. My eyes snapped open. Just as the monster's tentacles were mere inches away, Gavrel jerked me out of reach and into the twirling portal.

A rush of life-giving air filled my gasping lungs as the thought of my childhood drowning invaded again.

Gavrel had saved me then, too. I was sure of it now. The memory was once obscured either by the trauma or by Melina's ember, but the haziness had finally cleared.

A younger Gavrel swam toward me in the bubbling darkness. Then he was dragging my limp body from the pond that had tried to claim me.

The images flitted away as Gavrel's concerned focus locked on mine. Refusing to part from him, I mimicked his grip and locked my fingers around his wrist. We plummeted among a slurry of fizzing stars as they crashed into the rotating wall of liquid.

Unceremoniously, the portal deposited us in a soggy heap atop a moss-covered slab, just big enough for our tangled bodies to lie upon. We clung to each other like sodden weeds cast out of the sea, and the portal fizzled away into the aether as if it had never existed.

Exhaustion coursed through my muscles and my mind. Gavrel gently untangled himself from me, and I forced myself to sit upright.

Coughing, I winced at the muddy liquid fleeing my lungs and splashing onto the stone. I ran the back of my hand over my mouth, nose crinkling as a pungent musk stole space in my lungs. "What am I smelling? Please tell me it isn't me," I groaned.

A low chuckle reverberated as Gavrel glanced at me. My eyes narrowed at him. He shrugged, picking himself up. "You get used to it after a while—the peat. So much underlying decay throughout the mire." He scanned the area, adjusting his broadsword. "It's barely noticeable in the city."

I offered him a deadpan glare. "What a shame. I love the smell of rotten eggs in the afternoon."

He shook his head, an amused expression lining his face as he grabbed my hands and helped me stand. I rose, taking care not to slip into the muddy, debris-ridden water surrounding us.

My sodden rucksack shifted awkwardly along my back, making me keenly aware of how uncomfortably wet I was. The air was muggy, sticking to my skin and leathers in a clammy embrace. How I wished I could change into dry clothing, but everything in my bag was surely drenched. "You lose your pack?"

He shrugged. "It's no matter. It shouldn't take long to find our way to Helos." Reaching up, Gavrel seized two sturdy, long branches from an overhanging tree. With a swift, decisive motion, he broke them off, the sharp crack echoing like the sound of bones snapping. I shuddered, a twinge of empathy washing over me for the tree's pain.

In every direction, slim gray trees lurched from the murky depths, their contorted appendages scraping at the overcast sky. *Doombark cypresses*. I believe that's what Magister Barden called them during our lessons. Various vines and vegetation drooped from the boughs, clung to the peeling bark, or drifted solemnly along the shivering water.

"Thank you for saving me from drowning … for the second time in our lives," I muttered.

He nodded before stepping off the stone. The water lapped at his calves as he jabbed his stick into it.

I breathed in through my mouth, trying to avoid inhaling the scent of decomposition.

Hauntingly captivating, a chorus of swamp crickets chirped as I scoured our surroundings, and despite the humidity, I shivered.

It was rumored that the Perilous Bogs had claimed many wanderers over the centuries. There were many stories of deceased mortals floating up from the depths, their physical bodies preserved, albeit bloated and waxy, by the swamp.

My shoulders tensed, lifting a little as my imagination scratched within me. Perhaps the trees were the last remnants of bog bodies that had never escaped the muck—bones twisted, stretched, and planted deep.

A fetid waft of air rustled through the branches, causing the extremities to sway; the vines dripping from them shuddered. Far in the distance, I thought a pallid hand crept out of the surface, its crooked fingers groping at the sky. I blinked several times and rubbed my eyes. When I looked again, only murky, rippling water remained.

I pushed my shoulders down and back, squeezing my hands and then shaking them out at my sides. I was exhausted, and my mind was playing tricks on me.

Gavrel's chest rose and fell evenly as he studied the expanse. His calm composure comforted me, my mind sweeping away grisly musings. I plucked at the damp sleeves on my biceps; the snug cuffs were more and more like manacles. My brow furrowed. "What the void attacked me in the loch?"

"Something that had no business being in Midst Fall," he grumbled, offering me the second branch and helping me step into the tepid water.

"Was it a Void creature?"

"I suspect so. Which would mean the problem we've been having in Surrelia is spilling into this realm." The side of his jaw ticked angrily.

"You have thoughts on that?" I prodded.

He grunted.

"Your jaw is about to crack off. So, I think you just might have some ideas," I snickered.

He slowly shifted his jaw from side to side before regarding me from his peripheral. "The portals between realms are weakening. I'm not sure why or whether it's intentional. Perhaps it's connected to the thing trapped in the amber boulder—in the palace dungeon." His fist tightened around the walking stick. "Regardless, I mean to find answers."

I rubbed my lips together and lifted my chin. "We'll find them together."

His brow crumpled. "Seryn …"

"It's too late, Gavrel. I have my memories now. I'm tired of drifting through life … tired of pretending that we can't fight back. We'll find Kaden, and then we'll figure out how to save our realm." I breathed in, my chest expanding. "I'm not weak." My words rushed out on an exhale.

If I said it enough, I'd start to believe it.

Gavrel paused and turned to me, water slapping at his knees irritably with the sudden movement. My eyes were glued to his thickly muscled thighs as his breeches clung to the skin.

I braced myself for words of dissuasion. For him to order me to stay tucked away somewhere. Or maybe he thought everyone else would be safer if I hid so my abilities didn't tear them apart. Bitterness coated my tongue.

"Stop." He waited until I brought my eyes to his. "I can see your mind spinning. Weak is a word I'd never associate with you."

I scoffed, turning my face to the side. A heavy sense of disbelief and embarrassment dug into me. My boots sank deeper into the muck. Perhaps I was turning into a doombark.

Wetness splattered against my legs, the droplets cooling my heated, leather-clad skin for a moment before Gavrel gently cupped my chin. I resisted his touch, my teeth clenching and turning my chin to stone.

Gavrel's thumb brushed over the hollow of my cheek. The tension in my shoulders released, and I allowed him to turn my face back to his. His features softened, and he leaned forward a bit.

Surely, he could feel my pulse skitter beneath his fingertips. Gavrel's eyes searched mine, and I drowned within their emerald depths.

"You're one of the fiercest people I've ever met. You'll tear every realm apart to save Midst Fall and those you love … to find Kaden." He rubbed his lips together. "And you'll succeed, Asteria." The name still did something to me, warmth buzzing under my skin.

He studied every angle and curve of my expression, one surely of hesitant acceptance. Until finally, he pulled away. I wanted to drag his hand back, but I dug my fingernails into my belt instead. Straightening, he sighed wearily.

In silence, we moved through the swamp, prodding at the spaces ahead before stepping, avoiding hidden wells beneath the thigh-high water.

Gavrel took my hand, guiding us around sinkholes and

pushing decrepit, rotting logs out of the way with his stick. The sound of toads and insects, shifting foliage, and sluggish ripples of liquid serenaded us as we went, only to be interrupted by the occasional slap of my hand as I swatted away the flying insects biting every inch of my exposed skin.

Once more, he jabbed into the water, his chest expanding with a deep inhale as he calmly brushed a mosquito from his cheek. "Helos shouldn't be far now."

Carefully, I stepped beside him, unsettling a chunk of bark as it coasted across our path. Watching, Gavrel and I paused. Atop the graying wood, a tiny, brown toad croaked angrily before leaping into the water with a plop. I smirked, a rush of camaraderie washing over me.

"Almost accurate. If you weren't heading in the wrong direction." We flinched at the haughty tone to our right. Within our next breaths, we brandished our weapons as we spun toward the stranger.

My branch flew from my fingers, sinking into an unseen hole. With the swamp water waist-high, my body wobbled as I tried to regain my balance and not topple over.

Gavrel grabbed my rucksack, and I steadied myself while gawking at the man's very shirtless, very toned torso. My jaw dropped along with my hands.

His face was just as chiseled as his muscles, albeit coated in a thin layer of a greenish-tinged sap like the rest of him. The color highlighted his brownish-red hair, its wavy, russet strands skimmed the broad expanse of his shoulders.

Whatever the substance was, it didn't hide the various linear scars marring his upper body, including a jagged line that ran diagonally from his left temple, through his straight, thick brow, to the apple of his high, angular cheekbone. By the look of it, he was lucky to have his eye.

I breathed in, no longer smelling the acrid swamp aromas.

Either I was now used to it, or I had lost my senses. The man was *dangerously* appealing.

He moved forward, the water rippling around his clingy, dark breeches.

"Another step would be a grave mistake," Gavrel snarled, positioning himself in front of me and raising his broadsword a fraction.

I huffed, my slight lapse in attention broken. I remembered to glare at the stranger, but couldn't muster any fear despite his arrogant display of his body and approach.

A nearly imperceptible smirk tweaked his mouth. Flaring around his tall, athletic form, a midnight-colored aura licked at his skin like flames.

Gavrel widened his stance. My power was tucked away, and the Druik was entirely unconcerned. *He's flaunting his ember on purpose.* One of my eyebrows rose at his boldness.

"Now, now. No need for bloodshed. These waters have claimed enough bodies," he stated in a droll tone.

He held up one hand, making a come-hither gesture before turning to the side. Easily as tall as him, he held an intricately carved wooden staff. It was likely more a weapon than a walking stick. "I'd say it's a pleasure to meet you—Seryn, is it?— but I'd be lying."

8

YAYA

"Come. Unless you want to head directly into that crocodile den you were about to stumble upon. It's not a death I'd recommend." The Druik walked perpendicular to the direction we'd been heading in. As he took long, confident strides, his ebony flames melted into his flesh, revealing a mesmerizing raven tattoo that spanned across his shoulder blades.

His muscles flexed, bringing the art to life. The inky wings spread wide as if the bird were soaring into the air. When the light brushed across the feathers, the ink shone like an oil slick in shifting shades of midnight iridescence.

Glaring at the male's back, Gavrel's nostrils flared as he sheathed his sword. I took his hand in mine and followed, pressing my lips together to hide the smile that wanted to break free. He would move with me. Gavrel wouldn't let me fall into this Ancient-forsaken swamp.

We caught up to the stranger, and he glanced at me sidelong, his expression indifferent, and his straight nose lifted.

"So, how do you know my name then, Sir Swampy Bottoms?" I inquired, sounding extra precocious. This man seemed especially mercurial, and it made me want to poke his buttons. Not that he was wearing any.

His mouth twisted to one side. "The Augur informed Yaya you'd be here on this day. I had the *privilege* of fetching you," he stated, sounding extremely inconvenienced.

"Augur?" Gavrel's brow furrowed.

"She's revered in this region for her prophetic counsel ... assuming one finds such things credible," the male muttered.

A smirk pressed into the line of my mouth. "Well, sorry to burden you, but can you tell us who the void you are? Although Sir Swampy Bottoms has a nice ring to it."

A low chuckle vibrated in Gavrel's chest.

The male's arms flexed as he stabbed his quarterstaff into the water in time with his stride. He didn't look impressed as his brows pushed together and his lips puckered. He took a deep inhale and freed it, his jaw slightly shifting to the side for a moment before he responded, "Marek Skiya."

"Any relation to Neoma Skiya?" Gavrel asked. "We were told to find her."

"Obviously. Why would I be here otherwise?" Marek countered with a condescending tone. "Yaya. She's my grandmother." He stopped, and I nearly ran into him before bracing a hand against his biceps. "Here we are." He lifted his chin as I pulled my hand away, my skin sticky with the olive-colored sap.

He glanced at me, rolled his eyes, and scooped some water over my soiled palm. "You'll be fine. It's mucksap." I blinked at him, and he regarded me like I had the brain capacity of a gilly toad. "From the base of the cypresses ... it keeps the bugs at bay."

"Where is *here*?" Gavrel took a step and then halted, as though bumping into a wall. "Bloody void." He rubbed his fingers over his nose, glaring at Marek.

My face scrunched in confusion as I observed the dense bundles of spindled trees and mucky water ahead. Marek glanced at us, his dark blue eyes glinting mischievously before his ember flared once more.

Smugly, a hint of a smirk played on his lips before he faced forward and raised one hand before him. Dark flames guttered and twirled around his skin in a frenzy.

His shadows slithered over an invisible barrier, clinging to the air, ripping through it like parchment. All at once, the illusion of the unending mire crumbled.

I gasped, my breath catching in the back of my throat. Before us were at least a hundred dwellings balanced atop graying stilts or wrapped around the doombarks they clung to. Among the buildings, the trees were thicker, sturdier shades of gray than the ones we had passed along the way.

My eyes trailed up, focusing on the handful of homes perched higher up the trees. A series of plank and rope bridges interweaved between them, with various corkscrew stairs twisted around the trunks.

Between the buildings closest to the water, a smattering of footbridges zigzagged between and connected them. People, all dressed in varying shades of slate and soot, meandered along the walkways, chatting or working. Some openly stared as we neared.

Heading toward a rope ladder hanging from one bridge, we sloshed between two massive glass domes, submerged far to each side of us. I bent forward; my curiosity insatiable. My eyes followed the line of them to my left, peeking under and through the random spaces between stilts.

There were several submerged domes curving in a line

around the perimeter of the settlements. They were familiar somehow, but I couldn't determine why.

"What are those?" I inquired, straightening.

Marek grabbed the ladder, giving it a shake toward me and pressing his mouth together. I put my hands on my hips and stared at him, slowly blinking when he returned my glare.

His tongue pressed into his cheek, and he dropped the rope. "Conservatories."

My mouth formed an O, and he rolled his eyes and climbed up the corded steps, muscles bunching as he went.

I scurried up after him, not waiting for Gavrel to set foot on the bridge before rushing to the side to peek into the dome. Sure enough, ten gleaming Dormancy pods nestled within, forming a dark, foreboding flower. Watery sludge swayed against the bowed glass walls from the outside.

My top lip curled, and the sudden urge to slam an embered orb into the curved surface burned through me.

"Interesting," Marek mumbled, eyeing the iridescent halo around me. Although his tone said he was anything but interested. I focused on his smug face as if he were swamp water flooding my boots. My aura sputtered, sinking within me, and I winced, not realizing I'd let it simmer.

Gavrel now stood behind Marek, his face lined with annoyance as he took in the scene. "Neoma," he barked.

Marek remained aloof, but he slowly tilted his head toward the commander and then strode past him in the other direction without a word.

"Damn boggers," he grumbled as we followed.

"What was that, Gav?"

He lifted his chin; his back taut and unbreakable. I suppressed my amusement as he stalked forward.

Marek led us through the city, the soft murmur of Bog citizens flitting around us as we passed. He greeted each person we passed with a solemn nod and was met with kind smiles and hearty pats on the shoulder.

From the paths staggered at varying heights, drifting under the planks in narrow boats, or peeking out small windows, the people's stares were inquisitive as though we were intriguing curiosities they'd never seen.

Perhaps we were. I didn't suspect many outside of the region journeyed here.

The network of plank bridges gently swayed and creaked beneath our footfalls. Correction. The entire city seemed to move, as if the settlements were breathing or merely bits of debris adrift in the mucky current. In the distance, the faint hum of crickets warbled.

The sound of mud squelching within my boots accompanied every step. My mouth pulled into a grimace as I fixated on the feel of it between my toes. I exhaled slowly, the air, although cooler now, still stuck within my lungs. At least it no longer smelled of rot. Gavrel had been right.

Marek stopped at the foot of a curling stairwell; the steps fastened snugly around the trunk of a rather thick tree. Around it, the planks coiled below the small platform and into the water next to a narrow, rickety boat that was fastened to a nearby post.

Agitatedly, he poked his quarterstaff into the space above him. "Up you go."

Any retort fizzled into the damp air as I climbed the stairs, awestruck, holding onto the makeshift rope rail weaving along the outward edges of the spiral. I craned my neck to take in the weeping branches of the tree, which loomed far above us and cast dreary shadows over the nearby walkways and dwellings.

Nestled high against the trunk, the bottom of a substantial ash-colored abode perched. It was fastened to the groaning tree with numerous ropes and wooden supports.

As we drew close, the flight led into an open hatch, and a

flickering orange glow beckoned. I paused, drawing in the familiar scent of burning wood, and a mollifying swell of nostalgia rippled over me.

I flinched as Marek brushed past me, barging through the hatch. "Your *dirtlings* have arrived, Yaya," he jeered.

"Don't be rude, Marek," a strong, feminine voice scolded. Her words sounded as if they were wrapped in sturdy, well-worn leather.

I rose into the sizable space. Loosely knit macramé wall hangings, the color of storm clouds and trampled grass, were draped over the graying walls.

Various pieces of carved wood furniture were strewn about the space, with a small kitchen at the back to our right, and a cozy, yet neat bed in the opposite corner with an immense trunk at its foot. Along the wall and beside the bed was a privacy screen painted with scenes of flying black birds and wide, ruddy trees. I drank in the sight, fascinated by the panorama.

It reminded me of home.

Marek's scoff caught my attention.

"If this big, strong *warrior* continues to use derogatory language …" Piqued, Marek plopped his weapon against the wall, wood knocking against wood. "I'm obligated to return the courtesy." His sarcasm trickled off as the older female propped her hands on her narrow hips and squinted at him, her sharp elbows jutting out to the sides.

She was petite but sturdy. A wispy, slate-colored tunic and loose, flowing breeches in the same shade adorned her lean frame. Several dark necklaces made from a myriad of beads and knots swathed around her neck.

Before I caught sight of the small fire in a corner stove, I imagined the very essence of her crackling.

In a mesmerizing dance of light and shadow, the flames snaked over her chest-length strands. The curling, silver tendrils and elaborate braids weaving along her head glinted in the radiance.

Her eyes, the color of burnt autumn leaves, smoldered as she glowered at her grandson. Marek's shoulders dipped, and he looked out the small window by the bed as if something was fascinating beyond it.

With a grumble, the male's shoulders slumped ever so slightly as he shuffled over, placed a kiss on her cheek, and then trudged over to the water basin. With efficiency, he began roughly scrubbing the mucksap off his skin with a cloth.

I dipped my chin, trying to hold in a laugh, but the swish of a stifled snort escaped regardless. I peeked up at the sound of amusement coming from the woman. One eyebrow rose as she studied me unabashedly.

Positioned beside me, Gavrel bowed his head respectfully toward her. "Mistress Neoma Skiya, I presume? I'm Gavrel Larkin, and this is Seryn Vawn." He held his hand toward me. "Rhaegar Hale sent word for us to find you."

Slowly, she blinked at him, her elbows still poking the air.

His nostrils flared, and his mouth pinched. Resigned, he rolled his shoulders back and frowned as Marek faced us, his tanned skin ruddy and clean. A mask of smug boredom coated his handsome visage, his biceps bulging as he crossed his arms expectantly.

Several seconds slinked by, the only sounds in the still room were of the popping logs and sodden fabric squelching as I shifted. Finally, the men's standoff ceased.

"I apologize for using the term 'bogger.' It was ill-mannered of me. It won't happen again," Gavrel conceded. Marek nodded in response and sat at the oval table in the kitchen, propping his long, muscled legs atop the antique-looking chair beside him and leaning back, satisfied.

"You're damn right it won't. And it's Yaya," the woman snapped, stomping over to the chest by the bed and pulling out various pieces of dusky fabric. "Now, take off your boots and put your weapons by Marek's." Swiftly, she marched over to Gavrel, and in a flurry of movements, she removed his baldric and lowered his sword to the ground with ease. Stunned, his mouth hung agape.

From under her arm, she shoved clean clothing at him and then charged at me. She clucked her tongue and cuffed me on the arm when I took a hesitant step back. Eyes wide, I froze as she went through the same process, tossing my belt and rucksack into the pile.

She chucked fresh clothes at me and then went to the kitchen, placing a kettle on top of the stove. "Change behind the screen, and then come sit. We've much to discuss, and it won't do for you to track muck everywhere like a bunch of peat snails."

She moved with confidence and authority as if she were accustomed to being heeded. The mud coating my socks glued me to her floorboards.

Can I bottle whatever runs through her veins? Sweet Surrelia, the woman is a raging inferno. Of battle fever incarnate. Is she Athena, the Ancient of War, in disguise? I mused.

With a clink, she set some cups on the table, casting me a stern look from beneath her lashes.

"Yes, Yaya," I mumbled.

I scurried to the screen as Gavrel, in a fresh black tunic and breeches, hastily pulled out the chair that Marek's feet were on. The Druik scowled as his legs dropped and Gavrel's bulky form took their place.

While Yaya poured steaming brew into our cups, her expression pinched. In unison, Marek and Gavrel cleared their throats.

Whether from the earth or the mire, I supposed we could understand one another if we put aside our differences. Leaned into what tied us together.

In the city of Helos.
In this tree.
This home.
What tied us together was a healthy fear of Yaya.
No further introductions needed.

9

VEILS AND MASKS

GAVREL

The bitter tea swirled down my throat, warming me. Neoma leaned back in her chair, her weathered hand cupping her firm but delicate jawline as she studied us. Seryn boldly met the older woman's scrutiny, tucking away any lingering diffidence.

Quelling the urge to gather Seryn to me, I gripped my knees. She was an indestructible force. She didn't believe it now, but she would. I'd make sure of it.

I set my cup down, focusing on the older woman. She was something, I'd give her that. Not someone I'd cross intentionally.

Neoma's brow quirked, one corner of her mouth following suit. "The Augur mentioned you were both gifted your memories, and that you'd need guidance." Her eyes ricocheted between us. I frowned, glancing at Seryn as her chin dipped.

The ability to remember wasn't always a gift.

Neoma dropped her hand to the tabletop, bringing our

attention back to her. "She told me you each had a part to play—your journey was written in the stars."

"The Fates are in their cups again, I see," Marek scoffed.

My hands clenched, fighting the urge to punch him in the teeth. "The only guidance we need is information about my brother, Kaden. Kaden Larkin. Have you had any recent visitors?"

"My dear, you can deny the truth all you want, but the reality remains: each of you is marked for ... something greater. Despite your sour faces, your memories *are* an asset—a treasure we safeguard from the grasp of the Dormancy. Many of us risk evading it just to preserve them, unless we need eyes on the Elders. After all, information is a force that can shift even the currents of the Insomnis Sea." She clicked her tongue.

My eyebrows were surely glued to my hairline, and Seryn's mouth hung open.

The older woman chuckled. "Nevertheless, no. No, there haven't been any run-ins with strangers as of late. There rarely is."

I pushed my empty cup away and rested my elbows on the table. "Then why the embered illusion surrounding the city? I don't recall that being in place when I visited a few turns ago." My jaw tipped up, and I cupped it, resting my elbow on my crossed forearm. "Or the city having as many inhabitants, for that matter."

"Times have changed—" she started.

"I can see that. What with you *evading* the Dormancy. That is quite the feat."

Neoma continued, ignoring my words, "—but, also, we only showed you what we wanted you to see." Her chin lifted higher than mine. "There have been more and more reports of crea-tures, not of this realm, attacking our people once the dusk sets in. Rumors of the dead scratching at the barrier." Seryn and I glanced at each other, mirrored concern etching into our features. My thumb brushed against the stubble lining my jaw.

Neoma went on, "Not to mention, the Elders' sycophants and Akridais are getting bolder. Less formality and questioning. More impulsive violence." She shook her head, eyes hardening. "Why not make it as challenging as possible for hunters to find Helos, whether they be beast or mortal?" She glanced at Marek.

My mouth stiffened, and my heartbeat hammered behind my ribs. There was no way they knew what I'd done—granted, what I would no longer do—for Melina. I'd likely be dead if they did. I settled back in my seat, wishing my sword were nearby.

Marek nodded. "We've no use for Elder Laws here. Their only interest in our people is to seek potential Scions or raid our rations."

Slowly, he cracked his knuckles, deep in thought, and then blinked a few times, clearing whatever ran through his mind.

"How forthright of you. And so openly exposing your gifts to us earlier, which are quite impressive, I must admit. How do you know we aren't their sycophants?" Seryn cocked her head, fluttering her lashes mockingly at him.

I shifted my jaw to the side, trying to rid myself of the tic pulsing in it. *Didn't this bastard own any bloody tunics?*

Marek chuffed humorlessly. Neoma rolled her eyes, her fingernails tapping rhythmically atop the table. "The Augur has never led us astray. Nor has Rhaegar." She smiled brightly around my second's name, and my forehead lifted higher.

"Hale is quite valuable to the Korax's cause," Marek stated, a note of respect lining his words.

"Ah, so the rebel cause is alive and well." I'd suspected as much, especially after this conversation, but Rhaegar and I had danced around it over the turns, preferring to hold tight to plausible deniability and our friendship.

I had no desire to quell such a rebellion, but I'd spent so long cultivating my position in the Order. Playing my part to protect those I cared for and the realm in the best way I knew how.

In the shadows.

Melina's dutiful *pet*.

Or so she thought. The seam of my lips curled.

Though I couldn't always resist Melina's cruel demands, I had appeased her vanity and downplayed the unrest boiling among Midst Fall, trusting the rebels would evolve. Each time I'd heard whispers of the Korax, the coals of hope smoldered brighter within me.

"May the wings of the raven carry you," Seryn murmured, her fingers fiddling with the hem of her tunic.

Neoma sipped her tea, a knowing smile dancing on her lips as she swallowed. Seryn glanced from the woman to me. "The Draumr in Ceto. That's what he said before we left."

"And they shall carry you." Neoma stood, scooping up our empty cups and putting them in the washbasin. "Gather your things. Marek will show you to your accommodation. You'll have a day or so to acclimate before seeking the Augur."

"And why would we seek her out?" Seryn asked, her tone laced with genuine curiosity.

"Because, my dear, she's likely your only option if you want to find your friend. Off you go." With finality, Neoma rolled up her sleeves, unveiling an intricate black raven wing tattoo that ran down the inside of her right forearm from elbow to wrist. The firelight caught on its subtle, multicolored sheen as she moved. She nodded to the door, turned, and then began washing the cups, her silver hair glittering in the firelight.

We collected our things and followed Marek down the coiling stairs. The overcast sky was even gloomier as we approached the platform below. The air had cooled, but it still clung to my skin like a damp caress.

Marek paused at the base, locking arms with a man passing by. It was unsettling to see his lips curve upward. They shared a few friendly words before the man went about his business, and we continued on our way.

As we reached a bridge along the edge of the city's boundary line, Marek stopped, his body tensing as his blackened aura flickered. His face crumpled as he stretched one arm out toward the swampy horizon.

Seryn gawked at him, her eyes following the movement of his ember. It stemmed from the base of his spine, where the darkest ebony flames flared, rippled, and curled around his torso. The flames surged over his arm and extended from his hand, reaching beyond the gleaming dome of a submerged conservatory.

His power writhed outward as if it were burning through the very air surrounding the city. Within minutes, the hazy barrier was in place. Seryn's gaze drifted above and around, captivated by the illusion. The citizens went about their business, some smiling appreciatively in Marek's direction.

No alarm or fear crossed their features at his open use of ember.

They were used to this.

Accepting.

"Remarkable," Seryn commended.

Marek's tongue pressed against his cheek as he bowed his head and walked across a swaying bridge. He clutched his quarterstaff, holding it perpendicular to the path, effectively keeping us at a distance.

Seryn's voice rose, ensuring that he heard. "Does creating such an illusion drain you? I can't even fathom maintaining that barrier every day."

We snaked through the city, the planks creaking under us, weathered shanties swaying, and firelight flickering through the gaps between the dwellings' wooden faces.

"It's nothing. We've embedded protection runes along the

border. It's simply a matter of activating them with my illusion ember."

Seryn shook her head. "It's not that simple." He looked away, refusing to meet our eyes. "The people here are very fortunate to have your protection."

He adjusted his staff, pointing to a small abode at the end of the bridge. He glared at us, his mouth tight as a subtle flush crept up his chest. "This is you. There's enough food and fresh water to get you through the next few days. The fire and a hot bath are waiting. I'll find you if you're needed." With that, he strode in the other direction, his weapon jabbing into the boards.

"He's hiding something," I noted, following Seryn.

"Of course he is. As are we. We've just met these people, for Surrelia's sake." She pushed open the door with a creak and sauntered inside. I smirked at her sass. It meant she wasn't drowning in pain and confusion at the moment.

Next to one another, there were two narrow beds against the back wall. To our right, a small wood-burning stove, a kitchenette, tall barrels of clean water, a table, and a pair of chairs. Behind a wall of interlocking planks to our left, steam wafted to the ceiling.

Seryn groaned as she tossed her pack at the foot of one bed, dashing over to that corner. "Don't mind me. I'll be soaking the rot off me for a while."

I sat on the rickety chair, taking off my boots and watching her shadow dance into the crevices of the woodgrain as she undressed, her boots slouching against the outside of the makeshift wall. Her shadow lifted one leg over the rim of the tub, and my mouth went dry. I pictured her soft, pink skin sinking into the steam. Her contented moan floated through the air.

Calm the fuck down, you idiot, I scolded my unruly manhood, which stirred in my breeches. Reluctantly, my cock settled as I busied myself with cleaning our boots, our sodden clothes, and weapons.

Her footfalls sounded as I finished hanging up our clothes on a rope railing outside the front entrance.

"I'm a new woman." At the sound of her satisfied giggle, I turned, admiring her as she did a carefree twirl on the tips of her bare toes. She wore only the borrowed gray tunic, the hem brushing her damp upper thighs as her arms stretched above.

My throat dried as all the liquid in my body pooled on my tongue and in my obstinate cock, as if I were some inexperienced fledgling. Clearing my throat, I rubbed my palms on my thighs, pushing past her. "Indeed. My turn, I suppose."

Her arms fell as she stared at me, bewildered annoyance draping over her delicate features before indifference crept over her face. My muscles tensed. I loathed the masks she hid behind.

Displeasure bubbled under my skin. She could hide herself from others if it helped her manage what she was working through. But I didn't want her to hide from me any longer.

She toyed with the fabric at her hips. "Thank you for cleaning my things. I …" She paused as I tugged my tunic off, her lips pressing together tightly. After a moment, her words spilled out. "I'm sorry if the bathwater is cold and used. We can use some of the fresh water they've stocked."

"No need. Your bath water doesn't bother me." My gaze sank to her lips as they parted and then dragged over her face as she gawked at my chest.

I enjoyed making her mask slip. Apathy didn't suit her. She was anything but indifferent, and I grew weary of pretending otherwise. Giving her space and my silence was no longer effective. It was time to try a different tactic if I was to garner an authentic reaction from her.

Running my hand through my hair, biceps bunching, I let my next words tumble out. "It's better to conserve the supplies as best we can. Perhaps next time we should share the bath."

Her mouth fell all the way open, and her cheeks instantly burned. She shifted, her thighs brushing against each other, rustling the tunic's fabric. I swore I felt the heat between her legs, and it sparked something deep in my belly.

A slow smile spread across my face, and I didn't bother hiding my body's reaction to her. Seryn glanced down, her nostrils flaring as she, too, noticed.

My pulse quickened under my jaw. Her fingers curled into her palms, and she spun toward the barrels, scooping water into a cup and staring out the window as she took deep pulls from it.

With a contained chuckle, I moved behind the privacy wall, pushing my breeches off, and then sank into the cooled bath water.

Progress.

10

THE FECKING SPIRIT

SERYN

*M*orning light rudely poured over my face. I blinked away my momentary disorientation, one arm falling over the edge of the narrow bed, the other blanketing my eyes. From under my arm, I peeked at Gavrel, his bare chest rising and falling with his gentle breaths.

A stifled groan of annoyance hummed in my throat. It had taken me entirely too long to fall asleep. Uninhibited images of Gavrel's hot skin sliding over mine—his lips and hands and tongue all over my body—had scampered behind my eyelids well into the early morning.

I pushed my face into my arm, blocking out my view of him. Served me right, not being able to stare at his ridiculously honed muscles until my shameless eyeballs fell from my damned, drool-ridden face.

A sudden bang crashed against the front door, and I tumbled out of the bed in a heap, curls spilling over my face and shoulders haphazardly.

Gavrel lurched out of bed, his sword already in his hand as his gaze whipped to me and then the door as it slammed open.

"These are the slack-tits we're here to find? Bloody fecking void, Rhaeg. A desert snail moves faster than these shite piles. I'm not mad at"—she wiggled her fingers at Gavrel's body—"all this though."

"Breena!" I leaped up and charged her. A look of utter horror raced across her heart-shaped face, and her crimson aura sparked around her as she held her hands up defensively. I slammed into her, hugging her tense body tightly.

"Who attacks a stranger with a hug?" she groused, patting my back stiffly a couple of times before pushing me from her at arm's length. "You must be Seryn. I hear you killed me in the trials." She tilted her head toward Rhaeger, who filled the space beside her with a sheepish smile.

My expression fell at the reminder. Her arms dropped as a wry laugh fell from her grin. "Eh, don't get your panties in a bunch. If you bested me, then I like you already." She winked, and I offered her a glum smile in return.

Rhaegar lifted his hand loosely, palm up, as the corner of his wide mouth hung up in a lopsided grin. "Morning. I'd offer apologies, but you know very well I had no control over her entrance."

Gavrel sniffed, tossing his tunic on and then greeting his second-in-command with a brief squeeze on the shoulder before gathering his belongings. "It's damn good to see you, my friend." He nodded to Breena, and she smirked, dropping her arms from me and circling the small room. "Cordelya sends her greetings, by the by."

Rhaegar grinned, his eyes raising to the ceiling as he rubbed his palm on his chest as if reliving a pleasant memory. "I'll have to pay her a visit soon. Fine woman she is."

I hugged Rhaegar, and he returned it in a tight embrace. "I'm pleased we found you here before you moved on. I hear you've met Yaya and Marek." A wide grin spread across his teeth.

Gavrel strapped his sword onto his back. "I hear you are invaluable to the Korax," he countered. I pulled my breeches on, readying myself as I watched their exchange.

Rhaegar lifted his chin, "That a problem, Commander?"

Gavrel approached his friend, assessing him as he paused. He inhaled, squaring his hips. "Not anymore."

"New rebel in the making, eh? Welcome, Sir Grumbles," Breena teased. I covered a snort behind my hand, the sound making me lighter.

Gavrel ignored us and nodded toward the exit. He sighed, clicking the door shut behind us as we stepped into the late morning sun. "We need more information about the Elders. More than what we've gathered over the turns. What their weaknesses are. How to dismantle and suppress their supporters."

A look of pleased surprise rose across Rhaegar's visage. "Glad to hear it. And might I say … it's about time." He slapped a palm on Gavrel's shoulder and glanced at me. "We'll request an audience with Yaya tonight. Although I'm certain she'll find us first."

Breena nudged my shoulder. "So, Ryn-Ryn." I smiled and then remembered that this version of Breena didn't know me at all. "Have you been to the bog fields yet? Navigating them really works the thighs." She slapped hers for emphasis.

"Uh, no. We just arrived yesterday. Haven't explored yet."

Breena huffed. "And Marek was your tour guide. Pretty to look at, but what a salty ball sack."

"Ah, so you two have a history then?"

Breena's chin jutted to the side, her tongue poking at the inside of her opposite cheek. "We've crossed paths over the turns."

I giggled, and she pursed her full lips. "Enough of him. Come with me." She linked our elbows and tugged me past the men. The bridge swayed precariously as we rushed across.

"Seryn?" Gavrel called after us.

"We'll meet you later," I replied, holding my free hand up and shrugging helplessly.

"In the square this afternoon," Breena yelled in a sing-song voice as we rushed away from them.

We roamed through the city. Its citizens were friendly, and Breena knew a few here and there. I supposed she and Rhaegar visited often through the turns as part of the Korax.

We passed through the square Breena had arranged to meet in later. It was near the epicenter of the city, its massive platform filled with various huts and shop counters. People bustling, trading, and bartering.

We came to a textile merchant's stand, and I ran my fingers over a dress made of dark fabric. Metallic rainbow threads were woven through its gauzy layers in an intricate pattern.

"Gorgeous, right?" Breena said, poking her finger into the dress. "This thread is only found in the Bogs. Muckworm silk. Nasty little buggers, and difficult to find despite them being as big as my arm.

"But the muckers make good coin, swamp diving and hunting them down. And then those little, slimy assholes have a whole play area set up in a small Bogs town west of here where they live out their days in wormy luxury." Breena's hands were so animated I thought she might fly away. "I mean, would you rather live in the mud, or a cushy kingdom where you get to eat all day, relax, and shite rainbows?"

My laughter bubbled over, and I bent over, clutching my stomach.

Breena crinkled her nose as if I had gone crazy, then she started laughing hard as well.

By the time we settled, my belly was sore. I wiped the

wetness from my cheeks as we left the square. "I missed you, Bree. I know you can't say the same, but I'm happy you're here."

She wiped her cheeks and slung an arm around me. "Welp, that's where you're wrong. I'm positive I've missed you. I just don't know it yet."

My pulse fluttered. "Breena, I … I have something that could bring back your memories."

Her eyebrows crushed together, and her wide mouth pinched in confusion.

"We found a Mirage Orchid during the trials, and my chambermaid, Derya, made a tonic from it. It's how I regained my memories. Would you … would you want to use it?" I shuffled my feet, chin dipping slightly.

"Oh, damn right I do." She beamed.

I smirked. "Only works during the full moon."

"It's a date, then. Can't wait to remember all the shite probably best left forgotten." Chuckling, Breena slowed as we came to a quiet bridge and looked over the side. "Ready?"

"Ready for wha—"

Before I could finish, she swung under the rope railing and over the edge.

A surprised squeak flew from me, and I lunged forward, gripping the rope.

Breena was chuckling as she climbed down a swaying ladder and dropped into a small boat tethered below. She looked up, mirth dancing in her rich brown eyes. "Get in, we're going hummock jumping."

I shook my head and made my way down. Breena whistled. "No wonder Gavrel wants a piece. Just look at that arse."

I chuffed a laugh as I plopped into the boat clumsily. "He does not. You've only just met us—what was it—slack-wits? So, I doubt you've picked up on that so soon."

"Listen, *slack-tit,* if I know anything about the male species, and I do"—she wiggled her eyebrows—"that muscled hunk of meat wants in your breeches something fierce."

An awkward giggle reverberated in my chest as I grabbed one oar from her and jabbed it into the hazy water.

I pushed thoughts of Gavrel aside, like I had been for days. But I knew she was right.

That didn't mean *it* was right.

I needed to focus on finding Kaden. On destroying the Elders. Not pine after Gavrel like some bloody fledgling.

I sat taller in the gently rocking boat as I rowed behind Breena.

We passed a small group of people diving under the brackish surface, alternatively popping up and plopping slimy beasts into a woven rope basket on the side of their skiffs.

"Muckers!" Breena shouted gleefully, waving at them. Some of them waved back; the others were too busy diving again and again. I shuddered at the thought of swimming and excavating the muddy depths.

Sighing, I pushed against my oar, the monotonous movement both soothing and wearisome as memories of Gavrel slinked into the depths of my awareness. The way he always watched over me. When his plump lips formed a grim line. A smile that cracked on the sides when I said something funny.

Then his mouth on mine. His hardness straining at his breeches before his bath.

I bit my lip hard each time, chasing each unbidden thought away with the nip of pain.

Halfway through an hour, we reached the bog field, and my bottom lip was now raw.

Fuck.

Breena tied our vessel to a thick doombark nestled against an expansive field of water-logged hollows and bulky mounds of compacted bog moss—hummocks. A drooping fog slithered into the horizon.

She hopped onto a nearby knoll, her arms spread out at either side, stabilizing herself. She grinned. "All right, you 'lil snack. You can take your chances walking in the mud, but one wrong step, and it'll suck you right under. Never know if it's solid or just a bunch of peat floating in a hollow." She made a slurping noise, her cheeks hollowing before leaping to the next visible heap.

Hesitantly, I stepped onto her abandoned spot, the mass bobbing under my boots. Peat flexed uneasily over the viscous slurry like a mottled elastic bubble ready to pop.

My blood rushed to my head, and I trailed Breena as she bounced to the next, sounds of joy bursting from her as she landed.

I breathed in, expanding my ribs so they weren't clutching my lungs so tightly.

"Feck it!" I hollered and followed my friend as she leaped from hummock to hummock. My friend, who was alive and safely out of the Stygian Murk.

"That's the fecking spirit!"

We dashed and vaulted over and over. Cricket song crescendoed with each landing, only to pause as my boots met moss, then resumed behind me as I left.

A few times, the mounds threatened to collapse as I landed on them, the squelching of mud sucking at the air. My thighs burned from continually bouncing and balancing.

But I was free. Reckless and untethered. Pure delight ripped from my lungs; my gleeful squeals swallowed by the haze coating the bogland.

On my next jump, I veered off to the right as Breena went to the left, the fog absorbing her.

Unabashedly, I dashed across several, the breeze smacking into my teeth as I grinned. From the corner of my eye, an ebony shadow flew past me, the beating of wings whooshing against the mist as it tore into the obscured sky.

I whipped my head forward again as I jumped toward a smaller pile of vegetation. Too late, I realized my error as the peat licked at its wobbly edges. The lumpy moss quivered and crumbled under my feet, and my body was a stone swallowed into the thick pool of sticky muck.

With a yelp, I squirmed within the gooey sludge, but its gummy embrace dragged me slowly downward, my movements causing me to sink further.

"Breena!" I screeched, terror shredding free from my frame and leaving me to the muddy depths.

The murk and fog swallowed me, dampening my cries as my arms slapped against its viscous surface uselessly. The nearest hummock was out of reach.

My blood and breath whirled within me as I screamed.

"Calm yourself, child." I stilled as the soft demand grated over me. A gilded glow peeled through the haze, followed by the bent form of a woman atop the lifted moss.

The fog dispersed, and I blinked my eyes as if finally seeing clearly for the first time.

Her flowy, pale hair fluttered to her chest, wispy strands brushing against her ashen cheeks and dark, gauzy robes. Her skin delicately creased into a patchwork of wrinkles like a map drawn on crumpled paper.

"Would love to, but as you can see, I'm being eaten alive by a bog!" My voice rose at the end, cresting along the ridges of my panic.

Her lips set in an unamused line as she flicked her wrist nonchalantly. All at once, I flinched, sinking deeper, as a long, thick branch flew straight at me and landed near my hand with a splat.

I spit out flecks of gunk, glaring at the ancient woman. "Thank you for this … this stick. I hate to ask the obvious, but would you mind using your ember to get me out?" My words sounded shrill, fear squeezing my windpipe.

Patiently, as if she were dealing with a small child and not a woman about to be gobbled up, she folded her hands in front of her, glancing pointedly at the bough.

My eyebrows rose, forehead creasing as I realized she was insane. I hollered again, my throat aching and voice cracking as the gray goo met my collarbone.

I whimpered, ignoring the female and staring at the branch. Sucking in a lungful of air, I snatched the wood, gripping it at each end for dear life. It wouldn't reach the bottom and would only get stuck if I tried.

With an exaggerated sigh, I slapped it in front of me in annoyance. It clung a bit to the peat coating, and my brows rose.

I pushed my arms down against the branch, wiggling it against the muck. Painstakingly, I slowly leveraged my weight against its wider surface area until my body inched forward bit by bit.

Twenty minutes was a lifetime when you were struggling to survive.

The sludge tugged at my weary limbs, trying to drag me back down, but I pushed and writhed until I reached the hummock the female stood upon. I clutched the moss and pulled myself onto it.

Dragging in ragged breaths, I feared my limbs were made of mud as they wobbled. Standing wasn't worth the risk of toppling into the bog, so I plopped onto my back.

"Bleeding muck on a mound. Where've you been, Ryn? And who the void is she?" Breena landed near my shoulder as I stared dully at the sky.

Breena propped her fists on her hips as the female ignored her and pressed her mouth into an unamused line.

Pushing damp curls off my temples, I groaned. "I've been here, getting eaten alive by the bloody bog." I flopped my hand in the female's direction. "While *she* just watched."

Breena frowned, glancing at my left hand. "Rhaegar said that trinket on your finger makes you go—" She sliced her hand through the air, a buzzing sound vibrating between her teeth. "Why didn't ya just use it?"

I held my hand up, glaring at my ring, and then plunked it back down. I groaned, annoyed that I'd been too panicked to think of it.

Layers of wrinkles pushed up into the older woman's hairline as she studied me. "I hear you're in need of my guidance."

"Like I need a dagger to the face," I muttered weakly.

Her mouth quirking was the only sign that she'd heard me. "And after witnessing your determination, I'm willing to give it." She placed her bony fingers against her chest. "How can the Augur assist?"

11

AS THE RAVEN FLIES

GAVREL

The hunched female looked as if she had been created from the haze drifting far in the distance, and was about to crumble back into it.

Covered in peat and brown slime, Seryn's chest rose and fell fitfully as she lay at the woman's feet, scowling at her. I knew the moment the woman's words registered and overcame Seryn's annoyance.

Jerking and then scrambling to her feet, her eyes went wide. Seryn's gaze snapped to the woman's and then to mine as she realized my presence. Her brows lifted so high I thought they might disappear into her curls.

I flexed the fingers of my right hand, the burn of my tattoo easing. Rhaegar and I had been nearing the square when my rune lit up, like it had the day Seryn was first attacked by a mare wyrm in Surrelia. The deep bite of fear overtook me when I knew Seryn was in danger, as if her terror were my own.

Rhaegar didn't question me when I ran to a boat and let my rune guide us away from the city. I was grateful that my second —my *friend*—was with me. Not once had I ever had a reason to doubt his loyalty. His steadfast support.

He hopped from our vessel and bowed to the female perched on the mound opposite. "It's a privilege to meet you. I've heard a great many tales of your wisdom over the turns."

She lifted her chin and one palm, inviting Rhaegar to rise.

"You're the Augur? Well, color me impressed." Breena dipped her head respectfully before elbowing Seryn and giving her a pointed look.

Dear Ancients, the woman never knew when to keep her thoughts inside. My hands tensed at my sides, studying the Augur's response. She looked down her curved nose at Breena with an unreadable expression before turning her attention to Seryn, her light eyes assessing.

On unsteady legs, Seryn brushed her hand down her muddy tunic and then lifted her chin. I knew that look. She was about to get straight to the point. Resolutely, she took another step toward the female, chest expanding with her request. "Pleasure to *meet* you. I … We're looking for—"

"I know whom you seek," the old woman replied, her eyes twinkling knowingly. Seryn snapped her mouth closed, looking at her expectantly. "And you'll recover them once you embrace your Ancient-given gifts."

Seryn winced, her fingers digging into her palms.

Chest rigid, I stood, the boat rocking against the thick muck. Frustration skittered up my neck. I was completely sick of all the obstacles thrown in our path as of late. "With all due respect, we don't have time for your games. Do you have the information we seek? My brother's life hangs in the balance."

One of her eyebrows lifted as she focused on me. "As do all of *your* lives, do they not?"

My chin jutted forward, mouth smashing together so I wouldn't say anything I would regret.

Fuck it.

Likely sensing the shift in my decision-making, Rhaegar coughed loudly into his fist. No doubt trying to get my attention. I pushed my shoulders back even more, my tunic stretching across my chest. "Indeed. But—"

Her words, sharp and strong, belied her frail body. "It's as I said. Embrace her gifts, or the ones you love cannot be recovered." She looked at Seryn again. "Come to my home on the morrow, and we'll begin."

"Why would you help me?" Seryn asked, eyes narrowing.

The old female lifted her chin. "I help those who are vital to maintaining Kosmos—order and equilibrium. And who are important to … to the Fates."

"Aren't we *all* important to maintaining balance?" Breena quipped.

The Augur's mouth curled. "Some more than others."

Breena rolled her eyes.

"How will we find you?" Seryn asked.

"As the raven flies." A barely visible shimmer blinked over her, and in a burst of billowing sparks, she was gone.

Breena muttered a string of curses, grabbing Seryn's hand as they stumbled backward. Rhaegar jumped onto the moss and grabbed their hands before they tipped into the mud. "Shall we head …" He paused, bending to peek behind Breena.

I followed his line of sight as both women moved to his side. The fog was thickening a short distance away; the mist a breathing mass pulling the edges of itself inward.

"What the … Get to the boat." His quiet words were almost lost to the sound of his battle axe brushing against its sheath and the wavering chirps of swamp crickets.

Instead of heeding his words, Seryn and Breena drew their

blades. My jaw set, and I cracked my neck from side to side before readying my sword.

The darkened patch of haze pulsed a few times and then spun, drilling itself down into the muck with a splash.

The crickets quieted. A gelatinous ripple swept over the surface from where the throbbing cloud had disappeared.

"Uh, let's get to the boat," Seryn whispered, agreeing with Rhaegar. They jumped to the hummock nearest me as the sound of squishing and groaning rumbled under the surface of the peat.

All at once, the vessel lurched to the side, threatening to spill me into the bog. I grunted, swinging my sword upon the pallid, decaying hand clamped on the wood. An angry moan sank back into the water as the severed hand flopped at my feet like a fish.

"Gavrel!" Seryn yelped, darting toward me. Three sets of waxy bodies rose from the depths, their flesh and clothing in various states of bloated pallor. Jerkily, they lunged their torsos onto the mound, fingers creaky and stiff as they grabbed at Seryn. Hollering, she cursed.

Breena lunged, swinging the curved blade of her dagger into the creature's ear canal. Its bulbous eyes rolled back as it collapsed, lifeless, onto the moss. "Well, butter my arse and call me a biscuit. The bog bodies are awake," Breena tossed over her shoulder.

Rhaegar chopped his axe into another creature's skull as it skittered toward him. And then another. "I can bloody well see that," he retorted.

"Bog bodies?!" Seryn squeaked, jabbing her blade into a creature's eye as it grabbed her ankle, chomping the few teeth it had left in the air.

I cut off the heads of two more bodies lunging for me. One's graying skin was so puffy, it split like a grape up the center of its cheek as it toppled back under the layer of peat. "Fucking void. Get in the boat!"

Weapons slashing, they landed beside me, the small skiff dipping precariously low in the water. Hastily, Rhaegar and I paddled away as several more bodies lunged for us.

After several hurried minutes and no further signs of attack, Breena pointed at their raft tied to a tree. "Over there."

We sidled next to it, and Rhaegar stepped inside while nodding at Breena, who was pouting. "Just when things were getting fun."

"Come on, you." Rhaegar chuckled as she joined him.

Seryn's eyes were wide, her hand still tight around the hilt of her dagger. "Bog bodies?!" she repeated, her voice rising at the end.

Breena shrugged. "Well, they normally don't move. Being dead and all."

"They bury their dead in the Bogs. It's a sacred space. But alas, that fog." He frowned, forehead scrunching. "That fog wasn't normal. Likely another Void creature." Rhaegar tapped his pointer finger on his chest with each word.

My brows fell. "No doubt. Neoma mentioned the dead scratching at their wards, but usually at dusk. Just what we need. More damned Void beasts stealing into the realm." My blood boiled against my pulse points. "There was a sea monster in Lotus Loch as well."

Rhaegar's head dropped. "Shite. We need to meet with Yaya. Tell her what happened."

Suddenly, Seryn shot up and flung her hand out. Her dark blade whizzed past the side of my neck, barely nicking my flesh. I winced, turning just in time to see the point of the wavy obsidian sink into a bog body's eye socket with a squish. Its jaw went slack as it fell backward into the water.

The molten, rainbow-like mist in the pommel stilled, and I jerked to the side just as the weapon snapped past me and back toward Seryn's glowing hand.

Her chest pressed against her tunic with every ragged

breath, curling tendrils whipping against her rosy cheeks. As she gripped her dagger, warmth spread to my tailbone, my bottom lip dropping. I gulped, air sticking in my throat.

Ancients.

I wanted her hand wrapped around me.

She sheathed her blade, set her full mouth into a grim line, and dipped her chin as she claimed her seat. "Let's go find Yaya."

THE WINGS OF THE RAVENS

GAVREL

"I won't deny your logic is sound," Neoma admitted, one hand cupping her chin. "Void vermin are slipping in, and the full moon is when embers are most potent."

We huddled around one of the many rickety tables strewn about the rowdy pub dubbed *The Boggy Grog*. It wasn't more than a large box with a bar along the back, and crisscrossing wooden poles nailed to the ceiling and walls.

With fingers flying over fiddle strings, a lively trio of musicians sang, their jaunty music bouncing off the walls. Throughout the space, candles flickered and shadows danced over the secrets and laughter being shared.

I leaned back in my chair, pushing my tongue against the back of one incisor. "We need to figure out what is weakening the veils between the realms." I looked around the table. "I have my suspicions."

"Go on then. We're not getting any younger. Or sober-er." Breena snorted, taking a long swallow of her brew.

Rhaegar covered his mouth with the lip of his pint glass, shoulders shaking. At least someone found her funny. I blinked slowly at her, and the damned woman smirked, tapping on the tabletop.

Beside me, Seryn's eyebrows lifted, and she angled closer to me. "The dungeon?"

My fingers twitched, itching to pull her to my lap. Instead, I nodded, thinking of the mass of amber hidden within the obsidian cliff.

"Care to elaborate?" Marek scoffed as he approached, setting another round of drinks on the table.

Breena cocked her head. "The fecking dungeon," she shot back at him, rolling her eyes as if he were an imbecile.

He scowled, jaw ticking while he took his seat.

For a moment, my lips pinched. I was certain she didn't know about the underground chambers. She wouldn't have remembered them, regardless.

"The cells beneath Morpheus' palace," Seryn explained with a bemused smile.

Breena's eyebrows shot up, mouth forming an O. She smacked Seryn lightly on the arm. "Was I invited to traipse around the wee dun—?" She paused, collecting herself as Marek glared at her. "I mean, of course, the fecking dungeon." And then the blasted woman winked at him. Marek's eyes narrowed to slits.

I leaned forward, my voice low. "Something is caged in amber at the bottom. Every full moon, the Elders siphon energy from it. I think it may be the key to why the portals are weakening during that time. The Order always had more trouble fending off Void creatures beyond the veil in the Weald during lunation."

Neoma, Rhaegar, and Breena all sat straighter, giving one another knowing looks. Marek crossed his arms tightly over his wide chest.

With one eyebrow cocked, Seryn added, "Melina has Elders Guust and Strom imprisoned down there as well. Constantly wiping their minds clean for Ancients know how long."

"Damn. We knew they were holed up in Surrelia, but this is worse than we feared," Neoma hissed.

"Two fewer Elders to deal with, I'd say," Marek muttered.

His grandmother swatted his biceps with the back of her hand. "If we can't get to them all, Ascension will be damn near impossible."

Seryn's shoulders slumped inward as she looked around the room uneasily. "Ascension? Wouldn't it be better to dismantle them completely?"

For a moment, Neoma's mouth was caught between her teeth before she continued, "Ascension *must* occur. Not only does our history confirm this, but our prophecies as well."

Marek grumbled a curse under his breath, his scar pulsing at his temple.

Ignoring him, Neoma sat back, clasping her hands on the table. "The very fabric of our world depends on balance being maintained." Seryn's mouth slackened, and she ran a finger over her chin while Neoma went on, "Without honorable leaders, ember is a festering blight on the human realm. We'll tear ourselves apart as we once did. Well before the land claims us."

Movement caught my eye when a short, curvy woman with dark blonde, wavy hair whispered into one of the musicians' ears.

She seemed familiar somehow.

The man nodded enthusiastically and leaned back to shout something behind him at his fellow performers. Lilting notes swayed over a spirited melody. A weighted hush fell over the room.

Seryn flicked her attention over her shoulder, eyes widening as she caught sight of the female. Her hand gripped my wrist. "I know her. She ... she was in the Winnowing," she whispered.

I squinted at the female as she ran her hands over the bodice of her dark kirtle, her chest rising on a deep inhale. The memory skittered through my awareness. The Druik with the purple aura during the final trial. She had been one of the last competitors, and Seryn's ember had drained her after the woman had attacked Kaden.

Marek's elbows thumped atop the table as he leaned in. "You know the half-borne?"

Neoma shot him a glare.

"What?" he muttered. "That's what they're called when they have mixed embers."

Neoma ignored her grandson. "Her name is Caelora Aundyne." The older woman's eyes softened. "Her Haadran mother passed on long ago, and luckily, the girl found her way here. She never knew her father, but he hails from Pyria Island."

"Fire and water. Huh, well I'll be damned. Never met her or a half-borne before." A look of curiosity spread over Breena's face.

"She keeps to herself mostly," Neoma added. "I'm surprised to see her out, but I recall her fondness for music as a child. It was the only way to make her less fidgety when she first arrived."

Rhaegar grinned as the melody swelled, and his pint plunked against the wood. "Have you heard of the Hollowed Stars prophecy?"

"Ancients, not another bloody foretelling," Seryn muttered.

I set my glass down, swallowing. "Go on."

He adored storytelling, especially when he'd had an ale or five. "The Korax believe the era is finally upon us—to take our stand. We've prepared over the last few decades. It's been said that the Fates themselves gifted the founders of the cause a divination, and it has guided us over the turns. Listen." He nudged his chin toward the musicians.

My pulse hummed just under the skin of my jaw as rich,

dulcet tones spilled from Caelora, her voice ringing over our heads. Although the words bounced merrily over the fiddled notes, they were ominously morose.

Behold the call of the end,

When lo, the Aetherbind's seams do bend.
As withered roots the earth doth take,
The battle 'gainst the curse shall break.

A group to our left joined in, their voices harmonizing with Caelora's as their lifted cups swayed above their heads.

Dark beasts through veils shall creep,
And dreams shall rot in mortal sleep.
Unless the stone of light shall fall,
Within obsidian, night devours all.

Rhaegar and Breena joined in. And then more. And more. Seryn's hand found my wrist again, my heartbeat hammering into her damp palm.

Lest rise Dark Reaping from the scars,
Make haste with hollowing of the stars.
Earth harvests breath and misted pyre,
And flame be quenched by blackened fire.

One shall be two, and two turn three,
To break the curse o'er land and sea.
When the final threads are fully weaved,
Only then shall Khaos be cleaved.

The entirety of the pub filled with every citizen's shouted words, grins, and cheers peppering the final chords.

So speaks Kosmos!

All at once, the buzz of energized chatter and glasses clinking scattered around us. Of course the people of the Perilous Bogs crafted a jaunty song out of an unnerving prophecy. I shook my head, lingering unease simmering within me.

Quietly, Caelora left the musicians, settling in a shaded corner with a goblet between her palms. Looking curious and remorseful, Seryn caught Caelora's eye. I swore the female flinched as they regarded each other, but the moment passed, and she looked away, fixating on her cup with a somber expression.

"She wouldn't remember," I told Seryn. "Her memories would have been erased after the Dormancy."

Seryn sighed as we turned to the others.

"Er, well, that prophecy doesn't sound great," Seryn muttered, taking her hand back and clutching her neglected cup.

Rhaegar held up his fist, his thumb uncurling. "It's a warning passed down through the generations. Every omen has come to pass. The Withering. The Ancients vanishing. The Void creatures."

Rhaegar's fingers joined his thumb as he listed off the omens. Breena added, "Now, the stone of light. The amber trapped in the dungeon."

My second-in-command took a long drink from his cup as his ring finger straightened. Neoma squeezed his forearm. "We're at the last bit finally … It's the path to save our world," she said matter-of-factly, her eyes twinkling with wisdom and a quiet strength.

"Perhaps." Marek snorted. "Perhaps the Fates were bored. Or perhaps our insurrection was inevitable, regardless of their whims."

"Enough," she snapped. "It's the only hope we have." Marek sighed, bowing his head to his grandmother sheepishly, but with a clenched jaw.

Seryn leaned back in her chair, scrutinizing the older woman. "I can see why you're their leader."

"Oh?" Neoma's mouth puckered.

Seryn's head tilted to one side, genuine curiosity lining her words. "How did such a responsibility fall on you?"

"I had a lot of time on my hands. What with my husband passing on, and my daughters gone."

Seryn lifted her head. "I meant no offense. I'm genuinely in awe of you."

Neoma's shoulders relaxed. "When ... when Marek found me." She glanced at him. "I'd been helping Druiks take refuge in Helos for many turns. My husband and I had a lot of practice ... in keeping secrets. Even when he died, the need to keep doing so—to do what was right—lingered. The rebel cause had always been simmering, albeit unorganized."

She brushed her palms together as if that was that. "A few others and I took it upon ourselves to help the Korax take shape. To unify. To discuss strategy. The rest is history."

"And she so humbly forgets that the original followers collectively chose her as the leader. The head Raven," Marek added, pride lining his surly face.

Lost in thought, I studied the room of lively patrons. Surely, some were listening to our conversation. Did no one fear repercussions? Obviously not considering their choice in music. The hair on my nape prickled.

Seryn glanced at me with a look of concern and then around the tavern.

"Haven't you realized yet?" Neoma chuckled, sweeping her right arm in a wide arc while the other cupped her glass. In the dusky candlelight, dark iridescence rippled over her wing tattoo, making it appear as if she were about to take flight.

My eyes narrowed at the older woman. Hers flashed mischievously. "You must have suspected. Otherwise, a commander with your skill would have asked the question already."

She was right. I knew it deep in my bones. Seryn's confusion surfaced as she looked from me to Neoma.

The others at the table held their pints up, and everyone in the pub mirrored them.

Hints of feathered tattoos poked from under collars and sleeves throughout the room.

Caelora's warm, golden-blonde waves snapped behind her as she left the pub, a flash of dark ink peeking out from her nape.

Breena held her chin-length hair to the side and showed Seryn the dark feather tattooed behind her left ear. Rhaegar unbuckled his wrist guard from his left forearm, revealing an inky, opalescent bird on his deep brown skin. Its wings wrapped around his wrist, cuff-like. Seryn's eyes were wide now, realization capturing her.

Neoma continued after taking another sip, "Helos is where the Korax was born. Where believers and Druiks find refuge and hide in plain sight. We speak freely ... because we're all Ravens here."

A chorus of jovial salutes and clinking glass rent the air. My mind swirled with the possibilities. With the number of rebels—mortal and embered—harbored in the city, our odds against the Elders and their sycophants significantly improved.

A thundering chant rang through the tavern, louder than when they were all singing earlier, and then rippled outside along the walkways. "May the wings of the raven carry you!"

And in that moment, I hoped they would.

13

TO STRUGGLE IS A PRIVILEGE

SERYN

A faint string of cursing flit over the breeze from my left. Gavrel rolled his eyes to the sky as he pushed his oar into the water behind Breena. I giggled. "What was that, Bree-Bree?" I called from our rowboat to theirs. Propelling our boat forward, Rhaegar chuckled behind me as my biceps worked with my paddle.

"As the raven flies," Breena grumbled loudly. "That's a bunch of bollocks. There are bloody ravens everywhere!" She threw her hands up in exasperation.

I scanned the sky as I had been all morning, but there were, in fact, no ravens to be found anywhere. And she didn't mean us or the city of rebels at our backs.

I glanced at the space behind her ear as the wind tossed back her dark strands. Now that I knew it was hidden there, the tiny feather tattoo marking her olive skin was so apparent.

I chewed on my lip, nodding in solidarity. "If nothing else, we're having a little adventure. Yeah?"

Breena's shoulders fell. "Right. You always know how to calm me down, Ryn, unlike that knob-shite." She jerked her head toward Rhaegar.

My smile lingered at her words. She spoke as if she'd already taken the Mirage Orchid tonic. As if she remembered our friendship that started during the last Dormancy. The full moon was several weeks away, though. She and I were both eager for her to use it. But until then, her vial hid in her and Rhaegar's hut.

"Woman," he scolded, "Did you forgo breakfast this morning?"

She scowled. "Yes. What's it to you?"

I peeked at him. His smile was disarming. "No reason. I'll gladly be your pin cushion, my friend."

She sniffed, lifting her chin and jabbing her oar into the swamp water with a splash.

We'd chosen to head to the bog fields, considering that's where the Augur had found us. My mouth pinched. I vehemently hoped that the Void fog didn't infect the bog bodies today. I could do without the dead trying to eat me again.

We settled into a comfortable silence, our boats occasionally separating and coming together as we meandered aimlessly. I inhaled, enjoying the salt-tinged breath. Fortunately, the stench of rotten eggs was absent today, and despite the humidity, the damp air no longer bothered me.

My thoughts wandered to Letti. I hoped she was safe. I'd no doubt that Xeni had found her way to my sister. No doubt that Letti could handle herself with Father. He'd always treated her well, so all she had to do was pretend as though her memories were as they always had been.

Erased.

I heaved a sigh, feeling the weight of my responsibility.

To Kaden. To my sister.

To everyone I loved.

To Midst Fall.

"What's on your mind?" Rhaegar asked, his tone as smooth as the still water ahead of us.

After turning in my seat, I faced him with a sad smile that bent my mouth. "Do you ever feel … heavy? Like you're drowning with stones tied to your ankles. You know you need to break through the surface, but you're being pulled down anyway."

He shook his head. "Well, that sounds positively horrific." He laid his oar across his lap, scanning the sky as if we had all the time in the world. His eyebrows drew together, and he bowed his head, running his thumb over the wood. "But I know the feeling. When my sister Skye was ill, I felt helpless. It didn't matter that I was just a boy myself. I tried everything I could to find her more food—more medicine—as did our parents. But it … it wasn't enough." His forlorn gaze met mine. "It was my responsibility to protect her. And I failed."

Reaching over, I laid my hand on his for a moment. I didn't offer him words because we understood one another perfectly. Logically, he knew that it wasn't his fault. Deep down, I recognized the same. Yet, it was. We carried the burden of both protecting and fighting for those we loved … at whatever cost.

Even when the price was our soul.

He continued,"I wouldn't say it gets any easier when you aren't able to save someone you love. But time has honed the pain and guilt into a clear purpose. The realm is dying and doing its very best to take us all with it. The Elders are to blame in one way or another. Their laws are self-serving. A means to help them manage the masses. To maintain their power."

His hands fisted on his oar, conviction rumbling through his chest and through his words. "We *will* be the ones to bring them to their knees. To struggle is a privilege the elite will never know. They think fighting for survival is a weakness. But what they don't understand is that the more we've struggled, the more resilient we've become."

His jaw set in a firm line as he exhaled slowly, looking at the sky once more. "Like you said, you know … *we* know we must reach the surface, but the hardest part is discerning which direction to swim. Having stones weigh you down can strengthen you—make you all the more determined to break through. It leaves you in no doubt as to which way is up."

My eyebrows rose, and a renewed resolve straightened my spine. I glanced at Breena and Gavrel's boat as it swayed closer. My head slowly bobbed as I met Rhaegar's dark eyes. "We'll reach the surface."

In this moment, I believed it.

"Bloody right we will."

My belly grumbled, and I grinned. "All this talk of rebellion has worked up my appetite."

He reached into the small satchel attached to his belt, tossing me a chunk of dried meat, and then took a solid bite out of another piece. "You know how I love sharing food with my kin."

My smile didn't leave me as shining ebony streaked overhead, a rattling caw in its wake. As the majestic raven soared to the west, my gaze trailed after it. The sun tinged over its feathers, making the tips look almost blue.

I shared an excited grin with my *kin* and the others as their rowboat approached. "As the raven flies!" I cried, pure hope floating atop my reinvigorated fortitude.

Gavrel's mouth twitched but remained in a tight line, pushing his craft to the west. He'd probably reached his limit of Breena's sparkling personality today.

Good. I smirked at the thought. Struggling made you stronger.

As we followed, the bird weaved through the air, circling and diving as it waited. Thankfully, we skirted the bogs at a distance until we came to a copse of doombarks.

With a scratchy screech, the winged beast dove straight for the center, where the trunks bent inward, creating a triangular archway. There was nothing but a swampy horizon beyond.

"Another adventure?" A wide smile sliced across Breena's mouth.

"Always," I agreed, mirroring her expression as we propelled onward.

A dizzying hum of energy clung to me as we neared the entrance. Our skiffs floated through the trees, which were wide enough to allow passage side by side. Breena and I passed through first.

A damp chill washed over my skin as Breena shivered. A soft rush of cherry hues flushed over her. My aura shuddered and flashed over me as well. Looking over my shoulder, a rippling wall of reflective water covered the archway, blocking the men from view and making our boat appear sliced in half.

When the rowboat continued its trajectory, the men shook their heads as if clearing away a fog, runes glowing on their hands.

"Always a delight. Your adventures." Rhaegar winked at me. I smiled, facing forward as our energies vanished beneath our flesh.

Now, a tunnel of bent, graying boughs stretched several lengths before us. Drooping down, soft, wispy vines twined between the limbs. The raven flew ahead, disappearing as it reached the end and swooped out of sight with a final croak.

Swamp crickets and lapping water serenaded us as we made our way through to the end of the passageway.

As the clouded light seeped over my face, a plethora of twisting doombarks sprinkled outward, interspersed with mossy knolls and flat slabs of rock protruding from the gloomy water.

In the center stood a wooden shack, precariously balanced on thick, crisscrossing poles that creaked under the weight of the structure. Mixing with the fragrant dampness in the air, a briny breeze brushed against my cheeks. The weathered planks were adorned with a bright, painted medley of various flora, trees, and animals from all of Midst Fall's regions.

It was a stark contrast to the milieu cradling it. And the grizzled female rocking in a chair on the deck, observing us with steepled hands.

Gavrel moored our vessel to a tree, and I stepped onto a partially submerged boulder next to it.

As we leaped across the hummocks and stones, my heart thrummed faster, my inhalations shallow. If she helped us find Kaden, and hopefully Mama, all our efforts would be worth it.

With time etched into her joints, the Augur rose slowly, holding her arms out to her sides in greeting. My breath caught. "Hello, child. Come, let's begin."

She flicked her hands at the others as they stood their ground by my side. "Go on. This time is for me and the girl."

Breena examined her nails. "Pass."

Gavrel's body sidled closer, the heat of him brushing against my arm.

The female's eyebrow quirked, her forehead wrinkles creasing deeper.

I brushed my palm along his biceps as they tensed. "It's all right. If she wished it so, I'd already be dust."

The line of his jaw flexed, and he nodded to Rhaegar and Breena.

"Fine, Ryn-Ryn. We'll go stab one another over there." Breena drew her dagger and jabbed it toward a patch of hummocks several yards away.

Lifting my chin, I faced the Augur as they went off to spar. She tilted her head, studying me. "Show me."

14

THE THREAD THAT BINDS YOU

SERYN

Clammy dread caressed my skin, my pulse tapping under my star-shaped scar. The Augur's frail frame leaned forward as she waited. She'd be waiting forever before I unleashed my ember. My fingers curled into fists, heels digging into the spongy surface.

Sighing, she slowly lowered herself to the rock below her porch and then held her hand out in invitation.

Watching her, I moved across a few compacted peat mounds until she paused atop a smooth, level slab of charcoal-colored stone. My hips wobbled as I balanced upon the rounded perch.

Her gaze was direct, but a touch softer than before. "No need to be afraid." A sheen of sparkling power flickered over her. "Here you will find yourself. Show me."

My eyes closed, my blood pumping in time with the power vibrating under my skin. I opened my eyes and stared at my hands, letting myself feel the hum of my energy. Letting the echoes of its radiance simmer.

I loosened the reins on my ember. It sparked over me, clawing at the surrounding space agitatedly.

"You've been chaining your gift. Fearing it," the Augur observed.

My jaw shifted to the side. "Well, when it tries to suck everyone dry, that's what happens."

Her eyes narrowed, looking at the sky. "You have yet to commune with it fully." She held her palms out toward me, and warmth sizzled over my spine. "Let go. Breathe. Let it wander a little."

I wiggled my shoulders, concentrating on breathing. My aura burned, flaring in spurts. It was hungry. Frustrated. It boiled around me, grasping at the Augur.

Mine.

My chin jutted forward as I thrust my hands out. Iridescent boughs zipped over my forearms and hands. I grit my molars against the throbbing scorch.

Gilded sparkles curled up my arms, a cool, winding caress. My ember flinched, unsure if it was being attacked or soothed. "Breathe, child. Relax. Crown to heel."

My lungs expanded, jaw moving from side to side. I'd been clamping my teeth so hard they throbbed as I released my bite.

It's okay.

You're okay.

"Keep going."

I pushed air out, contracting my belly, concentrating on each limb and joint. The burn lessened, and my aura swayed rather than snapped around me, the fractured rainbows dancing instead of mauling the air.

Tentatively, it prodded against the Augur's energy like a cat pawing at a mouse.

Is it ... is it playing? Or hunting?

"Let it be what it'll be. One cannot fight their nature. Fight themself. It would be like cutting off the very flesh that holds you together." My eyes, like glowing ice, reflected in the deep honey pools of hers. A kind smile stretched over her lips. "One can only build fellowship with their ember."

My eyelids fell, threatening to spill the wetness lining my lower lashes. I wanted what she spoke of. I was so tired of the fear. Of the exhaustion coursing through every fiber of my body.

But I refused to hurt those I loved. Refused to burn the world down because I couldn't control myself.

Enough.

My chin wobbled at the demand. I wasn't sure if the thought was mine or my ember's.

Both.

We'd both had enough.

All right. Let's commune, I offered to myself, my palms rising to face one another in front of my chest. *But don't bloody kill anyone today, or I swear to the Ancients.*

My energy buzzed, dazzling incandescence pulsing in colorful waves along the branch patterns until a spinning glow formed between my fingers.

The female backed up, her slippers swishing over the slab. Slowly, her glittering light unfurled from my arms.

Warmth tingled from my scar to the bottom of my spine. I breathed in, counting the pulsing crests of my ember and blood as they poppled within me.

"More," the Augur directed, smoothing her hands down her wispy robes.

So, *we* listened.

"LISTEN, CHILD." She shuffled atop the flat rock, clasping her fingers in front of her.

I plopped onto the peaty mound with a huff, propped my elbows on crossed legs, and hung my head, sweat dripping down my temples.

"Ember isn't simply about bloodlines and elemental gifts. It's about energy. It's about how your very essence connects with the world around you and the Ancients. While it's rooted in the elements, it effloresces into the aether."

"Eh, it's story time, is it?" Breena jumped onto my hummock, making it wobble precariously. I swatted her ankle, and she laughed, situating herself next to me. The clash of metal sounded in the distance. Gavrel and Rhaegar were busy sparring.

The Augur ignored Breena, her bony fingers delicately weaving in front of her now, pale hair flicking around her. "Ember is present in every living creature. Every breath. Every vibrant human emotion. It's the light ... and the dark. It's Kosmos."

A spinning orb of golden sparkles fluttered between her hands before she clapped, and they dispersed in a twinkling billow. "Its thread weaves through everything, which is why some who are embered can wield beyond the elements. Can manipulate the body, mind, emotion, or aura. Can draw on the gifts directly relating to the Ancients that bestowed them. Evergryn lineage connects with the earth, but also with the body, whether it belongs to mortal, plant, or beast."

She waved her hand at Breena, and a breeze twirled around her, lifting her dark hair for a moment. "Pyrian Druiks are often gifted with heat or flame. Others can ignite potent emotions in others." The old female lifted a brow at Breena. "This one's ability to manipulate heat and morph it—like the sun's invisible waves—into a shield is sufficient." Breena grinned; it was quite the compliment from the Augur.

Breena shifted, propping a knee up and wrapping her arms around it. "Let me guess. Pneumalian is wind and breath."

Breena winked at me. "Once met a Pneumali Druik who could suck the air right out of your lungs."

The Augur nodded once. "Haadran: water and cleansing emotions. And so on."

I sat taller, curiosity overtaking my feelings of defeat. My forehead creased. "And this connection with Kosmos—with aether and pure energy—it's why ember needs to be pruned and expended. It has to go somewhere once it's summoned. Otherwise, it's too much for us to bear. It's why it drains you when you've used too much … We're so intricately tied together," I deduced, a note of awe lacing my words.

Nodding, the skin around the Augur's eyes crinkled. "If it isn't used to shape the physical world or bend the mind, body, or spirit, then it serves as pure energy. As a distinct weapon. How one wields it is up to the *embered*. Not the *ember*."

I sighed, disappointment seeping back in. My scar tapped against my nape, taunting me as my shoulders slumped.

"Enough self-pity. Such indulgences are composed of wasted moments." She stepped closer to the edge of the slab, eyes boring into mine. "Perilous Bogs' gifts connect directly to the aether. It's rare. Easy to lose oneself to its allure. Others covet or seek to destroy it. The ability to manipulate the mind, astral body, or aura is remarkable. It's the most unpredictable ember and requires the utmost patience and control." A flush of pink stained her papery cheeks. It was the most riled I'd seen her.

I bit the inside of my cheek, and Breena rubbed my knee.

"In time, you'll find the thread that binds you to your ember. For you are one and the same. As you said—intricately tied together."

"Bound together like a rune tattooed on your soul," Rhaegar crooned behind us before bouncing onto our hummock and jiggling his hand in front of Breena's face.

"Piss off, you," Breena groused, swatting his hand and knocking her head against his knees. He yelped, ungracefully circling his arms to steady himself, but fell into the mucky water, backside first, regardless. Beneath us, the peat bobbed precariously as if irritated by all the commotion.

"Bloody void, woman," he complained. "These were my last dry pair of boots."

Breena snickered. "Serves you right for sneaking up on a lady."

"Lady, my arse."

I giggled, swaying my head from side to side as I noticed Gavrel jump onto the mound beside us. "Spar with me?" he asked.

"Haven't you had enough?" Gulping, I eyed his heaving chest and the damp waves clinging to his forehead.

The hint of a smirk toyed with one side of his mouth. "Never."

Interrupting them, I bid Rhaegar and Breena farewell as they got into their boat to head back to Helos. Rhaegar's soggy boots squished loudly as he settled himself, and their bickering trailed after them.

Chuckling, I turned to say goodbye to the Augur, but she was no longer on her perch. "For someone who's so frail-looking, she moves quickly when it suits her."

He made a sound of agreement, offering me his hand as we mounted the slab. With a grin, I snapped my dagger from its sheath and twirled, holding the sharp edge against Gavrel's neck before he could draw his blade. I wiggled my eyebrows. "Lesson one: Always be ready," I purred, echoing his words from Surrelia during our first lesson.

15

MY YESTERDAYS. MY TODAY. MY TOMORROWS.

SERYN

His throat bobbed, the corner of his mouth curving upward. "Ah, there she is."

I smirked, backing away. He drew a dagger from his belt, raised one brow, and then swung his arm. I sprang away; my eyes glued to his every move.

His muscles rippled and bunched beneath his dark tunic. He jabbed toward me, and I blocked, pushing his forearm away with my other fist. We danced around each other, parrying and blocking one another, our weapons clashing and clanging.

I had honed my skills with a blade since our time in the Dormancy; muscle memory enhanced and responsive. Of course, Gavrel could best me if we'd been sparring with swords, but with daggers, we were equally matched.

As adrenaline surged through my system, months—nay, turns—of frustration condensed into this moment. My pulse roared in my ears, a frantic drumbeat, as my vision tunneled and locked on the glint of my dagger. Until all that was left was the burning need to defeat my opponent, the thrill of victory coursing through me.

Because maybe a win would momentarily offer me relief from the constant disappointment of not being able to tether my ember. Maybe it would make me forget my less-than-chaste thoughts about the man jabbing a blade at me.

A grin split across my face; I appreciated he wasn't holding back. He trusted me.

A soft breeze caressed my skin, making me acutely aware of a bead of sweat that dripped down my temple. Gavrel's eyes narrowed, a roguish smile dancing along his mouth.

Swiftly, I sliced my weapon through the air, the blade barely missing his tunic, and he jerked back with a wry chuckle. "One would think you're trying to draw blood, Little Star."

I beamed. "Never." And then stabbed toward him.

Gavrel feinted left, spinning out of the way, his thick arm wrapping around my waist from behind me, and cold metal nestled against my throat. Stuck between us, my curls tugged at the back of my scalp. His face bowed, and his ragged whisper dragged across my ear. "Do you yield?"

Would I really give in to the man who had shattered my heart?

The one who lingered in my thoughts, refusing to fade away?

Perhaps.

The beginning of a growl caught in my windpipe as desire pooled between my thighs. "Never."

Without thought, I flung my arm down, digging my nails into his upper thigh, precariously close to his manhood. A deep rumble vibrated against my back, and he pushed his hips into my bottom.

The blade at my throat drifted away, and my mouth curled. All at once, I dropped into a squat, kicked out my leg, and hooked behind his knees until he toppled onto his back. Swiftly, I straddled his waist, my blade pressed against his neck. "Do *you* yield?" I asked victoriously.

The clatter of metal against stone sounded as his hands bracketed my waist. Gavrel's pupils dilated, and I swore I stared into the eyes of a wild beast. He licked his lips and gently raised his neck to my dagger's edge. "Only to you," he murmured.

My eyes widened, my mouth slackening until my bottom lip dropped along with my weapon. Clanging bounced against the rock and somber trees. The cacophony of croaking toads and chirping insects was suddenly overwhelming, accompanied by the faint caw of a raven flying overhead.

With each heartbeat, I bent forward as if the force of it drove my ribcage closer to his. As if his pulse called to mine, reeling me in.

Was he my captive, or was I his? I thought as my hands pushed against the cool, damp rock on either side of his head. The chill sank into my skin. My face hovered a breath above his. "Damn it, Gavrel," I breathed. "Why do you say such things?"

"You know very well why, Asteria." His words were rough and barely restrained. His body practically vibrated beneath me, taut and rigid. The bite of his fingers moored me to reality when all I wanted to do was fall into this dream.

My eyes searched his, bouncing between the viridian depths. His nostrils flared, and his fingers twitched against my waist.

He would never lose control.

Unless I *wanted* him to.

And I was tired of holding back. Of the guilt and anger. Of denying whatever was resurfacing between us.

"Fuck it."

My lips collided into his, swallowing his escaping groan as his arms immediately wrapped around my back, one hand tunneling into my hair.

His plump lips were as I remembered. Firm, but supple.

Our mouths left each other.

Joined once more.

Over and over again.

His tongue invaded my mouth, demanding that mine meet his stroke for stroke.

We were still sparring. His patience and mine finally snapped.

My thoughts tapered, senses spiraling through me and condensing. Teeth and tongue and lips journeying over every inch of his kiss. It was as if my mind were creating a map of his lips for the times I'd want to imagine them on me in the future.

As a molten shiver swept from my throbbing nape to my tailbone, I moaned. Or he did. I wasn't sure as it vibrated through our mouths and where our chests connected. Our frantic heartbeats volleying against one another.

He sat up, my backside seated firmly against the hardness straining within his trousers. His palms dragged down my back, cupping my rounded cheeks, and I grabbed onto his nape.

I was going to incinerate.

Ancients, I wanted him. *Needed* him.

He tore his mouth from mine, breathing raggedly, and nipped at my jaw. "You taste like I remember. Fucking salted honey," he rasped against my neck.

I stilled, a chill slithering over my heated skin.

Confusion and unmitigated guilt clung to my awareness.

Kaden had said something similar to me months ago.

But whatever was happening between Gavrel and me felt different.

More potent.

Its talons digging into my spine.

But Kaden …

My fingers flinched against his nape, and I untangled them as I slowly rose from his lap. "I'm … I'm sorry. I can't—"

"Don't." His hands gently rested on my hips as his eyes met

mine, lips swollen. With a gaze that was soft and assessing, he pressed his fingers into my breeches ever so slightly, bringing me back to reality.

"This was a mistake. I … I can't do this. Kaden … He said something about salted—"

"Don't," he repeated, wincing as if I'd slapped him, hands dropping immediately from my body. Although his tone was low, the sharp edge of it cut through me. A shadowed look slammed over his face as he stood, brushing off his breeches and then picking up our weapons. His movements were those of a well-honed commander.

Efficient and precise.

Perfunctory.

He slipped my dagger into the sheath at my hip, his emeralds digging into the ice that was surely coating my irises. "It wasn't a mistake." He moved toward our skiff bobbing in the muck. He gripped his broadsword, the sound of it scraping through the air as it slid into its leather scabbard.

"Gav, I …"

He looked at me, a look of utter resoluteness sweeping over his features. His jaw hardened into a square, its edges ticking near his earlobes.

I sucked in a breath, certain that he'd keep what he so clearly wanted to say tethered. That he'd walk away like he had all those turns ago. Keep his thoughts and feelings locked away— buried beneath his secrets—so I couldn't reach him.

With my pulse slamming against my neck, he proved me wrong. All at once, he was in front of me. He cupped either side of my neck. Despite the barely contained restraint pushing at his tense muscles, his touch was gentle. So gentle, I thought he might be a figment of my imagination.

His nostrils flared. "I don't give a damn what my brother said to you. What happened between you two; it's a memory. I aim to be your today and every tomorrow after that." His eyes softened, and a fist full of fireflies fluttered through my belly. He stepped back, and his fingers slipped from my skin. The loss of them burrowed deep within my soul. "What happens between us is entirely our own. No one else's."

I blinked a few times, clearing away the fuzzy warmth. Unbidden, the memory of Gavrel tearing my heart out two autumns ago took its place like a bucket of iced water pouring over me. Ire bubbled up my throat, my eye squinting dangerously. "How dare you!"

He froze, eyes widening.

I poked my finger into his chest. It was like stabbing a rock wall. "How dare you say such things, you … you wanker!"

Tilting his head, he wiggled his jaw, but it didn't rid him of the ticking along the hinge. Several wayward ebony strands fell over his forehead.

A sound of pure frustration reverberated in my throat as I squeezed my nails into my palms, preventing myself from swiping my fingers across his brow. "My today? My tomorrows? How dare you so easily forget that *you* are the reason this" —my hand thumped against his chest and then gripped the fabric over mine—"was torn apart. You had me then. Until you tossed me aside."

He stepped into my space, nostrils flaring. My body stilled, vibrating with anger and anticipation and need. I looked at him from under my lashes, fists clenching. Was that the sound of my heart or his thudding feverishly against muscle and bone?

His chest expanded as his gaze bore into mine. Dropping his head, he sighed heavily before stepping back. "I could never forget, Little Star." The farther he got from me, the deeper the furrow between his brows dug into his skin. "I destroyed what we had. I won't deny it. The memory of that look you gave me. That moment I ripped your heart—*and mine*—into countless pieces. I *felt* your pain, and I knew I was the one who made you carry it. I'll regret it forever." He rubbed his palm over his left breastbone, staring helplessly at my boots. My skin warmed as if his palm was brushing over my sternum.

After a moment, his eyes met mine. "But I broke us because it needed to be done. And I'd do it again and again if it meant keeping you safe. From Melina. From myself. From the fucking Ancients themselves if need be." He reached out and cupped my cheek. "So, yes, I do dare … because, at last, hope is within reach."

Stunned, all I could do was blink.

He ran one hand through his hair and turned, climbing into the rowboat, holding it steady while I silently joined him. My blood raged as we paddled back, and my molars ground into one another as I chewed on the thick silence between us.

Aching remembrances crawled out of the shadows. I wanted to let the resentment go. Wanted to forgive Gavrel for breaking my heart. I *yearned* to trust him with it again, but I didn't know if I could.

My infatuation with him had always simmered beneath the surface. What began as admiration and awe in my childhood had evolved into a deep well of pining during my adolescence. When the spring of womanhood finally effloresced, there was no doubt of my feelings for him.

And two springs ago, when he finally acted on his affections, I recalled his expression—so full of reverence and remorse—when he first called me *Asteria*. In that moment, I believed it to be true, as the stars *finally* shifted into place.

Until they shriveled that following autumn.

My fingers tightened around the oar, lips smashing together, as other thoughts weaved through my awareness. My mind spun through everything that had happened between Kaden and me. Everything that led up to us crossing that line between friends and lovers.

Guilt twisted like a knife in my guts. My situation with Kaden. My feelings—old and new—for Gavrel.

Each recollection was like one of Medusa's snakes, threatening to strangle the others. I feared that if I looked at them head-on, I might turn to stone.

My heart banged against my ribs, and my ember hummed against my nape. I breathed in to the count of four, and then out again.

Slow down, I reminded myself. *One thing at a time.*

If I were honest, I didn't *entirely* regret what happened during the Dormancy. At the time, I had wanted more with Kaden. But even without recalling half of our lives, something had been missing. I just … couldn't give him every piece of my heart.

And that was all right.

A heavy sigh pushed from my lungs as I sat up and stretched my neck from side to side.

Kaden had said it himself. *Don't ever apologize for feeling.* Irritation bubbled up my throat, and I scoffed.

When we found him, I'd remind that cur he'd said that. He didn't get to make me feel awful for not reciprocating his affections. Not anymore. I wasn't culpable for his emotions.

A grimace dug into my features. *What is wrong with you? Your best friend is trapped somewhere, and you're planning on tearing him a new asshole? Hasn't he suffered enough?*

Spiraling.

That's what I was doing.

The vibration under my scar tapped wildly.

Bollocks. Hadn't it had enough fun today?

I jabbed my oar into the swamp water, and mud splattered against the side of my knee. Huffing, I slapped at my pants, brown sludge staining the fabric.

I glanced behind me, and Gavrel raised his brows, tucking his still-swollen lips between his teeth.

He probably thought I'd lost my mind. Perhaps I had. At

least, that's what it felt like with all these unfettered thoughts and emotions bashing around my skull.

Tossing my braid behind me, I turned to face forward.

Fucking void, Gavrel.

My *today*.

My *tomorrows*.

The fireflies were back. Bumping into my guts and trying to light me up from the inside. I clamped my molars together, willing the creatures away.

I could barely handle the next minute. So, Gavrel would have to wait an Ancient-damned second while I pieced myself back together and worked through my yesterdays.

Breathe.

16

THE VIOLET WRAITH

SERYN

The sun dipped, its luminous hues spilling phosphorescent ink over the vista. Like dark stains, the silhouettes of sleepy doombarks crosshatched along the horizon.

A cleansing inhale swirled into my lungs, and my eyelashes fluttered against my skin. The hum of crickets, toads, and lapping water drifted over me. All day, I'd been wandering around the city, the sway of its bridges and the chatter of its citizens comforting.

Here and there, I'd let my ability peek out, and I was in awe of the vibrant display of ember sprinkled throughout the city. Living things—trees and creatures and refugees—were communing, their multicolored energies frolicking, lustrous, and smoldering. Despite the lack of resources, like everywhere else, its people were bound. They were driven by their sense of belonging and the desire to bring the oligarchy crashing to its knees.

This place was burrowing into my soul, nestling beside my devotion to Evergryn. Something here tugged at my marrow, as if my very essence knew my roots came from the mire.

With a sigh, I pushed off the rope railing and made my way back to our lodging. It'd been a couple of days since the *confrontation*. Thankfully, Gavrel had given me space and hadn't mentioned what had happened between us. The words would have to be put into the universe eventually … but not yet.

Breaking into my distraction, the planks several lengths ahead creaked and then abruptly silenced. I dragged my attention toward the sound, and the female before me hesitated, her slender fingers tucking waves the color of burnished wheat behind her ear. A flicker of violet danced over her form before sinking back within her and her long, flowy steel-colored dress. Her fingers fidgeted with the belt around her waist, jostling the slim blade hanging from it.

Caelora.

I sipped in the humid air, letting it cling to my lungs before releasing it. Shame bubbled in my stomach as she tilted her head and slowly stepped forward. I flinched at the memory of her splintering into ash in the Winnowing arena.

My curls brushed against my flushed cheeks as I squeezed my eyes tight and turned toward the swamp, gripping the rope once more. My breath caught as she neared.

"Excuse me. Seryn, is it?" She settled beside me. The scent of lilacs mixed with something warm and comforting, like freshly baked goods. My eyes flicked open, glancing at her from the side of my vision, uncertainly.

Her chin dipped as she faced me, one hand clamped around the railing, mirroring my stance. Gulping, I turned to her, eyes skimming over her pretty, oval face.

At first, I thought her eyes were a deep brown, but as she turned to look over the horizon, the lingering sunbeams illuminated the rich, dark purple of her irises, which were mottled with specks of indigo. It was like gazing at a sunken bit of amethyst beneath a shadowy wave. I'd never seen such an eye color before and wondered if it was a side effect of her blended lineage.

She pressed her mouth together, gripping the rope tighter, waiting for my response. I tugged on the hem of my tunic. "Ah, yes, sorry. I am. And you are?" I thought it best to pretend I didn't know her until I gathered my wits.

"I think you know who I am," she replied, releasing the rope. "Just as I remember who you are."

Void.

I admired her frankness, but it was disconcerting all the same. My heart rammed into the muscles and bones restraining it. My scar prickled on my nape.

She raised her left hand, giving me a pointed look and then nodding toward the unblemished space between her thumb and forefinger.

I hesitated, the line between my eyebrows deepening before I let my gift take a peek. The small rune on her pale skin glimmered into view. The dainty lines of the now-visible tattoo glinting in the shape of two interlocking decagons. My bottom lip dropped, unspoken words escaping me.

Did she win the rune promised by the Elders? What does that mean for Kaden?

She pushed her fingers into her palms, lowering her arm to her side. My heels dug into the bridge as I cleared my throat. "How?"

Mouth pursing, her cheeks hollowed as she turned sideways and leaned her elbows on the railing. "I'm not entirely sure. As you know … I wasn't the victor." She lifted one eyebrow at me, and I sighed, shoulders slumping. "There isn't a turn's supply of rations to be found. But I woke up in my pod, with this rune glowing. And I … I remembered. At least through this last Dormancy." Her humorless laugh fell into the water.

"Damn me to the murk," I muttered and then grimaced at my choice of words. That's *exactly* where I had sent her after draining her.

The corners of her rosy lips dipped, the small V in the center of her top lip stretching. "You don't have to apologize for what happened in the arena. What is done in times of necessity—times of battle—well, there's no shame in doing what you need to."

I exhaled slowly through my nose and rested my forearms beside hers. "Nevertheless, I am sorry for it, Caelora."

She nodded, letting the warm breeze tug at her strands while her eyes roamed over the mire. There was something about her, like the quiet before an approaching storm. It was that moment when the air stilled, and you could taste the thickness of it. Although the thunder had yet to roar, you could sense its silent rumble beneath your feet.

My eyes fixed on the doombarks. "How is it? Having your memories?" I asked, although I already knew how it was to remember what was better left erased. Word likely got around that I also had mine back, but to what extent, I wasn't sure.

She pushed herself off the rope. "As is expected. Being a part of all this"—she waved one hand in a circle—"prepared me better than most. But it's still quite the journey, isn't it?"

Ah, so she knew I had mine as well.

"It's a boon and a curse," I agreed.

"It is." She seized the railing; her thumb rubbed against the rough threads. "It's sobering to feel the life drain from you … to know the breaths you're taking might be your last." She sucked in a quick inhale, her mouth parting. "Then they aren't. And you can recall every bit of that frantic, desperate agony. It seems cruel … selfish somehow. To have wished so long to remember, only to want to go back to forgetting."

My chest rose and fell in quick, shallow respirations. Her words dug into my own anxieties and recollections.

As if she understood precisely how I felt.

But she does.

A sad, humming sound of agreement left me, and she squeezed her eyes shut for a moment. My hand flinched, itching to reach for hers. But I fisted the air, keeping my touch to myself. I didn't know Caelora. Didn't know if it would be an intrusion in such a raw moment.

"You want to know something awful?" she whispered, and I looked at her, waiting. Her chest expanded, and then she continued, "My mom died when I was young. And though I'd give anything to have her back, I'm … I'm grateful that her suffering was put to rest. I wasn't able to admit that until now. And oddly, I have you to thank for that."

A burning roiled just below my ribcage, understanding and grief itching under my skin. "I … I don't know what to say to that except that I'm sorry. About your mother. Mine disappeared many turns ago, and I'm not sure if it gets easier. Rather, it's more like a constant hum in the background of everyday life."

Her head bobbed as she brushed her fingers over her hidden tattoo. "I like that. Thinking of her always with me. I feel her when I sing. When I hear a song that reminds me of home." She dropped her right hand, but kept studying the skin of her left.

"I wouldn't expect that rune was given out of the kindness of the Elders' hearts," I muttered.

With a soft exhalation, Caelora pushed her long hair behind her shoulders. "No truer words have ever been spoken. Take care, Seryn. I'm glad we talked." Gently, her fingertips touched my wrist before her chin dipped. She moved past me like a wraith, her form disappearing into the bustle of the twilit city, shades of purple cloaking her despite her aura being tucked away.

17

UNWRITTEN HISTORY

SERYN

There was so much sifting through my mind. The encounter with Caelora both comforted and unsettled me. My thoughts and emotions were like sediment drifting into place behind each step. Reminding me of things that pained me, and things I needed to atone for.

Kaden.

Hesitantly, I unpacked what had happened with my best friend during the last Dormancy. A lump stuck in my throat, and I swallowed a few times while my gaze unfocused and wandered aimlessly. I couldn't own his feelings, and I wasn't ashamed of the intimacy we had shared.

Yet, I played a part in hastening things. I could blame naivete and the sense of urgency the Dormancy fostered, but that would be the easy way out.

Deep down, I'd sensed the intensity of Kaden's affections, a silent current beneath the surface of our friendship, but I hadn't wanted to accept it. I'd chosen to take things down the path we'd taken, knowing that I didn't reciprocate them. And for that, I was sorry. I hoped I'd get the chance if—no, I *would* apologize … *when* we found my best friend.

As if a band had been loosened around my ribcage, my lungs expanded. My focus cleared, and a particularly verrucose toad came into view. He blinked at me slowly with his mouth gaping.

My eyes narrowed. *Why are these little bastards so damn judgment—*

"Tea to go with your introspection?" Yaya's voice poked through my thoughts.

Sticking my tongue out at the creature, I followed her up the winding stairs and into her home. A cozy fire sputtered in the hearth, and its warmth embraced me as I sat at her table.

She set the plain cups in front of me, taking the seat by my side. With a solemn expression, she poured a bit of lavender liquid into each. Lifting one eyebrow, I brought it to my nose. The scent wasn't quite sweet, but it smelled of some type of fruit. "This isn't tea," I teased.

The older woman shrugged, taking a sip. "Did I say tea? I meant a nip of mireberry wine."

I smirked, tasting the tart liquid as it tingled down my throat. My lips smacked together, eyes squinting. "I'd say just a nip will do ya."

"It gets better as you go." With one hand, she gestured for me to drink more.

I did, and its bittersweet heat was a pleasant comfort as I swallowed. I lifted my cup in thanks, and she reclined, her chair creaking.

"What were you muddling over out there? Or did you already tell the gilly toad all your secrets?" She smirked, resting one elbow on her crossed arm, her cup near her chin.

A breathy snort left me as I bent forward, resting my forearms on her table. "They are quite attentive." She waited until I gave in, "I was thinking about Kaden. And Gavrel. And my part in how our relationships have turned out."

"Ah, matters of the heart, then. That's good. It's good to have your wits about you. Ancients know it's easy to get your brains twisted along with your panties."

I choked on the drink I'd taken. She set her cup down and patted me on the back a few times. "Er, I suppose, um."

She clucked her tongue. "No need to be embarrassed. I've birthed two daughters. I know how it works." She settled in her chair. "So, which one is it, then? I'd put my coin on the commander. I see the way you look at one another. Can't imagine you'd be as jumpy if it were the younger brother. What with him being missing and all."

My chin dipped, and I ran my thumbs over my cup. "Kaden and I have been best friends since we were children. During the last Dormancy … we were more. He said he'd always loved me, and I didn't feel the same. Things ended poorly before he vanished. And now … now Gavrel and I are … well, I'm not sure yet, but it's something. It was something before. I just hadn't remembered it until recently."

Her mouth puckered, but she didn't dig further into what I meant. Instead, she drank the rest of her wine. She sighed. "Sounds like you know the part you played with your friend and are sorry about it. But you're owning how you felt and are figuring out your course of action with the older brother." She clasped her hands on her stomach. "Good on you, my dear. It takes a backbone to own your mistakes, not apologize for your heart, and then move on with it."

A flush scurried over my chest and cheeks. *Obviously the wine.* "Uh, thank you," I mumbled.

She nodded curtly. "You should be proud of putting one foot in front of the other. It's important to understand where we've been if we have any chance of knowing where we must go."

"That's true. History is so important." I looked around her

home, my forehead lifting. Now that I thought of it, I hadn't noticed any literature in Helos. "Do the Bogs not have any books?"

"Ah, good observation. We used to have more, but war and the elements claimed most texts long ago. Much of our history, though, is passed down orally and has been for quite some time. The people here believe each mortal must pass on our stories to the next generation."

I placed my hand on my collarbone. "That's beautiful."

"It is. I can tell you enjoy learning, yes? From the way you soak up what everyone around you is saying. How you study your surroundings. Like you are waiting for the story to unfold."

I shifted in my seat. "I … Yes, I do. I enjoy reading. Learning. My teacher used to say that I'd wear out all his books by the time I was done with primary education." A smile spread across my mouth at the memory of Magister Barden.

Yaya grinned and then poured more viscous liquid into our cups. "Do you know of the Nightbloom Sundering?"

"A bit. It was the last great celestial war. I've never been able to find much about it, or at least didn't have access to it. Growing up, Magister Barden mentioned it briefly. A century long and devastating to Midst Fall."

"Ah, that's because much of the texts were destroyed"—she held up her forefinger—"and devastating to *all* the realms." She tapped her temple. "And why our unwritten history and our music are so sacred." She drank, pressing her lips together.

The firelight flickered in her eyes, and a thrumming warmth spilled over me in anticipation. With a deep inhale, she began, "It's been said that when the humans were first gifted ember, war broke out through Midst Fall. The empire fell, and Druiks, ungoverned, wreaked havoc on the realm. Give a mortal power without edicts, whether ember or rule over others, and it festers. Mutates into something malignant." She sighed, swirling her wine in her cup. "Everything needs boundary lines to bump into. Otherwise, we fall off the edge or completely unravel the Aetherbind."

My brow furrowed at the unfamiliar term. "Aetherbind?"

Her shining gaze glanced out the window over her bed. "The seam that holds the aether and everything within it together. The very thing that keeps Kosmos in check."

"Ah. So, the Ancients intervened, yes?"

She shook her head. "Not at all. The Ancients don't entirely care for the affairs of mortals unless it affects them. Unless it *benefits* them." She took a drink, letting the liquid swish over her tongue before swallowing. "Jealous by nature, the Ancient of Nightmares envied his brother and took it upon himself to kill Morpheus' wife during the chaos of the mortals. Out for revenge, Morpheus shifted the tides of dreams; his creations displacing the torment of his brother's nightmares—a battle in the minds of the slumbering. Their feud rippled throughout the realms, and a war of epic proportions among the Ancients followed."

My eyes widened as I listened intently, soaking up the details. "How did it end?"

Yaya gave me a patient smile, holding up a hand. "After nearly a century of war ravaging the realms, the Fates were compelled to intervene. With no end in sight, mortals suffered greatly as both their and the Ancients' battles raged. The Aetherbind was fraying, its hold weakened. You see, Kosmos is the Fates' most precious gift to living things. It is universal order and balance. Life and death. Ancients and mortals. Dream and waking. If it isn't maintained, then everything goes—" She snapped her fingers.

Magister Barden never directly mentioned the Aetherbind, but his lessons on balance and chaos flit through my mind nonetheless. "What binds, protects. What breaks, devours," I murmured, echoing his words.

Yaya set her cup on the table and nodded. "If the Aetherbind breaks, Kosmos collapses. And then everything we know—ember, our realms, even the Fates—falls into Khaos. Unstable, chaotic nothingness." Yaya sighed. "The Fates warned the Ancients that they'd release the Primevals, the first beings that ever were and always have been. The very personification of creation itself. They'd unleash the Dark Reaping."

A shallow gasp flitted over my bottom lip. "Bloody void. They would cut us all down rather than face the wrath of Khaos."

"Indeed. At least with a Dark Reaping, the Fates would survive and could build a new universe. Faced with a dire threat to their existence, the Ancients had no choice but to negotiate a treaty. We know little about it, but we know it ended the war and spurred the establishment of the Elders, their sacred bloodlines, and the process of Ascension."

My fingers had slipped over the bottom of my chin and mouth. "Yaya, thank you, truly. You're quite the storyteller."

She grinned. "Historian, my dear. It's *our history*. And we've been figuring out where to go from it ever since."

18

I AM YOU AND YOU ARE ME

SERYN

The power between my palms wobbled, and I grimaced. My heart smacked against my ribs, more with frustration than fear. Practicing under the Augur's continual guidance had consumed the last fortnight. Had I made progress? I believed so. More than I had when I'd worked with it during the last Dormancy, to be sure.

The twirling, prismatic orb whirred and hummed, and, in response, I huffed. I'd rather be honing my dagger-tossing skills. At least I could do something well.

My thoughts meandered to the times over the last few days when Gavrel and I had practiced. I bit my bottom lip, imagining his warm body behind my back. His thick arm lay upon mine as he adjusted my wrist before I let the blade fly dead center into the heart of whichever doombark I was aiming for.

I jerked my head, trying to dislodge the wayward curls tickling my cheeks. *What was the point of a damned braid if my hair always escaped it?* My mouth scrunched to one side, and I blew a puff of air at the stubborn strand.

My power buzzed irritably, bringing my focus back to my weaving fingers. There were plenty of places to toss my uncontrolled creations safely. But I was sick of wasting everyone's time. Tired of my energy snapping at the bit I placed between its teeth. I looked over, and another blasted toad was gawking at me. *Hop along, you judgey bunghole.*

Or maybe it thought I was its brethren, since greenish mucksap was slathered over my exposed skin. Trying to nip me through the liniment, the annoying little bugs were excessive today. I glared at the amphibian. *Do your job and eat these little fuckers.*

"Child." The Augur slapped at the air from her porch, and my flailing ember orb zipped from my fingers and into the water several feet behind the toad. The ensuing explosion startled him, and he croaked irritably before diving into the murk.

"Concentrate."

"I *am.*"

She frowned, her wrinkles drooping over her gaunt cheekbones. Her bony fingers steepled in front of her mouth. "You and your ember are one and the same."

"That's what you've said," I mumbled.

"Then believe it. Otherwise, it'll continue to overpower you. Continue whispering its basest hunger in your ears." Her displeasure pulled the corners of her mouth further, and she hobbled into her hut while throwing her hands into the air.

Mockingly, the colorful wildlife painted all over the boards of her home stared at me. My shoulders slumped as I climbed atop the porch and sat beside Gavrel. I turned to him, sensing his eyes on me.

His brows lifted as he tucked a loose strand behind my ear. The deep green of his eyes shone boldly from his mucksap-covered face. "What do you feel when your ember takes over?"

My bottom lip pushed into the top one as I looked at the chalky sky. "I don't know."

"Try."

My cheeks puffed out as I released a frustrated exhale. I looked at my fists clenched in my lap. Uncurling my fingers, I swiped my thumbs over the base of each forefinger.

From the corner of my eye, Gavrel pressed his lips together for a moment as he waited patiently. The man had a bottomless well of perseverance.

I sighed. "Fear. Doubt. Rage."

He nodded. "And your meditations work. Until they don't."

"Until they don't," I agreed. "I'm failing. Kaden. You. Me." I dug my nails into my thighs. "Everyone."

He covered my hand with his left, and my fingers relaxed. "You're not a failure. You've made plenty of strides. I wonder what would happen if you simply *gave in* to your ability. Communed with it rather than trying to fight it."

A half-laugh, half-huff burst from my lips. "I tried that during the trials, and look where that got me."

"You said you felt rage and fear. But the moment doubt sinks in is when it all falls apart. I've seen it in your eyes. In Surrelia. Here." I looked at him then. The crease between his brows deepened. "It isn't something to chain or run away from. It's something to embrace. To partner with. It's ... it's *you*. And that's more than enough." My chin dipped, but his right hand cupped it and gently pushed my head up. "You are more than enough."

As his hand fell, my pulse sped up, and my nape tingled at his words. Was he right? Was I so terrified of what I'd done and what I might become that I was holding myself back?

He leaned into me. "You'll master this."

The Augur returned, settling herself in the creaky rocking chair. "Indeed, you will. Now, get up and try once more. The Fates wait for no one." Her invisible ember poked me in the side. Gavrel's other hand left mine, and I sighed, rising to my feet and jumping onto a nearby hummock.

Sometimes I wondered what her aura looked like. So far, she was the only Druik I couldn't get a read on.

She must be absurdly powerful. And disciplined ... And, therefore, pull your shit together and put your big girl breeches on, Seryn, I scolded myself. This was not the time for self-pity.

Widening my stance, I closed my eyes, concentrating on the vibrations within. *I am you, and you are me.* My scar buzzed on my nape. Gavrel's words brushed over me. *You're more than enough.*

With a deep exhale, I freed my ability.

I am you.

Let it flow over me.

And you are me.

I meditated, repeating my new mantra over and over until I believed it. Until *my ember* believed it.

I'm not sure how long I stood there as the world around me slipped away. But I felt the moment my ember and I reached one accord.

With a calm heart and even breath, my energy glided over my flesh and flowed through my sinews. It usually burned when it did so, demanding that its needs be fulfilled. Ignoring me in its quest for satiation. Yet, now its heat soothed, like a honey salve slipping down a sore throat.

I am you, and you are me, it whispered back.

We were one.

My eyelashes fluttered open, and I ignored the wetness lining them.

The Augur grinned, and a look of wonder lifted Gavrel's forehead as he gripped his baldric, his knuckles pale.

"Well done." With effort, she rose and shuffled to her door.

"Oh, and Belladonna." She paused, poking her crooked finger in the air, eyes going glassy for a moment.

My heart fluttered. I leaned toward her. "Are you … are you all right?"

A spark of tarnished gold flit over her pupils as they snapped to me. I jolted, and her lips curved, pushing into the creases lining her cheeks and eyes. "The Budding Moon is nigh, and the Fates are pleased." She waved a bent hand at us. "Off you go."

Gavrel's shoulders tensed, and I rolled my eyes, brushing my fingers under my lashes and tucking away my aura.

Another dismissal served with a side of cryptic declarations.

What an Ancients-damned delight.

THE NEXT AFTERNOON, Gavrel sat at the edge of the Augur's porch, his long legs dangling above the water as he shouted clipped instructions at me. "Keep it up … Eyes ahead." He stood, not one to rest for long, especially when barking orders. "You need to prune your power by feel, not sight."

"How about I prune you?" I glared at him, and the handsome bastard grinned.

Funny how he smiled the widest when bossing me around. My huff ended on a squeak as my leg muscles shifted. The hummock I stood upon wobbled with the prismatic, embered blob swirling between my palms.

For Surrelia's sake.

Steadying myself, and relieved the mossy knoll would not crumble, I spread my toes within my boots and planted my feet on its spongy surface. My hips adjusted, and I stacked my weight over my knees and exhaled my held breath.

I am you, and you are me, I thought over and over until my heart slowed and pulsed in time with my aura. Energy caressed my skin, purring. My eyes fixed on a gnarled tree in the distance.

"That's it, child. Commune with your gift. You are one and the same," the Augur called as she came out from her home and sat on the rocking chair.

I nodded, focusing on the sensation of my ember rippling under and over my flesh, the waves beginning at my neck and pushing outwards along each extremity.

"Splendid. Now guide it." She rocked forward, and I glanced at her. Her forehead raised, pushing into her pale hairline.

My lips pressed together, and I prodded my power down my arms, through the glowing bough patterns, and into my palms. My fingers weaved the sparkling light into a spinning orb.

Gavrel's rune lit up. Its energy tugged at my ribs, knotting around them.

Mine, my ember growled.

I breathed in.

I am you.

Breathed out.

You are me.

The coiling sphere kept its shape and grew, my arms widening to accommodate it. My focus flicked to the Augur, eyebrows lifting.

My body thrummed with frenzied energy, little sparks plucking and popping within every inch of me. With my eyes tightly shut, I focused on channeling my power so it wouldn't burn me alive. Cresting waves of iridescence leaked from my palms and fingers.

A darkened space formed in the center of my orb, its blackness slurping in the glittering light around it. It looked like stars being rapidly pulled into the void, much like water twirling and disappearing down a drain.

My mouth dropped open, and the line between Gavrel's eyebrows was quite severe.

The Augur lurched out of her chair. "Enough. Call it back,"

she ordered. My knees wobbled at her sharp tone, and I willed my energy to sink within, become a part of me once more.

The orb fizzled and unraveled into nothingness. My aura melted away. I flexed my fingers before rubbing them on my breeches.

A wide grin spread across my lips as I hopped onto the porch.

"You're incredible," Gavrel said, lifting me by the waist and spinning me around. I giggled and braced my hands on his shoulders. He set me down, clasping his hands behind his neck with a look of awe on his face. "Truly."

"You'll practice more tomorrow, but the boy is right. Progress deserves a cuppa." She hobbled into her hut and poured us each some tea.

"I'm pleased with you, Belladonna." She sipped from her cup and closed her eyes, savoring it. "As are the Fates." The corners of her eyes crinkled as she opened her eyes and studied me. Her elbow perched on the edge of the table, the lifted teacup hiding the coy smile I knew was there.

I snorted. Over the last several weeks, all the talks of the three prophetic sisters and their predictions disillusioned me. "So you've mentioned. Where were the Fates when the Withering cursed Midst Fall? Where were they when our loved ones were taken from us? When the Elders abused countless souls?"

Her cup clinked against the tabletop. She was most definitely *not* smiling. "Do not confuse my generosity with a willingness to accept such disrespect. It is not for us to understand the schemes of the Fates. But we must strive to navigate the road laid before us, no matter how obscured in shadow."

Chin dipping, bitter resignation coated my tongue. "Apologies."

The corners of her mouth curled. "I am quite close with the Fates, you see."

I nodded as if I believed her, and Gavrel's countenance maintained a look of impressive indifference.

Reclining, she clasped her hands, resting them on her stomach. With a faraway look, she stared off into the distance as if she could see through to the bogs outside her walls.

Damn me all the way to the void. She was settling in to rattle off a story that would prove her point.

"Long ago, there were two brothers. Quite different in every way, but close when they were young. Their father doted on his eldest son and his gifts. Bitterness festered within the younger one."

Gavrel shifted in his chair, his tongue pressing at the inside of his cheek. I leaned forward, bending slightly as I placed my forearms on the table and steepled my fingers against the wood.

"As they grew older and more powerful, they didn't take heed of the Fates' warnings. Their prophecy of a child who'd have the ability to take what they held most dear—their gift turned against the Ancients. They were too enamored with the roles they had to play. And they were tested. One was too trusting. The other too covetous.

"If they'd have respected their oracles and the divinations that were revealed, they'd have been on different paths. The Fates don't take kindly to complete disregard." She glanced at me and then at Gavrel with a raised brow. "Thus, one brother's jealousy destroyed the other, and will most certainly carry him to his demise. The other brother suffered for a long while, and it's yet to be seen if that will end."

With wide eyes, I gulped. "All right. Thank you for the … the lesson and the tea." I emptied my cup and stood. "May the Fates have mercy on us all."

"Only time will tell." And with that, she waved us off.

19

SISYPHEAN PEAKS

SERYN

"She's something else." I chuckled as we guided our boat toward the city.

Behind me, Gavrel dug his oar into the muck and propelled us forward as I did the same on the opposite side.

He grunted. "When she says little, she says a lot. And vice versa. I lose my damned mind trying to piece together her true meaning sometimes."

In agreement, a wry laugh sounded in my throat. We moseyed through the swamp, the sun dipping toward the horizon. Dusky shades of amber painted the doombarks. Shadows seeped over the mire.

Over my mind.

"Do you think we'll find Kaden?" I whispered.

"I've no doubt we will," Gavrel replied.

My oar stilled. "It's been weeks."

"And look how far you've come. It was time well spent." His confidence was a balm to my frayed doubts.

"I have a newfound kinship with Sisyphus. Constantly pushing a massive boulder up a mountain, only to have it tumble down again and again."

His dimple fluttered as he rested his elbows on his knees and leaned in. "Perhaps. And maybe it's because you're skilled at looking at the whole scene. You take in the entire landscape and are in awe of its might. But every peak was carved over time, whittled down by the elements. Perhaps it doesn't look altered, but it's ever-changing. You can overcome the mountain if you have the will. And you have that in abundance." His eyes swept over my body, and a shiver rippled over the places his gaze touched. "You're a force of nature, Asteria."

My chest expanded with shallow breaths, and I rubbed one hand along my forearm before turning back and digging my paddle into the water. The damp air didn't help the flush heating my skin.

My musings scampered about as we maneuvered through the swamp. The things we'd need to accomplish. But he was right. I needed to take one thing at a time.

We'd met with Yaya, Marek, and others often during our time here. To share information, dive into the Elders' weaknesses, and strategize the next steps. My mind wandered to our last meeting.

Marek bent over a map of Midst Fall in Yaya's kitchen. Yaya handed out cups of tea as the morning sun spilled over the lines and circles marring the weathered map's surface.

"We've pockets of ravens throughout the realm. Helos is the biggest stronghold, of course." He poked the marked capital on the map. Rhaegar, Gavrel, Breena, and I listened attentively as he went on.

His finger trailed to the south, into the Pneumali region. "But our second largest is throughout the deserts of Pneumali surrounding the capital. The Elders and their minions stick largely to the city. So, we've taken advantage of that. Learned how to traverse the lands least accommodating to dwelling. Same here." He pointed to the Ourea Peaks, the mountain range separating Haadra and Evergryn.

Gavrel's eyebrows scrunched in thought. "How many ravens do you estimate we have? The Order of Draumr is at least five thousand strong, not to mention at least five hundred Akridais. And those who worship the Elders as though they were Ancients."

"We're around the same, but as skilled fighters? Two-thirds more like," Marek noted.

"But we'll use our skills traversing the land to our advantage. We also have the element of surprise on our side," Rhaegar added. "We've been slowly recruiting over the decades, coordinating targeted attacks that undermine their following. That cast doubt throughout the realm."

Marek crossed his arms. "And it's working. But we need to make a stronger stand soon." He glanced at Gavrel, bracing his hands on top of the map. "Spit it out."

With his hand cupping his jaw, Gavrel's brow furrowed. With a heavy sigh, he looked to the ceiling and then around the room, meeting each of our eyes. "I agree that we should accelerate our timeline. I am loath to admit that Melina demanded that I ... I hunt Druiks and Scions specifically over the turns. Her obsession knew no bounds, but only worsened as time went on. I attempted to thwart her, but wasn't always effective."

Remorse glazed his eyes, his shoulders sagging. The rest of his confession stayed locked behind the grim line of his mouth. I held my breath at his admission, knowing it pained him to say the words out loud. He was likely disgusted with what he'd had to do for Elder Harrow. And if I knew anything, there had to be a good reason.

Neoma grasped Marek's biceps, silencing him before he could retort. Instead, he scoffed and glared at Gavrel. Rhaegar dipped his chin and slapped a hand on his friend's shoulder in a show of support.

Obstinately, Neoma pushed her shoulders back, nodding at the commander. "It's war, boy. We've all done things we'd rather not admit, and if you live long enough to confess your sins, you're doing something right."

Gavrel lifted his chin, uncertainty flickering in his eyes as he offered her a polite smile.

Marek cursed under his breath and stabbed a finger onto the map. "We should pay a visit to the deserts. Touch base with Keethan and his team. As for the mountains to the north, I haven't had word from Oren since his last missive. He mentioned some sort of flying animals attacking his camp. Took out a dozen or so. They were going to investigate and report back." His brow furrowed, rubbing his middle fingers against his thumb. "Last harbinger starling he sent nearly took my finger off," he muttered.

Yaya rolled her eyes and placed both hands on the edge of the table. "All right, so we send scouts to the Peaks and meet with Keethan. And now that we have the next piece of the prophecy, the first step is to find a way to Surrelia. To destroy that amber under Morpheus' palace."

"Without the Dormancy Pods. And without offing ourselves," Breena muttered.

"Bloody void," I grumbled, sipping my bitter tea. "May the wings of the ravens carry us."

A TOAD LEAPED over my oar, croaking loudly and bringing me back to the present. I pressed my lips together. "So, you think I'm ready?"

"Ready?"

"For whatever awaits us when we find Kaden. When we … when we go against the Elders." My tone hardened at the end.

"You've *always* been ready. When it comes to protecting those you love, there's no question," he retorted.

"You know what I mean, Gav." I turned back and tossed him an eye roll.

His mouth curved, and his muscles bunched and flexed as he worked. Heat zinged from the small of my back and burst behind my ribs, spreading over my limbs. My thighs pressed together, and my fingers slackened as I studied him. I jerked in surprise as the rod slipped in my grip.

Bollocks.

Why was this man so damned attractive? It was almost ridiculous. I spun forward, tightening my hold and digging into the silt once more.

An amused sound reverberated in his throat. He knew the effect he had on me. He just wasn't choosing to be as gentlemanly as he once was about it.

Damn him.

He leaned forward, slowly brushing his fingers over my back as he moved my braid over my shoulder. "As I said, you've always been ready. You just have to choose to believe it."

"*Can you believe it?*" Breena twirled later that night in her hut. She wore a silky, pewter-colored dress that hugged her curves as if liquid metal poured over them.

"You look lovely. What's the occasion?" I quirked one brow as she handed me a dark bundle, kaleidoscopic threads twinkling throughout.

"The Moonbud Revelry, woman. Open the present."

"The Moonbud Rev—" My words tapered off into a gasp as I unwrapped her gift. It was the dress I'd admired that first day in the main square. "Oh, my Ancients. Thank you, Bree. How did you—?"

She grinned. "I can't have you looking like rubbish at Helos' biggest party. Besides, I have plenty of coin from the *errands* I run for the Korax."

I inclined my head, studying the delicate threads as they shimmered in the moonlight. "Errands?"

Dismissively, she waved her hand at me. "A little stabby here. A little slice there." My eyebrows lifted as I looked at her, and her mouth somehow stretched even wider. "Anyway, the Budding Moon and Selene are sacred to this region. They act like absolute heathens during the celebrations. Drink. Dance. Feck." She winked. "Not necessarily in that order. It's absolutely delicious."

A laugh thrummed in my chest. "Sounds scandalous. When is it?"

Gavrel and Rhaegar joined us. "When is what?" Gavrel asked.

I glanced at him. "The Moonbud Revelry."

Gavrel leaned against the wall, and Rhaegar grinned while placing his boots by the door. "Ah, yes. Merrymaking is had by all. The citizens celebrate the Budding Moon and make offerings to the Moon Ancient. It goes until the sun rises."

"It sounds lovely. The way people hold on to their traditions here is truly inspiring," I remarked, my fingers brushing over my new dress.

Rhaegar nodded, tapping his fingers against his burly chest. "In the Bogs, where the tides hold dominion over the landscape, the moon's phases mirror the constant flux of life for the citizens. Here, the people hold Selene in the highest regard. The Budding Moon, in particular, signifies renewal and a link to the celestial dream realm. It's widely believed that Selene will aid Morpheus in the restoring of dreams."

"Well said, Rhaeg," Breena added. "And here I thought you loved the revelry because you wanted to indulge in mireberry wine and charm your way through all the willing females?"

Rhaegar snorted, dismissing his friend with a wave while

sweeping his eyes over Gavrel. "You'll need to get a proper overcoat."

The commander grunted.

"In a week's time," Breena added.

Gavrel grumbled under his breath, nodding at them before leaving and marching toward our lodging across the bridge.

Hugging my friend, I smirked. "I'll ask Marek if he has an overcoat for Gav. Thank you for my dress, Bree. It's beautiful. Want to practice dagger throwing with me tomorrow?"

"Absolutely. I'll meet you at your place with the sunrise. Not sure if I'll barge in or not, so it's up to you if you have clothes on." She wiggled the delicate slashes of her eyebrows as I chuckled my way out the door.

Marek's shanty wasn't far. I breathed in the crisp, damp air as I meandered to his door. As I lifted my fist to knock, his door swung open.

Bewildered, his mouth dropped until he collected himself. His chest was bare, per usual. Although he was fit, the sight of him didn't turn my eye. He didn't make my mouth water and heart flutter. Didn't make my mind and body a traitor like the sight of Gavrel did. I frowned.

"Happy to see you as well," he muttered. "Are you lost?"

With a heavy sigh, I suppressed my eye roll and pushed past him. It was tidy, but unadorned. Exactly how I would have pictured his home. Utilitarian, but comfortable.

"I just learned of the Moonbud Revelry," I said, turning in a circle, eyes roaming over his space.

"Congratulations."

A chuckle stuck in my throat. "Would you happen to have an overcoat Gavrel could borrow?"

He scoffed.

"Please?" My smile spread wide, eyebrows lifting.

He stomped over to a trunk in the corner, and after digging

through piles of fabric, he whipped out a piece of clothing and tossed it to me. "That should do."

"Why, I didn't realize you had proper clothing," I teased.

"If I could get away without breeches, I would. But I don't want to cause a commotion among the mortalfolk."

I cuffed him on the biceps, and it was like slapping stone. "Was that a joke? My Ancients. Have I died?"

He snorted, his head tilting ever so slightly. "I find it more efficient to go without a tunic. In this climate, the fabric clings, and anything that impedes my movements is impractical. One must always be ready for an attack."

My eyes slid over the scars marring his flesh. To the wicked scar skating diagonally across his face. Lifting his chin, he met my eyes without shame.

"Helos is lucky to have you," I repeated the accolade I'd given him the first day we met.

His jaw jutted forward, his chest rising and falling with even breaths. "Perhaps I am the lucky one."

"It's hard for you to take a compliment, isn't it?"

Conceding, he dipped his head, his russet hair brushing his shoulders as he moved his head from side to side. "You sound like Yaya. She's … she's a fine woman. I do believe my life would be on a different course if I hadn't found her."

Compassion welled up under my breastbone. It was nice to see this softer side of him. There was something more to Marek than the haughtiness and contempt he wore as a shield, instead of a tunic, most days.

He sighed, the white slash through his left eyebrow rising. "Anything else, Seryn?"

My mouth pinched in an amused line. "No, thank you. This'll do. Good night, Marek."

He showed me out, his tongue pushing against his puckered lips. "Good night," he mumbled, before closing the door behind me.

20

THE MOONBUD REVELRY

GAVREL

I couldn't breathe. She'd stolen the very breath from my lungs. On the bridge near our dwelling, I'd been staring off into the clutter of bristled ropes and water-worn timber. I shifted in Marek's borrowed overcoat, the sleeves snug around my biceps.

Initially, I'd mistaken a glimmer at the corner of my vision for the sun's reflection. I glanced in its direction, and then did a double-take.

Not the sun. Not everyone else's, at least.

That's when my breath hitched, my fingers clamping onto the railing as my world tilted.

It was my Little Star—radiant and otherworldly—looking like a celestial being that had fallen from the sky.

As she approached, one of her delicate brows arched as her icy-blue eyes glittered. "Tongue get cut out during your sparring session?" The corners of her eyes crinkled.

Her cheeks glowed; her skin scrubbed clean and painted in

the soft neons of the retreating light. Like wild auburn flames, her curls tumbled over her shoulders and down her back.

Mouth parting, I followed the line of her shoulders to the thin, woven straps that clung to them.

Down to the deep V of semi-exposed skin between her breasts, the sheer strips of ebony chiffon hugging the edges of the deep neckline were both demure and incredibly enticing.

It would be so easy to tear that off her.

"What was that?" she asked as the bridge creaked under her dark ankle boots.

Did I say that out loud?

Yes, you imbecile, I admonished myself.

I grunted in response, and her mouth curved. Gulping and setting my jaw tightly, my eyes glided over the rest of her.

Shimmering, sheer, black fabric skimmed over her curves, the hem kissing the tops of her supple thighs. Intwined throughout, kaleidoscopic threads glittered like the setting sun upon rippling water. With every movement, waves of moody, prismatic hues flowed over her body.

Though the material was sheer, the tightly packed pattern of the threads covered her, the hint of what lay underneath testing my restraint.

My hand itched to slip under the hundreds of delicate, dripping tassels decorating the hem. I drifted closer—pulled into her orbit—as she stood in front of me.

Enthralled, I reached for her hand and brought it to my lips. I kissed her knuckles and then interlaced my fingers between hers. She let me.

When a shy smile flitted over her mouth, an inhale forced its way down my throat. It was a relief to recall how breathing worked once more.

"You're stunning." My heart slammed into my ribs. I leaned closer to her. The sweet smell of her hair flooded my senses. "Like a wish come true, Asteria."

Her chin dipped, and I knew her blush was hiding under the sunbeams painting her skin. "Thank you." She reached up and pinched the fabric of one of the sleeves. "You're not so bad yourself. Marek's clothes look good on you."

At the male's name from her lips, a muted snarl reverberated in my chest, pushing me to my full height. She smirked and tugged me along as she moved across the bridge.

The city was alive. Vibrant. People were laughing and chatting. Giggling children rushed past us, their feet slapping as they ran. The walkway jiggled from the force of their merriment, and Seryn nestled closer, running her hand up my forearm.

I wanted her hands on me for the rest of our lives.

She tucked her arm into the crook of my elbow. My eyes closed for a moment as I savored the heat of her.

"Sweet Surrelia … It's … it's so …" A reverent sigh carried away the rest of her thought as she pulled away.

"Enchanting," I mumbled, staring at nothing but her. But she didn't hear me as she greeted Breena, a wide smile across her friend's mouth as they embraced. Rhaegar nodded at me from behind them and then focused on gathering a few goblets from a makeshift pub.

All the shops encircling the central gathering's vast platform were closed for the night in honor of the Moonbud Revelry. Cheerful music from local musicians, playing various stringed instruments and lively voices, rang louder as I approached.

Nearly a hundred citizens were already partaking in the festivities—dancing, drinking, and mingling. In muted shades of gray and coal, each person wore their finest clothing, some embellished with shimmering rainbow obsidian thread like Seryn's gown.

From what I understood, this was the biggest celebration of the turn. A time when people threw their worries aside and attempted to connect. To squeeze every bit of happiness from this night and revere the Budding Moon, which would show itself tomorrow.

I was honored to be a part of it. Humbled that, even among a cruel, dying world, the people of this region hid and protected this city. Fortified their hope.

Was that what was filling the last shadowed corners of me like a smoldering flame tearing the darkness to shreds?

Hope?

For turns, perhaps my whole life, hope had been elusive. Impossible. The only times I'd ever felt a flicker of its warmth revolved around Seryn. I glanced at her, and she turned as if sensing my attention. She offered me a genuine smile, nose gently scrunching in amusement, before continuing her conversation with Breena and Rhaegar.

Heavily, I sighed and clenched my hands briefly before releasing them. I'd numbed myself for so long that my doubt and fear were spiders skittering under my skin, desperate to burrow elsewhere while I burned their webs away.

A myriad of interlacing cords swept from the branches, ropes, and homes scattered around and above the space, with thousands of small glass globes of firelight bobbing from them. As the sun slipped into dusk, the flickering light and blissful joviality wrapped around the space, trying to strangle a smile from me. My jaw stiffened.

"Looks like you need some spirit, my friend." Rhaegar chuckled and handed me a snifter.

Seryn and Breena drank from their cups and then took turns twirling for the other. The tassels flared as Seryn spun, and the threads of her dress glittered as firelight sparked over them and her hair.

In the heart of the Perilous Bogs, Seryn had flourished. She was merging with her gift, its claws no longer deeply embedded within her confidence. The despondency that had pulled at her features over the last weeks had eased. Now, when she smiled, she meant it. It reached her eyes the way it used to.

The citizens here were her people just as much as those in Evergryn. My heart stumbled over its beats. Would she choose to live in this hidden bayou city one day? Would she choose the doombarks over the grymwoods? The wetlands over the forest?

I rubbed my palm over my chest, my scar pushing against my tunic. I didn't care where I lived. Anywhere Seryn existed was my home.

I swigged and then choked on the bittersweet nip sliding down my throat. A viscous lavender liquid sloshed within the glass as I held it up to the light, the liquor's legs sticking to the sides. "What the void is this?"

Rhaegar took another swallow. "Mireberry wine. It gets better as you go." He slapped his beefy hand on my shoulder. "I'm on my third cup and feeling fine. Just fine, indeed."

Cautiously, I took another drink, and the wine prickled pleasantly as it went down. He was right. The taste was a bit more agreeable this time; the tart sweetness chased the burn. I shrugged.

"I recall my first time," Marek taunted, settling on my right and crossing his arms. Rhaegar hid his smirk behind another sip.

This bleeding lout.

I'd grown to tolerate him during our time here. Marek liked goading me, and in all honesty, I enjoyed poking him back. It seemed to be the best course of action to take with him.

I cocked my head and narrowed my eyes at him. The fabric of his overcoat stretched across my shoulders as I tilted my glass toward him. "Ah, this must have been what you wore as a young lad. Would explain the fit of it."

The line of Marek's jaw went tight as he snorted, studying Seryn and Breena intently. Loosely tied back at his nape, the firelight flickered along the waves of his russet hair, making it more tinged in ruddy hues than normal.

I knocked back the rest of my drink and slammed the goblet on a nearby table with a clatter. If he didn't stop looking at Seryn, as if he couldn't decide whether he should throttle her or rip her clothes off, I was going to tear his bloody eyes right out of his fucking—

Jerking, I shook my head to dislodge my wayward violence and rubbed my temples. I detested not being in control. What the void was in that wine? Was I losing my ever-loving mind?

Seryn made her way toward us while Breena went to get more drinks. Her smile disarmed me, my pulse purring in anticipation of her proximity. Rhaegar pursed his mouth to the side in amusement, his head moving from side to side.

Marek glowered as he greeted Seryn with a nod. My brows rose, but my unspent jealousy left as quickly as it came. The male fixated on Breena, not Seryn.

Breena's rounded hips swayed as she made her way to us. The silky pewter slip dress flowed over her, a hint of skin flashing from the thigh-high slit with each stride. I could've sworn her steps faltered a bit when her eyes met Marek's, but it must have been a trick of the light. The woman never missed a beat.

His nostrils flared, shoulders tensing under his dark tunic. Seeing Marek fully clothed was odd, and the thought of his discomfort made my mouth quirk.

As Breena handed Seryn a glass, Marek's chin rose, his scowl softening as he looked at Seryn. "Find Yaya later, yes? She wanted a word with you." He rubbed his lips together, taking a deep breath, as if he wanted to say more. Instead, his jaw tightened before he bent his head and then strode away.

Breena rolled her eyes and drank deeply. "It's a shame his packaging is so pretty," she mumbled.

Seryn's carefree giggle had me stepping closer to her, my

mouth quirking up stupidly. "Bollocks. Don't tell me he's gotten under your skin, Bree." Seryn poked her friend and teasingly whipped her finger away as if burned. "Thought you were made of fire."

Breena's eyes squinted at Marek's back. "I am." Her voice rose as she pushed her shoulders back, the ends of her hair flicking at her bare shoulders.

"Yeah, you are!" Seryn and Breena high-fived clumsily. I suspected they were feeling the mireberries.

"I'm fecking made of fire. Here." She pushed her cup into Rhaegar's empty hand, lavender sloshing onto his boots from both his and her snifters, and stomped off in the direction Marek had gone.

"Bloody void, woman," Rhaegar groused, setting the empty glassware on the table and swiping his hands down his front. He sighed, tilting his head to the side. "Excuse me, I seem to be in need of another drink."

I nodded and then looked at Seryn as she hummed to the music. "Did you see the procession on the other side?" she asked.

I glanced in that direction and could just make out a line of people heading toward the other end of the city, carrying bundles of flowers and flickering lanterns.

Seryn put one hand on my forearm, delight lighting up her face. "They give bog flowers as an offering to Selene." Her touch left me to rest over her heart. "This place, Gav. The people. What they stand for. It's just … just beautiful."

"Quite beautiful," I murmured, but I wasn't looking at the crowd.

She sighed and then noticed my stare. Her chest flushed prettily.

"Seryn, I—"

Interrupting me, Rhaegar returned, an older couple in tow. If they were human, they looked to be around seventy turns old.

If Druik, they'd be ancient, considering how long the embered lived and how slowly they aged. "My friends, it's my honor to introduce Eliz and Keethan Wynt. They were the ones to recruit me."

Eliz, the shorter man with white hair, smiled kindly as the taller man, Keethan, dipped his rounded chin, his mouth lifting at one corner. "It didn't take much, son."

As Rhaegar grinned, I bent at the waist, my hand covering my heart. "It's a pleasure to meet you both."

Seryn bowed her head, placing a hand on her chest as well. "How did you all meet?"

"Well, you see, we often travel in the Pneumalian deserts. We prefer the dry lands, being that Keethan and I hail from the south. We came across Rhaegar in the city during one of our scouting trips, and the rest is history." Eliz looked at the male next to him with adoration. "Thank the Ancients, Keethan and I found one another decades ago across the dunes. I'd be lost without my khorda."

21

NEVER

GAVREL

Seryn sucked in a quick inhale, and the muscle within my chest flipped. Finding your fated was nearly impossible, especially nowadays. Most mortals were starving, lost to the Stygian Murk, or worse.

Keethan patted Eliz's hand. "Same, my love. We're quite fortunate indeed." The taller man sighed wistfully and then lifted his chin. "We've been part of the cause since the beginning. Recruiting, espionage, you name it. We give the Somneia a run for their coins." He tapped his forefinger against his temple. "It helps that our bond connects us. Mind, body, and ember, as they say."

Seryn's bottom lip dropped before she composed her look of fascination. "Excuse me if this is too bold, but I'm in awe of you. I've never met a fated pair before. At least, not that I know of. If you don't mind me asking. Is it difficult to ... to be so ... connected?"

Eliz tittered, leaning into his partner as if Keethan were

whispering something in his mind. He very well could have been. "It was quite the shock, let me tell you. Over time, you get used to sharing the spaces within you. Learn how to manage it as well." He smiled at Seryn. "Boundaries, my dear. Always boundaries. We're lucky in that we actually enjoy one another. Other fated couples aren't so lucky." His eyebrows rose. "I'm sure you've heard the stories about Elder Harrow murdering her fated."

Seryn's mouth pinched. "Ah, so the rumors are true? I suppose some consider having a khorda a weakness, even if you don't undergo the Kollao Ceremony."

Looking at his and Keethan's joined hands, Eliz shook his head. "I'm sure some view it that way. Melina surely must have, but I also heard tell that her fated was not a good male. That's neither here nor there, I suppose, considering the Elders are beyond salvation." Eliz's chin lifted, his conviction flashing across his eyes. "What others find to be a weakness, I see as a strength. Once we went through the ceremony, we were that much stronger. We were finally whole. If you fight the bond, it doesn't disappear. It's simply stagnant. But once you accept it, it blooms, and then the ceremony helps it flourish." Keethan's eyes softened as he looked at his partner.

I glanced at Seryn, my jaw ticking and fingers itching to take hold of her.

"When they met me, I was primed for recruitment. They didn't even need to do their little mind talking tricks." Rhaegar laughed. "We shared a meal and a pint, and we became fast friends over our fiendish dislike of injustice."

Nodding, Keethan chuckled. "Joke's on you, son. We're always doing the tricks, and always want to enjoy a pint." The older man thumped Rhaegar on the shoulder and then bobbed his head toward Seryn and me. "Wonderful to meet you both. If Rhaegar calls you a friend, then we shall as well. You make a splendid pair."

Seryn bit her bottom lip, and warmth swept over my chest. I didn't correct him.

"Enjoy the Revelry." Eliz wiggled his fingers as they moved along, hand in hand.

"They are lovely, Rhaegar. Thank you for the introduction. I would ask if you'd dance, but I respect my feet too much." He laughed as a playful smile curved Seryn's mouth, and I was unexpectedly tugged toward the dancefloor.

She guided us through the writhing throng of people. Bodies swayed and spun to the whimsical tunes spinning into the night.

Seryn stumbled, and I gripped her waist, fingers sinking into her soft curves as she grabbed my biceps to balance herself. I licked my bottom lip, staring down at her, relishing the feel of her in my hands. She was ethereal as the sputtering candlelight painted the dips and valleys of her face and chest.

Tortuously, she slid her palms over my arms, pausing at my shoulders, but then tilted her head and wrapped her hands behind my nape. Her fingertips teased the strands along my hairline. Wherever she touched, tingles swelled in currents, culminating at the base of my spine.

Her hips swayed, and my body followed as we moved within each other's arms. Lilting music cocooned us, and I didn't know if anyone was around us anymore or if I was dreaming.

Her eyelashes fluttered, and she looked up at me from under them. Her cheeks were flushed, and her lips were shiny. I wanted to drag my teeth over her bottom lip to see if she tasted like mireberries.

Bittersweet.

If that didn't bloody define our entire relationship, I didn't know what did. My molars ground together, and I clamped my eyes closed.

Gently, her thumbs brushed over my scrunched eyebrows. "They'll stay that way." She sighed as my eyelids slowly opened, then slid her hands from my jaw down to my chest, letting them rest over my thumping heartbeat.

I was going to drown in her gaze if she kept looking at me like that. I drew her in closer, knowing I shouldn't. But, once again, I succumbed to the pull, ignoring the many times my willpower had crumbled in her presence.

"Do you have regrets?" she murmured, her focus never leaving mine.

"Too many."

She glanced to the side, rubbing her lips together before looking up at me. "Us? Do you … do you regret what happened between us?"

Her face crumpled, and I frowned. *I'm a fucking blighter.* Two turns ago, I'd made damned certain that she *believed* we were a mistake when we were anything but. Disgusted with myself, I roughly dragged one hand through my hair.

Before I could withdraw, her fingers dug into my tunic. "Don't you dare."

"I—"

A lively tune began and cut my words short. Spiritedly, people bounced and stomped around us. I scowled at the interruption, whipping my arm around Seryn and towing us through the throng.

As we reached the end of the crowd, I grabbed her hand and pulled her past Breena, whose hair was mussed as she left a secluded shop at the edge of the main area. Behind her, Marek was slinking off in the other direction.

"Ryn?" Breena called after us, but I didn't stop to give Seryn a chance to respond.

Her hand tightened within mine. I kept moving, trudging across a quiet side bridge, ignoring her. A rabid frenzy of anger and lust and disgust was fueling me, taking over my better senses.

"Gavrel!"

Instantly, I paused, and she bumped into my side. I spun, gathering her close so she wouldn't fall, and she braced her hands against my chest.

She swatted at some strands tickling her cheek as she stepped out of my embrace, narrowing her eyes. My shoulders fell, and I took a deep breath and then held out my hand. My pulse still rapped against my ribs, but more evenly now.

She sighed and placed her hand in mine. Just beyond the bridge, I led us up a secluded, winding staircase. The stairs led to nowhere. Only some worn wood planks of a dilapidated platform remained of what I guessed was once a home.

Facing the swamp, we reached a hidden spot behind the massive trunk. We were both breathing hard as I let go of her hand and backed her up against the smooth bark.

Her breasts heaved, threatening to spill from the sheer fabric clinging to her cleavage. The strings of light flickered from below, a soft amber radiance dancing over her face. The notes of a hauntingly beautiful song began to play, and her eyes widened at the familiar ballad.

There it shall linger,
In the void where shadows creep.
Beyond Nether,
The nightmares decay sleep.

"Is that *Fated*? My humming song? Isn't that odd?" she whispered breathlessly.

My jaw ticked, and I braced one hand above her head, hoping to steady the energy buzzing through every limb.

Here you'll find me,
In the withering mist between trees.
Among shattered
Hopes and phantom breeze.

"Not particularly. It's from here." There wasn't much heat in my words, the melancholy lilt of the song wrapping around us, binding us.

Her eyes drifted closed. Muted words, suspended on the melody that had captivated her in Surrelia, flitted around us.

There, I'll find you,
In the blooming embers of your dreams.
Fated promises,
Sealed in moonbeams.

It seemed a lifetime ago when I'd gone to Seryn at the ball, drawn to her then like a faraway dream.

I'd watched all these turns as if she were a mirage I could never really touch. Had to stand by as others touched her. As my *brother* touched her. I loved him, and I didn't want him to suffer the heartbreak, but she was never his. Not really. Bitterness scratched deep within my throat as I forced the thought of Kaden away.

Our prolonged separation had gnawed at my resolve, and I was at the precipice of my patience. I couldn't tell her all I yearned to, but I could show her. My lips tucked between my teeth. Keeping her at arm's length wouldn't keep her safe any longer. And she was so damn strong.

Fierce.

Magnificent.

And I didn't just want her to be a dream any longer.

Because I wasn't fucking dreaming, and no one was going to touch her like I would for the rest of our days.

She was *mine*.

I leaned into her. My nose brushed her temple, and her rapid breaths fluttered against the base of my throat, errant curls tickling my skin at the open V of my tunic.

I wrapped my other hand below her jaw and around the side

of her neck. Her skin was hot against mine. Her energy prickling under my touch.

"Ask me again," I demanded.

"The song?"

A low, frustrated sound resonated in my chest. She whimpered, grabbing my wrist. Radiance sparked under my tattoo.

I shifted, putting my face above hers, and I slid my hand along her jaw, cradling her chin between my thumb and forefinger.

Her lips parted, eyes searching mine.

My cock strained against my breeches. I was at the end of my restraint.

Her dress glittered like the fallen star she was.

My fallen star.

Mine.

"Ask. Again."

"Do you regret … us?" Her voice trembled, and her pulse tapped frantically against my fingertips. Her aura materialized and quivered delicately around her in fractured, multicolored hues.

"Never," I growled and crushed my lips into hers, light bursting from my rune.

22

NO OBJECTIONS

SERYN

I couldn't breathe. He'd stolen the very breath from my lungs. He slammed his lush lips into mine, and an all-consuming inferno swept through my body.

Although the bark against my back was fairly smooth, it ground into my shoulder blades. I savored its bite because it meant this was real. And I very much needed this to be real.

Not another dream.

Gavrel's arm tensed beside my temple before his fingers burrowed into my hair, his fingers tangling in my curls, tugging. A jolt of heat zipped down my spine at the nip of pain.

His other hand gripped my neck.

Claiming me.

A deep throbbing pulsed within my core as his tongue pushed into my mouth. His broken groan spilled down my throat as our lips crashed and tongues melded and sparred. We were ravenous. Starving for the other in the turns we'd been kept apart.

The haunting chords of my humming song bled into our kiss as if the words were binding us, telling our tragic story and sparking something deep within me. Something bright and burning and laced in promise.

I dug the nails of my left hand into his wrist. My other hand fumbled under his coat until I clamped onto the tight muscles of his waist. I wanted to tear his clothes off and claw into his flesh until we were as one. Until I didn't know where I ended and he began.

Whimpering, I yanked at his jacket, and we scuffled with each other as he fitfully removed the snug material from his thick arms and tossed it onto the shaking stairs below.

He kissed me again, sinking his glowing hand into my hair and bracing against the trunk with his other. He pressed the weight of his body into me. His knee wedged between my thighs, and his straining arousal pushed into my hip.

My core rubbed against his thigh repeatedly, and a moan tore from me, vibrating between our lips as we devoured each other. His hand scraping down the trunk rasped beside me, and in the next moment, both of his hands gripped the thin straps of my dress.

He leaned back, dragging his eyes over my chest. Breathing heavily, he snarled, "You don't like this dress, do you?"

"Quite a lot."

His mouth tipped deviously to the side, and he tugged, snapping the fabric. I sucked in air, damp heat pooling between my thighs while I instinctively grabbed the top of my dress and held it in place.

As the dewy air soothed the sting along my shoulders, he bit his bottom lip and then dragged his teeth over it. I wet my lips in response. "That was very wicked of you."

With heavy eyelids, his emerald eyes glinted, and a feral grin spread across his face. His dimple flashed, and it never looked more roguish as he made a show of letting the strings flutter from his fingers and pushed his thigh more firmly into my apex.

I shuddered at the friction. At the throbbing.

He set his hands on either side of my head, caging me in. His hips pulled slightly away before returning and grinding his rigid cock against me.

My heartbeat thumped against my wrists, my scar, and my ribs.

My skin was vibrating.

I needed him as I needed my next breath.

More so.

Breathing was overrated.

I pressed the back of my head into the tree, sliding my hands down my chest and belly.

The sheer fabric covering my breasts peeled away like wilting petals. His eyes followed their path, eyes lingering hungrily on my puckered nipples.

He dragged his gaze to mine. "You're so damned beautiful." The crease between his brows peeked out, competing with his dimple. The man didn't know whether to be happy or concerned.

I grasped his wrists, my thumbs rubbing soothingly against his rapid pulse. His forehead relaxed, and he leaned down, kissing the side of my jaw.

Biceps tensing, he paused, his hot breath brushing against my neck. "Now's the time to avoid any regrets, Little Star," he whispered raggedly.

I swallowed, sliding my hands over his shoulders until my fingers clasped at the back of his neck. His head drooped, and his forehead nestled into the curve of my neck.

"Never," I countered.

He shuddered, and his hands snapped to my waist and lifted me against the tree. Instantly, my legs wrapped around his middle, his cock bumping into my damp underwear.

He sucked and nibbled his way down my neck and chest. "Fucking void," he groaned in between licking my taut nipple. A wild sound of need flew from me as he bit the aching bud; a scorching zap of energy raced over my spine.

"Gavrel," I moaned, cradling his head. He sucked hard and lapped at my breasts while grinding his erection into me. Hot, liquid desire throbbed within me, threatening to explode.

"I need you," I whimpered, meaning it to my very marrow. Every part of my being was reaching for him. My energy buzzed against my flesh, desperate for us to become one.

His head leveled with mine, flexing his jaw at the hinges, his pupils dilating. "Take what you need. Whatever I have has always been yours."

With heaving chests, our mouths crushed together again, and I slipped my hand between us, loosening his breeches and gripping his thick cock.

His breath caught as I rubbed my thumb over the tip, a bead of pre-cum coating it. His nostrils flared, and he wrapped one arm more firmly around my waist, muscles bulging as he held me up.

His other hand went to the fabric between my thighs, his fingers easily slipping beneath and gliding two fingers into my wet channel.

"So fucking wet for me, aren't you?"

I nodded, sliding my fingers down his length and gently squeezing on the way back up. His hips followed, seeking purchase. I smirked. "Good boys don't say such things."

"Yes, they bloody well do. Say it," he bade me, pinching my throbbing clit, and then tore my delicate underwear down the center.

A garbled moan clogged my throat, and my head slanted to the side.

His thumb circled and brushed over my aching clit, and I trembled.

"Please." He kissed me gently, dipping his fingers within me, his thumb moving faster.

He wasn't one to beg. That one ragged word splintered me from the inside out, and my breath whooshed from me. "You make me so *fucking* wet, Gavrel."

With palpable lust, he locked his eyes onto mine and growled, "Good girl."

His words sent a flame rocketing down my spine, and a mangled sob spilled over my bottom lip. The cresting inferno burst as I guided his cock to my convulsing entrance.

He cupped his hands under my backside and watched as I nearly broke apart. If he didn't fill me now, I'd fucking die.

"Inside me. Now," I demanded, pushing my core onto the tip. With a relieved groan, he thrust into me, fully seating himself to the hilt.

My body trembled in his hands. His eyes widened and then rolled back for a moment as my pulsating center settled around his length. I swear my heart pumped in perfect rhythm with his. We were one giant heartbeat.

I took a quick sip of air, and then, as his gaze connected with mine once more, he moved. He felt too good, too right as he pumped into me, my back slapping against the tree, the stairs quaking and creaking beneath us.

Burying his mouth against my neck, he bit me, and then sucked hard as he slammed into me over and over. Stars burst behind my eyelids as they fluttered closed, the heat rolling over me in waves and immediately building again.

Gavrel's eyes leveled with mine as he moved faster, his voice rough and low. "Come for me again, Asteria. I want your tight cunt weeping for me."

In a frenzy, my aura flared around me as scorching flames of lust ignited through every inch of me. My center clenched around his length, and my thighs quivered, eyes rolling back into my head. Heat buzzed along my spine until it burst in a flare of white behind my vision. "Fuck, Gavrel!"

Muffling my scream, his mouth devoured mine, and with a final push, he groaned and spent himself inside me as I trembled and burst into a million tiny pieces.

We stayed connected for several ragged breaths, as if we'd become one with the mire's wildness. A breathy chuckle spilled from me, the last of my nervous energy releasing. I was completely content for the first time in a long while.

He leaned back to look at me, a tender expression lining his face. Gently, he pulled out of me and set me down, helping me adjust the material of my dress in place.

Silently, he tied the torn straps at my shoulders and placed a kiss on one. My heart flipped. He cupped my face and placed the softest kiss on my lips before smoothing some wayward curls behind one ear. "Are you all right?"

I smiled, standing on my tiptoes, and pressed my mouth to his again. "More than all right."

He leaned his forehead on mine. "That's not entirely how I wanted our first time to go."

"Regrets already?" I teased, and a sound of discontent thrummed in his chest. "If you want to show me how it should've been, I'll allow it."

His expression wobbled between amusement and chagrin. "I've wanted you for so long. You deserved more than me taking you against a tree."

"I appreciate the chivalry, but I have no objections."

The corners of his lips quirked, and he scooped up his over-coat and wrapped it around my shoulders. He gently untucked my hair so it wasn't stuck under the jacket, and kissed the side of my neck before letting the curls fall over my shoulders.

He took my hand, guiding me down the stairs. Guiding me back from a dream. "Little Star?"

I looked at him, my eyes softening.

His dimple winked at me. "I'm glad you have no objections because we've a lot of time to make up for."

23

KINSHIP

SERYN

*A*s we moved toward the music, a thick breeze wafted through my hair, goosebumps sprinkling over the back of my damp neck. I pushed my arms through the sleeves of Marek's coat, rolling one. Gavrel reached over, tugging at the cuff so the edge was crisp and even, then rolled the other sleeve so they both hung loosely under my elbows.

My mouth quirked as he placed a gentle kiss against my temple and slung his arm around me, tucking me into his side as we walked.

"About damn time," Breena declared as we rejoined the festivities. She smoothed her palm down the side of my curls. "Hopefully, all that *fun* will make you both less twitchy."

Pinching her arm, I tossed her a deadpan look. She chuckled, swatting my shoulder and heading toward Rhaegar at the bar.

I scanned the revelers as they danced and laughed. A lively bunch of young men were arguing and guffawing at the edges of the dance floor. A group of older citizens watched the merry-making from the sidelines with wistful looks misting their eyes.

Although there were so many things to worry about, I was at ease. I felt alive. A part of something.

These people.

This place.

Gavrel.

I peeked at him, the corner of my mouth curling as he gazed down at me. His body wasn't tense as it usually was, in a constant state of battle.

I was sure that wouldn't last long. We needed to make plans.

To find Kaden once and for all.

To figure out how to defeat Melina and her cronies.

But these were thoughts for tomorrow.

Tonight, I'd relish being in this place with people I cared for. I'd savor Gavrel and I beginning anew.

My eyes caught a glint of silver at the opposite end of the dancing space. Neoma smiled dreamily, her chin lifted in a stubborn line as she sipped her drink and studied the crowd. On my tiptoes, I kissed the base of Gavrel's jaw. "I'll be back." He followed my line of sight and nodded. His stare lingered as I made my way over to her.

"Marek mentioned you wanted me to find you," I said with a smile.

"You remind me so much of my eldest," the older woman replied as I approached. The music wove around us, her words almost drowned out by the lilting notes. Gliding over my face and hair, her eyes misted as she took a nearby seat. My stomach flipped. I'd never seen Yaya look nostalgic. Or was it regretful? I wasn't sure.

"Oh?" I took a seat next to her, scraping my chair closer so I could hear her better.

She took a sip from her cup and then balanced it on her knee, fingers gripping the metal tightly. "She had the same coloring. As did I once upon a time." She clucked her tongue, fingers idly toying with the end of a graying curl.

My heart flipped, emotions welling in my throat. She wasn't one to open up much, and I wondered if the tart mireberry wine had anything to do with it. I leaned forward, placing my hand delicately on hers. "Tell me about her."

She glanced at me with a sentimental smile, and her hand turned, weaving her fingers with mine. Her touch was soft and warm. She watched the others commune and laugh, a dreamy look slackening the usually stoic line of her mouth. The reflection of the tiny, flickering orb lights danced in her burnished eyes, making them appear to be a smoldering campfire.

"One time she wept. She wept when her younger sister brought home fireflies in a jar. We called her 'Bug' after …" A quiet sound of amusement tumbled from her. She rocked, digging her heels into the floorboards as if bracing herself against the memory.

"Marek's mother, Deitra, was my sensitive one. But …" She crushed her eyes closed, breathing deeply. I slipped my other hand under our joined ones, encasing hers. Her lashes fluttered open. "But as soon as Bug caught sight of Deitra's lightning bugs, my oldest broke into a fit of tears. It's one of the few times I ever saw her cry … beyond her earliest turns. She was eleven turns old."

Yaya ran her thumb under her lashes and smiled wistfully. "She scolded Deitra, who was nine at the time, saying it wasn't right to keep such majestic creatures trapped. Deitra freed them at once and never caught fireflies again. But they'd watch them for hours, giving them names and telling stories about their imagined adventures."

My brows squeezed together as a deep sadness burrowed underneath my ribs. It made me think of Letti. "What happened to them?"

"Deitra passed on moments after giving birth to Marek. At

least, that's what I was told. I hadn't known she was with child. You see, she ran away with her lover when she was twenty. And this was turns after we'd lost Bug. Deitra was never the same after her sister disappeared. She found solace in bad decisions and worse men. I didn't know how to help her." Her mouth twisted as if she held a bitter lemon between her teeth. "I failed both my children. But I'll be damned if I do the same to my grandchildren."

Unease crept over my skin, mingling with the prickles skittering over my nape.

"I didn't even know my grandson until he was already a broken, unruly teenager. Made his way here, escaping whatever voidish nightmare he grew up in. Said he'd had a dream, and it guided him to me. There was no doubt he was my kin—looks just like his mother—and well, it's clear he's inherited our family's gifts. The Augur confirmed it anyway." Her hand slipped from mine, and she waved it in the air dismissively. Yaya turned to face me, her eyes boring into mine as she took a deep breath and cleared her throat.

My heart stopped, the air in my lungs throbbing as I forgot to breathe. "What was Bug's name, Neoma?"

Ignoring my use of her real name, her hand cupped the side of my cheek briefly before she drained her cup and set it on the ground. "I know my eldest is alive. The Augur shared a secret with me earlier as she's wont to do. That blasted female is *never* wrong."

I swallowed the burning taste pooling in my throat. "What was her name, Neoma?" I snapped, my heart slapping against its cage.

A dry laugh tumbled from her, and she leaned forward, resting her elbows on her knees. Slowly, she looked at me from under long, light-colored eyelashes. "It's Yaya to you, girl, as you well know." I squinted at her, and she smirked. "Our family has been hiding behind the Skiya name—among others—so long, our true surname feels forbidden, as if the Fates'll curse me if I dare speak it."

My arms crossed snugly over my chest, and I counted the pulse thumping in my neck, trapping my ember within me. She sat straighter, hands clutching her knees. "But we're cursed as it is. It's high time we're honest with one another before our time runs out. My eldest's name was Maya. Maya Nightshade. And I'm told you're my kin."

24

SURREALITY

SERYN

The breath within my lungs whooshed out. One hand covered my mouth, and the other gripped my middle as if I could stop my body from splintering.

"Told her, eh?" Marek strode behind Yaya—*grandmother?!*—and leaned against a doombark. "How you holding up, cousin?"

I shot out of my chair, tipping it over with a clatter as I stabbed my finger at the infuriating prick. He held up his hands in surrender, and Yaya stood next to him, widening her stance. "Even *he* knew? Are you bloody kidding me?" A wall of cold shock and betrayal blocked any sense of diffidence and empathy for the woman.

"Why are you doing this? I'm not a *legacy*. I'm not a *Nightshade*. Where's my mother? How do you know she's alive? How do I get to her? Who are you?" I cried, my body chilling and beginning to tremble. My ember scratched at my bones, but at least I was now strong enough to keep it within as my mind spiraled. People were staring as I broke apart.

Solid but gentle arms wrapped around me from behind. I melted into the familiar scent of leather and wood. "I've got you. Breathe," Gavrel murmured, rubbing his hand over my arm.

"What's going on?" Breena demanded, her eyes shooting daggers at Marek as she and Rhaegar joined us.

Marek rolled his eyes. "She's just learned we're related. She's pissed off about it. Her mother's alive. Oh, and she's a Nightshade. Welcome to the family, we're not that bad." He waved a dismissive hand at me. But his eyes softened as they roamed over my face, not matching his sardonic tone. I inhaled and exhaled, working through my initial stun.

"What a fecking shite show. Let me stab him in his wee cock, Ryn-Ryn."

"You know very well there's nothing wee about it. Besides, you're not hiding any blades under that scrap of dress." My *cousin's* brow lifted. Breena lunged at him, but Rhaegar grabbed the fabric at her back before she could progress any further.

"Rhaeg, I swear to Morpheus, if you want to keep that hand …"

"Enough!" Yaya snapped.

My breathing slowed, and Gavrel released me, standing silently beside me. His warmth calmed me further.

"I know it's a lot. It's too much to bear." Yaya touched my shoulder gingerly. My flinch nuzzled into her touch. "But I know you can, *granddaughter*, and you *will*. Your mother's life and yours depend on it. Probably your friend's, too. Come, the Augur has requested an audience with you at Hallowed End tonight." She stood tall, turning from the gathering.

Glaring at Breena, Marek set his jaw in a square and followed Yaya.

Breena huffed, shaking out her hands and flexing her fingers at her side. "I've got you, Ryn. And I don't care if you're related to that blighter, I'll bloody stab him right in his wank-stick if the need ever arises." The tail end of her threat rose an octave, and I could have sworn Marek's shoulders shook before settling into a line above his frame.

Distracted, I brushed my hand over hers and caught up to them midway over a bridge, Gavrel at my back, and the others behind him.

Solemnly, all six of us moved toward the very edge of the city. Gavrel stayed close, his hand often grazing the small of my back as we traversed various pathways, mooring me to reality when all I yearned to do was allow my mind to collapse. To obscure my racing thoughts so that they blended into the surrounding fog.

He squeezed my side, and his warm breath skimmed my ear, the scent of mireberries filling my inhale. Less than an hour ago, I was just Seryn *Vawn,* and he was just *Gavrel.* When his lips had been on mine, my worries had scattered away for a moment. "You're still you. I'm not leaving your side."

He always knew what fears haunted me; his words were a beacon clearing away the phantoms. I drew in a deep breath, held it, and exhaled. I reached behind and brushed my fingers over his hand before it left my flank. My mind quieted, and I shuffled through it. One fact at a time, I tapped my forefinger along the rope railing.

I couldn't be a Nightshade—a direct descendant of one of the five founding Elders. I scoffed at the thought. Everyone knew that bloodline had died out over a century ago … likely through Melina's extermination efforts. My jaw jutted forward, anger stirring and ebbing.

Breathe in.

Breath out.

It was impossible. Right?

Incessantly, my scar thumped in annoyed protest.

Nightshade, my ember whispered. *Scion.*

I gnawed the inside of my cheek, ignoring the words and

dread echoing within me. The chances of me or Marek being a Scion had just multiplied.

Another detail floated to the top of my mind. Optimism sizzled under the distress, trying to scorch through it. My mother was … *alive.* I'd always wished it to be true, but I couldn't accept one truth and snub the other.

Hope was a dangerous thing. Hope carried you even when you were torn apart at the seams. It made you believe the last strings binding you together wouldn't snap as you pushed onward. Even if they certainly would.

A single spark of hope could fuel a revolution.

It could topple corruption.

It could revive Midst Fall.

I rubbed my palms over my belly, soothing the fluttering within.

As I stared at Yaya and Marek's backs and felt Gavrel and my friends at mine, conviction tipped up the corners of my mouth. If there was to be a revolution—if I were to save Kaden, my mother, and our realm—I'd be grateful to have more family to lean on. Both by blood *and* circumstance.

If we were Nightshades, the Elders had something far greater to dread than the stirrings of hope. For the spark had already kindled long ago. They'd face our ember and the force of our united mutiny as we burned through the tethers of their corruption.

We'd be a nightmare haunting their every waking moment.

OUR GROUP REACHED the end of Helos, marked by a single bridge that stretched into the darkness. The only sounds guiding us through the misty night were crickets and gilly toads, the creaking of planks, and the occasional burble of water.

We stepped off the bridge and onto a decagon-shaped platform, surrounded by ten thick trees. Rope fastened each vertex to three of the nearest trunks. Piles of pale flowers were scattered over the deck—the citizens' offerings to Selene.

"Come closer, *Belladonna*." Crooking one knobbly finger, the withered female standing in the center smirked at the nickname. I was sick of the Augur's riddles.

I marched before her, the others hanging back a bit. "Let's get this over with."

She angled her head, scrutinizing me. "Always in such a hurry. When you rush, you miss the details."

"Well, I'm seeing them now. *Belladonna*."

Belladonna. Correction, *Nightshade.*

Silently, her shoulders shook. "How you amuse me. I see you've come to terms with your lineage on the walk."

"I bloody well have done no such thing."

"But you will." She sighed, lifting her forearms at each side. "During the Budding Moon, Hallowed End is where you'll find the next part of your journey."

My eyes swept over the circle of trees. "This place? What is it?"

"A place for blessings. A place for thresholds to be crossed, as long as you have the key." She lifted my left hand with her first two fingers. Her touch was steady and cool as her thumb ran over the carved obsidian circling my forefinger, and it tingled against my skin.

"So, it's a portal, and this ring ... this ring is the key to opening it. If this can open portals, why haven't I needed it for others like the one in Inksalt Loch?"

"Druiks who know the locations of such cosmic vortexes can traverse the mortal realm. They're a static source of travel within the region. Travel between Oneiric realms, however, is another thing altogether." She held her palms up, chin lifting.

"Other than the Ancients themselves, only those who

possess a celestial key can call upon and unlock the inter-realm passageways. As you know, without the right time and place, the ring's ember simply acts as a mechanism to transmit your physical body over shorter distances from one place to another. Yet, if you're close to a strong ember source or sacred location like this"—she gestured widely—"the key bearer only needs to imagine a destination to travel there."

"So, which realm would this portal lead to?"

"Where you will find what you seek—"

"My mother? Kaden?" I interjected; my words agitated.

A slight smile tipped her lips, her brows drawing together as she leaned toward me, lightly poking her finger into the space above my heart. "In a dismal place you've seen before. You weren't ready to face it then, but you are now. You must simply imagine it—here—and only during the peak of lunation."

My lips pressed into a white slash as my fingers shoved through the curls at the top of my head. I let my arms drop. "Always during blasted full moons. Seems incredibly careless of the Ancients to leave the portals so vulnerable every month."

The Augur's gaze unfocused, and her words softened tenderly. "There's only so much to be done when nature fuses with the Ancients' creations. The gateways between realms are no exception. All living things, whether a tree, mortal, or beast, are both wild and confined. Even the Ancients must obey Kosmos; their power limited to the realms and human affairs they preside over. If they leave the realm or source that gives their ember life, it eventually weakens. Just like when mortals physically visit other realms outside their own ... they'll be called to join the realm in which they've overstayed their welcome."

My energy tingled under my skin. "Why won't you give me a clear answer? Why speak in cryptic riddles?" I demanded, tired of games. My fingers dug into my belt.

The Augur cupped my chin, her skin warm and humming

against mine. "There's a design to the fabric that builds each of you. Yet, those exquisite threads of the Aetherbind that fasten your very essence to your physical self and destiny are elastic. As all threads are … until they break. I, too, must respect Kosmos and the design of the Fates' tapestries. For every knot I've shown you, elsewhere, another unravels." She stepped closer, dropping her arm, her eyes shining.

My lips parted, and I gaped at her. Beheld her golden eyes as they seized mine. Her pale brow quirked. A quick sip of air rushed into my windpipe. "Your eyes. They … I've seen them before." In a flurry, the images of the youthful seer from Ceto sped through my mind as her beautiful hands flipped over the oracle cards. "I don't … I don't understand. Who—what—are you?"

The liquid metal of her irises consumed the white as a dazzling, gilded aura spread over her. "Very good. You've assembled the details. You'll do well, *Belladonna*."

The others rushed forward, flanking my sides.

Yaya gasped, her hands reaching for the female. The men watched quietly, stances wide. Breena was Breena. "What the ever-loving fecking void?" she mumbled. "Who is this broad?"

A benevolent smile spread across the Augur's face as she hovered backward over the boards. Her long, pale hair and gauzy robes drifted around her form despite there not being a hint of a breeze.

"You're ready, child. Lean on your kin." Her melodious voice glided through the mist as her gaze connected with each of us.

My heart lurched as I struggled to comprehend what was happening.

All at once, the haze spun around her, melding with her glittering, golden aura. The deeply etched wrinkles smoothed, and her face morphed into that of the Haadran seer.

She'd sent the missive guiding us to her in Ceto.

Before that realization could register, her contours transformed into that of a young girl with the same stunning eyes. My mouth fell agape, my right fingers gripping the obsidian wrapped around my left pointer finger. The stone warmed and tingled against my fingertips. It was the girl from the Reverie Wield who'd gifted me the ring during the last Dormancy.

Breathlessly, I stepped forward, but paused as her brilliance flashed and twirled around her. My aura hummed through my muscles and sinew, yearning to connect with hers. Multihued flashes sparked at my sides. Everyone's powers were flaring.

The female's visage didn't stop shifting, features melting into one another as if they couldn't decide which shape to settle in. She lifted her arms above her head, and her body rose a few more inches above the platform.

She was *all* of these beings.

Young to timeworn.

She was none of them.

Made of mist and wild energy and messages from the Fates.

She'd helped me along the way, more times than I could count.

She roamed the wilds of the realms.

Spoke in riddles.

She was the definition of surreality.

The drawing from the book in Morpheus' library wavered in the back of my mind. *Ancient History: An Unabridged Bridge into Divine Yesterdays.*

The Oneiroi.

The celestial sister with the obscured face.

The aureate aura of an Ancient.

She … was … Was it possible?

My ember burst from me, reaching for hers, not to harm, but to revere. "Phantasos?" Her vibrant energy enveloped my faint, broken words. All at once, a collective gasp rent the air, everyone choking or sucking in shocked breaths.

Her ever-changing mouth curled. "Recollect … the dawn

does not fear the night. Protect the balance. Persevere." Her words were wind chimes tolling through my ears. Words she'd left me with in Surrelia. "We'll meet again."

The entirety of her burst into golden sparks and condensed into a beautiful black raven. It spread massive wings, immediately fading into the fog in a frenzy of gilded flecks.

"Wait!" I called out, activating my ring. My body was transported to the space she had occupied, but my fingers slipped through the scattering embers.

The Ancient of Illusions had left us again like the dream she'd always been.

25

MINE

GAVREL

*B*ewildered, we abandoned Hallowed End as the last of Phantasos' twinkling embers faded. We were apparitions in the night, depleted of words and lost to one another in revelations.

We exchanged somber goodbyes and plans to meet the next day before everyone went their separate ways. With dazed eyes and rigid shoulders, Seryn shuffled over the planks, and I shadowed her, ready to catch her if she fell.

But she didn't.

She never crumbled.

Just kept taking each step until we arrived at our lodging.

After we entered, she moved without thinking, undressing completely and plaiting her hair as she stared into the darkness outside our window. I slipped one of my tunics over her naked body.

As I pushed the beds together, the scrape of wood on wood permeated the air. Wordlessly, she took my hand as she sank onto the mattress, and I settled behind her, wrapping her in my embrace.

"I'm here, Little Star," I whispered into her hair, nuzzling into it. She nestled into me.

"She's … she's the bloody raven. Always a raven following …"

"Close your eyes. I'll be here when you wake," I murmured, hugging her closer.

After a while, the faint trembling of her body subsided. A relieved exhale left me, and with my next breath, her sweet, air-soaked scent filled my lungs.

"What if I'm a Scion?" The words were so faint, I questioned whether I'd heard them. Heart thumping, my jaw stiffened. If she were a Scion, then she'd be in more danger than I initially thought.

"Then so be it. I'll be beside you on whatever journey you decide to take." My arm tightened around her.

"But the Fates—"

"Damn the bloody Fates. You are who you choose to be."

Her back shook against me with a sardonic chuckle. "What if I ran away and pretended this was all a nightmare? Would you follow me then?"

I kissed the top of her head. "You know I would. But you won't. You've never run from anything in your life. Even when I asked." A stupid grin spread across my face before drifting away in our silence.

The sound of water lapping at the base of the tree wafted through the window.

Her fingers brushed against my forearm, and then stilled. "Would you hunt me if I ran? Like the others?"

My pulse lurched, and I propped myself on my elbow, my upper body slanting a bit over her. She tucked her lips into a tight line, giving me only her profile.

"Asteria," I growled. Still, she refused to look at me. Gently, I cupped her chin and turned her face until her gaze met mine. "Need I remind you? I'd go to the depths of the Nether Void to find you." Her chin wobbled under my touch. "But I'd sooner face the Ancient of Nightmares than hunt you for any other purpose than your rescue."

A whimper fell from her lips, and her eyelids fluttered close. I leaned into her and slanted my mouth against hers, my fingers resting against her jaw. She breathed deeply and pressed her warm lips into mine.

Her pulse scampered under my fingertips. Our tongues danced and caressed each other's for a few moments as I poured all my unspoken vows into our kiss.

A reluctant moan vibrated in my chest as I pulled away and rubbed my thumb along the underside of her jawline. I gazed into the glacial blue of her eyes, hoping everything I felt was sinking into their depths.

Into *her*.

Softly, I placed one more kiss on her lips before sinking down to the bed, my back melting into the mattress.

Within a few moments, she rotated in my arms and placed one hand on my chest. Her thumb stroked over the fabric of my tunic—over the thick scar above my heart.

"I know you'd never hurt me. I … I just want to understand what you went through. Why you had to do her bidding. And I'm … I'm scared." She swallowed as if the word was repugnant and stuck on her tongue. "So damned *scared*."

A tiny fissure splintered within me. Warily, Seryn looked up, and a stray tendril drifted over her cheek. I tucked it behind her ear and then covered her hand with mine as she snuggled her face into the crook of my shoulder.

My heartbeat thundered so violently that it pulsed through both our palms. I wanted her to know. *Needed* her to understand. Even if it meant exposing all the revolting, weak parts of me.

Even if it unveiled my failures.

My thumb brushed over her hand, back and forth like the pendulum of a ticking clock. My nostrils flared as I dug into the darkest recesses of my mind. Unearthing the buried nightmares I kept so tightly packed down.

Briefly, my lips rubbed together before my story tumbled from me. "When I joined the Order, I was looking for something I could never have. Something I was …" I glanced at the top of Seryn's head, and then back to the splintered ceiling panels. "… I was missing. But then my mother was culled, and Pa died. Honestly, the first couple of turns are a blur. Early on, Melina took an interest in me. She claims we were lovers during the Dormancies, before my rune, and I … I can't say that we weren't …"

Seryn's fingers flinched against my chest. Crushing my eyes together, I gulped. "The thought of it repulses me even now. To think I was that weak." My molars ground together as a memory from five turns ago played across the backs of my eyelids.

"Aren't you appealing?" Melina purred, running her pointed nails over my new rune tattoo. "It'll be much more enjoyable now that you remember our time together, Commander. Don't I deserve a thank you for such a priceless gift? You used to thank me all the time, in any way I saw fit." She cupped my jaw, her nails like lancets when I tried to jerk from her hold. "You were always my favorite playmate. Don't you realize? You're the only one—alive—I can't get inside. I need to pick you apart, bit by bit, until I break into that thick, beautiful skull of yours."

I gulped, willing the recollection away.

"You were grieving. Seeking comfort isn't a failure."

I humphed, disgust simmering in my gut. "Once I had my rune and senses back, her *gifts* didn't work on me anymore. Who knows how often she tried to use her ember on me before then, but it never worked because"—a searing pain sliced through my chest, and I winced—"Well, I wasn't interested in bedding her, and she couldn't break into my mind. So, she devised ways to control me. Unfortunately, my weakness was my brother. And *you*."

Seryn shifted against me, but her hand didn't leave the spot over my heart. A soothing warmth spread from the places our bodies met.

"Every turn, she threatened to harm you and Kaden. To erase your minds. To torture and break you if I didn't hunt down potential Scions. I did my best to delay or feign a failed mission, but that only infuriated her more." My pulse ticked in my clenched teeth. I stretched my jaw in a circle to loosen its hinges.

"She had Balor tie me down with his aura and demanded I watch as she fucked random citizens, or tortured them in unspeakable ways, *or both*. If I struggled or refused ..." My memories dribbled over my words like sticky blood. I went inside myself, not sure if I continued to speak the words aloud to Seryn ...

I sat on her silken settee, Balor's greasy ember strapping me to my seat, his pungent, hot breath heaving against my ear. He enjoyed watching. Excited and straining his soft body at the back of the divan.

Melina wrapped her naked body in a black satin robe, her latest victim wrapped in a sheet at the foot of the bed. I slammed my eyelids closed, trying to erase the scene I'd just witnessed. "Now, Commander. You know how I loathe it when you don't pay attention. Eyes on me, so you remember that it could be your attractive brother in my bed. Or that sweet, doe-eyed girl you're so fond of."

My teeth were going to crush within my mouth. I snapped my eyes open, boiling revulsion flashing over them as I glared at her.

She laughed, tapping her fingers along her chin and spinning to the dazed male. She'd stolen his memories as she came.

"Now, now. Balor, what shall we do with this one?"

I heard the wet lick of his tongue against his lips. "Mistress, why not the skin peeler?"

She clapped her hands in delight, trotting over to her vanity and plucking out a long, thin blade. "Balor, always such a good pet." She winked at me before strutting toward the man. "Eyes on me, Gavie. Although it was fun to fuck you. It's more fun to make you watch."

The echoes of her victim's screams bounced through my skull as I came back to the present.

"Then she'd wipe her abuses clean from their minds afterward. Send them to her healer Akridais. I …"

Shallow breaths spilled from me, and I clamped my eyes shut and squeezed Seryn closer. "I couldn't stop her. Couldn't break free. After a while, it was easier to go into this … into this hidden space within my mind until it was over. It was better to do as she wished and hunt for whoever she demanded. As long as it wasn't my brother. As long as it wasn't you."

Seryn's sob rent the air, and her arm coiled around me tightly. "I'm so sorry. I … She's going to pay. I swear it." She breathed my name, her hand moved to my chest once more as if checking my heart still beat under the weight of my admissions.

"She tortured them. The hunted. The potential Scions. I don't know what she did with them after, but I … I can only hope they were offered the solace of death." My words sank into my gut, disgust carving deeply. And I deserved it.

I brought her hand to my face, brushing my mouth over her fingertips and closing my eyes, urging the resurfaced nightmares back into the darkness.

Seryn's touch slid over my cheek, my grip slipping down her wrist. Gently, she pressed her palm into my skin until I looked at her. Her thumb swept across the hollow above my jawline, and a tingling followed its path.

"I swear it." Her whispered promise stamped into my ribs. My hold tightened, and I pulled her close until our chests met. I cupped her nape, guiding her lips to mine.

My need for her prickled over me. But it was more than desire. She was my safe passage. The one I'd always felt whole with just from being in her presence. I didn't deserve her, but I'd spend every damned second making up for that if she'd let me.

She was still wary. The memory of our first attempt at a relationship was a tender bruise upon her heart. It was in the slight hesitations when she looked at me, even though she wanted to embrace what was happening between us. There was so much left to tell her, but I couldn't yet.

Guilt mixed with my growing lust, but I pushed it deep into the shadowed cracks within me. There were some things she needed to unearth on her own. Things I couldn't reveal, no matter how much I yearned to.

Later.

I kissed her hard, our tongues and mouths dancing, devouring one another. She draped a leg over mine, eager to get closer.

Wearing my tunic, her honey-like scent melded with mine and the musk of our coupling earlier in the night. My cock hardened, and a rumbling groan sounded under my collarbone.

Sneaking under her clothing, my hand cupped her bare, round ass, my fingertips pressing into the softness, pulling her tightly against me.

Heat blazed down my spine as her cunt ground against me. Her soft moan vibrated through our mouths. I grabbed her by the hips and tugged her onto my lap.

She smiled as she sat up, slowly untying my breeches. My hard cock sprang free, standing firmly at attention between us. Before she could take me in hand, I bent forward, reaching behind me to wrench my tunic over my head, discarding it on the floor.

She bit her lip as her hands stroked over my pectorals, tracing the jagged outline of my scar.

Her head tilted, and her messy braid spilled over her front. "It's shaped like—"

"You're the only little star that matters." My breath hitched, heart slamming against said scar as my fingers unravelled the fiery plait. I loved her wild hair.

I shifted the loose strands behind her, and she smiled tenderly, leaning over to place a kiss on the thickened skin above my heart before trailing her lips and tongue up my chest.

Over my neck and jaw.

She wrapped her hand behind my nape, scraping her nails into the line of my hair as her slick core rocked against my hardness.

My muscles went rigid, and a raging need burned over my flesh, pulsing up my length. My fingers found the hem of her tunic, and I pulled it over her, lifting her arms.

She gathered me close again as I wrapped my arms around her, her full breasts pressing into my chest. I kissed the corner of her lips as my palms slid over her shoulder blades. "You're so damned beautiful, it hurts."

She smiled as we fell into each other's eyes. "Let me take the hurt away," she murmured as she lifted herself onto her knees and then reached between our bodies. Her hand guided my cock to her entrance, and she slowly sank onto my length, never breaking eye contact.

Her sweet, aching body gripped me, and I swear to the Ancients, her soul poured into me. It felt as though a string latched onto my rib directly from hers, and our heartbeats vibrated along it in time with one another.

The muscles of my neck and back tensed as her warm, wet heat squeezed my cock. I clutched her waist as she rose, nails digging into my straining biceps.

I wanted nothing more than to toss her down and fuck her tight cunt until she screamed my name.

Only my name.

Ever again.

But I also wanted the sweet torture. Because it meant she was in control, and she needed to know she had that power, not only over me, but over herself.

Asteria smirked, slamming herself onto my lap, my cock filling her to the hilt. She moaned, heat blushing over her chest and neck.

My fingers clamped, urging her to keep moving as her eyes glazed. She set a steady rhythm, her hips undulating against mine, her warm core squeezing around me, pumping me.

Mounting desire rolled across her features and spilled from her parted lips in fitful, breathy sounds. I pinched her nipple with my thumb and forefinger, and her head craned back, a moan vibrating within her as she moved faster.

"That's it, my star. Take what's yours." I leaned into her, latching my lips on her neck, licking and nipping at her flesh while she convulsed around my manhood; my name ripping from her throat.

A throbbing pulsed from the base of my spine and through my cock as her cunt spasmed around me like a fist.

In uncontrollable ripples, my orgasm tore from me, light bursting in my chest as I buried my eyes against her neck, my groan muffled by her damp flesh.

Dazed and sated, she drooped against me, cradling my head against her, her fingers clutching at my hair. I didn't dare move, for I feared the string connecting the bony cages over our hearts would snap if we parted.

For several quiet moments we breathed one another in, the cool air drying our sweat and leaving goosebumps behind.

At last, her whispered word shuddered against my cheek, harmonizing with the thundering beat of her blood.

One word that sounded suspiciously like *"mine."*

26

EVERYTHING

GAVREL

A contented stillness carried us into the next balmy day. Warm sunrays shifted over our naked bodies as we stayed in bed all morning, curled in each other's arms. Though I'd feasted on every inch of her to the melody of her breathy moans—my name rasping from her lips—I still hungered for more as we clung to one another.

I craved her taste.

Her smell.

Her skin against my tongue and mouth and hands.

I'd never be sated. But I would spend the entirety of my days trying to quell my hunger.

Her eyelids fluttered as she shifted within my embrace, and then she nuzzled into my chest. Her belly rumbled, pulling a chuckle from me.

"I need to feed you," I muttered against her hair.

"I'd rather stay here." She smirked, running her fingers

absently over my biceps and then sinking into my messy hair at my nape.

Groaning, I reluctantly unraveled from her embrace and covered her with a blanket.

"If you're going to leave me, might as well make me my preventive tea." She yawned, stretching her lithe body under the covers. Nodding, I did as she asked, bringing it to her in bed, and studied her as she sipped it.

She watched me over the rim of the cup, a mischievous smile reaching the corners of her eyes. "What are you thinking?"

A slow curl tugged at the corner of my mouth. "I'm thinking that I can't believe my good fortune." I stalked closer to her as she finished her tea. "And that you're in dire need of a bath."

Her laughter pealed through the room as I scooped her up and carried her to the tub. The water was lukewarm as I lowered her and climbed in behind her.

Leisurely, I washed and untangled her hair, and she sighed contentedly, her back pressing into my chest as I massaged her scalp.

"What do you think we'll find on the other side of the portal?" I murmured, enjoying the sensation of her against me.

She exhaled, goosebumps rippling over her chest in the wake of her breath. "I'm not sure, but I don't expect it to be pleasant. As long as Kaden is there. As long as it leads to my mother ..." She let her words drift off.

"We'll find them. And then, together, we'll find a way into Surrelia. Destroy the amber."

Her chest rose and fell evenly but deeply. She was likely doing her measured breathing, soothing herself. I shifted her hair over one shoulder and moved my fingers to her neck, massaging the tension out of it.

I breathed in time with her, our chests moving as one. My blood ran warm, flushing my skin. Most days, I couldn't fathom my luck. That this beautiful creature was giving me another chance.

She was so resilient.

So brilliantly stubborn.

And hopeful. So hopeful that it spread into those around her. Into me.

Even when her worries overwhelmed her, Seryn kept going. Kept using what she'd learned to temper them. And that's what mattered. It meant she was believing in herself *and* her gifts, even if her confidence wavered.

She wouldn't give up, and that was the thing that I admired most about her. Throughout our lives, she pushed away the shadowed embrace of defeat. The flames within her had always burned too bright to be extinguished.

Even when I'd pushed her away.

Even when my darkness tried to clamp onto her.

Thoughts from two summers ago spilled into my mind, sloshing at the edges. She'd given me her trust then, and I'd devoured it like the empty, starving man I was.

Am.

In those days, we would hold each other and share our fears, dreams, and hopes for Midst Fall. We talked about the injustices and cruelties of the world we lived in, but we also reveled in its beauty and the cherished moments spent with those we loved.

And then, when I'd broken us apart, even though it was for her protection, the rending of our hearts hurt just the same.

Yet she held her head high. Walked away from me as she should have, leaving me to my shame and bitter lies.

I had been a fool then. Not for choosing to protect her; I would make that choice time and again. No, I was a fool for convincing myself I could resist the pull she had on me. For far too long, I pretended she wasn't my Ancient of Stars, lighting my path while I clung to the shadows.

But we were inevitable.

And in her orbit was exactly where I always wanted—*needed* —to be.

My forehead pushed down; eyes squeezed shut. "Thank you."

"For?" she breathed, bowing her head so my fingers could get better access.

"For giving me—*us*—another chance."

"Gavrel ..." Her silence stretched for a few moments.

"I don't know what I did to deserve it, but I vow to never break your heart again. May the Ancient of Nightmares take me."

After a moment, one of her hands reached for me, her fingers brushing the top of mine. She brought my hand to her mouth and pressed a kiss into my palm. "Don't be foolish. Then, I'd have to hunt him down and rescue you. I'm full up on rescue quests at the moment."

I chuckled and curled my fingers over her kiss as her hand sank into the water. I rubbed my palm over my thumping heart and then brought it back to her nape.

Tentatively, she glanced at me with a soft smile curving her lips. "But I'll take your apology and the vow regardless."

"Thank you," I mouthed before she turned forward.

The pad of my thumb brushed over the dense scar on her nape. My nostrils flared, brows furrowing.

Maya had protected her daughter by hiding her gift with an implanted rune—the engraved stone that Seryn often stroked her thumb over absently.

Just as my mother had tried to protect me. I had gone along with it. Not for me; for Seryn.

Just as I always had.

And always would.

But that decision had come with a price, as they all did.

Enough. Now is not the time, I rebuked myself sharply, slamming my eyes closed. All of my focus narrowed to my hands as I kneaded Seryn's shoulders. Having her skin under mine was enough to take my breath away.

She was a living dream.

My every wish come true.

Every desire.

And I would rip apart anyone or anything that threatened to take her from me.

She moaned, and I ran my hands over her wet flesh. Her collarbone. Over her breasts until I reached her pebbled nipples.

My cock stirred, nudging her backside. Seryn's mouth curled as she wiggled against me.

This woman would be my end. And I'd happily accept it.

Shifting us deeper under the water, I leaned back as my left thumb circled and plucked at the tip of her breast. The sound of her breathy whimper shot down my spine, my length stiffening further.

I kissed the crown of her head, continuing my ministrations on her nipple as my right hand slid into the water and over her belly. Her knees trembled as they fell wider, inviting me to explore.

"You're everything I've ever wanted, Asteria," I whispered into her ear, my middle and ring fingers slipping into her wet channel. A soft purring vibrated under her collarbone.

She was so damn soft.

So greedy for my touch.

Languidly, I stroked over her clit, swirling and pressing until she squirmed. Water slapped against the sides of the basin.

"You're simply … everything." My lips rested against her temple as I played with her, her body heating and writhing against me.

Breathing ragged, my blood throbbed through me as her desperate whimpers draped over us.

"Gavrel," she sobbed, her voice hitching, breasts thrusting forward.

I nibbled at the top curve of her ear as my left hand pinched one nipple and then slid to her mound.

Seryn groaned as I sank the two digits into her heat, curving them so they rubbed repeatedly against the roughened pleasure point within her, my thumb rapidly circling her clit.

I bit my lip hard, hoping the pain would keep me from coming before I could slide into her. My left palm pressed into her lower belly as my right hand pumped. Inside her, my fingers repeatedly curled and pressed against her inner wall, against the spot that was making her eyes roll back and eyelashes flutter.

Ancients, this woman made me so fucking feral.

"Come for me. Come all over my fingers as they fuck your tight little cunt," I growled.

Her core squeezed around me. She screamed my name, her nails digging into the top of my left hand as it pressed into her. Her right hand flew up, clamping onto my nape, as she threw her head back in ecstasy.

With my hips grinding, seeking purchase, I groaned as she shattered. Seryn cried out—broken, gasping sounds—with each trembling spasm that skittered over her. Her cunt gripped my fingers as her walls convulsed, and then all at once, her entire body went lax in my arms.

Rolling her head toward me, a dreamy smile curved her mouth as she looked into my eyes. Her skin was flushed and dewy. My unspent cock twitched.

She turned within my arms, hovering over me on her knees.

The blue of her eyes darkened as she sank unhurriedly onto my arousal. "Your turn," she rasped.

All thoughts of food vanished.

We didn't leave the tub for a long while.

27

WHATEVER IT TAKES

SERYN

When we finally left our cabin, the sun had shifted into the early evening. As Gavrel walked behind me, he smoothed his hand over my backside. He was extra attentive when I wore leather breeches. Before we left, his eyes had lingered on me as I slowly strapped my dagger onto my hip and thigh. I smirked at him, adjusting my belt satchel as we headed to *The Boggy Grog* to share a meal with Rhaegar and Breena.

As we ate, he couldn't stop staring at me. Despite trying to wrangle his composure, a smile continually threatened the corners of his lips. I bit into my bread, letting its crusty ridges poke the roof of my mouth.

"Worked up quite the appetite, eh?" Breena snickered.

Gavrel narrowed his eyes, but she just stared at him, chewing and then jabbing her spoon at him.

Head swaying side to side, I snorted before taking a bite of my mushroom and mire rabbit stew. "Like you didn't. I saw you and Marek at the Revelry last night."

Instantly, Breena's amusement transformed into annoyance. "I don't have a clue what you're on about."

"What we should be *on about* is the fact that we've met a bloody Ancient. Not to mention where Seryn needs to direct the portal," Rhaegar muttered.

I lifted my spoon, pupils rising to the right, forehead crinkling. "I've been thinking about that—"

"When would you have the time?" Breena's eyebrows wiggled.

Ignoring her, I went on. "And I think Phantasos was hinting at the Stygian Murk. Last Dormancy, when I first arrived, there was this valley in the distance. Something was off. And in the nightmares I've had of Kaden … I can feel it in my gut. Not only his, but the misery of the Murk." With a shrug, my spoon lowered. "That's all I can think of."

Breena wielded her utensil against me now. "I think that'll have to be good enough, Firefly. Eh, how 'bout we talk about how much of a bleeding headache that tonic gave me this morning."

My eyebrows shot up. "You used the orchid?"

The skin on either side of her eyes crinkled. "You really did a number on me in the Winnowing. Proud of you, you ember-eating wench."

Squealing, I threw my arms around my friend, overjoyed that the memories of the Breena I first met had joined the new.

"Oy, woman! My stew—" Her words were cut short as a stout man crashed through the entrance. My stomach shot into my throat at the panic radiating off him.

"Arm yourselves! We're under attack!" he bellowed. Everyone in the pub froze for only a moment before shooting out of their chairs, brandishing weapons, and rushing outdoors.

With weapons in hand, we followed the rest. A booming

blast of oily neon exploded against the tree to my left, and I stooped as Gavrel grabbed me and hauled me away from the flying shards of wood.

The doombark groaned as the oleaginous ember slithered over its trunk and then over the roof of the pub. With a resounding crack, the building caved inward, the broken tree plunging backward into a nearby conservatory. The thick dome remained unharmed.

Of course it did.

No matter what doom befell Midst Fall, those damned things survived.

My eyes followed the path of the tainted ember. Atop a roof was a female Akridai, a fresh assault forming between her palms.

"Get to Yaya's," I ordered as a Helos citizen pushed the oblivious enforcer off the building she perched on.

Hurriedly, we weaved along the bridges and plankways.

Below our grandmother's home, Marek, bare-chested as usual, was spinning and jabbing his quarterstaff between two Draumrs. His raven tattoo moved with his shoulder blades as he shifted gracefully and struck his weapon efficiently between both attackers.

When the guards noticed Gavrel approaching, they faltered, Marek's staff knocking one off the bridge. Dodging my cousin's next attack, the other warrior crouched and retreated. The woman's face pinched, confusion lacing her tone. "Commander?"

"The Elders are a farce. Do with that what you will," Gavrel replied as Marek stepped toward her like a predator. The warrior's face crumpled before she sprinted away.

Yaya barged down the stairwell, a bow gripped in her hold and a quiver of arrows strapped to her back. "Get a move on! Protect as many innocents as you can, but get my granddaughter to Hallowed End. Whatever it takes."

She didn't have to tell us twice. As a unit, we navigated the pathways.

There were droves of Draumrs pouring in from all sides. My heart galloped, trying to push me onward as ember thrummed along my body. The knowledge that my blade would be sullied today had my fist tightening around the hilt.

"It would seem we have an Elder sympathizer among us," Marek snapped. "On the south bank, several boundary runes were destroyed. The illusion fell shortly after."

My grandmother's nostrils flared irritably at the information, but then her head snapped up. "Let's move!" she barked, nocking an arrow and letting it fly over my head.

A pained cry sounded, then breaking boughs as a body hurtled through the air, and then a final splat into the water.

Gavrel's mouth pressed into a firm line as he nodded approvingly at Yaya. Then we ran, rune tattoos and embers flaring among us. White light zoomed over Gavrel's and Rhaegar's weapons.

A few straggling Draumrs met us as we made haste. A pained expression flicked over Gavrel's face with every warrior he thrashed his weapon or fists at. It must have wounded him to harm his fellow warriors, but it couldn't be helped. The majority who joined the Order of Draumr were doggedly devoted to the Elders and their laws, conditioned to harm first and ask questions later.

But Gavrel had chosen his cause, and he would stand against anyone who got in our way.

He blocked a sword swinging at me from a shaky bridge running parallel to the one we were on. The guard gritted his teeth at the impact and then stumbled as the planks under him swayed. Using the full weight of my body, I rammed my shoulder into his, and the man cursed, tripping over the side and falling into the water.

As we stepped into the main square, at least forty warriors

blocked our path. They spilled onto the platform from various pathways. My knuckles turned pale around the hilt of my dagger, its kaleidoscopic mist swirling in the pommel.

On my left, Yaya and Marek hurried to a winding staircase. As the older woman darted up them, Marek struck a man in the neck with his quarterstaff as the guard lunged for her.

"Let's dance!" Breena roared, charging toward our opposition, her crimson aura blazing around her.

Rhaegar laughed and followed his friend, swinging his battle axe into the approaching opponents. "I'll clear the way!" he bellowed, yanking his curved blade from a man's flank.

A ball of Breena's blistering ember zipped over his shoulder and through a woman's arm. The warrior's sword slammed into the platform as she screamed, grabbing at the empty space her limb used to be.

Gavrel spun at the sound of stomping boots, his sword slashing and clanking against another. A second guard jabbed his blade at him, and he lurched backward just in time, knocking his weapon off course.

Frozen by the combat, I watched his skirmish unfurl. The sense of impending doom skittered over my scalp. Like it had during the final Winnowing Trial.

From every corner I beheld, limbs and blades thrashed, flaming arrows whizzed overhead, and gleaming energy flashed.

A streak of russet caught my eye, and I glanced at my cousin as he spun gracefully, his staff sweeping around him in a wide arc.

A brutal grin spread over his teeth; I didn't think I'd ever seen him as delighted. Another of Breena's heated orbs slammed into the warrior Marek had smashed, and he scowled at her as the guard fell to his knees. She tossed him a jaunty smirk before twirling and slicing her curved blade through another opponent's neck.

Rhaegar and Gavrel's tattoos were brilliant shooting stars,

tracing intricate patterns as they expertly swung and thrust their blazing weapons in combat.

Gavrel had once shared how these mystical symbols heightened their strength and agility, but witnessing their prowess in battle was another thing altogether. They moved with the swift precision and force of at least two or three warriors, effortlessly dodging and striking with otherworldly grace.

My halo sputtered around me, the patterns along my arms blinking. But I couldn't feel it. Numbness saturated my very soul.

Fuck.

I was *useless*.

It was happening again.

Each clash of metal clanged against my skull.

Gavrel blocked and lunged, alternating between the two guards he was fighting. The first guard jabbed, and the commander swiped sideways, knocking the sword from the man's hand. Gavrel rammed his boot into his stomach, and as the Draumr fell backward, Gavrel spun to the second guard just in time for his sword to clash against the other's blade.

My ember sent a surge of heat through my spine, and I staggered on the planks, electricity zapping through my fingers and toes. Suddenly, I remembered how to move my limbs.

From my side, a guard rushed toward me. As I pivoted on the balls of my feet, I flung my arm out, my blade sinking into her neck.

With a look of stunned terror, she fell to her knees, and before her hands could clutch her split throat, I called my dagger back to me. Revulsion and pride burrowed into my chest as I spun to Gavrel in time to see him and the other warrior retreat from one another.

Before either could deal another blow, Gavrel dropped to one knee and drove his blade into the space beneath the other man's ribs. Wide-eyed, the guard responded with a gurgling death rattle before crimson spilled from his mouth. Gavrel tugged his sword from the Draumr's body.

Satisfaction scurried through me. I wasn't sure if it was me or my ember, and I no longer cared. We were the same, weren't we?

I called upon it, weaving a twisting orb between my fingers. At the buzzing caress, a smirk plucked at the corners of my mouth. The glow reflected in Gavrel's eyes as he looked at me with pride.

There was movement behind Gavrel, and in the next moment, I lobbed the weaponized radiance over his shoulder. It was the guard he had kicked. The man's broadsword clattered to the wood at Gavrel's heels as my energy smeared over him, flashed outward, and contracted as if his body were absorbing the light.

With terrified eyes and mouth agape, his limbs flung out, and his back arched. With a final flash of brilliance, his form combusted. Ash and glittering mist were all that remained.

I cried out, horror and fascination lining my features. It was odd that killing someone with my ember was more distressing than doing so with a blade. I shoved the thought away as three guards froze in their tracks and whipped nervous looks toward me before scurrying in the other direction.

Good. I was a bloody monster.

As Gavrel gathered me in his arms, I choked on my words. "He ... he was going to ... going to kill you."

"I know, Little Star. Breathe. It had to be done." He kissed the top of my head as I set my jaw, nodding, finding the truth in his explanation.

We turned, arms around each other's waists. The battle roared, and fire licked at the wooden bones of the city. A deep rage boiled within my belly at the sight.

The city burned like a field of scorching wheat, the smell of charred wood and flesh sinking into my lungs. My eyes darted between the blazing infernos and my kin as they fought against the Elders' legion of warriors and enforcers. Yellowish putrescence pulsed behind each Akridai's neck hieroglyph, making it look as if a plague of inky locusts was swarming Helos.

People—the Ravens—were who mattered.

People could rebuild cities from the ashes and lift one another after the fall. And they'd rather raze Helos to the muck than let the Elders take their home.

My home.

Among the chaos, a stillness tunneled into my bones because I knew something in my very marrow that our enemies didn't.

No matter what firestorm raged around us, our roots were safely buried beneath the mire, biding their time before blooming once again.

28

SHOW ME YOUR TEETH

GAVREL

*D*usk set in, the full moon already bright and shining over the fighting and gore around us.

A shower of arrows poured into the mass of bodies. Draumrs and rebels in the constant motion of combat, battling one another while the city croaked and shuddered beneath our very feet.

Citizens jumped and swung from the treetop homes and stairwells, sturdy ropes and daggers clutched in their hands as they attacked from above.

"Commander!" Rhaegar bellowed from the other side of the square. Several Draumrs looked my way, shock and uncertainty slamming over their visages. I recognized one or two, but ignored them as Seryn and I charged toward him.

Neoma shot a final arrow before setting her bow across her chest and then grabbing a nearby rope. Before she could swing from the platform, a pair of Akridais appeared, one yanking her by the hair and the other's oleaginous aura slipping around the enforcer's form. I couldn't reach her, but russet strands caught my attention at the base of the tree.

"Marek! Neoma!" I bellowed, and his eyes snapped up, a look of rage lining his features. He jabbed his quarterstaff into a guard's face and charged up the stairwell, his halo flaming furiously.

At the sound of my voice, Seryn stumbled. "Keep going! Marek's got her!" I shouted. A grim expression settled across her face as she stabbed her dagger into an opponent's thigh.

Already deep in battle, we both knew it was futile to turn back. We wouldn't make it to her grandmother before her cousin. As we fought our way through the square, blocking blows and metal clashing against metal, I caught glimpses of Neoma as she struggled against the enforcers.

With a roar, Marek clenched his fists, muscles straining. A slithering shadow made of sooty flames burst from him. The dark inferno rolled up the stairs like a nightmare and engulfed the two Akridais. At once, they released Neoma, clutching the sides of their heads and screaming in terror.

As Marek's feet met the deck, his face was a mask of wrath. A savage grin sliced across his jaw as he watched his enemies collapse to their knees. I swore his pupils overtook the whites of his eyes as the Akridais clawed at their cheeks, eyes unseeing and full of horror. Whatever illusion he'd implanted was tearing their minds apart from the inside.

I deflected a blow and spun, thrusting my sword into another belly.

Tentatively, Neoma placed her hand on her grandson's shoulder, and he winced. He crushed his eyes closed and shook his head as if clearing away pollution. His ember melted into him while Neoma swung over the length of the square, landing safely on another tree deck.

Marek prowled near the trembling enforcers, who whimpered feebly. His eyes narrowed before he kicked one off the edge of the platform and whipped his staff into the other. Both fell limply into the water below. With his face set in a dour expression, Marek swung over to where Neoma had landed, and they joined us below.

"Holy tits, Yaya," Breena praised the older woman. "You've still got that battle fever in you."

Neoma laughed, charging ahead. Breena tilted her head toward Marek, eyeing him curiously. The male pushed past her, his jaw set in stone.

At last, we reached the bridge to Hallowed End, and I let out a breath I hadn't realized I was holding. Its creaking span vanished into the darkness, too long even for the moon's grasping tendrils to fully reveal.

We crossed in silence, the weight of something unseen nipping at our heels, pressing down—thick as the smoky air and the groan of timber beneath our feet. Fog curled along the ropes and planks like pale serpents. Beneath us, the swamp pulsed, its black water shifting with sluggish menace.

As the decagon-shaped platform came into view, my heart slammed against my ribs. A droning cacophony bubbled up from the murk, silencing the swamp critters. We froze, staring into the water.

Breena snarled as swollen, ashen bog bodies broke through the surface, bulging eyes and vacuous sockets alike fixating on our group.

We snapped into action, stabbing and kicking away the undead. Again and again, Seryn's dagger lodged into the undead's soft bits, instantly returning to her hand. The others swung their weapons and let their embered light slash a path over the bridge.

Sweat coated my brow, and as we rushed onto the platform, cracking fingers and chomping jaws lunged at us. I stabbed one of the beast's temples. Its one bulging eye rolled back in its head before it slipped into its watery grave.

The Budding Moon hovered above, watchful and steady, its beams spilling across the planks like a quiet blessing—as if Selene herself approved, marking our destination.

Seryn rushed forward, activating her ring and ember simultaneously. She closed her eyes, lashes fluttering, imagining the Stygian Murk as we'd discussed.

A swirling, amber vortex materialized as both Seryn's and the moon's light fed the embered gateway, its sparkling edges widening until the center of the misty haze beckoned us.

"Go! I'm not sure how long I can hold it!" Seryn cried.

Rhaegar and Breena leaped into the mist. Frowning, Marek hesitated as he looked at his cousin and grandmother.

"We'll be right behind you. Go on, boy!" Neoma barked. His jaw tensed, but he walked grudgingly through the threshold.

I stepped forward as Seryn's eyes met mine, her curls snapping in the portal's wind.

Neoma whirled, a scowl cutting across her features. My shoulders stiffened at the sound of a familiar voice calling my name like a tinkling chime flitting in a breeze. It slithered over my vertebrae.

Melina.

I drew myself to my full height as I turned, my teeth grinding into one another. Seryn's hand gripped my waist, her warmth pressing into my back in fear or comfort. Both.

Like a feral cat, Melina grinned as she stalked toward us over the swaying bridge. Her cape snapped behind her, and her gauzy, black dress gripped her curves.

The two Akridais who'd been hunting us since we'd escaped Evergryn flanked her, their greasy, yellow auras licking at her smoke-like energy.

Another female trailed behind them, her pretty, oval face familiar. She wasn't fazed by the dead bodies groaning and grabbing at her feet.

"Caelora?" Neoma snapped, ignoring Melina and glaring at the woman. "How could you?"

Ah, the traitor.

Seryn's forehead scrunched and then lifted as Caelora squared her shoulders, and her violet aura surged around her, amethyst eyes glinting like jewels. She tossed Seryn a defiant look—everything about her was defiant—as her honey-colored waves snapped in the breeze.

Although an Akridai rune didn't brand her throat, perhaps the Elders had recruited her. Her gift hailed from two bloodlines, which was a rarity Melina would covet.

My mouth pinched, sympathy for the traitorous female creeping over my anger.

"Enough chatter. I wish I could say it's a pleasure to be home again, but I find other things pleasurable nowadays." She licked her crimson lips and raised one perfectly arched brow at me and then at the Korax leader. "Neoma. It's been too long."

Acid boiled up my windpipe. She made me fucking sick. My head lifted, and I raised my sword, eager to impale her. Slice through to the evil core within her.

"Haven't you missed me, Gavie? You've been such a naughty boy. We've much to catch up on." She sighed and then flicked her wrists to either side irritably.

The female Akridai immediately flung her power toward the closest bog bodies, and the creatures froze, their moaning silenced.

As Melina cocked her head, her platinum hair flowed over her shoulder. The male enforcer at her back slashed his energy over the undead, and they collapsed into cloudy depths.

Melina twirled her hands as if conducting a music ensemble and continued, "You've done as I asked." She wiggled her eyebrows at me. "Found my pet *and* potential Scions. Well done, Commander. I'll reward you as usual."

Seryn's aura was buzzing against my back as she leaned into

me, her voice carrying over the bog bodies' cacophony. "Touch him, and I'll tear your pretty face off."

Melina clapped her hands, tittering. "Ah, my little pet bites. Come closer and show me your teeth. I would love to tame you. As I have Gavie."

Seryn growled, and—fuck me—if it wasn't the sexiest noise I'd ever heard. Heat surged to the bottom of my spine. Reaching behind me, I brushed my fingers over her waist. "Go on, I'll be right behind you."

"I'm not leaving you," she snarled.

And she wouldn't.

Desperately, I flicked my gaze to Neoma behind us. She met my eyes, stiffened her frame, and nodded.

I stepped back, forcing Seryn to do the same. My jaw clenched as I dipped my chin, eyes locked on Melina's slippers. She savored the taste of submission. "Mistress, I've done what you asked. I'm at your disposal."

She tapped a claw-shaped nail on her chin. "Have you, though? It seems as if you've been avoiding me. As if you're back to choosing *her*. I think there's *plenty* you haven't told me. That won't do, Commander."

A slow smile curled at the corners of Melina's lips, cold and knowing. A nagging spasm ticked under the scar on my chest, more dread than usual skittering along my nape at her words.

Elder Harrow was a predator savoring the moment before the kill. Her smoggy aura flicked angrily about, and I nudged Seryn closer to the portal.

"Stop. I know what you're doing," Seryn hissed.

I didn't stop. Melina and her enforcers were getting closer, and there wasn't time to distract them further.

Melina narrowed her eyes. "Ready the nearest pod," she snapped at the Akridais. "It's time for a culling."

"Now!" Neoma screamed as one of the Akridais' embers shot forward. She threw her weight into me, effectively pushing

Seryn and me into the churning haze of the portal as greasy tendrils locked around her waist.

Seryn called out her grandmother's name, her fingers grasping for Neoma as the woman's body jerked backward into the moonlight.

And then we fell, mist and firefly-like lights cocooning us.

29

A MURKY SITUATION

GAVREL

As if we were rancid morsels of food, the mouth of the portal spewed our bodies in a heap, the stench of decay filling my lungs. Seryn's howl followed us as we slammed into the pallid, cracked ground. The portal spun until it collapsed and vanished in a puff of sparks.

A heavy sense of hopelessness immediately blanketed me, all color sucked from my sight. I glared at the gray, dreary hues around us, infuriation blistering over me and replacing the despair. Pushing onto my elbows, a grunt tumbled from my throat. An acrid breeze rustled the strands hanging over my forehead.

The Stygian Murk was always such a fucking pleasure.

Marek, Breena, and Rhaegar splayed in a tangle of monochrome limbs, and Seryn trembled next to me. She sobbed once, dragging herself upright. Without thinking, I pushed onto my knees, ignoring the ache in my ribs, and gathered her to my chest.

"She'll be all right," I murmured, cupping her head and brushing my thumb over her strands.

She sniffled, choking around another sob. Her words were scratchy, as if her throat were raw from screaming. "We don't know that, and there's no use pretending otherwise." She squeezed her arms around me for a moment before clumsily standing, surveying the land.

I stared up at her, my mouth set in a rigid line. She was still forcing down the hard feelings so they wouldn't break her. The weight of them pressed into my stomach as if they were my own. I'd need to remind her later that she *could* break in front of me. That I'd help put the pieces back together so they didn't cut her soul to ribbons.

"Ah, always a treat visiting the Murk. I just adore my will to live being sucked from me." Breena's sardonic tone sounded as the others gathered around us.

Marek brushed the dust off his bare chest and picked up his staff. "Yaya?" He stared at Seryn expectantly. She shook her head and glowered into the distance.

"Melina and her Akridais showed themselves, and Neoma pushed us through the portal before it closed," I informed him.

His biceps tensed, and he looked away. "Bloody stubborn woman," he muttered.

"The traitor," I added. "Caelora Aundyne."

Marek sneered at the name. "The half-borne will get what she's owed. I knew she was more trouble than she was worth." My brow lifted to the sky as Marek reached for Seryn, and I stood. "We will rescue Yaya, cousin," he breathed.

She planted her feet in a wide stance and gave him a curt nod. "They'll pay. And I choose to believe that she's alive." Marek squeezed her shoulder once before gripping his quarterstaff with both hands.

Following Seryn's line of vision, I squinted. Not too far ahead, a deep, shadowed valley loomed between monstrous mountain peaks. Above it, the sky was enraged, coal-colored clouds heaving and crashing into one another.

"That's the valley I spoke of." Seryn's thumb rubbed along the pommel of her dagger. "This is where I ended up at the start of the last Dormancy."

"Did you—" Marek began, studying the horizon.

"No," she responded without letting him finish. She glanced at him apologetically, speaking more softly. "No. We went the other way toward the Surrelian portal. But"—her hand brushed against her nape—"but my ember *wants* me to go that way." Like a wraith, she moved toward the valley.

Her ember was true. I knew it in my marrow. My own hooked around my bones; its insistent energy urged me in that direction as well.

Kaden was in there. I was sure of it.

A fleck of black caught my eye in the space she'd left. Reaching down and picking up the gleaming stone, I ran my thumb over its etching. It was Seryn's protection talisman. She went nowhere without it. I pocketed it and trailed after her like the shadow I was.

I'd follow her anywhere.

Behind us, the booming crash of rock sounded. Powdered clay sprayed over our backs, and a distinct fissure carved the ground between my steps.

"Bloody void!" Rhaegar hollered while running past me, followed by Breena and Marek. Pale dust coated their backsides. Seryn and I glanced behind at the massive boulder that had plummeted from one of the teetering, hovering islets overhead and sprinted after them. *No need to be crushed today.*

As we dashed across the desiccated terrain, nearing the vale, the floating landmasses above quaked violently, shaking loose more and more chunks as they wept tears of stone. We darted and dodged the dropping rocks but couldn't avoid being pelted entirely.

Fortunately, the islets were shrinking as we neared the entrance, so mostly it was pebbles that rained down. Still unpleasant, but they weren't enough to cave in our skulls.

We paused, gawking at the angry, parched expanse before us. Shadows and shades of taupe and muddy gray mixed across the mountainous dips and ridges.

A crack above Seryn's head had me whipping my attention to her. A few gravelly shards struck my cheek as the tail end of Marek's quarterstaff jerked toward him, a massive cobble as big as my fist crashing in front of Seryn's feet.

He'd save her skull from being bashed in. Forehead furrowed, I nodded at him, and he did the same in return, digging his weapon into the ground.

"Thanks … cousin." Seryn blew a shaky breath out, her puffing cheeks turning a darker shade of gray. I could have sworn Marek's eyes softened before he muttered no thanks were necessary.

From the corner of my vision, a frenzied flurry of darkness buzzed on the horizon. "Shades are getting curious. Let's move."

Breena hurried forward. "Don't have to tell me twice."

"I overheard the Elders discussing them once." Rhaegar clutched his baldric, his axe handle bobbing against his back. His lips twisted to the side, and he exhaled heavily. "Apparently, they're Druiks who never escaped limbo."

Seryn's head dipped, and she rubbed her hand down her face. "Ancients, that's horrific. Those poor souls."

Breena gave Seryn a side hug, her hand rubbing her biceps. "Lesson learned. Don't linger in the Murk," Breena groused. She lifted her chin, her eyes shiny with unspent tears. "We're making it out. We're not shade material."

A sad smile lined Seryn's lips as she looked at her friend. Breena's grandmother had perished here. Seryn put her arm around her, and Breena crinkled her nose with a sniffle. Then they both marched forward, one stride in front of the other, with determined expressions. These women were made of pure backbone.

We traversed the arid, rocky terrain, following the empty riverbed carving down the center of the valley. This realm had likely never seen water a day in its existence, so who the void knew how it came to be.

This plane offered no remorse or logic. Its sole purpose was to suck the will to live from you while you tried to escape its clutches.

"The Ancients wanted to make it as difficult as possible for mortals to stumble into other realms, eh?" Marek grumbled as if reading my mind.

Rhaegar chuckled. "Why make *anything* easy for mortals? That would hardly be as entertaining. Eternal life, I suspect, becomes rather boring in time."

"Living is never boring," Breena snorted, bumping her hip into Seryn's. "And if it is, you're doing it wrong."

Seryn's lips wobbled, a small smile threatening. My heart lurched, overwhelmed with gratitude for Breena's ability to make Seryn smile. I nodded at the female, and she wiggled her brows at me, the corner of her mouth curling.

Every so often, thunder would crash as if upset that we dared walk through the vale. Lightning blazed above us, stirring the clouds into a frothy vat of agitated gloom and illuminating the living shadows stalking us. None yet were bold enough to attack.

With shades, it was best to go about your business unless they pounced. Their hunger for ember seemed collectively linked, and as a whole, they became more ravenous and menacing the instant one of them got a taste.

The deeper we went, the narrower the path became as the jagged edges of the mountains squeezed together like guards forming a barricade. The atmosphere became thick and oppressive, crushing into my muscles and making it more difficult to drag air into my lungs.

"We're not wanted here," Rhaegar said, rubbing a palm against his chest. "The very air is shoving against us." He glanced back and brandished his axe. As I drew my sword, both of our tattoos ignited, lighting up our blades.

"Fecking fantas—" Breena muttered at the same time Marek huffed, "We're doing something right then." They looked at each other, Breena rolling her eyes, her vibrant cherry-red ember snapping and sparking over her form. Marek's frown dug deeper into his jaw, and he clutched his quarterstaff more tightly while a halo of flicking ebony flames embraced him.

Seryn's gaze bored into me, and I met it. My sword's radiance reflected in them. She breathed slowly, allowing her aura to bloom in a dazzling display of fragmented rainbow hues. It was as if her body were a crystal prism that shattered her inner light and caught the broken fragments in her orbit.

My lips parted as I lost myself for a moment, my arm wilting and heart skipping several beats. Amusement flirted with the corners of her mouth. Tilting her head to the side, her smile never fully formed before concern darkened her face.

The intensifying buzz of swarming bees came closer, stealing my attention away from her. The shadow creatures advanced quickly now, their darkened mist coiling hungrily as they neared, yellow eyes blazing. They were ravenous for our activated ember.

An image of Seryn trapped within a shade's gluttonous smog flashed through my mind. Last fall, when one of these beasts attacked her, I had almost lost her. Acid boiled in my gut, threatening to burn through muscle, bone, and skin.

Back then, I hadn't been able to reach her in time.

I failed her … once again.

But I wouldn't allow that to happen now.

"Run!" Breena bellowed, sprinting toward the narrow gully cutting through the craggy walls.

The rest of us dashed after her. The atmosphere blackened like a candle being snuffed out. Lightning flashed, illuminating Breena, Rhaegar, and Marek as they pushed through the constricted passage without hesitation.

With a hand resting on the edge of the opening, Seryn paused, her eyes searching. Her expression relaxed as they landed on me, but then her brows shot up. "Behind you!"

The droning oozed into my ears, and a frenetic energy seared across my back. My will to live bled out, my rune's glow sputtering before snuffing out entirely.

It flared again as she stepped toward me.

"Go. Go now!" I shouted.

Her aura crackled, and bough-shaped radiance raced down her arms.

She wouldn't listen. *Per usual.*

This damned, uncompromising woman would be the death of me—and I'd gladly accept such a fate because it meant I'd perished in her orbit.

For whatever reason.

But these fucking shades were not claiming either of us today.

A frustrated snarl shook my ribs, and I forced my leaden arms to move. I flipped my sword within my hands so my blade jutted backward, cradled next to my flank. With a swift and forceful push, its shank sank into a gummy mass. The specter screeched, its cloying shadows spilling over my shoulders and dissipating along with the sharp hum.

I spun around, thrusting my sword through another creature as it skittered closer to take its brethren's place.

Whizzing past my ear, Seryn's dagger impaled a shade on my right, the faceted pommel glinting before the creature burst apart. For a fleeting instant, the liquid-like haze remained motionless before being sucked back into the crystal end of her weapon, reuniting with Seryn's glowing hand as if an invisible elastic band connected them.

I stabbed another shade to my left, and several more piled behind it. "Go! I'll be right behind you!" I bellowed after killing another, my rune and blade blazing again at full power. As a unit, the shades jerked away, fearful of my embered weapon.

"You damned stubborn ass!" Seryn hollered as she hurled her body through the channel. I backed up, squeezing through the constricted space after her, a sharp rock snagging my clothes.

With a final push, I wrenched myself out of the passage. Stumbling, my feet clumsily caught me. I blinked, fearing I'd lost my vision. An all-consuming gloom obscured the spaces around me.

"Seryn?" I shouted, not caring if any lingering evil heard me. "Seryn?!" The fog gobbled up my words, the volume shrinking despite me roaring her name over and over.

Dark silhouettes moved haphazardly, some darting around me, others barely moving. When I tried to focus on them, the shapes crumbled away. I held my sword up, pushing my ember over my blade once more. The fog swirled unpredictably, swiping across my vision like splashed paint one moment and then like thick, slow-dribbling honey the next.

"Bloody fucking void," I rasped.

My molars slammed together as a solid form knocked into me. Soft, sweet-smelling strands tickled my neck, and my left arm instinctively wrapped around her waist. "Little Star." My words fell out with a relieved sigh.

"Thank the Ancients." She slowly pulled from my grip and fumbled until her hand found mine. Energy prickled between our joined skin. "Don't let go." The fog shrouded her, but I could just make out bits of her when her aura twisted, slicing through the haze.

"Never will," I murmured. Her hand tightened in mine.

Her body lurched as someone bumped into her. "I've had just about enough of this fecking place," Breena complained, her fingers wrapping around Seryn's biceps. "Hold, please."

With her gift rippling over her, Breena lifted her other hand, a twisting orb of ruby sparkles and heatwaves sizzling within her palm. She bent her knees and shot up, whipping her arm above her head. The sphere flew high into the air, exploding in a shower of dazzling sparks.

"Brilliant." Rhaegar laughed as he joined us out of the smog.

With a smirk, Breena grabbed his hand. "Pleased you know that about me."

My second-in-command chuckled as Marek found us as well. "If you've finished congratulating yourself, we need to keep moving."

Breena's mouth pinched, her nostrils flaring before her features settled into a confident grin. "Lord Prickton of Twatsville is right. Let's do this." She cocked one brow at him before she tugged Seryn and Rhaegar forward, and, in turn, me. Seryn shook her head and held onto my hand tightly. Marek pushed his shoulders back, his embered halo snapping.

I stretched my neck to each side, and a sharp burn bit into the space between it and my shoulder. I pushed into the muscle and winced; my hand was coated in blood.

"Gavrel, you're injured," Seryn said, her brows furrowing.

"It's nothing. Let's keep going."

She narrowed her eyes, but swallowed her words.

As a unit, we pushed through the dense fog. At times, my muscles strained as if we barely moved. Other times, our limbs ripped through, our bodies slicing through the mist with ease.

Finally, my vision cleared as if a veil was torn away. Our feet met the blanched, dusty terrain once more. All of our embered light blazed bright for a moment before sinking within our skin. Seryn let go of me, stepping forward. I followed her gaze and drew in a sharp breath at what loomed before us.

It was a gleaming, mammoth structure. Glossy, jet-black panels, rather than glass, formed the concave walls, reminding me of our ten-sided conservatories. Instead of a domed roof, it curved inward, sharp spikes jutting upward from the intersections between the panels like a melded onyx crown.

An unnatural sense of dread prickled along my skin, scratching at my flesh. The others shifted on their feet uneasily beside me, faces scrunching and bodies tense.

"Steady now," Rhaegar said, pushing his axe forward as a slinking ebony mist began spilling from the base of the edifice.

Marek and I squared up, our weapons also at the ready. Seryn leaned forward with the blade of her obsidian dagger in front of her.

"Do you hear that? What the ever-fecking feck is that?" Breena asked, her words clipped. She squinted, pulling her daggers from the sheaths at her hips.

All at once, the screaming started.

LIVING NIGHTMARES

SERYN

My hand tightened around my dagger as terror and nightmare-like mist leaked from the building. It crept toward us, shrieking with every undulation and slow-motion caress against the broken clay. Or rather—it projected a symphony of horrified wailing.

My ember slammed against my scar in erratic bursts.

I lifted my chin.

"Likely from whatever's inside," Rhaegar mused.

Gavrel nodded and moved forward. "That's what I'm thinking. Stay together."

As we neared the slinking darkness, my power buzzed under my skin. The atmosphere chilled the closer we came, the screams filling my head, and apprehension sinking its fangs into my guts. Overwhelming despair carved into my ribs; the urge to curl into a frozen ball was unrelenting.

Marek sneered, and Gavrel rubbed his chest hard. I paused, swaying, yearning for the black fog to cradle me within its heady embrace. Breena glanced back at me, her eyes squinting, before whipping back to the mist that was almost upon us.

"Gather 'round me," Breena barked, her words caught in a cloud of icy breath as she came to me. She sheathed her daggers and concentrated on her cupped hands. Cherry-red aura spilled from her, and her energy enveloped us in a hazy film of sparking crimson.

A collective sigh filled our sanctuary as a balmy warmth soothed my body. I shook my head, helping my mind to clear the wicked miasma that had been tampering with my senses.

"Well done," Rhaegar said, allowing his rune to ignite. Setting his jaw, Gavrel did the same, and their weapons pulled the radiance along their blades. His injury was bothering him, but he wouldn't admit it.

Begrudgingly, Marek grunted in something akin to agreement.

Breena smirked as we moved again, and as the mist clawed at her protective shield, its whirling eddies skimmed over the edges and agitatedly folded back into themselves before slinking away.

Rhaegar and Gavrel prodded at the bolder tendrils of vapor creeping up our bubble. They, too, shrank away with each stab, rearing back and screeching before slithering off to join their brethren.

Approaching the structure, our group, protected by Breena's shield, reflected in the shiny panel. Marek tapped the surface with his staff as Gavrel poked it with his sword. They looked at one another with matching droll expressions.

Amusement stirred in my throat, but I swallowed it as a thrumming pulse of ember forced their weapons away from the building. I hovered my fingers over the panel, and prickles of icy energy needled at my flesh.

Gavrel grabbed my other wrist before I could fully touch the wall. I shook my head, and he sighed, knowing I was going to do it anyway. Power zapped my skin when I pressed my finger to the surface. I snatched my hand back and shook it out to rid myself of the lingering sting.

Brows furrowed, Marek reached out, his dark flames skating over him. Breena squeaked and smacked his arm. He hesitated, raising an eyebrow at her.

She crossed her arms and sniffed, pushing her worried expression into a mask of indifference. "Just felt like smacking ya. Go ahead and touch this death trap."

Marek pinched his lips and narrowed his eyes before slapping his palm on the wall. He groaned, his eyes crushing closed as his power zipped over his arm and slammed into the surface.

All at once, a sharp, grating sound throbbed through the air, and I cringed. The hairs on the back of my neck and arms raised, and my ember prickled down my spine.

"Marek!" I shouted as muscles tensed across his arm and back, the raven tattoo on his shoulder blades twitching with each painful twist of his expression. The stone rippled beneath my cousin's touch like ink, creeping over his hand with sticky fingers that sucked him in. Marek fought back, battering the panel with his flames and quarterstaff, but it was no use. "It's … it's not enough. I can't pull free," he snarled.

Rhaegar and Gavrel grabbed my cousin's torso and shoulders, yanking him out, but the blackness coated his forearm now, dragging him into the wall like quicksand.

My heartbeat filled my ears in time with the pulsing screak of the structure. Panic gripped my bones and vibrated through my limbs. I unleashed my gift, fractured rainbows splintering over me, and breathed in deeply.

Breena pushed her shoulders back, and her shield burned brighter. "Blimey, woman. Take my ember and help 'im!"

My brow crumpled, my mouth hanging open, and hands numb. *I am you, and you are me.* I focused on Breena's ember, and my power purred as it lapped at hers.

Her jaw set as she concentrated, the orb around us sputtering. I looked at Gavrel and Rhaegar, and they nodded. My halo grabbed onto their radiance, too, their light twisting and melting with Breena's as it bled into mine.

I focused, pushing the combined energy through my body and down my arms. The branch patterns zinged and rippled along my forearms, the colors melding as my ember consumed and blended the others' gifts into something new.

Now.

Pulsing in time with my measured breaths, a blaze of iridescence covered my hands. I moved toward Marek and gripped his biceps just as the structure's molten tendrils coated his elbow.

All at once, I forced my power into my cousin's aura. My halo exploded around me, and his was a blazing ebony inferno. He sagged, and a look of astonishment quickly turned into determination as he slammed his enhanced gift into the liquid shadows.

They reared back with a squelching screech, releasing him. The last of my borrowed ember poured into Marek. He forced his power over the wall, which splattered and gurgled in an outward ripple until a tall, undulating opening presented itself to us.

Breena's shield dropped, her power sinking. Without hesitation, we all barged through the doorway. As the screaming mist sucked back into the base, the passage sealed itself with a loud squish behind us.

Mine and Marek's auras fizzled out, and my shoulders slumped, exhaustion pulling at my frame. Marek jammed his staff into the floor, his fist tight as if he would topple over without its support.

The Murk's heavy weight of despair lessened, but a skittering sense of unease took its place across my shoulders.

"This place is fecking exhausting," Breena complained, rubbing her hands over her arms.

Rhaegar turned slowly as he nodded. "The Murk is draining everything more quickly. Our strength. Time. Ember. Best be moving along."

Gavrel and Rhaegar's glowing tattoos and weapons guided us as my sight adjusted to the dimness.

Taking a step back, Rhaegar bumped into something solid. A light flickered within. He spun, his axe swinging into the object, but the glowing blade simply bounced off the glass surface with a clack. "I'll be damned." He retreated, sucking in air as the light within the glass snuffed out.

With wide eyes, we all turned in place, taking in the scene around us. There were countless hovering glass spheres filled with slithering vapor. Sporadically, honey-colored light flashed in each like watching lightning crashing around a storm cloud.

They scattered throughout the massive open space, from floor to ceiling. The midnight-black walls, ceiling, and floor blended seamlessly, making the glass vestibules appear to be giant bubbles frozen in a fathomless, glinting void.

"There's something ... there's something inside." I reached out to the nearest container, and it flickered to life. Its haze twirled agitatedly, weaving with the amber light and pulsing within like a heartbeat.

Mesmerized, I moved closer to get a better look. Suddenly, a hand slammed into the glass from within. I yelped, stumbling. The others flanked my sides, weapons ready.

The older man pushed against his prison; a silent scream carved into his face. He writhed in terror, his eyes glassy and unseeing.

In horrified fascination, the group wandered, observing the prisoners. None of them were aware of anything outside their entombment.

Scenes of intense fear or sorrow surrounded us; people

rocking or curled in a ball. Women tearing at their hair and skin. Men writhing or grasping at their chests. Running, falling, slamming into the glass.

"We need to help them." My whisper echoed through the darkness, bouncing off the globes. In response, my scar tingled faintly. Shadows moved along the edges of my vision, but maybe I was seeing things. The weight of fatigue pulled at my joints, but so did the guilt of not being able to save everyone.

A brief glimmer of empathy flickered across Marek's face— the most I had ever seen from him. Breaking the moment, the look dissolved so quickly that I wasn't sure if I'd imagined it, reminding me of the walls he had built around himself. Marek tapped the orb floating above us, and it lit up with a younger woman within. He frowned. "You're not wrong, but we need to conserve energy if we're to help your friend and figure out a way out of this. Get back to Yaya."

My spine wilted; he was right.

Rhaegar nodded. "We'll devise a plan, but he's spot-on. In our current state ..."

His words tumbled away as he was distracted by the female above us.

"Ancients take me," Breena muttered, staring.

Light hair and clothes fluttered around the young woman as if she were in water. Her limbs sluggishly paddled through the mist until her body jerked, and she pawed at her throat, choking on invisible liquid.

My lungs seized with hers as she drowned, anxiety and memories tumbling through me as she convulsed. Then her limp form hung within the glass for a moment, mist caressing and sticking to her.

I sucked in the breath she couldn't before her form arched painfully back and animated once more. The horrific scene replayed all over again.

"They're trapped in their nightmares," I blurted, panic

tearing at me as my fingers grazed my neck. Images of my near-drowning and Kaden writhing in agony poured over me like icy shards.

Gavrel's brows dipped, understanding in the deep wells of his eyes.

A wisp of movement brought my attention back to the female, my eyelids disappearing under my browbone.

"Everyone, step away. Now!" I snapped; my eyes glued to the thing creeping from the darkness beyond.

The creature was made of night itself. At least seven feet tall, its bony frame stretched thin under a robe made of black shadows with a gauzy veil that draped over its bone-white visage. The netting sank into pits where its eyes, nose, and mouth should have been.

Hovering above the floor, there were no legs under the wispy fumes wavering below, but long, spindly fingers stretched toward the glass we'd been observing. Moving like fog drifting over a twilit horizon, it didn't show any signs of attacking us.

Yet.

Rhaegar's brow rose along with his sword. "Is that what I think it is?"

"Er, stabbing practice?" Breena muttered, mouth dropping open.

Marek stepped toward the creature, but I blocked him with my arm across his torso. "Dream reapers. Don't you recall the stories?"

Breena shook her head, her short hair flicking against her jaw. "Ryn, you know you're the only one who read all the beastie books ever written, yeah?"

Gavrel blinked slowly at her. "They used to tell us bedtime stories about them. They can't see, hear, or smell."

Breena snapped her fingers. "Oh, right. Gran mentioned them once, but stopped when she realized they didn't scare me into behaving."

I moved my head from side to side. "They feed on your night terrors … the crumbs that Phobetor doesn't consume. They won't attack unless they sense a nightmare … or extreme fear."

Head tilting, Breena's mouth twisted. "Still, what if I stab it?"

"Breena." Gavrel narrowed his eyes.

She grinned.

Amusement tugged at my lips. "If you touch them, they'll likely attack."

"Let's move. It looks like more are drawing near."

Within the globe, the woman's nightmare sped up, playing faster on repeat as more bony fingers crept from the dark. Shadow-like cloth dripped from waxen wrists as their brittle phalanges scraped over the glass.

Carefully, we moved, giving the ghouls a wide berth as they sucked in the woman's terror, their filmy veils pulling into the hollows of their skulls.

"You think they stole in through a weakened portal, or someone stationed them here?" Marek pondered.

"Either is likely, but I'm leaning toward stationed. A prison needs keepers," Gavrel responded.

Now that we'd seen the reapers, their presence became clearer. Thank the Ancients, because I didn't want to find out what happened if we bumped into one.

As best we could, we hurried through the darkness, our embers lighting the surrounding spaces. I searched for Kaden within each bubble, and with each face that wasn't his, my heart knocked into my ribcage until I thought it would escape through my windpipe. Unease settled heavily in my belly.

From my side, a glimmer caught my attention. Lava-like silver and smog coiled in the ground to our left. As we approached, we slowed, scrutinizing it. I squinted, following the hazy veins of light creeping from the basin and latching onto every visible globe. Where the tendrils touched, amber energy slurped into the streams.

Numerous reapers drifted in a wide berth around the pool, avoiding it.

The deep line between Gavrel's eyebrows dug into his skin as Rhaegar stood next to him. His second-in-command whistled, air puffing his deep brown cheeks. "That doesn't seem promising."

"It's the same as the dungeon," Gavrel muttered.

My ember whizzed over my body, and I stumbled. Breena held tight to my belt until I steadied myself with my left hand on Marek's raised wrist. His aura flickered around him as well. His eyes were wide as he stared at the molten matter.

Follow.

Startled by the voice—the same one that had led me to the dungeon in Surrelia—my muscles froze, and my eyelids blinked rapidly.

Gavrel's hand warmed my lower back. "What is it?"

I glanced at him with wide eyes. "The voice is back. I'm guessing you didn't hear it?"

Gavrel shook his head, understanding softening his features.

I squeezed my eyes closed. I breathed in, counting several heartbeats, and then exhaled slowly. Everyone else faded away as I envisaged my best friend.

His smirk.

His clover-colored eyes.

His laughter.

How he had once been my rock when I needed stability.

Unbidden, a picture of him arching back on his knees and roaring into the sky flashed behind my eyes.

Follow.

My lids snapped open; my eyes drawn to a cord of radiance brighter than the others. It stretched into the distance to our right. "This way," I urged, turning in that direction, not cognizant of whether the others kept up.

Weaving through the jumble of hovering spheres and

reapers, I followed the bright thread until its fingers fanned out over an orb above. A fist of power thumped into my chest as if a hook latched onto me.

My arms reached for him.

For there was Kaden. Trapped in his torment, back arching just as I dreamed. The sob tore from me as I called his name.

But he couldn't hear me.

And I couldn't hear the cries of anguish so clearly ripping from him.

31

BREAKING THE VICTOR

SERYN

Frantically, my attention snapped to each concerned expression. Breena's mouth puckered to the side as she looked up, studying Kaden's prison.

"Bloody void," Gavrel snarled, stalking in a wide semi-circle, looking for a way to free his brother. Rhaegar moved the other way, studying the angles opposite the commander.

The shadows churned not far off. The reapers were getting curious.

Studying Kaden, Marek blinked several times, his deep blue irises looked almost black. His nostrils flared and, without a word, he backed away several paces, his brawny form slipping into the shadows.

"Wanker." Breena scoffed at my cousin's retreat.

Desperation scraped up my spine as I focused above. Kaden's nightmare had moved along as every muscle in his body stiffened, the veins in his neck bulging. All at once, his body went lax, and he was standing, leaning against the curve of the glass with anguish hanging off his gaunt features.

I'd seen that look before.

When we were thirteen turns old.

The day Hestia was culled.

Was he reliving his mother's death? This place was draining him alive. The sickening realization that Kaden had been suffering for so long tunneled through the marrow of my bones.

Two dream reapers emerged, their skeletal fingers scratching at Kaden's pen.

The slapping of boots sounded behind me, and in a blur, Marek leaped, digging his staff into the floor and vaulting his body on top of a nearby sphere. It wobbled as he steadied himself.

"Not a wanker," Breena muttered, taking back her earlier insult. Her eyes were wide as we watched my cousin leap onto another bobbing globe.

And another. Until he was near enough to Kaden that his quarterstaff could touch the glass.

The creatures were already imbibing, greedy to feed on my friend's pain. A few more began drifting toward their brethren.

Marek's ebony flames flickered around him, and he held one palm out. His ember seeped over his arm in a rolling black fire, shooting forward and over the orb.

His energy wrapped and clung to the bubble like it had over Helos' illusion barrier. Marek bared his clenched teeth, shoulders tensing.

Lurching back, the specters' veils dispersed from their faces like a gust of wind clearing away smoke. Crimson flames flared behind the cavities of their skull-like faces as they hissed.

My pulse skittered, and my iridescent aura twirled around me restlessly.

Marek's dark power throbbed around the sphere, and the

silver streams that had been drinking in Kaden's nightmare recoiled. Their slinking tentacles lashed over my cousin's flames, trying to reattach themselves to the glass.

"Incredible. His illusion ember is confusing it," Rhaegar murmured in awe. "Well done. Bloody brilliant!"

Breena narrowed eyes fixed on Marek. "It's all right, I guess."

And as the lambent edges of his gift neared Kaden's head, my friend's clouded irises brightened into a clear green. He bobbed his head from side to side, and his brows rose as his attention snapped to my cousin. To the reapers scratching furiously at Marek's barrier.

Then, his frantic gaze locked with mine, and my scar throbbed in time with the illuminated branches pulsing and creeping over my arms as I reached for him once more. "Kaden!"

Next to his temple, he slammed his fist repeatedly against the glass, but then Marek's ember enveloped the orb entirely. "Seryn, now would be the time to help!" he bellowed, his scowl digging into his mouth.

I blinked a few times and then focused on the ball of dancing black fire and called upon my ability. It happily obliged as it pumped over me, through my arms, and exited my outstretched fingers.

As it rammed into Marek's flames, a chorus of screeches pierced the air. The reapers tried to scurry into the shadows, become one with them, but my ember latched onto them. Light contracted within each one and then burst like a star. Shadowy ribbons and ash fluttered about.

I pulled a deep inhale into my lungs, coaxing my gift to ignore my cousin's energy and to dig through to the amber light within the glass.

The prismatic glow beneath the boughs covering my arms swelled as if disgruntled. Then heat zipped along my spine, and a rush of coiling light tore through the air, nudging aside the ebony blaze before slipping underneath, where it clung to the orb from below.

Immediately, my ember siphoned the swirling amber, overtaking the bottom half of the orb so the top was a flickering black blaze upon a curling, multicolored cloud of fractured hues.

As the saffron mist seeped out of the globe, Kaden bashed his boot into the glass floor to no avail. I wrenched my ember back, its glow still clinging to the amber energy. It sank into my hands, the burnished light churning through the pattern along my arms.

While it distilled what it had consumed, my aura buzzed against every inch of me. I felt the transformation deep within and breathed in and out several times.

I am you, and you are me.

Sated, my ember purred along my nape, and I took that as my cue to channel the purified energy back to my palms as my fingers weaved a churning ball of light between them.

Glancing at Marek, he nodded, retracting his flames and leaping down the way he'd come. I thrust my hands above me, and my twisting power slammed into the prison with a sharp crack. The glass splintered, fractures rushing over the surface like jagged spiderwebs.

With one last stomp, Kaden's boot broke through the weakened orb. Gavrel jumped toward me as my body slumped, gathered me close, and shielded me from the sprinkle of shards raining down. Kaden dropped and rolled as his feet met the ground in front of us.

"Let's not do that again," Kaden huffed as he stood unsteadily, swatting his hands over his tunic.

On shaky legs, I left Gavrel's embrace and crashed into my best friend, throwing my arms around him. A whoosh of air barged from him as he balanced himself against my assault, and then he squeezed me back. I held him at arm's length and then cupped his jaw. "Kaden," I whispered. "Are you … are you okay?"

He tucked his lips between his teeth, and his brows fell. He looked down for a moment before his gaze slowly met mine, and the skin at the corners crinkled as he pasted a smirk on his face. "Just fine, Ser. Just fine."

I didn't believe him.

He left my hold, greeted the others, and slapped his hand on Gavrel's back as they hugged. Kaden's brows lifted when he noticed the blood smeared across his palm. His eyes shot to his brother.

"What happened?" Gavrel demanded, stepping away and sheathing his sword with the slightest of winces.

"Well, honestly … it's all a blur. Were those … were those dream reapers?" Kaden's aura flickered around him, and he reached for Gavrel's shoulder, pushing his healing clover-hued energy over his brother's injury without a word.

"Unfortunately. Use care while we move." Gavrel rolled his healed shoulder, nodding at his brother with concern and pride etched into his countenance.

I put my hand on Kaden's biceps. "What do you remember, Kade?"

His mouth pinched as he looked up, and then all around us with wide eyes. "Well, one moment I was in the arena, and Gav ran off with you. I was going to play my part as the 'victor,' and then Melina was in front of me, congratulating me on my win. Needless to say, I didn't reap the rewards."

Kaden sighed. "She gave me that rabid smile of hers. Had her Akridais drag me to a dungeon—did you know there was a fucking dungeon under the palace?—and then, I'm not sure. Think she said, 'enjoy your nightmares.' My body was being torn apart, and then I was trapped in that fucking fishbowl. Reliving my worst nightmare over and over." His face sagged for a second and then settled into a mask of indifference. His fingers flexed before he rubbed the base of his head.

"I'm sorry we couldn't get to you sooner," I said, sucking in a breath. I couldn't get enough air. "We—"

"You're here now, and that's all that matters. Let's get the void out of here. Wherever *here* is." His brows lifted as he took in our surroundings.

Gavrel thumped his hand on his brother's shoulder, his eyes squeezing closed for a moment. A relieved breath flared from his nostrils. "Stygian Murk."

"Course we are," Kaden muttered, moving away from the group. "I suppose that's better than being trapped in these things." He frowned, touching a nearby globe. A look of pained sympathy washed over him as he observed the trembling man within curl into a ball.

"We can't stay long, and we … we don't have enough power left to save the others right now and try to escape." I placed my palm on Kaden's wrist, and he focused on where we touched. "Kaden, you should know. You're most likely in your physical body. Yours wasn't in a pod when we returned. They must have pulled it here when you were imprisoned. I … I was in my physical form during the last Dormancy. We all are now."

His brow furrowed as he looked at me and then the others. "I suspected as much when you didn't burst into ash during the Winnowing."

"How abso-fecking-lutely spectacular we all are. Can we move it along?" Breena groused. "Unless we want to be sucked off by these nightmare beasties?"

Kaden rolled his eyes. "Yeah, Breena. That's what we all want."

Breena stabbed her middle finger into the air, aiming it squarely at him.

Rhaegar cleared his throat and shifted his battle axe to his other hand. "The longer we stay, the greater the risk of being trapped." He scanned our surroundings, squinting. Quite a few reapers lingered nearby. "I say we head back whence we came."

"Agree," Marek said.

Kaden studied him as if finally noticing him. "Who the void is this?"

"The guy who saved your dreamy ass," Marek retorted, his sardonic voice a stone dropping to the ground.

"This is Marek Sc—Nightshade." A heavy sigh left me. "My cousin."

Kaden balked. "Your what?"

"For the love of Ancients. Get a move on, people," Breena ordered, marching past us and into the shadows.

Marek pushed his tongue against the inside of his cheek, and Rhaegar's eyes softened as his lips pursed. They both followed Breena's cherry halo.

"We'll look for Maya as we go." Gavrel shifted the strap across his chest and nodded at the others before setting his mouth in a thin line and walking away.

He was giving me the space to be alone with Kaden if I needed it. Even if it hurt him to do so.

My brows pinched at the distance between us, unease festering within me. Would he slip away from me now that we had found his brother?

I rubbed my lips together, following the others, with Kaden silently at my side. He looked haunted; shadows hung on his bottom lash line. What could you say to someone who'd been reliving their worst nightmare?

Nerves fluttered in my stomach. It felt like a lifetime had passed between the Dormancy and now. So much had happened, and I couldn't forget that I'd broken Kaden's heart not long ago. And that mine was undoubtedly entangled with Gavrel's.

Kaden glanced at me as we walked, avoiding looking at or

touching the hovering globes and reapers as we went. "So, what's new?" His words sounded playful, but had a darker edge.

Still, I snorted a dry chuckle, and a brightness flickered through me. It'd been too long since he joked around with me. "I'm more concerned with how you're doing."

"I'll be all right."

"You know I know you're lying."

A small smile curled the corner of his mouth. "It was the day Ma was culled. *Over and over.*" His eyelids scrunched closed for a moment before he sighed. "There's no need to dissect it, Ser. And I don't want to rehash what happened in Surrelia either. My memories weren't wiped, so … yeah. We're fine, and that's that."

I swallowed, a thick lump sticking in my throat. "I'm sorr—"

"We're going to be okay." He rubbed his hand over his chest, digging the palm into his rumpled tunic. It sounded like he was convincing himself, and my heart skipped several beats, trepidation skittering over my neck. He continued, "Now, give me some details."

"Well—Gavrel and I fled home after Akridais were sent after me. Melina realized I wasn't in my astral body. She'd suspected for a while that I … that I might be a Scion. That Mama might have been, too." My fists clenched. "We made it to the Bogs. Met Marek. And his—*our*—grandmother. Phantasos has been helping us this whole time. Taught me how to work *with* my gift. And she said … my mother is alive. She helped us find you."

I let out a shaky breath.

"Damn, Ser." A long exhale puffed out his cheeks. "Give a guy a stiff drink when you blow his Ancient-damned mind."

I gave him a deadpan look. "You asked."

"Yes. Yes, I did. All right, go on." He rubbed his forefinger and thumb over his eyelids.

I nodded, the words tumbling out faster. "The night before the Winnowing, I took one of the Mirage Orchid elixirs Derya had made. I remember everything—from *every* Dormancy. Melina had erased a bunch of my memories, but I have those back now, too. I had three vials left. Letti and Breena each used one. Xeni is with my sister. And Father … He …"

I paused, grabbing his hand.

His brows fell as he narrowed his eyes. I gulped and then continued, "He's part of the Somneia, and he … he's the one who reported Hestia."

Kaden looked away, his jaw clenching so hard I thought his teeth would crack. His nostrils flared as he looked back at me, his aura skittering around him. "That doesn't bode well for him."

"I didn't think it would." It was my turn to look away now. My words were a ragged whisper. "I won't stop you from doing what you need to do."

He squeezed my fingers as we neared the others. At once, Gavrel noticed our interlocking hands, a dulled look sweeping over him. He was putting his shadows back in place.

Gently, I brushed my fingers over Kaden's as I let go of his hand and reached toward Gavrel's. But before I could touch him, all the globes illuminated, soundless screams lining each prisoner's countenance. The muscle within my chest plummeted.

There were thousands of them.

Thousands suffering endlessly.

Thousands of bony specters cloaked in shadows sucking at their terror like leeches.

A few nearby slowly turned their veiled skulls, necks cracking as they gave us their full attention.

My fear was palpable.

Ancients help us.

Far in the distance, the wall where we had entered opened, shrieks spilling into the space once more. I squinted, my vision adjusting to the brightness.

Amber bounced off the platinum sheen of slick hair, black smoke curling around the simpering female. The male Akridai stood beside her. The other appeared glued outside the passage as it closed, her frantic eyes beseeching as the structure's liquefied darkness crawled up her neck.

"They've found us," I whispered, not knowing which monsters I spoke of—living or undead.

32

———

ENOUGH GAMES

SERYN

*M*elina's voice echoed through the prison as the globes dimmed once more. "No need to scurry away. There's nowhere to run anyhow, pet. Have you found your mother? She's around here … somewhere."

Ire and crimson skittered over my flesh.

We wouldn't find Mama now.

"I'm going to stab her eyes out," Breena growled before both Marek and Rhaegar put their hands on her shoulders.

"That's what she wants. For us to react. To come to her. Keep your heads. There's always a way out," Rhaegar reasoned. Breena rolled her shoulders, dislodging the men, and then turned with a huff, gaze scouring our surroundings.

I did the same, eyes locking onto the visible threads of energy flowing from all directions, weaving between glass and ghouls.

If we were near a powerful source of ember, *then the key*

bearer simply has to conjure a destination. Phantasos' words flit through my distress.

"The siphon," I said.

"Worth a shot," Marek mumbled.

Breena let out a sound somewhere between a curse and a roar as she unknowingly stepped behind her into a reaper. Instantly, it dug its bony grip into the back of her shoulders, a trail of inky smoke sucking from her crown and into its shrouded cavities. Within moments, her cherry aura sputtered, her objections falling limply to her boots.

"Bree!" I shouted, fractured rainbows splintering around me. I stumbled, weakened by the excessive use of my power.

The Larkin brothers gripped my biceps on either side, steadying me. With a stern look of concentration, Marek's dark flames scurried over his forearm and poured over Breena. His illusion created a barrier between her and the enraged beast. A shriek followed its veil as it flew up.

"Move!" Marek ordered, his shoulders slumping.

As if waking up, Breena shook her head, jerking away from the demon's hold. On her flesh, bloody stripes were left behind, her tunic torn where the reaper had grabbed her. Baring her teeth, she swung and stabbed her dagger through Marek's embered barrier and into the wraith's robes for good measure. It screeched once more, but her attack only infuriated it rather than harming it.

"Damn it. I told you stabbing them likely wouldn't work," Gavrel groused as we backed away.

"I fecking know, but it made me feel better." She shrugged as Marek's aura faltered. The flames inside her attacker's eyeholes flared as my cousin's illusion dissolved. When they locked on Breena, her bravado slipped a bit, and she darted in the opposite direction.

Boots slapping against the smooth surface, we all bolted as Melina's cloying laughter chased us. We dodged reapers as their veils flew from their carcasses, skulls ablaze from within like pyres, their hisses scraping against our ears.

My halo flickered as Breena's kindled. "No, Ryn. We need your ember to get us out of here."

She, Marek, and Kaden, flung what power they could muster at oncoming reapers. It didn't stop the monsters, but it made them pause, giving us precious seconds.

Nerves buzzed along my spine, my eyes darting as we ran. My thumb brushed against the cool tourmaline of my ring. There were only so many minutes to spare. I could give everyone else more.

I glanced at Gavrel to my right. Dark strands flopped over his forehead, some sticking, others bouncing as we moved. It made him look charming and youthful. He was going to be so pissed off. But it couldn't be helped.

Narrowing his eyes as they met mine, dread already coated his irises as if he knew what I was about to do. I wondered what my tell was.

"I'll meet you there," I rasped. "Promise." He shook his head, reaching for me, but I didn't wait as my thumb ran across my ring. My eyes locked on the cleared space to our left.

His frantic shout evaporated as my body splintered and stretched, the ring burning into my flesh. I concentrated on my destination as my physical and astral forms split and merged and twisted and churned through time and space. Shattered, iridescent streaks followed me through the coiling path. I was a prism.

Nothing.

Everything.

Color, light, and time—all at once and not at all.

Seconds later, I stumbled from the burst of light, arms circling as I righted myself before I smashed into an unsuspecting trio of reapers. My heels dug into the stone as I backed away, glancing around. There, on my side, was another opening.

Again, I transported, missing globes and ghouls by a finger's breadth. An exhale whooshed from me, and sweat stuck to my back as I retreated.

Melina called out my name tauntingly once more. Stiffening my frame, I clenched my fists. "If you want to chat. Come find me!" My shout reverberated and blended with her responding titter, closer now.

I zipped to another location, provoking her, calling her name. And another and another in short bursts. Only traveling to spaces that appeared to offer at least a partially safe landing.

"Now, now, pet." A flash of white rushed at me and blew loosened curls back from my cheeks. "Enough games," Melina hissed as she materialized in front of me.

I jerked away, my mouth contorting, my ember burning over my limbs. Her face slackened, lips parting slightly. I couldn't tell if it was curiosity or fear.

Both.

I didn't care.

"This time I agree, Melina. *Enough games,*" I sneered, thrusting my glowing hands toward her, mustering a small orb of power between my palms, and slamming it into her chest. Stunned, she staggered back, nearly knocking over a reaper who turned slowly toward her, veil flowing upward.

In a blink, I whisked away from her, my ring's ember carrying me. With each landing, I yelled for my friends. For Gavrel. At last, I heard my name—a fragile sound—and I followed it like a prayer answered, while Melina's furious cry pursued me.

Light broke through the shadows just as my stamina was about to give out, and with a final push, I transported to them, hoping I didn't meet any undead skeletons along the way. Gavrel's arms locked around me, catching me before I toppled into the churning pool.

"Damn it, woman. It's not right that I want to both kiss and slap you." Breena grinned from the other side.

Gavrel released me, and I shook my head. "We don't have time. Reprimand me later."

His nostrils flared. In moments of frustration, Gavrel and his brother shared the same expression. Pinched and barely repressing the indignation bubbling under the surface. Ignoring them both, I breathed in, calming the frenetic energy still sizzling inside me as I stepped to the edge.

Without further comment, everyone formed a circle around the basin with me. The reapers stalked around us, an agitated halo of shadow and bone.

Marek and I glanced at each other. I knew he felt the tug within his stomach, as if the molten silver had hooked its claws into us, urging us to sink into the unknown.

Once more, the tourmaline prickled against my left forefinger. I held my hand up, studying it as all our auras and rune tattoos flared.

Surrelia, the deep baritone pushed into my mind.

My eyelids closed; a neon image of the Reverie Weald flashed behind them, and my ring seared my skin, but it barely registered.

I held my hands in front of me, allowing my power to flow over my limbs, bidding it to mingle with the ring's energy and craft some sort of escape like they had in Hallowed End. Hoping I had enough. My eyes opened, and the mist from the pool swirled like a maelstrom, lifting above the silver.

"Come now," Melina's voice skittered over my back. It was less an echo. Closer. "My patience is wearing thin."

My eyebrows scrunched as the liquescent metal pulled into the haze.

At my sides, I took Kaden and Gavrel's hands. The others did the same, grabbing their neighbors until we formed a chain around the spinning mist.

I willed my gift to drink in everyone's aura. Their bodies flinched, but their focus stayed true. Their energies pulsed through me, filtered and condensed until I pushed my palms forward. Not disconnecting, Gavrel and Kaden's grips shifted, wrapping around my wrists.

I pushed my ember into the whirlwind. The silver within snapped angrily, spitting and clawing, trying to escape as it weaved together.

A chilled breeze ruffled my hair. Ice slithered up my spine.

"Enough!" Melina snarled behind me suddenly. My gaze snapped to the Elder as her hair settled around her shoulders, cape fluttering. The shadowy remnants of reapers dissolved on either side of her. Clearly, her ember wasn't as weakened as ours.

I'd let her know when it was *enough*.

Her aura slithered around her, and I whipped my attention back, imagining the vibrant hues of the Reverie Weald, pulse threatening to smash out of my veins.

Her claws sank into my shoulder, black smoke coiling around my jaw. Acid and rage boiled in my stomach, the touch of her ember and skin enraging me.

With a furious scream, I ripped my wrist from Gavrel's hold and raked my nails over her flesh. Shrieking and yanking her hand away, the ring on her thumb gave way. Gavrel's fingers locked around my wrist once more while I clutched the carved tourmaline in my palm.

"Jump!" I roared.

With Gavrel and Kaden's holds tightening, we all leaped into the twisting portal. The whirlwind following us upward, fizzling as Melina's screams and billowing darkness scratched uselessly at the vanishing wisps behind us.

33

AION

SERYN

𝓔xhausted, my eyes blinked open as I looked up at the violet-tinged sky, sunrise already hooking into the clouds. My breath twirled above me in a glittering eddy. The corners of my lips curled.

Surrelia.

A bright glint prodded at my peripheral, demanding my attention. With effort, I sat up, squinting toward the blinding reflection.

My heart fluttered at the sight, the others strewn around me. As we stood, our breaths stirred the air, curling and sparkling around us, and the glow beneath the moss rippled under our feet.

A gleaming city lay ahead of us on the other side of a curving, obsidian coastal cliff.

An ocean of colossal towers climbed up the side of a gently sloping mountain. At the summit, the largest citadel perched. It was entirely gold with a halo of twinkling clouds revolving around the zenith. White opal covered the rest of the semi-translucent edifices, mixing with shimmering, shifting spectral hues as the early light shifted over them. Gold melted over the tip of each tapered spire as if they'd been dipped into the looming fortress at the heart of the city.

A curtain of gushing water spilled over the coastline, hugging the edge of the city and into the ocean far below.

Like the hands of a clock, gilded statues of the Horai circled the perimeter. I'd read about these females. They were the Ancients of Hours who guarded Aion, Surrelia's capital.

I recalled an ink drawing of the beautiful celestials dancing in a circle around a globe, laughing and holding hands. They were the keepers of time. Of the passing seasons.

Kaden shuffled over to me, gently pushing on my chin until my gaping mouth closed. He chuckled and stared off into the distance.

"What have you got there?" His head bobbed to the black stone my fingers fidgeted with.

My eyebrows wiggled. "Melina's ring. It might take her a while to find her way out of the Murk now."

Breena smacked a kiss on my cheek. "You beautiful, devious wench."

Shrugging, I smirked and tucked the ring into my belt satchel.

"Well played, Seryn." Rhaegar came to Breena's other side. "Incredible, isn't it?" He shifted his battle axe on his back. "The first time I saw Aion, I nearly fainted."

"I'd love to see that. You, a big pile of mush and muscles, falling over like a grymwood," Breena snickered, slapping his shoulder while his head swayed from side to side.

Marek rolled his eyes, mouth pinching as his eyes flicked over the Surrelian capital.

"I couldn't have imagined it," I murmured, still in awe of the city's ethereal exquisiteness. Gavrel stepped beside Kaden, his hand resting on his brother's shoulder. He glanced at me, face impassive, and then to the city.

My shoulders dropped as I took in the endless metropolis. It beckoned to me, inviting me to explore the winding streets and nacreous buildings.

This was where the dead ended up. Where their astral bodies found solace throughout the rest of eternity.

At least that's what scriptures proclaimed.

Unless Phobetor collected them and stole them away to the Nether Void.

I glanced at the raging waters below. Maybe the Insomnis Sea was caught between the two clashing realms. A churning threshold, restless and waiting for one of them to cross the line.

After all, the line between dream and nightmare was a thin thread, constantly ready to snap.

WE MADE our way along the coast, the Larkin brothers flanking me. The silence was tense, spongy earth squishing pleasantly under our soles the only sound. The others were far ahead, Breena and Rhaegar's repartee swallowed by the distance. Marek trudged behind them, studying the rippling glow of the moss as they moved.

"All right. Say what you need to," I said, breaking the quiet.

"You could've been—" Kaden was cut off as Gavrel rasped, "Ancients grant me strength with you, Little Star."

Kaden cracked his neck from side to side. "You could've been killed, Ser."

"But I wasn't. And it bought us time." I looked at Kaden, his jaw ticking. "I'm stronger now. My gift and I are one ... and I know that now." I focused on Gavrel. "And you can ask for all the strength you need, but you know I did what had to be done."

Gavrel sighed. "I don't doubt you can handle yourself." He crushed his eyes closed for a moment, rubbing his palm over his chest. "I fear losing you."

My shoulders softened as his lips sealed. He wouldn't say anything more in front of his brother. With a deep exhale, I placed a hand on both of their forearms. "You aren't losing me today."

Gavrel's muscles loosened, and Kaden's tensed a bit before relaxing into my touch. My hands went to my sides, leaving the brothers to their thoughts.

Without any further conversation, we caught up to the others. Within an hour, we stood upon a massive, golden bridge. A gate made of curling aureate posts blocked the entrance. On our left, rushing water spilled under the bridge and into the cascading waterfalls surrounding the city's borders.

As we neared the gates, they glowed white and swung open. No sign of the Horai were present other than their looming likenesses standing guard at the edges of the city.

A twinge of unease shuddered through me. Of course, the Ancients had vanished. This was nothing new. But to think the very Ancients of Time had abandoned us. Were we truly on the edge of destruction? Was Midst Fall's time up?

A gentle swirl of twinkling air spun away from me as I exhaled. Subtler than in the Reverie Weald, but just as mesmerizing.

We wandered through the streets. Lush, glit-leafed trees were scattered about the opalescent cobblestone and buildings. With each shift of sunlight, fragmented hues danced through the opaque surfaces as if the sunrise was caught in the milky moonlit stone.

A pleasant, sweet-smelling breeze teased my senses. I couldn't quite place the scent, but it was nostalgic. Cozy. Like when I used to smell the flowers at home when I ran through hanging lines of freshly washed clothing.

Countless residents went about their business—walking, laughing, chatting, and tending their homes behind round-paned windows. Contentment permeated the air.

Gavrel lifted his chin. "We should find a place to rest."

"And make a plan to sneak into Morpheus' dungeon," I added.

A young female with short, ashen hair approached us. Her voice was welcoming and melodic. "Are you lost? How can I help?"

My breath caught as a set of white wings, with feathers tipped in gold, shifted behind her. They hung delicately from her shoulder blades to her ankles. Her pale robes fluttered about her.

"How'd you know?" Kaden's dimple peeked out as one corner of his mouth curved. He was entirely unbothered by her wings.

Warmth fluttered in my chest. Maybe he truly had moved on. Had forgiven me.

She gave him a sympathetic look, completely oblivious to his charm. "Well, it's my job as an astral guide and all. But new astrals have a look about them. Confused, lost children. The lot of you."

Kaden's mouth fell, and he coughed. "Ah, yes. Well, we're looking for lodgings for the night."

She giggled, her image flickering like a translucent mirage. My eyebrows rose. "For the night? I'll do you one better. How about forever? You fresh ones slay me. Come this way. My name's Wren, by the way."

As the guide turned, I tucked my lips inward, suppressing my humor, and shared an amused look with Breena. She grinned, holding her finger to her lips.

No one bothered to tell our guide that we weren't deceased yet.

"Nice try," I teased, bumping my shoulder into Kaden.

He gave me a halfhearted smile. "Bit rusty, I guess."

I gave him a side hug, and he tensed. My arm dropped, letting the awkward silence creep between us as we walked.

Wren led us to a tucked-away courtyard nestled between a circle of buildings. "This is a community space, so feel free to enjoy it whenever you please."

She waved her hand to the back corner where a wide, golden table overflowed with colorful foods and drinks. "Eat if you wish. Most astrals still enjoy mortal comforts. And why not, I say."

My gaze roamed over the dream-like space, a gentle peace settling over my shoulders. Was Yaya here? "Excuse me, but have you heard of a woman named Neoma Nightshade arriving in the last days?"

Marek stepped forward, head tilting and tongue running over his teeth. Wren looked up at the sparkling, clear sky. "No, I don't believe so. If I hear any news of her, I will let you know. Family?"

My hands fisted. "Yes." If Yaya wasn't here, there was still hope that she hadn't been executed.

Stay strong, grandmother.

With a kind smile, she crooked her finger at a young male with wings, standing by the food table. He straightened instantly and hurried over, placing six gold decagon-shaped coins in her palm. She smiled, and his cheeks flushed as he bowed and went back to his post.

"Here are your room keys. Just slip them in the door and in you go." She pointed to the building to our left and then placed the metal, engraved with a number, in each of our hands. Gavrel's room was next to mine.

"If the rain doesn't bother you, there's a beautiful ceremony tonight at Morpheus' citadel celebrating Selene and the Budding Moon. She did so love the rain. Said it reminded her of renewal and new beginnings." Wren sighed.

"You knew the Moon Ancient?" Rhaegar asked, his tone full of wonder.

"Of course. The Ancients used to visit Aion regularly."

My eyes widened. "They don't any longer?"

"No." Our guide paused, eyes narrowing. "But it's widely believed that they went into hiding and are staying close to their realms or sources of ember as a way to preserve themselves. When the mortal realm was cursed, more and more mortals stopped believing or died off. And without acolytes to worship them"—she snapped her fingers, her body flickering between solid and see-through—"Ancients cease to exist."

"I've heard that Ancients can't wander for very long away from their ember source. What would happen if, let's say, a mortal were trapped in Surrelia ... in their physical form?"

Wren's eyes rounded, her pert nose crinkled. "What an odd one you are. Luckily for you, that isn't an issue. Because if you were here in your physical form ... well, you'd have about a month before the aether claimed you. Kosmos has its limits, and neither mortals nor Ancients can outwit it."

I guessed as much from what Phantasos had said. We'd have to find a way out of here before Khaos destroyed us all.

34

COUSIN

SERYN

*U*nbothered, Breena slapped her thighs. "What a bloody travesty. Well, I'm going to freshen up and nap before I cease to exist. Toodles."

"Wait a moment. I'll come with you," I stated, rummaging through my belt satchel until I found the last vial.

Turning to Kaden, I put the powered tonic in his hand. "This is for you. Mix a drop of your blood in and drink it within the next couple of days. All your memories from previous Dormancies will come back, but it'll knock you out for a bit."

"Don't forget the headache. And the regrets," Breena chimed in.

"You'll have a raging headache afterward. Likely not worse than when you've enjoyed a night of mead."

His smile didn't reach his eyes as he lifted the container to his eyes before tucking it into his pocket. "Thanks, Ser."

My mouth tipped up at the corners as I looked at Gavrel. It seemed a lifetime ago since I'd felt his skin against mine, even though it was just yesterday. But so much had happened in such a short amount of time. I reached for his hand and ran my thumb over his rune tattoo. It warmed under my touch. "Why don't you two catch up?"

The weight of Kaden's glower settled over me as he followed my thumb's path, and with a sigh, I reluctantly released my hold on his brother.

I'd have to speak with Kaden about Gavrel and me. About any lingering resentment he might have. I wanted my friend to work through whatever he needed to, but I wouldn't hide what I felt for Gavrel either.

The commander closed his eyes for a moment, arm dropping, before they moved toward the food table with Rhaegar.

Marek went toward his room, a deep frown furrowing his brow, his footsteps heavy on the cobbles. I watched him walk away, our unspoken thoughts fading into the distance. Was he thinking of what had happened to Yaya?

I'd no doubt that she was culled or imprisoned. My hands fisted at my sides.

Another wrong. Another fresh wound upon my already lacerated heart. During the last Dormancy, Melina had laughed as she likened Elder Strom and Guust's minds to scabs she kept picking, as she erased their memories over and over.

She enjoyed causing pain.

Delighted in the suffering of others.

But what did it say about me that I understood?

That I would relish Melina's agony?

By the Ancients, I didn't bloody care what it said about me.

"I'm going to end her," I snarled.

Breena's brows rose. "I thought Wren was quite nice. Eh, well, I'll help you hide the body, but the wings might be a problem. Maybe she'll just turn to dust." She tapped a finger against her mouth in thought.

I cuffed her on the arm with a wry chuckle. "Appreciate the support, Bree. But I'm talking about Melina."

"Ah, even better. That twat-wafer needs to go."

My shoulders sagged, and Breena wrapped her arm around my waist as we moved toward the tower before us. "Yaya is the toughest broad I've ever met. She'll either berate her captors to death or haunt them into eternity. Either way, she'll make them pay." She squeezed me tighter. "As will we."

With a watery smile, I paused and wrapped her in a hug. She rubbed my back and then turned me by the shoulders, pushing me through the entrance to the building.

Our rooms were on the ground floor down a long hallway that curved along the circular bend of the tower. The floors were made of smooth opal slabs.

"Do you think of your Gran often?" I murmured.

The hollows under Breena's cheekbones sucked in as she nodded. "Yeah. She would've liked this place. I'm sure she didn't go down without a fight either."

I thought of my friend's ashen face in the Stygian Murk last autumn as she'd mentioned finding her grandmother's husk. A shade had consumed the poor woman before she could find her way to the Surrelian portal. It was likely that her astral body eventually turned into one of the shadow beasts as well.

"If she's as fierce as her granddaughter, I've no doubt." I took her hand in mine, and one corner of her mouth lifted.

The Dreamreaper's angry red claw marks still scored each of Breena's shoulders—four vertical lines on either side.

"Why didn't you let Kaden heal you?" I asked.

She shrugged. "I've had worse. Makes for a good story, eh?"

She looked up, blinking away the subtle wetness lining her lower lashes. "So, how are things with Kaden, the man-child?"

Snorting, I lifted my shoulders. "I'm not sure. He says we're fine, but I know he's lying. He still hadn't forgiven me before the end of the Winnowing Trials."

"You're a good friend, Ryn, but don't get lost in the muck. Is it a shame your relationship didn't grow into more than smooshing private bits?"

"I—"

"No. The correct answer is no. You and Gavrel give off more heat than a fecking volcano. And while I can understand how that'd be a tug on the bollocks for Kaden, he'll get through it. You can feel however you damn well want to. Derya wasn't wrong. Living is messy. Love is messier."

A flame wavered within me, and I pressed my tongue to my inner cheek.

Breena smirked. "Yeah, I said love. You bloody know it deep in your womb."

My eyes rolled as I waved my hand at her. "Tell me about what's going on between you and my cousin."

Her mouth went taut, eyes looking down the hall. "Ah, dodgy. Well played, my friend. But the answer to your question is nothing. Our brains loathe one another, but our bodies ... not so much. We haven't introduced our bits, if that's what you're thinking; more like wrestled until we came to our senses."

One of my eyebrows rose, my mouth twisting. "And what's the story behind this extreme aversion?"

"Damned if I know. I'm fecking delightful." Her bottom lip pushed forward. "I met him turns ago when Rhaegar recruited me to the cause. Riled up is Marek's constant state of existence. As soon as I enter the room, the stick up his arse shoves deeper."

I turned, laughing. "Perhaps you should make it your mission to find out why."

"He can keep his stick and his secrets," Breena huffed.

"Whatever you say, Bree."

My room was a few doors away from Breena's. I pulled out my room coin and slid it into the glowing slot above the metal knob. With a click, the door unlocked.

Before heading to her accommodation, Breena squeezed my fingers. "Ryn, I'm happy to know you. To remember you."

Before I could respond, her chin dipped, and she marched off to her quarters.

A grateful smile lingered as I went into my room. It vaguely reminded me of Morpheus' palace, but with a fireplace, a small sitting area in front of the hearth, and black silk sheets on the four-poster bed. The opal floors and walls shifted in the sunbeams in shades of coruscating aqua, pinkish-orange, and chartreuse. It was like walking through a refracted cloud of rainbows.

Tranquility enveloped me, pushing on my muscles from all sides. As if floating, I moved to the nacreous tub in the corner and turned on the faucet.

There was a hazy white globe hovering next to the basin, and I didn't hesitate to brush my fingertips over it.

A gentle, pulsing glow suddenly emanated from the orb, and a hauntingly beautiful melody echoed in my mind. Its other-worldly chords flowed through every part of me, as if a celestial enchantment were seeking out the bruised areas of my soul that needed healing.

With a shuddered sigh, I undressed and sank into the fizzing bubbles. A slightly citrusy, floral aroma drifted through my body as I washed. I reclined, letting sleep take me while the ethereal harmonies, scents, and water soaked into my aching limbs and ravaged soul.

WITHIN THE HOUR, I awoke, rejuvenated. After drying off, I wandered over to the armoire nestled in the opposite corner near the bed. Not one to question the mystical ways of Aion, I shrugged and opened it. Inside were various pieces of clothing, all in my size. I chose a silky copper-colored slip dress and sighed as the cool fabric slid down my body.

I turned toward the door at the sound of someone knocking. Thinking it was Gavrel, I opened the door with a bright smile, but the sullen line of my cousin's mouth met me.

"Marek, how dashing you look with clothes on," I teased, repressing the outward expression of amusement. I reached for him, resting my fingertips on his forearm. He flinched at the contact, so I withdrew my hand. "Come in."

He hesitated, stepping back into the hall. "No, I …" He looked down, his ruddy waves curtaining his high cheekbones. "… I just came to check on you."

My arms wrapped across my middle. "That was kind of you. I'm all right. What about you? Are you thinking of Yaya?"

He winced. "Yes, but I'll be fine. With all the things you've learned in the past days, I can imagine it's been … difficult."

My heart cracked a bit as I studied him. *My family.* I still couldn't believe it, but it was burrowing within the concept of my identity. Who I once was, and who I was becoming.

I gathered a lungful of air and let it flow from me slowly. He waited patiently, eyes assessing me. Like he did everything. He was all sharp edges and pent-up shadows, but he was here, making an effort.

For all we knew, I was the only family he had left. "It has … been trying, but it's the same for you. For all of us."

His jaw ticked, and he held his tongue to the inside of his cheek as if to stop the pulse of it. "She'll make it. I know she will, and we'll be there to see her free."

Swallowing, I offered him a weak smile, and I swore the seam of his mouth wobbled. "Marek, I … I am thankful to call you my kin, and I hope … I hope to get to know you and our family history better. Would that be all right?"

His shoulders slumped. It was a rare bit of softness in him. "In time, cousin. I will share what little I know, but for now, let's focus on surviving the next part of the prophecy. I can almost hear Yaya chastising us for dragging our heels."

A wry chuckle left me. "Same, and if one of us is the Scion, my vote is for you."

His eyebrows furrowed. "I would gladly give the honor to you."

"We'll let the Fates decide. If they're in their cups like you often think they are, it'll be entertaining to see what happens."

He shook his head, the side of his mouth finally curving upward. I wasn't sure if it was the start of a smile or a grimace, but I'd take it. As he turned to leave, my heart flipped, and I had the strongest urge to hug him. To seal whatever invisible bond had taken shape.

Before I thought better of it, I cast myself into his arms, giving him a tight hug. For a moment, his large body stiffened before he tentatively wrapped his arms around me.

"See you soon, cousin," I said, squeezing his arms before releasing him. This time, he didn't flinch.

He pulled at his collar, nodded while looking down the hall, and then strode away, tugging at the sleeves of his tunic.

35

THE JESTER AND THE MOON

GAVREL

Kaden stuffed his face with all the courtyard feast had to offer. Mostly, he was acting like himself, but his gaze—his tone—had an edge to it. He was currently gulping down a goblet of honey wine.

"Doing all right, brother?" I asked, chewing on some type of berry.

He shrugged. "Don't worry yourself on my account. Thank you for coming for me, though."

"Always." I thumped my hand on his shoulder twice. "I'm glad you're safe. You had me worried."

Staring off into the distance, his head bobbed, and he took another sip. "You think Ma is here?"

My brows furrowed, and I shook my head. "I honestly don't have faith that she is. Culling doesn't seem ..."

"I know, but there's always a chance." He sighed, glancing at me. "What's our next step? I know you've got some sort of plan. Don't deny it."

With a heavy exhale, I briefed him on what we'd gone through during our time in the Perilous Bogs and the prophecies leading the Korax's cause.

"Seryn's work with the Augur—Phantasos—was invaluable. She's stronger than she knows." I scrubbed my fingers over the stubble lining my jaw. "And now, learning of her lineage and newfound family, I have no doubt she'll conquer any obstacle in her path. I suppose we're all ravens now."

One of my brother's eyebrows quirked. "Damn. How's she taking it? Not being a rebel. Ancients know she was born for it. A Nightshade, though? That must've been a shock, and that Marek fellow, he seems like a good time."

I grunted.

"That fun, eh?" He chuckled, and the sound made my lips lift along the seams.

"She stopped at nothing to find you, you know. I ... I'm grateful you're here ... with us."

My brother's head bowed, and he rubbed his palm along his nape. Kaden puffed his cheeks out. "I suppose the next step is to figure out a way into that dungeon. Since you've gone and become a right rebel." He wiggled his fingers at me. "So, we destroy this rock. Then what? There has to be a backup plan. I mean, you can't tell me this entire thing rests on the back of some prophecy. Depends on the word of an Ancient. What have they ever done for us? Bloody fuck all is what."

"You're not wrong."

"So, we make some plans. We take the offensive. We fight." His eyes lit from within. Just a flicker. But it was more than I'd seen since we'd rescued him.

"Then we fight, but we do it with strategy. Without impulse," I conceded. "We discussed missions with Neoma and Marek, tactics that would take us to the Pneumalian deserts, Ourea Peaks, and Pyria Island. All the least inhabited areas are where the Korax has its strongholds. Where they recruit and make headway. If we can gather our forces, we can decide where to strike first. Where it makes the most sense."

His shoulders slumped. "Fine. Dungeon first. Stratagems next. Destroying the Elders last. I know you're right, but it doesn't mean I have to like it."

Shifting my baldric, I rolled my eyes, and he snorted, staring at his feet.

He pushed his shoulders back, chewing slowly. "Something going on with you and Seryn?"

My chin pushed upward, jaw ticking at the swift change in topic.

"You can tell me, you know."

My heart knocked against my chest, and my jaw tightened. "Kaden—"

"Sure, she ripped my heart out. But she never promised she wouldn't." With a sardonic chuckle, he rubbed his palm against his collarbone.

"Mind your tongue when you speak of her," I warned, eyes narrowing.

His expression pinched with a look somewhere between guilt and pigheadedness. "I often suspected there was something between you. Two summers ago, especially. I was bloody sure of it. But then … nothing. I'm not as oblivious as you think, Gav."

"I don't think—"

He interrupted, his words rising with the color of his cheeks. "I know what you think. What you *all* think. Kaden, the jester." He tossed the bread he'd been eating on the table. "Well, I'm finished being everyone's joke. Let's figure out how to destroy the bloody Elders." He drank from his cup and then pointed it at me. "And then you and my best friend can ride off into the sunset."

His goblet clinked against the metal table as he strode away.

Confusion and frustration rippled over me.

Seryn had ended things with Kaden. That much, I was sure.

But seeing them together again. Did she have second thoughts? Was she questioning our relationship?

She sure as void would when she finally learned everything.

But this wasn't the time or place.

And I ... I couldn't tell her even if I wanted to.

You damned failure.

My fists clamped around the leather strap on my chest.

I couldn't bring myself to regret what Seryn and I had done. I wouldn't apologize for any of it. What we had ... it was everything.

Yet, his reaction wasn't my brother's typical outburst. It lacked heat. It was more ... subtle. Laced in regret and despondency.

Kaden had gone into that glass prison as himself. But now, something had finally splintered within him. Or maybe he'd come out more himself than he'd ever been.

Frustrated, I shoved my hands in my pockets, looking up at the cerulean sky. Cool stone met my fingers.

A spark lit within me, trying to carve through the murky shadows. A faraway smile curving across my mouth.

Seryn's talisman.

LATER THAT DAY, we gathered together for dinner and then wandered the streets toward the citadel. Twilight painted the sky in shades of cerise and electric orange. Kaden was to my left, and Seryn on my right. Her shiny curls cascaded down her back, reflecting the burnished copper of her dress.

My fingers itched to burrow within the fiery strands and then glide over her curves to check if the dress was made of liquid, since it looked like it had been poured over her. Instead, I offered her my elbow, the silvery sheen of my overcoat shifting over my joints.

We all wore borrowed clothing in varying metallic shades as if we were a collection of precious metals.

The astrals seemed content. Chatting, wandering, living their eternal dream. Something stirred within me, seeing that such peace could follow a life well-lived.

"If the Elders live in Morpheus' palace through the turn, then they likely have some Order unit or perhaps their most trusted Akridais guarding it," I noted.

In front of us, Breena flipped a small dagger in the air, catching it by the hilt as it twirled. I raised a brow at the rough, healing wounds on her shoulders—cleaned but still inflamed. She wore them with quiet pride, a sharp contrast to her usual brashness.

"What if we find a way from below? Like we did during the trials? There were plenty of underground tunnels under the training field." she offered.

Seryn's eyes lit up. "You beautiful genius, Bree."

Next to Seryn, Rhaegar's lips pursed. "But how do we get to the other side without being seen? We can't very well march over the bridge and start climbing down the cliff face. Trying to enter by the sea is surely asking for Poseidon to claim us."

"At least we'll already be in Surrelia then," Kaden muttered. He'd been quiet since we reconvened, his fingers kneading his temples. I studied him from the corner of my eye, concern etched between my brows.

I leaned toward him. "You all right?" I whispered.

"Took the bloody tonic."

Across my chest, Seryn reached for him. My brother waved her away. "I'll be fine. Don't fret."

Her arm dropped, along with her smile. I shot a frown in my brother's direction, irritation churning in my chest, but he didn't notice. I kept my thoughts sealed behind the tight line of my mouth.

"What if we flew?" Marek muttered from behind us.

"What are you on about? Did you eat the ambrosia? I told you *all* not to eat the ambrosia. It makes mortals lose their fecking senses," Breena scolded.

No one bothered asking how she knew that. The woman was a wellspring of random bits of information.

Marek closed his eyes, nostrils flaring. He'd left his quarter-staff in his room and donned a platinum-colored tunic and gray breeches. Evidently, he didn't find this place to be a threat, and he was being respectful of the impending ceremony. "Earlier, I saw a man flying on a Pegasus. This place isn't in short supply of winged creatures."

I cupped my jaw. "We've had more impractical ideas. I suppose it's something."

"Indeed." Marek scoffed.

"Indeed," I echoed in the same tone, hoping it was like a splinter under his skin.

Kaden and Seryn shared a wry look, and that annoyed me even further. When did I get so damned petulant?

Huffing, I seized Seryn's hand in mine and pushed ahead, marching up the twisting stairwell leading to the citadel. Kaden's glare dug into our backs.

"Gavrel," she groused. She sounded tired. "What's gotten into you?"

My pace slowed, and we let the others pass us on their way up. "I'm sorry. It's … it's difficult seeing you with my brother. I'm relieved that he's safe, but something is off. And I don't know what to do about it."

"I'm not sure there is anything we can do. But he knows we're more than friends. Yes?" She cupped my cheek.

My eyes searched hers. "He mentioned something along those lines earlier."

"Well then, it would seem the hard part is done. I'll talk with him."

I glanced up the stairs at my brother's slumped form as he climbed. It was as if he carried a heavy weight on his back.

What I wouldn't give to carry some of his burden.

If only he'd let me.

I shook my head and ran my fingers through my hair as we continued.

At last, we entered the citadel. By the looks of its wide expanse and the ten colossal pillars marking the vertices at the edges, I was sure it was shaped like a sacred decagon from above. Citizens poured in from every side, slipping between the columns in steady waves.

In the center was an enormous pile of flowers in all shapes and colors. As people arrived, they knelt at the base of the mass, bowing their heads reverently, placing their offering among the others, and then raising their hands toward the open sky.

The golden spire we'd seen from a distance had split open like a bursting star, the glinting vertices bent back to reveal the aether and glittering halo cloud above. The moon's radiance spilled into the holy space.

Hovering embered lights scattered above the open pinnacle. They looked like suspended, sparkling stars visiting from the blackened sky. As Seryn swayed, a haunting melody drifted, its ethereal notes caressing invisible strings. Dreamily, she smiled at me, and I rubbed my palm against my scar, ensuring that my heart still beat.

It did.

But only for her.

Only ever for her.

She took my breath away.

After running her thumb over my tattoo, she slipped away toward my brother.

They needed time. And space. So, I'd give them that. I'd give her anything. I stood back and distracted myself with the rituals playing out before us. People prayed and sang and danced.

Several astral guides, including Wren, filled gilded baskets with flower offerings and then flew high into the dome, tossing the flowers about. As they dropped to our feet, the gentle rhythm of raindrops filled the sanctuary.

The rain spilled around the outside of the citadel, but despite the open turret, the showers didn't fill the inside of the sacred space. The night sky was clear, the glittering halo marking the boundary of the downpour.

"Exquisite. Isn't it? I'm pleased." The young woman's voice slid over me like a song. Her silver hair drifted about her delicate frame, and she offered me a kind smile. "I loved another once." She looked at Seryn, whose pale skin was radiant. "Endymion and I yearned to be together forever, but it didn't work out as expected. It never does when the Fates are involved."

My pulse ticked in my jaw, goosebumps rippling over my flesh.

"But we take what we can. He slumbers eternally, and I visit him every night."

Wistfully, she sighed. "You know something of longing, I think. You have the look of it. Breathe in every moment you can, for you never know when the tides will pull you under."

"Um, pleasure to meet you, Miss ...?" I paused, turning to find her. She'd disappeared.

From above, Wren drifted to me, a look of veneration shining in her eyes as her wings relaxed. "What a blessing."

"It's a beautiful ceremony," I agreed, still looking for the young woman.

She giggled. "I meant your visitor."

My eyebrows lifted.

"Don't you know who you were just chatting with? Oh, of

course you don't. You're too young." She gave me an incredulous look.

I shook my head.

"Selene. She hasn't graced us in nigh a century. The offerings must have pleased her. Oh, I wish I could've communed with her before she left." She looked at the shining moon, kissed her palm, and raised her hand toward the night.

"Excuse me. Are you saying that I was just talking to the Moon Ancient?" I scoffed.

"What a blessing," she repeated, pumping her wings and soaring among the other guides, whispering and pointing in my direction.

Wide-eyed, I stared at my boots and scraped my fingers through my hair. More and more Ancients were coming out of hiding. And I wasn't sure if that was an omen or a boon.

Before my mother passed, I had a healthy skepticism regarding the Fates and their prophecies. I figured that if the Ancients didn't intervene in saving Midst Fall, they didn't deserve my prayers. So, I made decisions and dealt with the consequences because no one was coming to save us.

To save the people I loved.

My eyes searched for Seryn among the flowers and the dead.

Yet here these celestials were, invading our dreams. Offering guidance. Popping in for a bloody chat.

With an exasperated huff, a sharp twinge tugged along my ribs. Warily, I caught sight of Seryn and my brother. Unease shivered up my back, breaking through the tranquility and musings this place had cultivated within me.

Seryn recoiled as a look of frustration whittled over Kaden's features. She shook her head, curls bouncing over her shoulders.

My pulse slammed against my scar, and my blood squeezed through my veins as if a string was constricting the wild muscle thrashing behind my ribs, trying to cut its way through the meat of it. Seryn's hand pressed against her sternum.

His arm flung out in my direction, words tumbling from him freely. Desperation and agony contorted his face.

Seryn said something, her shoulders slumping, fists clenched.

Kaden looked like a cornered animal, his eyes darting, searching for a way out.

She held up her hand and then left him there.

Listlessly, Seryn wrapped her arms around her middle, shoulders imploding, eyes hollow and burrowing into mine.

Time stopped. I held my breath.

And the look she gave me—it stabbed into my gut and tore its way through my hopes and dreams of our future. The look she gave me indicated I'd broken my vow. That the Ancient of Nightmares would steal me away from this most sacred of places.

Because I'd done it again.

I'd shattered her heart.

And I felt every jagged piece as it carved through mine.

36

THERE'S ALWAYS A CHOICE

SERYN

I'd gone to Kaden to check on him, to rebuild our friendship stone by stone.

But it was going terribly wrong.

He was trying to hurt me, lashing out because *he* was hurting. The splinters of his pain wedged between my ribs.

"Gavrel and I … We're taking things day by day. Two turns ago, we'd been *something*. I think you know that."

Kaden's mouth pulled taut, jaw jutting forward. "I suspected. Well, I wish you all the luck—I'll even toss in a prayer to Tyche, just for you. Glad to have been your training dagger."

I flinched as if he'd slapped me. "That isn't fair, Kade. I miss you. I'm sorry for hurting you. I … I don't want to lose you."

"I told you then, what happened between us—how I felt— was on me. I know it, but it'll take me some time to process … everything. You don't have to keep going on about it." He crossed his arms.

"I want to be here for you and to know that we'll be all right."

I put my hand on his wrist, and he dropped his arms so that he slipped through my fingers.

"Ser, I don't know what you want me to tell you." The clover hue of his eyes sparked as he sighed. "Do you want to know that I'm pissed off? That I'm confused? That you picked him? That my fucking heart is a sieve, and I'm drowning in my own bloody resentment and regret. Ancients damn it!" he barked.

A few citizens looked our way, and I tucked some strands behind my ear. Panic and anger bubbled in my belly. My breaths were short and desperate as my lungs constricted.

I inhaled, digging my nails into my palms.

Enough.

"I care about you. I know you're hurting. I'd give anything to take that from you. But I'm done apologizing for what I feel. And if you recall, you asked that very thing of me not too long ago," I retorted. "Or was that a lie?"

His head jerked back as if I'd struck him. Mouth pursing, he whipped his arm toward Gavrel. "He's the liar—the one you *chose*. But the joke's on you because you never even had a choice. Just like my parents. And you'll die for it."

I narrowed my eyes at him, fingers stretching irritably as my heartbeat pounded against my nape.

"It's bloody true. Now that I remember *everything*." Closing his eyes, he let out a hard sigh. He pushed his palms over his brow and through his messy hair and then flung his arms down.

"Melina did something to me. Maybe she thought I'd escape eventually, and she didn't want to risk the truth. You know how obsessed she is with Gav. But she took a memory from before Ma was culled. I was thirteen, and I overheard them arguing. Ma had a dream. Said that my brother had to bury a rune above his heart." He pressed the base of his palm into his, and my own lurched. "You want to know why, Ser?"

I shook my head, ember and goosebumps skittering over my skin.

"I'll tell you anyway. To block your bond. Your fucking *fated khorda* bond." He spat the words at my feet as if they tasted bitter. "I always thought that my parents were fated. You could see it in their eyes. Could see it the day my father died, not long after Ma. He wanted to go to her. To be near her again."

I stopped breathing. Laughter and music flicked around us as my mind crumbled within my skull. A flicker of something akin to regret and trepidation tapped at the back of my ribs. Something that wasn't my own, a shadow that slipped in when I wasn't paying attention. I turned to look behind me as if someone were there, but Kaden's barbed words stung me. My torso slumped as I regarded him, waiting for the stone to smash into my back.

"And Gavrel did it, didn't he? He buried that rune above his heart. Then ran off and joined the Order, never wanting what the Fates had planned for you." Again, he swung his hand out toward his brother. "Yet you chose him anyway."

"Kade, you know I didn't know, but it doesn't change what happened between us. We wouldn't have been more even without ..." Something he'd said pecked at my temple. My mouth fumbled as I fisted the hem of my tunic. "You know ... you *knew*. When?" I whispered raggedly.

He rubbed one hand along the back of his neck. "Maybe it didn't change us, but it definitely didn't help the—" He stopped mid-sentence. "What did you say?"

"When did she take that memory?"

He stepped back, licking his lips. "Right before she tossed me in that nightmare prison," he admitted quickly, voice raised.

I swallowed, bile rising in my throat. "So, you both knew all along. You *both* kept this from me?"

Pinching his lips together, his face fell. For one moment, he looked as devastated as I felt. But then he crunched his eyes closed before slipping his mask back in place. "Ser, I—"

I held a shaky palm up and left him among the scattered flowers.

I'd never known him to be cruel. But he wasn't himself now. He hadn't been for a while.

Numbly, I stared at my boots, thoughts slamming around my mind.

Gavrel's scar.

His secrets.

He'd *known*.

My best friend had kept something so monumental from me. Why? Because he was envious? Because he was terrified of losing us if one of us died … like everyone else he loved?

Fated Khorda.

Whatever threads were holding me upright snapped, and I curled in on myself, arms wrapping around my center to hold myself together.

Slowly, my gaze locked with Gavrel's. Surely everything I felt—the riot of confusion and doubt and grief—poured at his feet.

His breath hitched, the deep line between his eyebrows severe. He stepped toward me, but I stepped back.

I wished I could just vanish. Fly into the aether and burn alive like a star. Raze the feelings that had festered within me over the turns. Even when Melina had tried to snatch them away.

Because there was no doubt that I loved Gavrel.

I loved him.

Loved him so much I wanted to tear my bloody heart out of my chest and tuck it behind his ribcage for safekeeping.

Gavrel winced as if he'd felt the surge of my emotions.

But he'd broken his vow again. Hadn't he?

Did I *ever* have a choice?

There's always a choice, Ser. The Fates can bugger off, Letti had once said. Ancients, I missed my sister. I wished she were here. But the only one here was Gavrel. And he was holding my bleeding soul in his palm while it slipped through his fingers.

Bitterness swelled over my tongue.

He was an Ancients-damned liar.

He never truly wanted me.

He had rejected and toyed with me all these turns.

I sucked in the sweet air and pushed my shoulders back. As I moved toward him, his chest rose and fell fitfully.

My eyes narrowed as I stood before him, anger fizzing over my spine. I opened my mouth to speak, but nearly choked on the sob clogging my throat.

He reached for me. "Little St—"

I held up one hand, blocking him. "Don't you dare. Don't you dare touch me."

Hundreds of people flit about, but it could've been just the two of us for all I cared. My hands trembled, and I shook them out, agitated by the sign of weakness. Spinning away, I rushed outside into the blessed rain and down the stairs.

He followed, grabbing my wrist and turning me to face him. Rain streamed down his jaw as if the Ancients were pouring their tears down his beautiful face, attempting to wash away the deception.

My chin lifted, and my eyes bore into his. "Kaden told me about your talisman." I poked my finger into the thickened skin under his tunic, and a zing of energy poked at my skin. "About how upset you were to find out we might be *khorda*." I spat out the last word.

Shame settled over his features, wide shoulders drooping.

"Seryn, I wanted to—"

"I don't want to hear it. This is the last time I'll allow myself to be broken by you."

He cupped my cheek, but I turned away from his touch as if it burned my flesh.

"Please. I couldn't—" he pleaded, but I was drowning in pain. He couldn't save me this time.

"Enough," I sobbed, my tears mixing with the rain. "My heart can't take it."

And then I ran, just like Gavrel had done so many times before.

The further I got from him, the more the thread wrapped around my ribs constricted.

But I didn't care.

It was my turn to flee.

37

PENANCE

GAVREL

I knew she'd find out the truth eventually.
And that it wouldn't come from me.
I'd lost her, and I fucking deserved it.
This was my penance.

38

BIG GIRL BREECHES

A soft knock sounded at my door. Uncurling from my side, I brushed my fingers over my face and through my hair. Moonlight danced through the window, accompanied by the pattering rain. It filled me like a hollow vessel left out in a storm.

When I reached the door, I opened it a crack. Breena booped me on the nose. "Thought you might need a chum," she commiserated as I let her in with a sad smile.

She plopped herself on my bed, and I lay next to her. We stayed like that, letting the rain serenade us, for a while.

I turned on my side. "Thank you for being here."

Breena sat cross-legged, and propped her elbows on her knees. "Of course I'm here. And which brother do I have to stab?"

I snorted and then pressed my palms over my eyes. "Kaden told me he overheard his mother and Gavrel arguing when he was younger. About Gavrel being my ... my fated khorda. And he kept it from me all these turns. Gavrel, too." My heart flopped against my chest. "He did something to block the bond. Put a rune in his chest."

Breena's head dropped. "I can't say I'm surprised about you two being bonded, but, hot damn, woman. That must've been a shot in the tit."

My hand rested over my heart. "Right in it."

She rubbed my knee, mouth twisting. "I'm sorry, Ryn-Ryn. I'm sure Kaden isn't fitting into his big boy pants yet either. If you want me to cause physical harm, just say the word."

A chuckle burst from me at the hopeful glint in her eyes. "No need. Who made you so stabby, my friend?"

She poked my side. "First off, I was born this way. Second, that's a bit 'dagger calling the sword pointy,' innit?"

I huffed a laugh as I sat across from her. The momentary lightness sank, pressure pushing between my ribs once more. I leaned forward, clutching my tunic. "It hurts."

Breena sidled closer, wrapping her arm around me. "It always does. Love isn't for the weak. And you sure as void aren't fecking weak."

A dry sob spilled from my lips. "They both … He lied to me. What I'm feeling … I don't know if I can trust it. If it's the bond or just … just me."

My friend's embrace tightened. "Now, listen well. Until you have all the facts, you don't know why Gavrel did what he did. That man looked like you kicked him in the balls and ate his soul at once. But what you can be sure of is that your mind and heart are your own to give. I see the way you look at him. Bond or not, you'd still want to climb inside him."

I leaned my head on her shoulder. "What would I do without you, Bree?"

"You'd have a cry and then put on your big girl breeches." She ran her hand over my curls. "You could teach Kaden a thing or two about that."

I wiped the back of my hand under my nose as my shoulders shook with silent laughter.

"I'm proud of you, you know," she murmured.

My head lifted. "For what. Being a mess?"

Her mouth pinched. It wasn't often that her features settled so somberly. "You keep pushing. Doing what's right even when it's fecking hard. And don't get me started on your bloody ember. You've come so far, and I'm fecking living for it. Truly— watching your bitty wings take shape? It's everything."

I swiped my fingers under my damp lashes, and Breena nudged my shoulder with hers. "I'm here for you, always. You won't be getting rid of me, so don't even try." Her palm slapped against my thigh. "And I hope you're the damned Scion just so I can see the look on Melina's face when we destroy her. And Marek's. Because that twat better not be. His head is already too bloated."

Dread and humor vibrated in my belly. This woman was the only one who could make me want to crawl in a hole and laugh until I cried simultaneously. "You're stuck with me, too. But I'd rather pass on the Scion bit."

She tapped her finger against her full lips. "Hmm. I'm pretty sure we already went over your big girl breeches. So ..."

My foot connected with her shin, and she yelped. "I know you, Ryn. Whatever the Fates throw at you, you'll survive. Because that's what we do."

I wrapped my arms around my bent knees. She was right. We were survivors, and I'd be damned if I allowed *anyone* to take that from me. "That we do. Thanks, Bree. Oh, and I'll let you know if anyone needs a good stabbing."

Breena grinned and slid off the bed. "I knew you loved me. Now, get some rest. We have a fecking rebellion to get back to."

"Love you, too, Mistress Stabberton."

Her chuckle followed her out. With the click of the door closing, I sank into my bed and my thoughts once more.

There were too many rebellions to attend to. Those within me and without threatening to burn everything I thought I understood to ashes.

IT'D BEEN HOURS. Hours of staring blankly into the darkness, body curled tightly in a ball.

At last, my mind settled, and my muscles went slack. I unfurled my limbs and sat up, the silk of my nightgown slipping along my skin. Lulled by the soothing rhythm of the rain outside, I closed my eyes for a moment and wrapped my arms around my chest.

My mind had weaved through all the turns.

Memories.

Every smile and touch.

My relationships.

Friendships.

Kaden had kept the knowledge of what he'd heard as an adolescent all these turns. It was wrong, and I was certainly upset, but I didn't think he'd ever intended to hurt me. Ancients knew feral emotions made mortals more beast than human.

Jealousy.

Grief.

Fear.

Love.

Regardless, it was up to him to ask for my forgiveness. To make it right when he was ready. I needed to let him heal; no one could do it for him, and I was tired of being his excuse to avoid doing so.

I scoffed, my pulse quickening. With my knees bent in front of me, I propped my elbows on my thighs, wrists dangling between them.

Gavrel is my fated.

Cradling my head, I raked my fingers through my hair.

My bloody khorda.

A long exhale puffed my cheeks. I sat, meditating my way through. My spinning thoughts. The facts. The memories.

Why had *he* held on to such a secret?

I sifted through my anger and shock. There was something glaringly certain.

Something was missing.

Gavrel had never done anything to harm me over the turns. Nor anyone he loved. In fact, everything he did was to *protect* those he loved.

So, why? Why would he do this?

If he didn't want me, he would've stayed away. Ancients knew he tried.

Unless the rune wasn't as potent as he hoped.

A heavy sigh fell to my sheets.

Fuck it.

The only way I was getting answers was to ask the questions myself. Then I could deal with the repercussions.

My bare feet padded to his slightly ajar door. His boots lay in a soggy mound between the door and his bed, like he'd simply stumbled his way inside.

He held his head in his hands, elbows resting on his thighs. His damp hair was a mess, as if he had wrung his fingers through the ebony waves too many times. Strands hung over his brow, shielding his face. His breeches slung on his hips, and his wet tunic clung to every corded muscle visible in the hearth's flickering glow.

I stepped further from the shadows, walking into the fire-light, toward him—into his burning orbit. My silken shift rustled against the corner of his bed. His head snapped up, his dark eyes a blazing emerald inferno scorching through my very soul.

"Leave," he rasped and then let his head drop. Pain sank into his features as he stared at the stone floor like he was trying to bury himself beneath it.

I knew him like I knew my own breath. He was deep in self-loathing. I didn't need to reprimand him again because he was torturing himself far worse than I ever could.

"No," I whispered. I crept closer to him, my spine taut with anticipation. Of what, I wasn't sure.

"Little Star, you must leave me." His words were defeated, ripe with regret and shame.

I stood in front of him, my curves invading his space, gently nudging his legs to accommodate me as I planted myself between his muscled thighs.

His lips pressed together in a scowl, a warning rumbling behind his caged teeth. His long fingers slid over his upper legs and clamped onto his knees, tense and stiff.

My heart slammed against my ribcage, threatening to crack it open. To escape and reveal everything I'd been hiding from him.

From myself.

"I can't, Gavrel," I murmured.

Tentative fingers trembled as I reached for him. My fingertips grazed the side of his face, smoothing the loose strands over his ear. I pressed my lips together, my pulse throbbing within them.

He leaned into my touch, squeezing his eyes shut. He looked as if he was in pain. His fingers dug into his thigh muscles, his wide chest straining against the clinging material. "I broke my vow. I don't deserve you. I can't … I can't tell you why."

"Try." My fingertips pulsed against his skin. "I'm here."

His neck strained, fighting something within. He groaned, thumping his fist against his heart. "I *can't*. It won't let me," he growled. "But I … It had to be done, and doesn't matter now. It's better if you leave me—safer that way."

It was a struggle to breathe. Every ragged lungful tore from me, tumbling into his throaty inhalations. Our breaths blended and twirled as if trying to become one.

A place behind my ribs seared into the bony cage. Was I feeling a fraction of what he felt?

"Does your talisman … Does it prevent you from telling me about our bond?" The words were husky, full of hope.

He crunched his eyelids closed, nodding shakily, biceps tense.

"Then I'm right where I want to be." The words were the most honest thing I'd ever said aloud. "Besides, if I left, you'd find me … to the Nether Void and beyond, yes?"

39

LITTLE STARS

SERYN

*H*is eyes snapped open. They were wild, the black of his pupils overtaking the green as he studied my face. He was a hungry beast looking for any sign that I'd run.

I squared my feet, my fingernails raking through his hair. My palm rested on his nape, steady and warm. I wasn't going anywhere.

His gaze penetrated mine as his jaw ticked. His skin was still wet from the rain, yet my fingertips burned from the heat radiating from him. He smelled like the meadow after a storm.

He smelled like home.

He was my home.

I leaned into him, my nipples straining against the soft fabric of my shift. He drew in a shaky breath, his thick chest heaving.

Twisting tendrils slipped off my shoulders, ruddy curls dancing in the firelight. They grazed his chest and shoulder as I whispered, "And I'll always want you … to find me."

Emerald flashed across his irises in response. Erratic puffs of air swept against my neck and down my chest. His pulse crashed against my palm, echoing mine.

He would not break unless I let him. He would never do anything I didn't want … But I wanted *this*. I was done with excuses. Finished with denying the truth. I needed him, just like he did me. I needed him like my next intake of breath.

"I thought I'd lost you," he murmured, his words cracking. "I agreed to have this … this thing buried within me because it meant they wouldn't know." He pulled in a deep breath. "That you wouldn't be vulnerable. It meant you had a choice."

"I'm right here. Whatever you've done. Whether or not we're khorda … I need you. I choose *you*."

As I pulled away, his sense of control shattered. His hands ripped from his thighs, sinking into my waist, crushing into my shift. He thrust his face into my stomach, pushing his cheek into my body as if trying to melt into me.

To keep my balance, I dug both hands into his hair, holding him close. His arms wrapped around my hips, his hands roaming my body, skimming over my bottom, my thighs, my ribs.

He squeezed one hip, making my shift ride up my thigh, the cool fabric caressing me and leaving a trail of fire along my skin. I gasped, overwhelmed by the sensations. My pulse throbbed in my core.

The flames in the hearth reflected in his ravenous eyes as he looked up at me. He rested his chin below my ribs, his muscled thighs gripping my legs.

With an unhurried pace, he smoothed one warm palm from the middle of my spine and down my bottom, cupping the back of my thigh possessively. His thumb lifted to caress the round curve of my backside, keeping me in place.

He pressed his entire face into my belly once more, inhaling deeply, and then his lips were on me, kissing and nipping at my skin through the silk. His other hand crept up my side, his long, thick fingers spreading wide over my flesh. His thumb swept over the underside of my breast, and my head fell back, my hair cascading between my shoulder blades. My hands found his biceps, squeezing the solid mass.

"Look at me," he demanded, his voice gruff.

Without hesitation, my gaze locked with his, my head tilting forward. His hunger was palpable, licking me from my belly to my throbbing core. I bit my lower lip, sliding one hand to rest on his chest over his galloping heart.

His grip tightened on the back of my thigh and then pushed upward, over my fleshy cheeks and spine, bunching the hem of my shift as it rose. Achingly slow, his other hand also slid over the mound of one heavy breast. His calloused thumb found my nipple, pressing teasing circles over the achy bud.

I whimpered his name.

His mouth moved hungrily up my stomach, biting and kissing my skin through the fabric, helping it ascend. My shift pushed under my breasts, the firelight caressing my exposed skin.

He breathed into me, his hot exhale leaving damp trails along my skin. He licked the underside of my breast, kissing it and then between my ribs. I shivered, even though my insides were melting and pooling in my core.

Everything inside me was boiling.

It was too intense.

It wasn't enough.

My hips had a mind of their own as I rocked into him, breeches pulling tight across his solid, straining length. His hardness rubbed against the damp fabric of my underwear.

I tugged the wet tunic from him with fumbling hands. He lifted his hands from me for a moment to help rip it from his body and toss it to the floor.

My skin prickled with goosebumps where his hands had been, my shift slipping into place again.

"This won't do," he said, gripping my waist and wrapping his lips around my other neglected nipple over the silk.

I felt his smirk as he sucked in the tender peak, the wet fabric chafing over it, making me pant. His fingers dug into my waistline as I slid my hands over his thick arms and then to the sides of his head. I pulled his face away, his lips plucking my nipple gently as they left me.

"I'll kill you if you don't get me naked immediately," I rasped breathlessly.

"Always choosing violence." He chuckled as I glared at him.

My lips dropped open as he suddenly stripped the chemise from my form, the silk fluttering behind me.

His mouth swallowed my gasp as it crashed into mine, his tongue slipping inside. We devoured each other, lips and tongues teasing, crashing, and melding over and over.

Our hands raked over each other's heated skin. Squeezing. Grasping. Hard muscles and soft curves pressing into the other.

One of his rough palms reached up to cradle my jaw, positioning my face so his lips could merge with mine more deeply. His hungry kiss was that of a starving man.

He was consuming my very soul.

Energy vibrated down my vertebrae.

Panting, 1 jumped and wrapped my legs around his waist as he filled both hands with my backside, his fingers digging into the round cheeks as he stood. He broke the kiss, and a voracious smile spread across his face.

There was his dimple.

He kissed me hard and then tossed my body onto his bed. I bounced once, my breasts heavy and breathing ragged. I propped myself up on my elbows, licking my lips as I took in his body. He undid the ties and pushed down his breeches, his solid cock springing free. A sharp gasp slipped from my throat at the sight of him.

His body was glorious and surely carved from marble. My

eyes trailed over the expanse of his muscular chest, bracketed by thick, powerfully built arms. His sculpted abs tapered into a delicious V-shaped expanse, guiding my vision to his impressive arousal. I swallowed, my mouth beginning to water.

He prowled toward me; his gaze feral as he stared at me with single-minded intent. He reached the edge of the bed. His eyes flashed before he wrapped his hands around my ankles, pulling me toward him in one swift motion. My backside was near the edge, legs dangling freely on either side of his hips.

"You're the most exquisite creature I've ever seen. Every delicious inch of you," he breathed, sliding his palms from my knees to the seam where my core met my legs. His thumbs drew light circles over the damp fabric covering my aching juncture, torturing me. His smile was pure wickedness.

He looped his thumbs under the undergarment, slipping it down my legs. He brought them to his nose, inhaling reverently.

A burst of flames spread across my face and chest, a choked whimper escaping me. I didn't have time to process such carnality. This man was driving me insane.

He slid one hand up my leg. My hip. My belly. His broad, wet tongue licked a path up the inside of my other leg, now bent and propped on the edge of the bed. He leaned forward, stretching his hand out to cup my breast, his palm kneading and plucking at the pebbled nipple. His lips met the crease of my thigh, kissing and nipping, his stubble rasping against the sensitive skin.

My whole body trembled in waves. I would not survive him —had nothing tethering me to reality.

My hands slammed into Gavrel's hair, hips lifting from the bed, seeking relief. His deep chuckle hummed along my skin, his breath hot against my thigh.

"Impatient as always."

"I'll have you know—"

He dragged his tongue through my slit, already soaked with

desire. Smirking, he looked up at me from between my legs. He licked his bottom lip and then scraped his front teeth over it. "Delicious … you were saying?" I shook my head, unable to find the words.

He smiled, and then gently sucked the pulsing nub at my apex. His tongue circled and flicked the bundle of nerves over and over until I was squirming and vibrating with need. My feet were planted on the bed, heels digging into the quilt.

"Gavrel, I … I can't handle… It's too much," I cried.

He placed one large palm on my thigh, ensuring that I couldn't escape his relentless attention, his tongue flicking faster and faster. With his other hand, he pinched my nipple one last time before slipping his palm down my slick skin. Two thick fingers slid easily into my drenched center, pumping in tandem with his tongue.

A scream ripped from me as my mind imploded, and a burst of my ember zipped across my skin, illuminating Gavrel's glowing emerald eyes.

My body vibrated, the trembling starting in my legs and rocketing up to my chest. My release exploded through me in waves as I moaned wantonly and squeezed my thighs around Gavrel's head.

All at once, I was boneless, my legs falling to the sides, my glowing arms flung above my head, heavy and tingling. He languidly licked up my core one last time, placing a kiss above my mound.

A dreamy smile curved my lips as he helped me shift onto the plush bed. My spent muscles sank into the soft mattress. He crawled over me, resting his hips below mine, our bellies touching. His brows softened as he looked at me, his eyes simmering.

I wrapped my arms around his back, running my fingers over the flexing muscles. He looked into my eyes.

"You are the beginning and the end for me, my star. I would burn down every realm to get to you."

My fingers trembled as they grazed his cheek, lingering before I smoothed a black strand behind his ear. I stared into his soul and into the devastating honesty he blanketed me in. He wasn't hiding from me anymore.

His hands were still and gripping the silk beneath us for dear life.

He was my fated khorda, and I chose him not because of this … But because I needed him more than I needed to breathe. He was the very heart beating within my chest, and no talisman could take that from me.

His lips hovered a fraction from mine. My words skimmed over his skin. "You are my beyond, Gavrel. I chose you long ago, but I was too terrified to admit it. And I don't need the bond to tell me that."

Our mouths met again, tenderly this time. My center began to throb again, my chest pulling in deep, shaky breaths between our mating lips.

His cock pulsed between us, impossibly hard and slick with my arousal as he rocked his length against my heated sex. His arms trembled as he restrained himself from entering me.

I needed him to break.

Damn his self-control.

My hips pushed into his, searching for more friction against my throbbing apex. Little moans of pleasure caught in my throat, only to be swallowed into his as our kiss deepened. My legs trembled, and need tingled from my nipples to my belly each time they grazed against his damp chest.

To my dismay, Gavrel paused and lifted his head, a worried look pulling at his brows.

"This is it. If we go further, you are mine. In body and soul." He hesitated. "Do you understand? This is your last chance to leave, to have a different path. I'm … I'm not strong enough to let you go again." He breathed in shakily, then repeated the words from the night of the Moonbud Revelry. "Now's the time to avoid any regrets, Little Star."

A small smile lifted the corners of my lips. I bowed forward to press a kiss into the tense line of his lips.

"Never," I whispered against them, digging my nails into the muscles of his tensed back, my hips rocking eagerly. "I am yours. And you are mine. Make it so."

We couldn't complete the Kollao Ceremony with his talisman still embedded, but I meant every word. I'd stand by him until the end of forever.

A relieved groan fell from him as he shifted, his biceps bulging. Then he surged forward, pushing his hard length into my molten center, slick with need. A satisfied cry fled from my throat. He stilled inside me, my core adapting and gripping around his erection.

The rune on his right hand was burning brightly now, his fingers entwined with mine. The skin of my arms and hands shimmered, iridescent light flickering within the wild, weaving patterns, glowing cracks in the shape of twisting tree branches.

He brushed some curls from my forehead, kissing me gently on the side of my brow, and then my cheek.

Tenderly smiling, he placed one more kiss on my lips.

A hoarse moan fell from him as he slid from me and then pushed back in. Bright, throbbing light encircled our entwined hands, spreading along our skin like liquid spilling from our palms.

"You feel … too good," he groaned, moving in and out of me, my center clenching around his thick girth. "I feel you *inside* me."

"More, Gavrel. I need …"

He began pounding into me, my breasts bouncing with each thrust. Our sounds of passion and me calling his name echoed through the room.

Slapping skin.

Whimpers.

Moans.

I ignited once more, this time a slow, throbbing burn deep within my belly. Light enveloped our joined bodies, cocooning us in a pulsing orb of kaleidoscopic ember. Our energies mingling and sweeping between and through each other.

We were two burning supernovas crashing into one another. Scorching infernos of passion, breaking and spinning back together over and over again. Until finally I couldn't tell where he ended and I began.

A blaze of heat zipped over my spine, and we both stilled, our souls sinking into one another through our locked eyes.

And then we burst into a million little stars.

4O

PROTECTORS OF THE MIRAGE ORCHID

SERYN

*T*he luminous meadow swayed around me, its towering flowers brushing against my biceps. Gavrel stood beside me, his hand in mine.

A gust of wind pushed against us, and I flung one arm up to protect my face. Gavrel threw his weight against it, tugging me behind him as he carved our way through an ocean of neon petals.

With a final lunge, we spilled toward the edge of the obsidian cliff. Frantically, my hair whipped at my cheeks, and I grabbed his wrist with my free hand. I tried to back away. Take him with me. We didn't need to dive into the void before us. Into the shadow realm beyond.

Bright flicks of pink and yellow wavered, the cracking of stems making me flinch. Oh, Ancients. The protector of the Mirage Orchid was back. Stalking us.

With fearful eyes, Gavrel tilted his head, and then suddenly pulled me into his arms, dove, and plunged us over the brink of the cliff. "It's the only way!" he bellowed as the darkness consumed him.

As we plummeted, my scream sliced through the murky emptiness. I blinked, and time slackened as if we fell in slow motion, my nails scratching toward the cliff's edge. Gavrel was lost to me. Gobbled up by the cold abyss.

With a swooshing flap of wings and a spray of loose stone, two enormous, serpentine-like shadows pitched themselves over the precipice. My lashes fluttered, trying to clear the sheen of tears from my eyes so I could see the beasts diving for us.

Within my next blink, a flash of gilded scales filled my vision, and my body jerked painfully in midair, cold bone wrapping around my torso like a cage. A rumbling snarl vibrated through the creature's foreleg and my sinew. Terrified, I gripped the curving ebony talon as we soared through the never-ending darkness.

The edges of my vision blackened, my consciousness surrendering to the looming faint. One last word flashed in my mind before the shadows seeped over my mind.

Wyvern.

WITH A GASP, my eyes fluttered open, and I struggled against the heaviness wrapped around my middle.

"You're all right. You're safe." Gavrel kissed the back of my head, his hand sweeping damp curls off my temple.

A deep breath surged into my lungs, calming the frenzied images bouncing around my brain. "I dreamed," I said, shifting on my back so my side pressed against his front.

"I know," he replied, his fingers twining with mine.

"I know how to get into the dungeon."

"I *know.*" He propped himself on his elbow, waiting for me to realize what he was saying. The crease between his brow deepened. I reached up and smoothed the pad of my thumb over it.

"You were there, in my dream, weren't you?"

"Yes. It would seem our b … b … it's trying to overpower the rune's ember. Join us … together." He cringed as a ripple of pain ran through him at the mention of our link.

I rose to kiss the corner of his lips, and then I ran a hand over his jaw.

"Well, you know we need to pay a visit to the wyvern that guards the Mirage Orchid then."

His brows shot up, hidden behind the messy strands flopping over his forehead. "Abso-fucking-lutely not."

"You have a better idea?"

His mouth pinched, and he sagged onto his back. I sat up, placing my hand on his taut stomach. "I can do this, Gav. It didn't harm me the last time. I … I saved its hatchling."

He scowled, giving me a sidelong glance. "*We* will do this."

Smiling, I leaned over and kissed where his dimple hid. "Deal. Let's fly."

"You're crazy. But I like that." Breena's grin sliced across her visage. I wasn't sure whether she was going to kiss me or bite me.

"I recall *someone* mentioning winged creatures the other day," Marek mumbled.

"Someone's wittle staff is showing," Breena chided.

Marek's knuckles turned white around his quarterstaff, jaw ticking as he glared at Breena.

"Hmmm, I don't—I don't remember anyone saying anything of the sort. It was all my brilliant friend's idea." Breena slapped her hand against Rhaegar's chest, and his breath puffed out of him. "Wasn't it, Rhaeg? Wasn't it Firefly's idea?"

I didn't think someone's eyes could roll *that* far back, but my cousin proved me wrong.

Rhaegar shrugged helplessly at Marek.

I brushed my hand over my cousin's hand. "The idea was brilliant, cousin. Our dream just confirmed what path to take." As the seam of his mouth softened, he gave me a tiny nod.

Arms crossed, Kaden lingered at the group's edge, staring off into the courtyard. He didn't offer me any sort of apology, and I didn't offer him my attention. I'd leave him to his brooding and contrition.

Gavrel's hand rested in the curve of my lower back. "Get your fill of food, gather supplies, and we'll head out."

As the others went to prepare, a soft rustling sounded behind me as Gavrel stepped closer to me. I chewed on my lower lip, turning my face toward him. His mouth curled. "Lift your hair."

I did as he asked, looking into his eyes as he fastened a delicate but sturdy golden chain around my neck. After dropping my hair, I reached for the pendant that had plunked between my breasts, the raven-black stone humming against my skin.

Wetness immediately glossed over my eyes as I gasped. My other hand fumbled at my belt. When my fingers met the empty leather bottom of my satchel, I looked at Gavrel from under my lashes, running my thumb over the carved face of the pebble.

My talisman.

"Where ... how?"

"I found it in the Murk. Must have fallen out when we came through the portal." He took the stone from me, placed a kiss on it, and then tucked it between the V of my dark tunic. "I found a shop in the city yesterday. Thought you'd like to have it with you always. It's of no use if you lose it."

I closed my eyes, not caring if tears trickled down my cheeks.

"Thank you. This means more to me than you know. I love"—my breath hitched, fear clinging to a different kind of declaration—"it."

His emeralds shifted over my face, diving into the watery depths of my gaze. "I know," he whispered, his words heavy. "As do I." He wrapped one arm around me and cupped my jaw, guiding my lips to his.

I sank into his kiss, tasting the wet salt of my gratitude and unspoken words.

When we separated, he placed one last kiss on my brow and swiped his thumb over my cheek, drying my skin. His dimple flashed. "Now, let's go find the wyverns."

We joined the others as Breena, Marek, and Rhaegar readied their rucksacks, taking portions of food that would travel well. Kaden chewed on an apple, his bag nowhere to be found.

"You ready?" Gavrel asked his brother, one brow lifting.

"I'm staying here for a few days. Going to see if I can find Ma."

Gavrel's eyes widened. He breathed in, and his mouth parted as if he was going to argue, but then he thought better of it and simply nodded. "If anyone can find her, you can."

Kaden's shoulders relaxed, his bottom lip dropping for a moment before he composed himself. "I'll find you," he murmured, hesitantly placing a hand on his brother's shoulder. A pained expression slipped over his face as he looked at me. As his arm dropped, so did his shoulders. Sighing, he bowed his head and left the courtyard.

The odds that he'd find Hestia were slim, but if it gave him a purpose, something to do while he worked through her death, his nightmares, and heartbreak, then so be it.

"Excuse me." The melodic words made us all jump. Wren appeared out of nowhere behind us, her wings settling down her back. "Did I hear that your friend was looking for another astral? Can I be of assistance?"

"He's trying to find his mother. She was culled when he was young," I explained, my hand finding Gavrel's.

"Oh, by the Ancients. He won't find her here," the guide said, head bowed. "Culling is a nasty business. It not only takes the physical, but the astral body as well."

My heart lurched. Marek's jaw twitched as he sealed his rucksack, his knuckles turning white as he gripped the fabric. We hadn't seen Yaya in Aion, not that I had expected to with so many citizens, but still. She could be alive. My stomach knotted, thinking of the alternative. Or she could be …

"Say more," Gavrel ordered, taking a step forward.

She wiggled her fingers above her head, and a puff of glittering mist burst and fluttered in a halo around her. "Culling returns beings to the aether whence they came." She looked at us with pity. "They simply cease to exist."

Gavrel cursed, rubbing his hand on his chest, jaw locking, and my heart bounced.

"Sorry to deliver such sorry news. 'Tis a burden I don't wish to bear, but honesty is the best tonic." She ruffled her wings and turned to leave. "Safe journey to you all. I'd be careful of those beasties. Just because you're astral doesn't mean getting chomped on doesn't hurt or that you won't get yourselves sent to the aether."

Wincing, I stepped toward the exit, following Kaden, but Gavrel held fast to my hand. "Let him go. He needs hope now more than the truth. He'll take it better if he finds out his own way."

"Like how I found out you were my khorda?" I retorted, and then immediately regretted lashing out as Gavrel's mouth pinched.

"What the?" Rhaegar croaked, dropping the banana he held. Breena picked it up from the ground and shoved it in her open rucksack as Rhaegar found something particularly interesting inside his bag. Marek ignored us completely, but one eyebrow raised ever so slightly.

Gavrel looked at me, his expression patient as he rubbed his thumb over the back of my hand. Too stubborn for my own well-being, I scowled at him, my mind working through his words and mine until my jaw and shoulders slackened.

"Sorry. I know you're right," I murmured.

Although grief manifested differently for everyone, I wasn't certain Kaden had ever allowed himself to feel the full weight of his mourning.

When I thought of my mother and Hestia, though the sorrow lingered, its sharp edges had dulled with time, its presence fading into a subdued hum in the back of my thoughts throughout the turns.

But Kaden … I'd watched him mask his pain over and over. Unchecked, his rage had been simmering for far too long. I feared that either his soul would evaporate, leaving him hollow and brittle, or it would boil over, consuming him entirely.

BRACE YOURSELF

GAVREL

By sundown, we'd reached the flower meadow. A crisp breeze shuddered through the flowers, making them twitch and creak. The field spanned at least twice the length of the training field outside Morpheus' palace.

"Stay together and step lightly," I instructed, pulling my sword from its scabbard.

The others nodded, moving along the edge with their weapons in hand, gently navigating the stiff blooms and scanning the surrounding area. We didn't know exactly what to expect, but hopefully it wasn't an immediate death by wyvern.

Seryn put her hand on my wrist, her face lost in thought until a flame of curiosity flashed over her eyes. "Yesterday, you said something. Something about your talisman. You said, 'they wouldn't know.'" I gulped, tension rolling over my back. "Who wouldn't know? Why would it matter if someone knew we were fated?"

I wanted to tell her everything, but the words lodged in my

chest like a blade. With every effort to release them, they sliced deeper into my bones, and the rune stone boiled my blood. It wouldn't let me release the words I so desperately wanted to free.

I grit my teeth, doubling forward. "I … You're—you are more," I ground out, pushing my palm hard into my chest and gasping.

She brushed her hand over my back, her plait falling over her shoulder as she soothed me. "All right. Stop. For Surrelia's sake, Gav. We need to get that thing out of you."

"Fine by me," I panted, grimacing. "The day we figure out how to do that will be a good one indeed."

Her mouth curved. "We can't just get Breena to stab it out?"

"As much as I'd like to see her attempt it," I muttered, tucking my mouth between my lips. "It won't allow it. I've bloody well tried." My nostrils flared as I breathed in the crisp air, letting it swirl inside me to ease the pain. I glanced at the others as they continued through the flowers prudently.

I straightened my spine and exhaled. "My mother—you know she dreamed—used to get messages from the Fates. When I turned eighteen, she came to me saying she'd been sent a warning." I grimaced as my talisman burned again. Seryn rubbed my biceps.

Tentatively, I continued, my words tumbling over the next, "Yes, we argued. Not because I didn't want you as my—" Heat sliced into my marrow, stealing my breath before I continued. "But because I was young and foolish. I didn't have faith in her auguries then. She said that we were—that you were—more." The sweltering behind my ribs spiked, and I wheezed. "If exposed, you'd be endangered. From the Elders. From the Ancients. I know not."

For a moment, I cupped Seryn's cheek, ignoring the simmering beneath my scar, and she leaned into my touch. Then my hand found hers, and I placed it over my heart, the contact easing the rune's attack ever so slightly. "It was enough for me. I agreed to be silenced in exchange for your safety, and to give you the choice of whom to ... whom to love. It's all I've ever wanted for you."

Heart thundering, my tattoo lit, the glow reflecting in her eyes as tears pooled in them. Her hand left mine and slid up my chest, her fingers resting under my ear. "You've sacrificed enough. All these turns. All the memories and secrets you've carried alone." Regret and disgust lined her clipped words.

Like some sort of celestial being, her aura shimmered around her in a halo, and a look of determination settled along her features. She was the most beautiful creature I'd ever seen. "You watched from the shadows, giving me the choice to live how I wanted. My mother. Hestia. You. You all paid the price for my safety. But I won't have it, Gavrel. Won't have those I love sacrificing themselves for me any longer. I can protect myself. I'm strong enough, and I'll be damned if I allow you to stay in the darkness a moment longer."

She stretched onto her tiptoes, clutching my tunic. Her face neared mine as I bent, her words brushing against my lips. "I'd choose you again and again. No one else. I'll be by your side, with or without the bond, until my dying breath. And I'd like to see you or anyone else try to stop me."

My fingers clutched at her lower back, pressing into the soft flesh. Pride swelled within me. She'd found herself. She'd found the strength she'd always feared. My mouth was a breath away from hers, drawn to her as if I were the aether being pulled into a supernova. Like we couldn't draw air unless it were from one another.

She was my everything.

The sole reason for my existence.

A delicate sheen coated the deep well of her eyes. I felt her pulse within me. I swore the edges of her thoughts were scratching at the dark corners of my sentience, thrashing against the stone barrier blocking them.

A ragged whisper dragged from me and over her lips. "Asteria, I lo—"

A frenzy of shouts and snarls ripped through the air. Seryn jerked from my embrace, her gaze snapping toward the commotion in the middle of the field.

"No!" she screamed, her body imploding in a flash of warped light and reappearing several lengths in front of her cousin and our friends in my next blink.

"Seryn!" I bellowed, charging in the direction of her and the others, my sword illuminating.

My pulse thundered, pumping in time with my arms. Seryn's braid whipped behind her as she faced the massive beast.

The wyvern had found us.

Its bulbous nostrils flared, and its broad, gilded chest heaved. As it puffed, the glittering air swirled in eddies around Seryn's rigid frame. Wings covered in olive-green feathers, tipped in cerulean, spread wide as gleaming indigo plumage trembled in a ripple down its massive, serpentine body.

Slowly, she sheathed her dagger and held her palms up to the creature. Shelf-like brows narrowed over its fiery glare as it considered her.

"Fecking shite, woman," Breena hissed as Marek bit out, "Cousin!"

I reached the others, slowing my pace and lowering my blade. "Let her do what she must," I snapped. From what they told me, the wyvern didn't attack her last time. We would put her in more danger by causing a scene. I sheathed my sword, holding my breath as I observed Seryn's every movement.

"Unbelievable," Rhaegar muttered, replacing his axe. He cuffed Breena and Marek's biceps. Warily, the others lowered their weapons.

A gnarl vibrated in the beast's chest, its spade-shaped tail flicking in the air as it lowered onto its stocky forelegs and brought its gilt snout closer to Seryn's face. Against my better judgment, I stepped nearer, hands fisting at my sides.

"Don't," Seryn ordered, not breaking eye contact with the beast. She stretched out her fingers. "Do you remember me? I saved your hatchling. I … We don't mean you any harm. We're here to ask a favor."

The dragon grunted, its lips shivering over jagged teeth as if it understood.

Seryn continued. "We need to find a way into the dungeon below Morpheus' palace. To … to fulfill the next phase of a prophecy. The Hollowed Stars prophecy. Do you know it?"

Irritated, the wyvern huffed, blowing stray curls around her face and leaning even closer, its diamond-shaped pupils dilating. So close, I saw the gold flecks swimming in the orange of its eyes. My heartbeat thrashed behind its confines as my khorda tenderly touched its lowered snout.

A ripple shivered over its roughened muzzle, and it pushed into her touch, brow bones prudently lifting.

Its gaze snapped to the side, a sonorous grumble vibrating in its gullet.

"Seryn!" Her name thundered over the meadow as my brother hurtled toward us from our left. All at once, my hand shot out, willing him to yield, but the words choked me as a second wyvern dove toward Seryn on our right.

The bigger creature reared its head, and Seryn stumbled backward.

I wouldn't reach her in time.

Pure terror exploded through me.

It was smaller, but still monstrous, with scarlet feathers streaking over its head and body. Its golden underbelly glinted in the sun as it stretched its dark claws and snatched Seryn from the earth, teal-colored wings flapping powerfully into the sky.

A resounding series of barks shot from the bigger wyvern,

and the smaller one's piercing shriek rent the air in reply, drowning out Seryn's garbled scream.

Kaden zoomed past me, and I cursed, following him as we chased them.

"Damn it, I can't lose you, too. Why the bloody void are you here?" I barked, my words clipped and choppy.

Arms pumping, his brows furrowed, and his mouth twisted. "Because I made a fucking mistake!" he yelled breathlessly.

The sound of wings rhythmically beating against the wind stalked us. I clamped my molars in trepidation as shadow blotted out the sun's rays.

"Brace yourself, brother!" I bellowed as the first wyvern's enormous talons wrapped around us, our legs and arms dangling from each of the beast's paws.

My jaw set, hands gripping the curved talons that caged me. If this was how we met our end, it mattered not where the monsters took us as long as I was by Seryn's side.

Always.

NOT MY IDEA OF FUN

SERYN

The beast studied me from the side of one teal eye, the scaly shelf above lifting curiously. My dread died in my throat as I met its gentle gaze, familiarity clicking in the recesses of my memory. I craned my neck, trying to get a better look at the wyvern protectively cradling me in its claws. I recognized the beastie's colorful plumage, and the recollection fully formed. One where Sebille slashed her blade at us while I helped a hatchling break free of its egg.

It blinked at me, its pupil contracting before focusing ahead. It *was* the young wyvern I'd saved, grown to nearly its full size in the last months. In awe, I hesitantly reached up and ran my palm along a hardened scale, and a purr hummed within its cavernous chest.

Was it taking me to the palace? We were heading in the right direction. We soared over the Reverie Weald. Wind slapped against my cheeks, and I squinted as electric shades of orange and cerise blurred below us.

I'd heard Kaden call my name before the wyvern claimed me. He'd come back. Found us. Perhaps it meant he'd already figured out his mother's fate. Or he'd regretted staying behind.

With a jarring swerve, the beast dove to the right and over the edge of the cliff. My gut roiled as the crashing waves of the Insomnis Sea zoomed closer. A keening cry ripped from the youngling as it banked and then evened out, our bodies coasting parallel to the aqua depths.

I gulped, my head snapping to my right as the mother screeched back, sidling next to her offspring. The deepest sense of relief flooded me as my eyes locked with Kaden's and then Gavrel's, both safely tucked between long talons. They both looked as if they could breathe again, eyes roaming over my body.

We didn't have to wait long before Morpheus' palace peeked through the last gilded rays of twilight. A quick intake of breath flooded my lungs. I wouldn't ever get over the ethereal beauty of the moonstone structure blending within the gleaming black stone islet.

In unison, the wyverns' flights curved farther into the sea, as if they understood they should keep out of sight as best they could. I brushed my palms over its belly, and it vibrated under my touch contentedly.

We approached from the back of the cliff; the ebony climbed higher over the moonstone here than it did at the entrance.

The fading remnants of sunlight caught on the moon-phase windows, which ran vertically down the center of the structure. I blinked at the soft glints refracting from the crystal turrets, casting faint rainbows into the dusky air.

My stomach dropped as we swooped near a jutting stone lip nestled near the base of the wall. Waves slapped at the ledge, the foamy edges slinking into a hidden grotto.

With a chuff, the wyvern got as close as its wings allowed and stretched its talons open. Yelping, I plopped into the sea, my limbs flapping through the water. Two more bodies joined me in the surf with muffled curses.

The mother flew toward her offspring, letting out a disgruntled screech.

Bobbing, I called out my gratitude to the pair. The smaller one circled once, blinking at me, before soaring after its mother.

The waves carried us to the ledge, and I pulled myself onto it, grateful that the ocean was not as violent today. That the salted liquid made me buoyant rather than bringing up past fears.

Gavrel and Kaden climbed beside me. Kaden tipped his head to the side and bounced, extricating the liquid from his ear. "So, that happened."

Still frustrated, I ignored him and moved toward Gavrel at the entrance of the cavern. "Well, we made it this far. No use stalling now," I said, sloshing through the thigh-high water.

Beside me, Gavrel stretched his neck from side to side. "You gave us quite the scare." His hand rested on my lower back.

I laughed. "Must have made an impression on that hatchling. That wasn't exactly how I pictured getting here. Yet, here we are, nonetheless."

Kaden positioned himself on my other side. "Glad you're safe."

"Thank you." My murmur sank into the splashing water. The grotto was just big enough for the three of us to walk side by side.

"I ... Wren found me. Told me about what happens when someone ... when they're culled." His words cracked. "I can't say it's a surprise, but I thought ... No, I don't know what I thought." He jammed his hand through his wet hair.

With a frown, I glanced at him and took his hand in mine. He tightened his grip as we reached a tunnel, which inclined gradually upward.

Gavrel cleared his throat. "I'm sorry you had to find out that way."

After taking a deep breath, Kaden nodded at his brother. "It was better I found out on my own rather than either of you trying to tell me. I've been … difficult."

Gavrel looked at me, eyebrows pushing together, and then moved into the burrow.

Pausing at the passage, Kaden released my hand. He stared into the blackness, his words tumbling out in a flurry. "Ser … I … I know I've been a right twat, but I can't seem to help myself when it comes to you. I've ruined things, and I'd deserve it if you never talk to me again."

I tilted my head, letting him go on, curious about how much he'd concede.

"I should have told you long ago about what I'd overheard. Maybe it was jealousy. Maybe it was just weakness. I needed you to myself, like that would somehow fix the rest of me. Gavrel is a better man than I'll ever be. I've been a mess for as long as I can remember, failing at everything that matters."

"Kade—" I breathed, shifting closer.

He held up his palm, going on, "And you … I've wanted you for so long. I convinced myself that my feelings were enough— that if I held on tight enough, you'd eventually feel the same. But all I did was ignore what you needed and punish you for not reciprocating. That's not just unfair … that's cruel. And you deserve so much better. If that is my brother, then so be it."

His head dropped, following a heavy exhale. "But there's more to it. It's like this blade in my belly. That everyone I care for will perish too soon. If you and Gavrel … if you go through with the ceremony. Then the odds are higher that you'll both be taken from me at once. And I'll be alone."

The wall around my heart trembled, and my breaths were shallow.

"I don't think I have it in me to fix all my wrongs right now, but I'm going to try. When I was alone in Aion, I regretted not coming with you. The terror I felt when that wyvern took you. Damn it." He cringed, fists clenching. "I'm just so fucking angry all the time. And in between, I am … numb. Confirming Ma's truly gone. Losing you. And my brother. It's too much to bear. I'm going to keep fucking up, even though I don't want to."

The final stones chipped away at his admissions. *My* Kaden was still underneath all the caustic layers. He just needed to dig his way to the surface.

"You're my best friend, you sod. You'll never lose me." I touched his shoulder. "Even when I'm gone, you'll still have me —right here." I tapped his chest, then brushed my palm over his cheek.

With a sigh, I let my hand drop. "I'm still cross with you. I need time, but we're not broken. *You're* not broken." I met his eyes. "And if I hear you call yourself a failure again, I swear I'll stab you."

A rough chuckle shook Kaden's chest. I continued, a breath easing out of me, "Just take it one day at a time—you'll figure out what you really need."

He nodded, his body shifting uneasily.

The corner of my mouth tugged upward. "Come on. Let's go fulfill a bloody prophecy and see what happens next."

A forlorn smile fluttered over his lips. "Fair. Let's get on with it then."

Together, we activated our auras as we entered the tunnel, Gavrel's glowing tattoo leading us forward.

Kaden touched his brother's shoulder, his face apologetic. Gavrel studied him for a moment and let his shoulders relax before he cupped his brother's nape in return. "Always, brother," Gavrel murmured, and touched his forehead to Kaden's.

Hope was there, just within reach. We'd taken a step toward mending our relationships. With any luck, we'd live to see it grow another day.

We sloshed through the tunnel until the water gradually dispersed. Our path twisted, leading us deeper and deeper within the cliff.

As we finally neared a stairwell leading down, the air thickened and chilled, pushing into us as if trying to shove us back. "We must be close," I whispered, peeking down the steps.

Irritably, my aura snapped around me the further we walked.

"This is not my idea of fun; I'll have you both know," Kaden groused.

"I don't think walking into a massive pit of despair is anyone's idea of fun. Well, perhaps Melina's," I retorted as we came to the end of the stairwell.

Before us lay the dungeon's massive pit, embered sphere torches lit the space along the edges of the spiraling ramp. I pushed my energy within me, and the Larkin brothers tucked away theirs as well.

Gavrel glanced at us, putting his finger to his mouth and then to one ear. Cautiously, I leaned toward the side of the pit, my stomach dipping a bit at the sound of metal rasping against metal.

From a few levels below, Balor Drent's words slithered up the walls. "Mistress bids you to eat. She said I could have some fun with you if you didn't. I always enjoy our time together."

With a look of disgust, Elder Marah Strom spat on his face through the bars of her prison. Thick metal cuffs bound her hands, a chain tethering her to the wall.

Balor snickered, "Now, now, Marah. No need to be so bold after all this time. It's a shame that your fetters bind your ember. It'd be more fun if you could put up more of a fight."

With a grunt, he rolled the circular gate along creaking grooves, and a flash of royal blue scurried out of sight within the cell. Her chains scraped across rock as she tried to put distance between herself and the Akridai.

Quietly, we made our way down the ramp while Balor was distracted.

"No!" Marah screamed, and something clattered to the rock, the sound bouncing off the gleaming walls.

"Lea … leave her be, you fiend," Elder Endurst Guust protested from the cell next door. He fisted the bars, and his cuffs clanked against them angrily, but his words sounded limp and feeble.

Slowly, we each drew a dagger. The weight of my blade felt good in my hand. But it would feel even better sinking into Balor's flesh.

We neared the cages, the sound of scuffling and dissent ricocheting. I pressed my body against the obsidian between Gavrel and Kaden. Gavrel's eyes narrowed as he pointed toward his chest and then to the cell. He jabbed his finger toward Kaden and then to Endurst's cell.

His palm faced me then, telling me to wait. I shook my head at the sound of Marah's pleas. Mouth pinching, his face fell as he realized I wouldn't stay put.

43

BET HIS TEETH TASTED BETTER

GAVREL

Rolling his eyes, Kaden darted across, holding his finger against his mouth as Endurst gasped. I was grateful my brother had found his way back to us. I'd heard a bit of his apology earlier, and although much of his recent behavior disappointed me, it was a step in the right direction.

Seryn stared at me, stubbornness burning within her eyes. She wouldn't mind me, but I had to try. My jaw clenched, and I sent a swift prayer to whoever listened that no harm would come to her.

She could handle herself, of that much I was certain. It didn't stop dread from splintering over every inch of my being. I'd tear anyone who so much as looked at her the wrong way to shreds, bit by bit. If she didn't do so herself first.

Gritting my teeth, I lifted my dagger, fingers gripping the hilt as I barged into the chamber. Seryn was close behind. "I'd think twice about where your hands are," I snarled, pressing the tip of my steel against Balor's spine. Disgust and fury skittered over my neck at the sight of him.

The Akridai grimaced, his embered tentacles and arms dropping from Marah's robes. With wide eyes, she tumbled out of reach as far as her chains allowed her. Seryn positioned herself so that she stood next to me and slightly in front of the female.

Slowly, Balor turned, the sharpened point of my blade dragging along the fabric of his pewter cape. "My, my, my, Commander. Mistress will be extremely pleased you've come home."

I stepped into him, my dagger slitting a hole in the front of his tunic, pressing into his soft belly. Seryn's mouth twisted as her halo curled around her, prism-like power snapping at the greasy coward.

Balor's beady eyes shifted, trying to figure out if he could harm us or escape before I sliced into his middle. His buttery aura thrashed against his flesh when I held out my palm. "Keys!" I barked.

Simultaneously, he threw them at Seryn's feet and slippery, embered tendrils shot toward me, snatching my blade and flinging it away.

Seryn lunged for him as his power wrapped around my neck, lifting me off my feet. My fingers tore at my throat, sliding through the clammy mist. I choked as his slimy ember squeezed.

Another oiled arm knocked Seryn's weapon out of her grip as Kaden rushed in, throwing his dagger into the enforcer's shoulder. Balor's thin lips pulled over his teeth, and with a garbled howl, his energy unceremoniously dropped me.

I dove for my blade, and Seryn thrust out her hands, eyes glaring in concentration. Her ember ruptured from her taut frame, latching onto him. A look of shock carved into his blunted features.

As she consumed Balor's aura, Kaden scooped up the keys,

and the vague rattle of metal sounded. The Akridai's phosphorescent ropes whipped toward Seryn, but her halo dissolved them on impact, sweeping the particles within the fractured rainbows.

Balor fell to his knees, eyelids fluttering as his pallid skin lost any semblance of color. Kaden dragged the tethers he'd removed from Marah to the male and locked them around his limp wrists. Silver rune etchings flashed brilliantly for a moment before fading into the iron cuffs. Balor crumpled in a heap on the obsidian.

Seryn summoned her ember home, and it heeded her call, iridescence rippling under the skin of her forearms in its bough design, humming and ready to be pruned.

"Holy fucking Ancients, Ser," Kaden breathed. "You weren't kidding when you said you'd been practicing."

One of her shoulders lifted, and pride scorched through me. She was bloody incredible. My brother smirked and took the keys to release Elder Guust.

I offered a hand to the freed female Elder behind us. "Mistress Strom, I'm Gavrel Larkin, and this is Seryn … Nightshade."

Marah's eyelids fluttered. "Nightshade, you say? You have the look of her. Maya, yes?" Feebly, she rubbed at her wrists.

"You know my mother?" Seryn asked, eyebrows rising.

The Elder nodded. "Melina feared her and spoke of her often. She was convinced that Maya was her Scion. If your ancestry is Nightshade, she had good reason to believe just that. To fear you as well."

Balor's hands jerked at his restraints. "You'll get your tongue cut out for your insolence," Balor hissed weakly, the sallow skin behind his locust rune quivering.

Nostrils flaring, Marah ignored him. "Your mother … We sent her to the Murk prison." Her head lowered, and straggly, brown strands created a curtain around her cheeks. "We sent many mortals there over the decades at Melina's bidding.

Mortals she thought might be our Scions. Innocents who riled her in one way or the other. She kept Endurst and me trapped in here"—her forefinger spun in the air, and then tapped her temple—"and here. If there had been a way to escape, it was lost to us for the better half of a century."

Elder Guust stumbled outside the entrance. He looked like he was about to collapse, but also stubborn enough not to grant his bony frame the privilege. "Mel … Melina made an alli-alliance. She used us like puppets at her whi-whim. Wouldn't let us break our blo-blood oath. Despite us not being in our right mi-minds—and it'll never be enough—but I'm deeply sorry and ashamed for my p-part in your mother's impris-imp-imprisonment." He held a hand to his chest and bowed his head.

My heart tripped as Seryn breathed in deeply. We knew they weren't to blame. That pleasure was all Melina's. And Elders Craven and Ash for their willingness to go along with her atrocities.

"As am I, young one. Thank you for our deliverance," Marah murmured as she went to Endurst's side, shaking her head free of Melina's cobwebs.

"Disgusting dirtlings," Balor sneered.

Kaden scoffed. "You're as limp and useless as your cock without ember, and that must be a brutal bit of shit to swallow."

Loathing burned in the Akridai's glare, and I wanted nothing more than to thrust my blade into him. Watch him bleed for all the times he'd taken part in Melina's games. For harming innocents.

The hilt of my weapon was heavy against my palm.

Forehead creasing, Seryn looked to Elder Guust as we met him outside the cell. "What alliance do you speak of?"

A soft swish distracted me, and I angled my ear toward the pit. "Did you hear that?"

Balor continued his rant, his flaccid body now propped against the wall, "Your demise is near, you filthy—"

Kaden punched him squarely in the mouth. The crack of enamel echoed as the enforcer's eyes rolled back in his head, and he collapsed like a corpse.

Kaden shook out his right hand, flexing the fingers and then wincing. "Bet his teeth tasted better." Kaden chuckled and cupped his other hand over his injured knuckles. His healing ability flickered and sank into his flesh and bone within seconds.

A scrape against stone echoed again. My eyes narrowed as I moved closer to the edge of the ramp, craning my neck. "There's movement up there."

My attention snapped down toward the flash of amber glass levitating from the depths.

"Get on, we'll deal with them once they make their way down," Marah ordered, her voice calm.

As the whirring neared, Endurst's lemon-colored halo twirled around him, and he thrust his power toward the conveyor. Wobbling in the space below, the writhing ember cradling it twitched against the Elder's.

It stalled, but then quivered as his energy reeled it in. We mounted the circular platform, and he stretched his fingers, pushing his palms downward. Sweat gathered on his brow as we sank into the dark well.

Platinum hair flicked over the edges of the ramp above as the person rushed down the endless spiral. *Melina.* But we were closer to the raw amber boulder than she was to us. My mouth stretched across my teeth. The thought of us succeeding in our quest would infuriate her.

As the massive stone came into view, my blood throbbed, and warmth skittered over my now-glowing tattoo. The ember under Seryn's branch-shaped markings surged and flickered. It was as if the coiling ebony and silver lava lapping at the amber's edges called to me. To her. Hungered to wrap its tentacles around my spine and drag me down.

With a shiver, I leaped onto the perimeter, grabbing Seryn's hand as she followed. A torrent of buzzing heat swept over where our skin met. Her lashes fluttered before she looked into my eyes, the whites of hers showing entirely. Lifting her hand to my lips, I set a kiss on her palm before weaving our fingers together and holding her close to my side.

While my gaze roamed over the chiseled rock and the shadowy bulk inside, I swore it trembled, tiny fissures creeping outward from the blurry figure trapped within. Whatever or whoever it was had had enough. Could probably taste its freedom.

This prophecy better not be a fucking mistake.

I craned my neck, heeding the rhythmic slap of leather against stone that spilled from the darkness above. I glanced at Elder Guust as he held the conveyor with his power. I repeated Seryn's unanswered question from earlier. "What alliance did Melina make?"

Marah's face scrunched, her slight lips disappearing completely. Endurst's jaw tensed, and he took a long pull of air. "Why, wi-with the Ancient of Nightmares, of course."

44

CORRESPONDING RIBS

SERYN

estroy, my gift whispered urgently in my mind. But the demand wasn't what it had once been. It wasn't laced with malice or hunger. It was akin to the anticipation of a reunion. Of affinity.

Vaguely, I heard Gavrel's words as he asked the question I'd posed earlier.

"Why, wi-with the Ancient of Nightmares, of course," Elder Guust responded, as if it was obvious.

I stacked my spine, hand squeezing Gavrel's.

"Phobetor? Are you bloody serious? Where the void has he been?" Kaden puckered his mouth and then chuckled. "I suppose in the Void."

"What kind of deal? How do you remember that if she wiped your memories?" I murmured.

Marah's glazed stare shifted to the protruding boulder. "She wiped our minds clean often, but left some details behind. The mystery of what happened haunted us; a torment without an end. What I know is that we've outlived our life spans. Ascension should have occurred long ago, but Melina's made it her mission to hunt and annihilate anyone who could be a Scion. She could never be certain of controlling or imprisoning a new Elder, and our blood bond intricately connects us and our enhanced gifts. Her life's purpose is to live and rule into eternity."

One of her hands fluttered toward the amber, and Endurst placed one of his on her shoulder. "For the last century or so, Mel-Melina and the other Elders gathered us every so often. It's like looking through clouded water, but there are glimpses of being d-down here. Of th-that thing's power shooting through us."

Marah cringed, her voice distant, as if she was drifting away in the sea of her lost cognizance. "Melina's fated. He ... he wasn't a good male. He was cruel. Violent. Melina wasn't always ... Their relationship twisted her into the monster she is today. Something ... something broke within her. And then she broke anyone who stood in her way." She dipped her chin, eyes closing. "She refused to die once her khorda was gone. So, she beseeched Phobetor. Agreed to his demands."

My breaths came in uneven gasps. Melina's footfalls were closer, the beat of them controlling my pulse. "We have to destroy this. She's too close."

"We'll stall her. Do wh-what you must. I've no doubt a Nightshade is more than up to the task." An encouraging smile lifted Endurst's mouth as he and Marah went off to meet their peer. Matching looks of retribution flit across their features as their halos burned around them.

"Prophecy time," I said, trying to convince myself that I was, in fact, up to the task. *You can do this. You must.* Pushing my jawline up and my shoulders back, my aura burst around me. My mantra bounced around my skull.

I am you, and you are me.

Blinking iridescence snapped over my skin, the patterns on my arms writhing. My fingers weaved until a gyrating ball of variegated radiance formed.

"You've got this," Kaden murmured, allowing his clover-like halo to flicker. He wasn't as apprehensive of my power as he once was.

Gavrel's rune blazed as I pushed more power between my hands. The pull of Gavrel's energy to mine droned through me. It wasn't just that my aura was latching onto his—his was reaching for mine as well.

The orb was as big as my head now, and my heart stuttered as the center imploded, sucking in the light directly around it as a black hole would. It was like looking into the eye of another universe with twinkling stars caught in its web.

Through the intense buzz reverberating through my every sinew, Gavrel's hand found my lower back. A tether to reality. Trembling, I bit down hard, concentrating and sifting my energy through my limbs.

"Let go, my star," Gavrel whispered.

My forehead furrowed, and I followed the prickling burn driving up my spine, prodding it until it flamed through my arms and sank into the center of the twisting halo. Fear and doubt gnawed at my confidence. I didn't yet know what I was capable of, and Phantasos had stopped me when the void had formed before.

I am you, and you are me. I breathed in, held it, and then exhaled, wiggling my jaw.

Before the epicenter could get any bigger, I lobbed my creation toward the boulder, and it bonded with the carved surface and oozed over it. I continued to push my ember into it, my face pulling taut.

Golden brilliance burst within the boulder, light seeping through every tiny fissure until it escaped in a rush of blinding luminosity.

A few levels up, flashes of smoke, azure, and yellow burst. The Elders' shouts fell upon us. Kaden's halo flared around him, and he placed his hand on my shoulder.

"Take it," he offered, bracing himself.

Instantly, my ember siphoned his. It pulled at Gavrel's energy as well, but he felt different. The current of his resolve whirled along the cord that tethered us, strengthening my will.

Kaden's shoulders slumped, but he squared his jaw as I fed our combined power into the stone. Finally, a crack rent the air, and a wide fracture split down the center of the boulder. Kaden's hand slipped limply from my shoulder, and he dropped to his knees.

My pulse was trying to break free from my veins, but still, I forced the rest of my incandescence into the crevice.

The skirmish above grew louder as the massive stone quaked. Melina's angered shrieks skittered over my back, forcing goosebumps over my flesh. I'd never heard her so distressed before.

Good.

I hoped she was suffering. Was frantic knowing we were about to destroy whatever was keeping her alive.

With a final gilded spasm of coruscation, the cobble exploded upward in a blazing fit of flashes and amber. Veiled behind a cloak of shimmering haze, the being collapsed in an unmoving mound as the burnished pebbles rained upon it, splashing into the molten pool around it and blanketing it in a sheet of fragmented bronze. If the creature wanted to harm us when it awoke, we'd need to deal with that then. My control was slipping, darkness creeping into the edges of my vision.

Enough, I rasped within my mind.

Fizzling into the air, my ember dissolved, and the tingling sway of it under my flesh stilled. My knees hit the obsidian, and I grimaced at the bite of pain that rocketed through my bones. I slung one limp arm around Kaden and the other around the back of Gavrel's knee.

The glow of my fated's rune simmered when he brushed his fingers against my cheek, tucking loose curls behind my ear. A humming warmth melted into my flesh at his touch, and I relished in the soothing relief it offered. Leaning, just a bit, on his sturdy frame. His thigh and calf muscles flexed as he braced his leg more firmly to support me.

"Breathe, Little Star. You've done it," he murmured.

"Well, at least it's not some beast that'll bite our faces off," Kaden joked. The color in his cheeks was returning gradually, overtaking the paleness.

I squinted my eyes at the bronzed mass. "Not yet."

Its skin had an aurous sheen and almost blended into the resplendent gravel scattered around it. It breathed, the side of its chiseled flank rising with each inhalation.

With unsteady limbs, Kaden stood. He reached down to give me his hand. I let him and Gavrel help me rise. My muscles were loose, unattached, and floating in a haze of fatigue.

Too late, the eerie silence registered in my awareness. There weren't any flashes of the Elders' ember above. No infuriated shouts.

"What have you done?" Melina's outrage sliced at my back. I tried to turn, but my legs buckled beneath me. Gavrel and Kaden bracketed me, holding me steady as we faced her together.

Melina's platinum hair was a mess; her usually porcelain skin was florid, and her diaphragm heaved against her dark sheath dress. I'd never seen her so deliciously disheveled.

Without her tourmaline ring, she hadn't been able to transport herself quickly, and she was delightfully breathless.

Balor Drent stumbled behind her, missing a couple of teeth from Kaden's assault and looking quite put out.

Lifting my chin, a grin spread across my enamel as my

thumb rubbed the faceted pommel at my hip. "Looks like you're having a bad day."

Her palms whipped up, talons spread wide. "I've had enough of you, pet," she hissed, her voice sharp with annoyance and her smoggy halo billowing around her.

"Like you had enough of your fated?" Kaden chided.

I glanced at him. The corner of his eye creased slightly. He was stalling.

"Shut your pretty mouth, or I'll shut it for you," she snapped, cracking her neck to the side.

Kaden smirked, goading her further, "But I hear that you so enjoyed your time with him."

She bared her teeth. "I think I'll keep you after I rid Gavie of his *khorda*. Show you what I learned from mine. The commander can attest that I was an apt pupil. Besides, you must be pleased that they won't complete the ceremony. At least you'll still have your brother." Her tone was scathing, her neck muscles looked as if they were going to burst, and one eye twitched.

Balor sniveled, inching closer to Melina. It was either the bravest or the dumbest thing the male had ever done. "Mistress, you thought Maya was—"

"Silence!" Melina barked.

He recoiled. "Yes, of course, but what if this one is—"

She whipped a smoky tendril of energy toward him, his body flinging to the stone. "Enough! I'll deal with Phobetor's wrath. It'll be worth it to watch the light in her eyes dim." She licked her bottom lip, flicking a half-lidded gaze to Gavrel. "And for Gavie to watch as I drain her mind completely."

All at once, her ember swooped toward my face. My gift reared back, weakened and thrumming below the surface, but my hand was steady as I flung my dagger toward her heart.

With a garbled yell, Balor dove in front of his mistress, my blade sinking between his ribs with a satisfying thunk.

He crumpled at her feet as I beckoned my weapon to my hand, and Melina's face twisted into an ugly mask of fury. Stalking closer, she pushed more power toward me, and my vision clouded with shadows.

Gavrel roared, twisting his body in front of mine and wrapping me in his embrace. The brunt of her attack pummeled into his back. His name tumbled from my throat as a billowing wall of blackened mist swept over him.

With a frantic look, Kaden charged Melina, clamping his arms around her middle, their bodies crashing to the stone. Her aura seeped into her skin, but the residual haze still clung to Gavrel, its shadows slinking into his ears and nose.

His jaw was taut as he resisted the intrusion, muscles straining.

His rune blinked on as he cupped my face, the ten-pointed star reflecting in his pupils. "She can't take them, Asteria. Our memories are ours. I won't let her take them. I won't let her take you."

"Gavrel." The breathless whisper was like a knife dragging up my throat. Trepidation slithered up my spine while my fingers clung to the front of his tunic.

My aura sputtered. An embered thread twined tightly to the bone hovering over my aching heart, and I knew, with soul-deep certainty, that the other end fastened securely to my fated khorda's corresponding rib.

Reverently, his thumbs brushed over the hollows of my cheeks. My soul pulled taut on the thread.

Why did it feel like he was saying goodbye?

Footfalls rushed toward us.

"To the Nether Void and beyond—"

His mouth crashed into mine, and then he spun, pushing my body back toward the wall. The breath was knocked from me, and I choked on his name.

Gavrel hooked his arm around Melina's waist as she lunged

for me. His biceps bulged as he caged her flailing body against his torso.

Stunned, Kaden watched, a look of horror and realization contorting his face. Elders Guust and Strom stumbled onto the landing, shock and disorientation twisting their features.

Shifting stones crackled as the being shifted under the rubble at the center of the pool.

Pure, unconcealed love shone from Gavrel's eyes as they met mine.

As if time stilled, the image of him from my dreams flashed before me.

Of him falling backward into the dark abyss.

"It's the only way," he'd said in our dream.

And as Melina flung her weight backward, Gavrel's boots slipped on crushed stone and then tipped over the edge of the pool.

I reached for him, desperation tearing at my chest. "No!"

Greedily, the metallic-lined blackness gobbled them up, coiling around them and dragging them into its depths.

45

A GOLDEN THREAD

SERYN

With a sob, I lunged toward the pit on my hands and knees, not caring if I was about to meet my end. Flashes of all the times Gavrel had saved me from drowning flooded my mind, and I choked on hiccupping breaths.

My eyes were fixed on the twisting metal and smoke, the tiny spark of hope that he would break the surface extinguished. In that moment, all my fears fell away. I no longer cared if the lava-like shadows filled my lungs and consumed every space within me. I would gladly drown if it meant saving the man I loved. If it meant joining him in the aether.

How cruel were the Fates to give me my heart, and then tear it away? The thread that bound us sliced into my rib, and tears flowed freely down my cheeks. My ember thrashed against my vertebrae.

Before I could throw myself over the edge, Kaden's arms

clamped around me, pulling me to his side as I struggled against him.

"Take c-care, girl!" Endurst cried, Marah's fingers covering her mouth.

"Where were you?" I screamed at the Elders. An irrational sense of condemnation boiled within me. "Why didn't you stop her?" My nails scraped against the stone as I tried to drag myself into the molten pit.

Marah's brows fell. "We tried, my dear. Our ember was lacking, and she stunned us for a moment."

I barely heard the female; my heartbeat was thrashing about my skull so violently. "Let me go!" I raged, pushing and slapping at my friend.

"Seryn!" He shook my shoulders. "Ser, look!"

Distraught, I whipped my attention toward the being as he unearthed himself from the pile. His chin lifted as he stood to his full height, wide shoulders rolling back under the pale gold wrapped around him, the fabric draping down to his feet. Frosty blue eyes flashed as he looked down at us over his strong nose, the bridge slightly curved.

The two Elders fell to their knees, foreheads touching the stone. My chin lifted, tears flowing freely over my cheeks.

I knew that face. All its robust angles. The face from my favorite painting in the palace. My favorite book in the palace library.

His palace.

"Well done." His voice—*the* voice that directed me time and again—boomed through the pit. "Rise, Elders."

And they did, eyes wide.

"It's … it's you," I snarled. "*Morpheus.*"

Kaden's mouth dropped open. "Holy fucking Ancient."

My pulse hammered as I stood, and I planted my heels into the obsidian as they itched to leap into the basin.

One of Morpheus' brows lifted as he glanced at Kaden and

then at me. "True. Now to the business of retrieving our khordas from the Nether Void."

"Bloody Nether Void." Kaden gripped my wrist as if I would jump. He wasn't wrong. My very marrow was screaming at me to dive in after Gavrel.

My words slid between gritted teeth as all-consuming pain and resentment shivered over my spine. I didn't care if he was an Ancient, and even though I desired nothing more than to do what he asked, the contrary words spewed from me like acid. "You can't do it yourself?"

A halo of twinkling gold and mist flickered around him, pooling at his feet. He floated to the perimeter as if riding on a cloud and then stepped onto the stone. A glint flashed over his irises. "There's nothing more I'd like better than to pay my brother a visit." He rubbed his knuckles against the steep angle of his jaw. "But alas, the treaty forbids it. My brother and I are rulers of our domains, but exiles of each other's."

Kaden's eyebrow quirked. "*Treaty?*"

My fingertips swatted at the dampness clinging to my cheeks. Yaya's teachings flit through my mind. "During the Nightbloom Sundering, he and Phobetor almost destroyed Kosmos. The Fates were so furious that they threatened to summon the Primevals."

Marah shifted, wringing her hands. "Who were here long before flesh and ember, and will exist long after."

Endurst rubbed his forehead. "The Pri-Primevals stir beneath our f-feet. We walk on their graves and call it the world."

Morpheus closed his eyes and took a deep inhale. "So eloquent—the mortal scriptures."

My tongue pressed against my bottom teeth. "If the Primevals awaken, everything and everyone, except the Fates, will be destroyed. The very fabric of life would unravel so that the process of creation could begin anew."

Swallowing, Kaden ran his fingers through his hair. "Ah, sounds like a good time." His reply didn't carry his usual light-hearted sarcasm.

Morpheus' eyes narrowed for a moment. "It's quite the opposite," he said humorlessly.

My mouth pinched, anger roiling deep in my belly. "Regardless, Phobetor got the upper hand, it would seem," I muttered. "He doesn't fear the upheaval of order and balance. You've been trapped for over a century, people's dreams have vanished, and Midst Fall is dying."

His jaw lifted. "He knew well enough that he could neither rid Kosmos of me nor directly break the treaty. But he's always been impulsive. Shortsighted." He frowned, his gilded aura brightening. "Perhaps he believed that if my dreams were trapped here with me, his nightmares could freely take root." He shook his head, staring at the coiling, metallic magma.

Scoffing, my hands flexed. "But the Withering took root instead. The fool cursed us all with his greed and jealousy. Without humanity, he'll fade into the aether. You need worshippers to exist."

"You aren't wrong," he conceded. "I doubt he regrets the consequences of his actions. Knowing him, he'll take his pride to the aether. And I have nothing but regret … I shouldn't have been as trusting. I should've heeded the Fates' predictions." He held his hand out to the pile of amber. "My brother used the Elders for his bidding. Tricked Melina into the deal that would imprison me, gave her eternal life and power, and provided him with an endless stream of nightmares to feed off."

His head dipped, and his fists clenched at his sides, matching my own stance. "You see, Ancients can merely whisper in a mortal's ear, but it is up to the mortal to choose their path. I can see that your khorda bond is strong enough to withstand the Void." His eyes softened. "Despite your fated's rune blocking your thread's full potential. It's why I need you, once again."

I yanked my wrist out of Kaden's grip. "Good, then let me get on with it," I said, nearing the edge of the molten pool once more.

My best friend's pleading tone made me pause. "Ser, you can't be serious."

I glared at him.

"I mean, you can't think I'm not going with you. I can't lose you both."

My shoulders slumped. "You're needed elsewhere. The others need to know what happened, and Elder Craven and Ash are still out there. You need to be here for what's next." I waved my hand at the two Elders behind us. "Perhaps you can heal Endurst and Marah."

Their brows lifted as they looked at one another. Marah's hand fluttered to her chest. A deep line dug between Kaden's brows, so similar to Gavrel's. I brushed my thumb over the line. "I can do this, but I need to know you're here. *Please*," I whispered.

His eyes darted between mine, and his chest heaved. "Go get the commander." He pulled me into a tight hug, and then, as if he was fighting his movements, he stepped beside the Elders.

I turned to Morpheus, nails digging into my palms. The warmth of my gifted ring tingled against my skin. I pulled Melina's stolen band from my belt satchel. "I believe this is yours, yes?" With a nod, his handsome face softened. Morpheus took it from my outstretched hand and slipped it on his left forefinger.

His head tilted, eyes studying me. "I won't be able to offer you guidance down there."

I tossed him a deadpan look. "Oh, no. No more mysterious words spoken inside my head? No more dreams full of premonitions?"

"I'm sorry if they vexed you, but they were a boon, were they not? It pained me not to be able to do more over the turns. But once

I realized I could offer you the little I did, hope fueled me. Hope that you'd be the one to release me. To save the mortal realm ... and my fated, so we can finally be bound through the Kollao Ceremony."

"Because you can't leave Surrelia," I spat, scowling. "All-powerful Ancients can't save us."

"As I said, we can only influence. The Fates and the treaty forbids direct intervention. I would think the time spent with my sister would've made that clear."

Kaden rolled his eyes, and I scoffed. "Nothing is ever clear with Phantasos."

Kaden scratched his jaw. "Why hasn't sissy been sucked into the aether? Seems like her ticket between the realms doesn't have an expiration date."

Morpheus closed his eyes for a moment, wide chest expanding, as if preparing to talk to an unruly toddler. "She's always been quite adept at appeasing the Fates; her intentions cloaked in riddles. My sister need not worry about her power depleting like the rest of us, for her ember is sourced—"

"From the wilds. She can traverse any realm's wilderness and thrive," I interjected, recalling my studies this last winter.

The corners of Morpheus' mouth curled as my ice-blue eyes narrowed.

As if I were looking at my own reflection.

Acid boiled in my stomach, apprehension sliding a frozen finger up my spine.

"Who's your fated?"

The Ancient of Dreams moved closer to me. "After I was caged, loathing, in its purest form, festered in me. I vowed to destroy my brother. Treaty and Kosmos be damned. For you see, each time humanity dreamed during the Dormancies, all that ember had to go somewhere ... The pods siphoned it directly into me every month. Until my very essence nearly burst from my flesh. Until my sanity was pushed to the brink of darkness again and again. I would've ripped through everything and everyone in my path if I had been freed then."

I gulped, my heart hanging on every word.

His smile pushed further into his high cheekbones. "Then one day, many decades into my captivity, our bond called to me. A single golden thread broke through the rot and shadows, consuming my soul. I reached for it, tethering it tightly to my left rib so it wouldn't get lost in my torment."

He rubbed his chest, his golden aura shimmering and pulsing. "Selene smiled upon me that day. From then on, during the full moons, I met my love in her dreams." I flinched as his warm hand cupped my chin tenderly. "Your mother—my Maya—brought me back from the brink of insanity. And I've been waiting a long time to have her by my side … and to meet you … Daughter."

EPILOGUE

GAVREL

"*It's the only way,*" I had said in our shared dream last night. That seemed so long ago. Although I had no sense of time, I plummeted into the nothingness devouring me. My limbs flailed, spine whipping and bending as flashes of metal snapped and sparked in my vision. Smoldering blackness raked against me, coiling and scorching my flesh as it dragged across my body greedily.

I hadn't known what the dreams meant then. All the times I imagined the darkness claiming me as I fell from the edge. But when Kaden charged at Melina, her sickening shadows clinging to my face, it was as if every hazy crumb that had been offered during my sleep had fully formed.

I had to do it.

It was the only way.

Even if we had been somehow able to end her—which I highly doubted considering how drained we had all been—Melina wouldn't stop.

And I couldn't risk my brother.

Seryn.

Melina wouldn't take any more from them.

And when I kissed my little star for the last time—when I told her, "To the Nether Void and beyond"—nothing had ever felt as true.

My khorda.

My *love.*

While I clamped my arms around the evil that was Elder Harrow, our bodies tumbling into the molten pewter-lined blackness, I hoped it would all be worth it. Seryn, my brother, and the others ... they would make things right. They would save Midst Fall. And my fated would find happiness. She'd be safe.

Either way, it was too late for any regrets now. I'd done it, and even though I couldn't see Melina, I knew she was stuck in this void with me.

And I hoped it tore every inch of her apart with agonizing efficiency.

The abyss was wet and sticky like warm blood, but when the metal-like veins sparked in my peripheral vision, jolts of slick ice sliced across my skin.

Wherever it was taking me ... I hoped to reach the end soon. A burning sickness roiled in my guts, acid threatening to spill from me. Or perhaps it was the caustic substance rolling around me, its energy trying to tear me open and sink within my organs.

It clawed into any hollows and seams it could find. My mouth filled with its metallic tang, and my eyes and ears burned with its sticky fumes. I choked, unable to get control of my arms as my fingers so desperately scratched at the dark.

Images of Seryn's beautiful face, each vivid expression crossing every dip and valley, zipped through my mind. With her as my heart's core, my mind grasped at our bond, aching for her to share in the love and sorrow vibrating through the cord that bound us. Imploring her forgiveness for what I'd done, fully aware that my rune still stood as an unyielding barrier to such hopes.

Without warning, I slammed into crude, rough stone with a crack, ramming the visions of my fated out of my head. A whoosh of air burst from me, liquid smog fleeing from my throat. I wheezed, palms clinging to the rock at my sides, sharp pebbles cutting into my skin.

Every bone screeched as I rolled onto my side, coughing and gasping for breath. As the last drops of the portal's elements left me, I pushed myself upright. I was a giant, throbbing bruise. Shakily, I stood, testing my aching joints and muscles as I took in my surroundings.

It was as if a film of gloom coated my vision. I rubbed my eyes, but they had already adjusted, and still everything was in shades of shadow and despair. Except for the sky. The sky was vermilion, the color of smoldering coal, and the clouds were eerie wisps of sable hues.

As far as I could see, sharp ebony boulders jutted from the soot-covered terrain. Every so often, a geyser of black fire with azure-tinged edges would spew from the cracks or chasms scattered across the land. The air was unnervingly still, and flecks of glowing ash were suspended in the air as if this realm was perpetually holding its breath.

I shook my head, my brain rattled inside its thick, bony walls.

Everything was upside down and back to front—all the colors inverted and obscured in night, umbras, and dark flames.

In the distance, the outline of a gothic castle rose imperiously; numerous serrated turrets resembling barbs pierced the sky. The atmosphere shifted over its glossy, obsidian surface, making it seem breathing as red and orange hues flowed over its many rounded depressions, shaped like scalloped shells. A massive islet of black opal, flecked with vibrant green, sapphire, and ruby chatoyancy, cradled the stronghold.

It was familiar, but also not. Unease skittered over my skin and left a trail of goosebumps in its wake.

It reminded me somewhat of Morpheus' palace, if it were turned inside out, with the brutal edges and raw seams visible and twisted.

Phobetor's castle? Was I in the Nether Void?

My heart pummeled the back of my ribs. I clenched my fists and pushed my shoulders back. A rasping moan sounded behind me, and I drew my sword, its weight solid and comforting as I spun around.

A few paces away, a fan of platinum hair and splayed limbs spread across the ground. I stepped closer, ire bubbling within me.

Melina.

She was breathing raggedly, her eyelids fluttering. Her head jerked, mouth peeled back across her teeth.

My arm rose, the tip of my blade rising above her heart.

I thought of everything she'd done to me.

To Midst Fall.

To those I loved.

And here she was, the Void displaying her like an offering. She was mine to eradicate.

Finally.

She flinched, her chest heaving as her eyes snapped open, head turning side to side as she took in her surroundings.

The sky burned across the silver of her irises as her eyes locked with mine. A slow, satisfied grin split over her face. "At last, you've sent me to the Void, Commander. How does it feel to join me?"

Both hands clutched the hilt of my broadsword, biceps ticking in anticipation, the blade hovering above her like the pendulum of a clock. My nostrils flared as I lifted my weapon higher, preparing for a swift retribution.

But just as my muscles tensed, ready to deliver the blow, words like cool velvet skimmed over my awareness. "I hate to intrude, but I must." I froze, turning warily toward the voice. And a stutter of breath clogged my windpipe. From the shadows, the being emerged and uttered one word.

"Gavrel?"

NOT YET THE END ...

<u>WANT MORE?</u>

BOOK 3: Don't miss the next breathtaking installment in the Fate of the Embered series—a spellbinding tale of passion, peril, and profound sacrifice—where only the fiercest hearts endure the price of destiny.

Of Hollowed Stars is available on Amazon at:
https://books2read.com/ofhollowedstars

EXCLUSIVE CONTENT: Be the first to learn about Rowyn Adelaide's new releases and receive exclusive content!

Join Rowyn's author newsletter:
WWW.AUTHORROWYNADELAIDE.COM

GLOSSARY/PRONUNCIATION GUIDE

CHARACTERS/CREATURES

- **Akridai (Ack-reh-die)** – very powerful, elite Druik enforcers who wield their power at the discretion of the Elders and the Elder Laws.
- **Alette Vawn (A-let Vawn)** – a.k.a. Letti. Younger sister of Seryn Vawn. From Evergryn.
- **Alweo (Al-weh-oh)** – Seryn's chestnut stallion.
- **Ancients** – powerful gods who created the mortal realm and gifted magic to certain mortal bloodlines.
- **Asteria (A-stare-ee-ah)** – The Ancient of Stars.
- **Augur (Awe-grr)** – A revered female of the Perilous Bogs who offers prophetic counsel to those who seek it.
- **Breena Cadell (Bree-nah Kah-dell)** – friend of Seryn Vawn. Lives in Pneumali City, but originally from Pyria Island. Possesses red, fire-related magic.
- **Caelora Aundyne (Kay-lor-a Awn-deen)** – a half-borne Druik that was in the final Winnowing trial

with Seryn and Kaden. Her combined lineage hails from both Haadra and Pyria Island. She has a violet-colored aura, which manifests as lavender water that turns into flames on contact.

- **Chasm spider** – giant, cave-dwelling spider beasts with camouflage abilities.
- **Derya Atwater (Dair-yah At-water)** – friend of Seryn Vawn and her chambermaid. Lives in Surrelia, but originally from Haadra. Possesses blue, water-related magic.
- **Draumr (Draw-mer)** – warriors in the Elders' warrior legion, the Order of Draumr. Uphold laws and order within realms.
- **Druik (Drew-ick)** – one who wields magic. Lives longer than non-magic mortals/humans.
- **Elders** – extremely powerful, chosen/ascended Druiks granted extra celestial powers through the Ancients' Ascension ceremony and rule the mortal realm as an Oligarchy. They hail from divine lineage from one of the **five founding bloodlines**:
  - **Aerides (Air-id-eez)** of Pneumali
  - **Celosia (Suh-low-sha)** of Pyria
  - **Lotus** of Haadra
  - **Nightshade** of Perilous Bogs
  - **Oleander (Oh-lee-an-dur)** of Evergryn

Current Elders:

  - **Endurst Guust (En-derst Goo-st)** of Pneumali – possesses yellow, air-like magic.
  - **Lucan Craven (Loo-can Cray-ven)** of Evergryn – possesses green, earth-like magic.

- o **Marah Strom (Mar-ah Strawm)** of Haadra – possesses blue, water-like magic.
  - o **Melina Harrow (Meh-leena Hair-oh)** of the Perilous Bogs – possesses smoky, memory-erasing magic.
  - o **Ryboas Ash (Rye-bow-es Ash)** of Pyria Island – possesses red, fire-like magic.
- **Eliz Wynt (Ee-lie-z Win-t)** – friend of Rhaegar and fated khorda of Keethan Wynt. Keethan and Eliz are recruitment scouts for the Korax and recruited Rhaegar for the rebel cause.
- **Elysium (Eh-lis-ee-um) Tree** – the oldest and most sacred, banyan-like tree in all of existence. A source of life-giving ember. A place to pray or offer oaths to the Ancients.
- **Emmet Larkin** – Gavrel and Kaden Larkin's father. Husband of Hestia Larkin. Died shortly after his wife was culled.
- **Fates** – three powerful sister entities who write, alter, and determine the destiny of mortals, realms, creatures, and Ancients alike.
- **Gavrel (Gav (like have)-rel (like fell)) Larkin** – Seryn Vawn's neighbor and friend. Brother of Kaden Larkin. Elite Commander in the Order of Draumr. Has a rune tattoo on his right hand that grants him some ember and enhanced strength/stamina.
- **Gideon Vawn (Gid-ee-on Vawn)** – Seryn and Alette Vawn's father. Husband of Maya Vawn.
- **Half-borne** – Druiks born of two lineages and display mixed ember abilities.
- **Harbinger starling** – starling-like birds that deliver missives across the realm.

- **Hestia Larkin (Hess-tee-ah Larkin)** – Gavrel and Kaden Larkin's mother. Wife of Emmet Larkin. Was culled when Gavrel was eighteen turns old and Kaden was thirteen turns old. Possessed green, earth-like and healing magic.
- **Horai (Ho-rye)** – the Ancients of Hours. Twelve Ancients who once guarded Aion, the Surrelian capital.
- **Iben Burlam (Eye-ben Burr-lamb)** – librarian and begrudging friend of Seryn Vawn. Lives in Surrelia, but originally from Evergryn. Possesses brownish, earth-related magic.
- **Jace Barden (Jay-s Bar-den)** – Otherwise known as Magister Barden. He arrived in Evergryn several decades ago. He teaches the students of the region.
- **Kaden Larkin (Kay-den Larkin)** – Seryn Vawn's best friend. Brother to Gavrel Larkin. Possesses green, earth-related and healing magic.
- **Keethan Wynt (Keith-an Win-t)** – friend of Rhaegar and fated khorda of Eliz Wynt. Keethan and Eliz are recruitment scouts for the Korax and recruited Rhaegar for the rebel cause.
- **Korax (Core-ax)** – The rebel group fighting against the Elders and their Laws. The leader is Neoma Skiya (i.e. Nightshade) from the Perilous Bogs.
- **Mare wyrm (Worm)** – Nether Void, leech-like creature that tricks you into thinking it is your loved one. Once they have you in their slimy hold, they suck the life and magic out of you.
- **Marek Skiya (Mare-ick Skee-yah)** – Member of the rebel group called the Korax. His hidden lineage hails from the Nightshade bloodline of the Perilous Bogs. Grandson of Neoma Skiya.

- **Maya Vawn** – Seryn and Alette Vawn's mother. Wife of Gideon Vawn. Disappeared when Seryn was seven turns old. Has some sort of magic related to the Perilous Bogs, where she was originally from.
- **Morpheus (More-fee-us)**– the supreme Ancient of Dreams. Presides over Surrelia.
- **Neoma Skiya (Nay-oh-ma Skee-yah)** – the leader of the rebel group called the Korax. Her hidden lineage hails from the Nightshade bloodline of the Perilous Bogs. Grandmother to Marek Skiya.
- **Oneiroi (Oh-knee-roy)** – the dream Ancients. Siblings. (Also see Morpheus, Phantasos, and Phobetor).
- **Order of Draumr (Draw-mer)** – the Elders' warrior legion.
- **Pegasus (Peg-ah-sus)** – Surrelian winged, horse creature. Mortal-bred horses that were gifted wings by the Ancients once they reached Surrelia. Very rare.
- **Phantasos (Fan-taz-ohs)** – Ancient of Illusions (and surreal dreams). Wanders across the realms and likes wild landscapes.
- **Phobetor (Foe-beh-tore)** – Ancient of Nightmares. Presides over the Nether Void.
- **Pixie** – mischievous, winged creatures that are as big as a mortal hand. Reside in Surrelia in the Reverie Weald. Skilled at finding portals in Reverie Weald.
- **Rhaegar Hale (Rag-ar Hail)** – friend of Seryn Vawn. Gavrel Larkin's second-in-command in the Order of Draumr.
- **Scion (Sigh-on)** – descendants of one of the five founding bloodlines. The only type of Druik that can undergo the Ascension to become an Elder. Only one exists at a time.

- **Selene (Suh-leh-nee)** – The Moon Ancient. Her true love was a mortal named Endymion. He was put to sleep eternally so she could visit him every night for eternity.
- **Seryn (Sair-in or like the name Erin) Vawn** – Our main female leading character. Alette is her younger sister. Gideon and Maya are her parents. Has some sort of mysterious magic that hails from the Perilous Bogs. Has lived in Evergryn her whole life.
- **Somneia (Som-nee-ah)** – the Elders' covert network of spies.
- **Tyche (Tie-kee)** – the Ancient of Luck.
- **Wyvern (Why-vern)** – Surrelian creature that lives along the cliffs in the Reverie Weald. Massive, reptilian-like creature with wings, feathers, scales, and two forelegs. It can spray poisonous spit. Protects the Mirage Orchid.
- **Xeni Reed (Zen-ee Reed)** – friend of Seryn Vawn. Girlfriend of Alette Vawn. Warrior in Gavrel's elite Draumr unit.

PLACES

- **Aion (Ah-ee-own)** – Capital city of Surrelia.
- **Ceto (See-toe)** – Capital city of the region of Haadra.
- **Evergryn (Ever-grin)** – Northern, wooded region of the mortal realm. Magic that hails from here is earth-related and often shades of green and brown.
- **Haadra (High-druh)** – Eastern, water-ridden region of the mortal realm. Magic that hails from here is water-related and often shades of blue and aqua.
- **Hallowed End** – A sacred place at the edge of Helos

where Seryn opens a portal that leads into the Stygian Murk.

- **Helos (He-low-s)** – Capital city of the Perilous Bogs region.
- **Insomnis Sea (In-sawm-niss Sea)** – fabled dream realm sea that surrounds Surrelia.
- **Lochs of Haadra (Locks of High-druh)** – A series of three large, brackish lochs that border the Haadran border. The northernmost loch between Haadra and the Ourea Peaks is Lotus Loch. Below that, Inksalt Loch borders Haadra, the Ourea Peaks, and the Perilous Bogs. Aerides Loch, the southernmost loch that borders Haadra and Pneumali.
- **Midst Fall** – the mortal realm
- **Nether Void** – Ancient nightmare realm. Phobetor presides over this realm. It is a terrifying, dark realm where those who pass on may live out their eternity in eternal suffering.
- **Ourea (Oo-reh-ah) Peaks** – Mountain range that borders the easternmost edge of Evergryn and westernmost edge of Haadra.
- **Perilous Bogs** – Western and center, swamp/bog region of the mortal realm. People avoid this area and not much is known. Magic that hails from this area is mysterious and can manifest in many different ways and is often shades of black or iridescent.
- **Pneumali (New-mall-ee)** – Southern, desert region of the mortal realm. Magic that hails from here is air-related and often shades of yellow and orange.
- **Pyria (Pie-ree-ah) Island** – Southernmost, volcanic island of the mortal realm. Magic that hails from here is fire-related and often shades of red.

- **Reverie Weald (Rev-er-ee Wheeled)** – a beautiful and neon-colored forest that separates Morpheus' land and palace from the rest of Surrelia.
- **Stygian (Sti-jee-uhn) Murk** – a colorless portal realm or limbo between realms where time slows and travelers easily get lost while their will to survive and exist is drained.
- **Surrelia (Sir-el-ee-ah)** – Ancient dream realm. Morpheus presides over this realm. It is a beautiful, vibrant realm where those who pass on live out eternity.

TERMS

- **Aether (Eth-er)** – the pure, invisible essence that permeates space and time throughout all the realms. The fabric of the universe.
- **Aetherbind (Eth-er-bye-nd)** – the seam that holds the aether and everything within it together. The very thing that keeps Kosmos in check.
- **Ascension** - the ritual in which the Scion metamorphoses into the new Elder.
- **Dark Reaping** – in the event that the Primevals are unleashed, they would destroy every living being in Midst Fall. Without worshippers, the Ancients demise would soon follow.
- **Dormancy** – the process the mortal realm is mandated to undergo from every Autumn Equinox to Spring Equinox in order to preserve resources.
- **Ember** – magic that was gifted by the Ancients to Druiks and is inherited through bloodlines.
- **Fated khorda (Core-duh)**– a Druik's mirrored or twin soul. The three sister Fates helped the Ancients

weaken Druiks so that mortal ember would not become overwhelmingly powerful. It was believed that Druiks were born with half their soul, the other half cleaved from them and gifted to another—Druik or human.

- **Hollowed Stars Prophecy** – The prophecy warning of the end of Midst Fall once various omens come about, and potentially how to prevent this. The Korax believe it is the path to saving Midst Fall.

Prophecy/Song:

Behold the call of the end,

When lo, the Aetherbind's seams do bend.

As withered roots the earth doth take,

The battle 'gainst the curse shall break.

Dark beasts through veils shall creep,

And dreams shall rot in mortal sleep.

Unless the stone of light shall fall,

Within obsidian, night devours all.

Lest rise Dark Reaping from the scars,

Make haste with hollowing of the stars.

Earth harvests breath and misted pyre,

And flame be quenched by blackened fire.

One shall be two, and two turn three,

To break the curse o'er land and sea.

When the final threads are fully weaved,

Only then shall Khaos be cleaved.

So speaks Kosmos.

- **Khaos (Kay-ah-s)** – Unstable, chaotic nothingness. The opposite of Kosmos, which is balance and order.
  - **Proverb:** "What binds, protects. What breaks, devours."
- **Kollao (Kah-lay-oh) Ceremony** – the ritual through which a Druik is bound to their fated khorda and becomes whole in soul and magic. Their life is also bound together.
- **Kosmos (Caws-mows)** – Fates' most precious gift to all living things. It is balance and order. Life and death. Ancients and mortals. Dreams and waking. If it isn't maintained, then everything spirals into Khaos—unbalanced, chaotic nothingness.
  - **Proverb:** "What binds, protects. What breaks, devours."
- **Nightbloom Sundering** – A monumental war that spanned nearly a century and crossed multiple realms. The conflict erupted when humans were first gifted ember, leading to chaos throughout Midst Fall. The empire collapsed, and the Druiks, left unchecked, unleashed destruction upon the realm. Seizing this opportunity, Phobetor killed Morpheus' wife. In response, Morpheus infused dreams into the slumbering, banishing his brother's nightmares. This rivalry ignited a war across both the dream and nightmare realms among the Ancients. After nearly a century of turmoil, the Fates finally intervened, as the Aetherbind had become vulnerable. They threatened the release of the Primevals, which would trigger the Dark Reaping.
- **Primevals (Prime-evils)** – the first beings that ever were and always have been. The very personifications

of creation itself. If released, would cause the Dark Reaping.

- **Turn** – one year
- **Winnowing Trials** – a Surrelian festivity at the end of the Dormancy where Druiks and Draumrs can compete to win a grand prize.
  - **Weeding** – first trial of the Winnowing Trials
  - **Wilting** – second trial of the Winnowing Trials
  - **Winnowing** – grande finale trial of the Winnowing Trials
- **Withering** – the progressive decay of the land in Midst Fall.

ACKNOWLEDGMENTS

I'm so grateful that you, reader, are sharing this wickedly dreamy ride with me. I honestly would not have been able to finish this story without the support and encouragement from my husband, friends, family, and readers like you! For all the days and hours I spent hunched like a shrimp in my office or on the couch, thank you to my husband for his endless patience and cheerleading.

Thank you to Bethany, T. Nerdy, Courtney, Chey, Joy, and Christiane. Their constant encouragement, guidance, and support as my beta readers was indispensable. I wouldn't have been able to push through this second book without them. You all are the real MVPs. Now, I'm going to go cry in a corner thinking about how grateful I am for each of you.

Katie (Spice Me Up Editing), my wonderful editor, thank you so very much for your expertise, your humor, and patience through this whole process. You are an amazing editor and all around human!

Thank you to all of my readers, my Wicked Dreamers Street Team, ARC readers, and reviewers who took a chance on an indie romance author with a dream and a magical, steamy story to tell. I appreciate each and every one of you for reading, reviewing, sharing, making reels/posts, and generally just being amazing.

I can't even with my character art. Thank you to the amazing Sarah of Spooky Yeti Art (IG handle: @spookyyetiart), Hope Garrity (IG handle: @hopegarrity), Koti Komori (IG handle: @kotikomori), Mori Di (IG handle: @moridi_art), Lesya (IG Handle: @lesyablackbird), Indigo (IG handle: @scarletwildcard_), BrieeZiee (IG handle: @briez.draws), Sarah (IG handle: @sarah_and_dipitous), Elle (IG handle: @elleillustrationss), Isabella McMurry (IG handle: @im_arc_), and Scorpi (IG handle: @sobr.scorp). You should check them out because, I mean, their art is freaking gorgeous and brought my crazy characters to life. Thank youuuu.

ABOUT THE AUTHOR

Rowyn Adelaide is an insatiable romance reader, advanced practice MSW social worker, and the author of the *Fate of the Embered* series. Her debut novel, *Of Withering Dreams*, launched the dark fantasy romance series with a haunting blend of passion and peril. Her work fuses atmospheric world-building with emotionally driven romance, often exploring themes of transformation, angst, and resilience. When she's not writing or devouring stacks of romance novels, she's usually globe-trotting, rocking out at concerts, counting down to spooky season, or singing karaoke (very poorly). She lives in the Midwest with her favorite creatures: her husband, their dog Audrey Shepburn (aka the goodest girl that ever lived), and their chaotic cat Stormy, who is equal parts villain and sidekick. For more information, visit www.AuthorRowynAdelaide.com.

Get your books, follow Rowyn, get updates, & join her newsletter!

www.ingramcontent.com/pod-product-compliance
Lightning Source LLC
Chambersburg PA
CBHW030742310726
48969CB00005B/1284